A FEARFUL DESTINY

Cranford Hataway

Acknowledgements

I would like to express my appreciation to my wife, Heidi; our children, Jackson, Beth, and Ann; and my brother, Mack, for their encouragement. In addition, I would like to thank Cindy Dyer who retyped and updated the text. Good friends read early versions of the book, gave feedback, and encouraged its publication: Danny Graham, Larry Ross, and Larry and Ann Web.

Foreword

Our father left us this unpublished book about Thomas Becket. The life and activities of Thomas Becket and King Henry II of England have been the subject of many books. This one is unique as it is written from the perspective of a lifelong manservant of Becket's.

Our father would probably not have been able to go college where he found his lifelong interest in early Western civilization, but the passage of the GI Bill enabled him along with other veterans of World War II to attend. He earned his undergraduate degree at Troy University in Troy, Alabama, and later a master's degree from Mississippi State University in Starkville, Mississippi. After retiring from the U.S. Air Force, he made a second career of teaching college students about his favorite topic of early Western civilization.

We are pleased to present this book about Thomas Becket's England using a Saxon's viewpoint. We hope you enjoy reading about this exciting period in early English history.

Mack and Jack Hataway
Montgomery, Alabama
July, 2013

CHAPTER 1

It is very cold in this drafty stable, but it is better than being out in the cold wind and rain that is blotting out the country side. The straw in here is dry and the heat from the animals is better than no heat at all. A useless old ostler should be thankful to have food for the stomach and a warm place to stay.

I have been told that I will be moved within a monastery, but promises have always eluded me. A destructive illness would be welcome. It is my time to die. I must beg for what I eat and wear and where I am allowed to stay. I cannot accustom myself to this meanness, yet I do not have the strength of character to kill myself or let myself starve to death. The thoughts of damning my eternal soul by self-destruction frighten me beyond words. I must not think on it, else I must confess to the good father the cardinal sin I am thinking on. I have in my day, had too much and too many good things to allow me now to revel in starvation. Oh, if only the good would just return in small measure!

Then I get ravenously hungry. I recall the days when I had my fill of rich gravies, fine wines and red meats. And all the fresh, warm bread I could eat. I would gorge until the savories drooled down my chin, then I would feel guilty when I had to wipe the rich drippings and few drops of good red wine on my clothes or the clean straw that I got to know and like so well. I developed a sad liking for full wines, clean houses, much travel and to my sorrow, I will know them no more. When I eat the few moldy crusts of bread that I can manage to beg and the thin soup that is the charity of nobles of this day and time, I cannot but help but yearn for the full, exciting days that I have known.

This threadbare clothing, although plentiful, is not as warm as were nice woolens that I have worn so many years until I cannot count them. I wash my clothing as often as I can, but the vermin still creep in and I cannot tolerate them any longer since I have become accustomed to not scratching and itching in public as well as in private. Ah when I think of the beautiful clothing I used to wear. And I had a changing of them too. One was a soft yellow, the other a brilliant green. I learned to like the feel of soft silk next to me. I gloried every day in the feel of velvet and fine wool. I could never stop the habit of caressing those magnificent clothes even though the blessed Saint Thomas would chide me from time to time about my worldliness. But he would only laugh and be gentle, forgiving me the luxury of a small sin of pride.

If my memory serves me correctly, I was in my fifth year when my father told me that his master, Gilbert Becket and his wife Rohan were blessed with the birth of a strong and healthy son. He told me to thank God every day for this blessed event because it meant a continuing of this prosperous house and continued employment. I dutifully thanked Saint Withan and the Virgin Mary whenever I prayed and asked for their continued good blessings.

I have been reminded forever that my family has been handlers of horses for the gentry for all their time on this earth and even though we are of ancient Saxon lineage it is no disgrace to work for Normans if they are kind and considerate. The Beckets are the souls of kindness of gentleness and consideration. I cannot understand this, because the Norman nobleman will run you down with their horses on the streets, or strike you with their riding crops or swords if you glare at them or plead for mercy.

My family has always been proud of its family history. We have taken pride in our independence and ability to do a good job for our masters. The yoke of the invader weighs heavily on us at times, and were it not for the fact that we are employed by good and considerate people, my father has often said that he would rather hide out in the forests and eat acorns with the swine than to be in bondage. I have to stop at times to remember that I am in a house of the conquerors because the Beckets never remind us of our condition. Thus, I am the son of Wat, ostler to Gilbert Becket. The Beckets have chosen to name their newborn Thomas. All augurs well for a quiet and orderly future.

In my young years I was always fascinated by the history of the Becket family. They did not discuss their continental ancestry much, but they always talked of Gilbert's travels on the Crusades. I cannot imagine such far distant places and what it would be like to be among people who know nothing of God and the Universal Church. It is not real to live in this civilized day and age and not know anything of salvation and heavenly rewards. But the accounts of the wild, faraway lands, the savage Turks and the dry sunny lands where rains seldom fall sounds unnatural. I believe I would die in the heat and dust without water and green things around me, even if I have always suffered somewhat from the dampness and cold of my native land. But sire Becket would tell of the many wonders and privations. Many times he would laugh, but often he would shudder in recollection of the savagery and brutality of the infidels.

Gilbert Becket would tease his wife unmercifully and remind her that she was a conquest from those faraway lands and that she should be grateful for the comforts and ease of his home. He would tell of this good woman following him all the way from the Holy Land and even though she spoke not a word of English, she wandered the streets crying his name until some priests called the constabulary who located the Becket house for her. Mother Rohan would scoff at these wild tales and go about her business. At times if she felt particularly harassed, she would flare up and remind her husband that she was of as good a Norman ancestry as his and that he knew perfectly well that her home was in Caen. Her parents, like his, had migrated to the islands to make their fortune.

"Wife," Gilbert would laugh, "prepare the fine dishes and serve the food of your country to show these people that you know other things."

"Husband," she would return, "teach me the manners of food preparation by the infidel and I shall do my best. I hear that the ingredients are hard to obtain here in England, but that those strange people did use lots of peppers. We have that vegetable here in quantities. If you cannot furnish me with the material for preparation, I can get pepper and from now on I shall give you your fill!"

"Hold," he would cry, "fill not my food with too much foreign matter. I could not eat the stuff when I was there. It would be too much to inflict it on me in my own home. I will forego attempting to locate those stranger foods if you will abstain from scorching my insides with fiery preparations."

"You should not tease me so, my husband," she would reply softly. "I pray for my mortal soul each time you do so, because I would not have it that I practice heathen ways or think godless thoughts. It is my eternal joy that I was born a Christian and I would not jeopardize my happiness in the hereafter."

"There, there, don't worry yourself so, my plump little squab. I would not cause you concern. I was only speaking in jest."

At this point Madam Becket would find me some errand to do. It was quite often that of emptying the slops into the streets, something I thoroughly enjoyed doing. To take the refuse, hold it high, call out shrilly, "Beware! Beware!" and let fly was a great delight. If I struck or splashed someone, despite the torrential flow of invective, I dared not look for fear of being identified. If I thought that I could recognize the language, I felt a secret delight in knowing that I had at least discomfited a Norman noble or beldame or some of their progeny. At the tender age of five I was old enough to understand that one must resist the foreigner however possible.

I had many occasions to observe Gilbert Becket. I found him to be a short, stocky beefy faced man who loved stout and kidney pie to the exclusion of all goods. He would eat other foods but reveled in beef, venison and mutton. I would watch many times from behind a tapestry or screen while my backside literally froze as this florid, sandy haired, red faced man would eat enormous amounts of meat and bread and wash them down with liquid. He was always willing to laugh, pinch a serving maid when his wife was not looking and make conversation with guests. His clothes were always a conservative gray or brown but he always managed to look prosperous. He preferred to be clean shaven as opposed to the current fashion for beards, thus his countenance was an open book for anyone who wished to read it. He was forever jesting with someone or singing a mildly ribald tune. He said it was the fashion on the continent for gentlemen to sing and that it was a pity that the habit had not become common in England.

Madam Becket, on the other hand, was quite serious and sniffed at the singing. She always expressed herself that such matters were offensive to the Church. If one should sing, she always said, it should be in praise of God or some of the saints. Madame was as plump as her husband was stout. She was flaxen haired and red cheeked although again, she frowned on the servant girls using color to redden theirs. I never saw her with color about her but her complexion was too beautiful to compare it to the common sallow faced English woman. She dressed soberly in black or gray, only adding lace or a fine woolen shawl to her attire when she went calling, shopping or to church. Her bright hair was a great contrast to her dull clothes and I would peer at mother's brown hair and wonder why people could be so different.

"You have no business peering so closely at your betters," my mother would snap at me when I wondered aloud at the differences." You should apply yourself to learning the ways and manners of these people and to bringing home more meat for food." This would depress me because here I really would wonder why we rejoiced at meat twice a year in my house and the Beckets had it constantly. I was good at snatching and concealing bones that were set aside for the dogs and scraping plates and pots behind the cooks back. My leather satchel always had something for my hungry brothers and sisters when I would come from the big house to the stable. Even at five there are many things that can be learned. Foremost of these is survival of oneself and one's family.

There were days when meat was scarce at the Becket table. If the butcher did not come or the king needed food for the army, they would eat whatever meat was available, which was generally the undesirable parts of the animal that could not be preserved. Madam Becket would instruct the cook to mix the meat particles with wheat, vegetables and water and prepare the best dish possible. The cook would grumble but I would like these instructions best of all.

"Always I am put upon to prepare something from nothing," the cook would complain. "It's not possible to prepare a good meal without roasting or boiling sound red meat. Ears, hoofs, tails and intestines are hard to work with because they spoil so easily. I must use spices of all kinds to conceal the taste and odor of spoiled meat. If the master detects anything wrong, I get cuffed about and threatened with being sent to the country. If they did not go hungry in the fields and forests I feel I would be better off."

I learned early to take no notice of the cook's grumbling. She was fat and greasy from eating the rich foods that she served. She had developed a taste for things of foreign places and she was really excellent in making the best of breads and crusts for pies. The days of meat shortages were the best days. Much food was left over and it was not hard to dip a hand in the steaming dishes and eat all one could hold and not be accused of stealing. On these days, I would hurry with my chores which were generally light, make myself appear often and hurriedly in the kitchen, run some small errand for the cook and eat constantly. At the end of the day things would have gone very profitably and when my father closed the stables and came for me, I would only have a knapsack of bread but I would have a full belly of meat scraps, crusts and gravy. The family would grumble at me although I never ate of the food that I brought home but they would ferociously gobble the tasty baked goods.

Many times when the weather was raw, I would have loved staying in the warm Becket house and curl up by the fire, rather that facing the cold wind and bitter rain. The Beckets never suggested it in those early days and I doubt seriously if my father's pride would have let me stay there. I cannot remember being warmly dressed until Master Thomas became grown nor did I sleep warmly until I was required to attend him day and night. There were enough people at my home to keep each other reasonably warm but there was never enough wood, bed clothing or outer clothing to be satisfactory. I huddled with the other children in the straw in the bedroom but I was always chilly from the damp and wind that seeped in through the shuttered windows. One does not become accustomed to being cold.

On the very, very raw days, I envied the Beckets as my father and I trudged home. Although the stone floors were chilly in their house, the great fireplaces roared and the areas near them were deliciously warm. I would stand near them as often as I could and make myself inconspicuous among the dogs and servants and luxuriate in the delightful glow that would spread through my body as the warm rays from the flames would caress my clothing. If I was not careful, I would doze while standing in the heat and step on a dog that would snap at me or lean against a servant who would cuff me ungently. My ears are a great source of discomfort to me now and I attribute my troubles to the hard knocks I received in the Becket household while I was growing up. As I grew older, my strength and position with Thomas aided me in subduing both dogs and servants, but the time came too late to undo the damage done to my ears.

Gilbert Becket was the customs collector for the city of London. I found his house to be exciting at all times. He was always bringing home some impounded goods that had to be redeemed at a later date, or hearing from disgruntled merchants about charges, damaged goods, and unscrupulous seamen.

"But your lordship, I can't pay these excessive taxes," a seedy, threadbare importer would complain.

"Don't lordship me my man," Becket would speak to him in modest tones, "I'm only an honest agent of the king and I must do my duty. I don't write the rules for the operation of the port; neither do I set the charges. That is done by his majesty's councilors and I am bound by their decisions."

"But your honor, can't there be some adjustments made? Some small amount that be perhaps in your favor?" the leering one would smirk.

"That could get you and me in trouble," growled Gilbert Becket. "Be gone you devil, lest you implicate both of us in a nasty plot to defraud the king and the kingdom. My job is not one of bribery but one to collect the revenue of outgoing and incoming goods. I could not hold a job very long after I established a reputation for corruption and bribery. Especially among small thieves. Appeal your case to a court and redeem you goods."

"But your honor, you haven't heard me out yet," whined the merchant.

"I've heard enough. There are many people awaiting me and my decisions. You've had your time. Be off with you or I shall be required to call in the sheriff and report this conversation."

I know that I should not have been listening to this case, but it was seldom that port business was done in the home and I learned much from hearing the honest official fend off the dishonest proposal. The house was always full of visiting merchants from all over the world. I learned much from them. Someone was always leaving a cut of silk or velvet or lace for Gilbert or Rohan to admire and they always failed to reclaim the objects. Objects of brass, silver and gold were placed throughout the house to be admired and occasionally stolen by some untrustworthy visitor or servant. Some of the merchants would bring in hints of the world abroad and I longed to see Italy, Greece and other faraway places. Gilbert Becket always maintained an interest in the east after his adventures there. A traveler from those places was always sure of an invitation to his board if he brought news of interest from the Holy Land or the Land of the Greeks. I remember one well.

This man was tall, thin, olive skinned with elaborately curled hair and whiskers. He wore a tall peaked hat of silk and swirled about in red silken robes. He smelled of musk and spices but was exceedingly dirty. He had come to London with a cargo of golden objects, Cathay silk, precious stones and finished leatherwork. His cargo and conversation impressed Gilbert Becket greatly.

It was in the winter, if I recall correctly that this bearded, perfumed one came. Madam Becket was still abed with the new born child and I was called on to run more than my share of the errands. I quickly attached myself to the great hall and the fire and made myself indispensable to the master by anticipating his demands.

"How now sir, what is heard of the east," Becket queried the visitor.

"The war goes well for the Christians," replied the bearded one. "Here child, take these and see that they are well turned in salt," he said to me.

I stood, looking expectantly at the master, because I did not understand one word he said.

"Take the bag and run down to the kitchen," Gilbert ordered me, "and tell the cook to sprinkle them generously with salt, then heat them. Tell the oaf to take care that they do not burn, and serve them on one of the good silver platters while they are still warm."

I nodded my understanding, took the small bag the stranger proffered me and sped off to the kitchen. Cook was aghast. "What are they?" she whispered, "some kind of good luck nut from far away. Or are they perhaps evil and intended to poison someone?"

"I don't know," I informed her, "but I am to wait and serve them after you have heated them in salt," I said.

"I'd best not smell them," said cook as she wiped the sweat from her greasy brow with the dirty apron she usually wore. "They might poison my innards or put weevils in my guts."

I was frightened by what she said but not too much so, because I thought to help myself hastily to some cold boiled mutton and as stealthily as I could, conceal some cold bread on my person. I could take it or send it home by my father where it would be ever welcome. Cook quickly warmed the flattish brown nuts stirring them slowly and put them on a silver dish and covered them with a clean napkin. As I rounded the corner going into the hall to the great room I hid some of the nuts in my garments. I wanted to see what they did. If they were evil, I would toss them in the fire, if they would turn out to be good, then I had something to gain.

Becket took the dish from my hands, uncovered the nuts and extended the dish to the visitor. The man took a small handful and began to munch on them. My master did the same.

"Ah, good, good," murmured the dark haired one.

"Yes, yes, a taste of the Greeks," murmured the master appreciatively.

I turned my back and quickly popped a nut into my mouth. The salt was good, but the bitter taste almost caused me to retch. I decided to save the reminder of these curious items and take them home. Thus it was that almonds were introduced into an English family other than one of high rank or one of Norman descent or origin. "Do things go badly for the Christians in the Holy Land?" my master asked the trader.

"Not so badly for the Christian but for the Greeks," answered the Levantine softly. "It will be a pity to see that great trading nation fall. They are between a great nutcracker. The Christian west with the Pope demanding religious supremacy, the Normans demanding land and a voice in the government, and the Turks invading by the millions spells doom for the Comnenus family and the fall of Constantinople. Things are in a great ferment. Religious persecutions occur daily. Trade is seriously declining, the Genoans are greedy for every type of coin that exists but I believe the Venetians are worse. Few people in this day and time can withstand the Norman mailed fist except the Turks and they do so with sheer size of numbers. That part of the world is not safe anymore for anyone. Government and protection are almost nonexistent."

The master looked a bit disturbed.

"But the seasons change as they ever did. The pomegranates are as sweet as ever. You can see for yourself the almond knows no change in man and its fruit is as tasty as any found on earth." The merchant looked at master.

"Yes, you are right," said Gilbert Becket. "The world still lives despite whatever havoc man may wreak. I would have thought God in his wrath might have destroyed things long ago and started anew. But here there is peace among men. Business is good and people like you renew us with the news of other lands. I hope the infidel will be subdued in the Holy Land and devout, religious people can visit the tomb of the eternal Christ without fear of loss or life and limb."

"The Turks will not lose the Holy Land," the merchant said softly. "They are there to stay."

"Why do you say so?" demanded my master excitedly.

"It is their home and that is a strong motive to fight. They do not have the long supply problems that the Christians face and the food problem for them is not very great. They have unity in their ranks. Neither the western Christians or the eastern Christians trust each other and this war within wars will finally eliminate them from the Holy Land."

"It is hard to believe since the kings and the Church demand unity of purpose in the conquest of Christendom from the infidels."

"Kings cannot command the natives in the near east and the Pope is far away when one wishes for a kingdom of his own. Especially when one desires the kingdom of another Christian prince. Western manpower is very short in the Levant and it is quickly exhausted if the fighting is heavy.

"But we ship horses and men all the time to augment what we have over there," my master said heatedly. "There is forever new taxation and new levies of foodstuffs and clothing. Ships leave the port at all times heavily laden for the fighting forces. We rent ships from many nations to assist us in transporting people and supplies. There must be many westerners and much western supplies in the home of Christ's birth. England, France, Germany, Italy....all send much of everything they have, including men and horses."

CHAPTER 2

The merchant continued his conversation as he toyed with a candied lemon rind, a great delicacy the world over.

"The elaborate requirements of great men from the west to live are not available in that land whatever you might send. The non-fighters that attend them are as big a drain on their resources as are the fighters. In some cases, I have seen it more so. It took more to supply the camp followers than it did to keep the men in the field. Your kings do not cooperate. They are determined to rule wherever they are, thus you have conflicting ideas about who rules where and what. I have again seen serious efforts to subdue the enemy come to naught because two kinds or princes disagreed on who was to rule."

"True, true," my master sighed, "I know that Germanic desire for orderliness is irksome and even my own kinsmen, the Normans, are very difficult when it comes to ownership of the land. I cannot say that I truly like the Italians myself, because I never know whom they are supporting. It seems that all they want is payment immediately for whatever they do, even if the Pope does order them to serve the cause of God. But I thought that with a renewed effort we would defeat the infidel and restore the Holy Lands to the Glory of our Maker."

"It will not come in yours and my lifetime," smiled the merchant, "so why worry about something we, as individuals, cannot resolve? I, myself intend to survive and live the life I know as best I can live it. If I do not die on the high seas, I will die somewhere in what you call the Holy Land. It is my home. I am a city dweller, not a nomad, so I shouldn't really judge the matters that go on in the interior," he smiled wanly, "but I long and yearn for peace and a return to normal trading ventures. Taxes on merchants have always been oppressive but wartime taxes are almost forbidding. I must pay at every port and every city where I trade."

"Perhaps if the Christians triumph, there might be standardized prices established throughout the land," suggested master, "perhaps coinage can be made that everyone will accept and a common language established so that travelers and people can make some sort of understanding."

"The Christians will not triumph. They cannot muster the manpower nor the unity. If they did triumph, who would establish the common coinage and language? The Pope? The Germans would not tolerate that, neither would the Normans. The Italians? They are universally hated as avaricious mercenaries. The Turks and Jews hate the Christians and the Christians feel that these two groups of people are only to be tolerated as slaves and movers of commerce. The Popes are the only ones who could possibly bring order to the Christian world and the Byzantine and Italian ones cannot agree. The Turks and Jews would never accept the decisions of these men. Venality, greed, and belief in who is right will always stand in the way of universal unity. The only thing that anyone agrees on is that there is a God but they are even willing to fight about whose God is the God," the Levantine smiled wearily.

"Of what persuasion are you?" asked Becket.

"I am a Levantine," replied the merchant, "I profess no particular faith or race. Being born in the crossroads of the world my ancestry and religion is one of all. I generally manage to blend with all faiths and peoples wherever the occasion demands."

"What would you do if you had to choose?" demanded my master.

"I do not know. I do know that I would not make my God white or black or brown or in the manner of any known race or country. I would not make him militant nor would I make him a native of the land. I believe God is for everyone and all things and that he cannot be personified in man or in man's philosophy if man persists in identifying Him with a certain group of privileged people. I believe God is universal, all embracing, all unifying and as considerate of one people as he is another. Man is made in the image of God, so God has to be faceless. His son Jesus, who died on the Cross, was a Jew. The Christians and Turks hate Jews. Yet they stream across the land and sea in countless numbers to reclaim Christ's birthplace from the Turk who worships God but not Christ. Both groups persecute the Jews, yet tolerate the Jew to conduct the commerce of the world. Neither is at war with the Jews, yet the contempt for anything Jewish is barely concealed. The God I worship is not concerned with these things. He is wise, loving, tolerate, and above all not contemptuous nor enslaving. I can feel at home in any church that is dedicated to the true worship of God or in any house where he is revered. My God goes with me wherever I am. I feel the universe is God's especial house and he gives me .living space."

"You speak heresy, my friend. Be careful where you say such things and in front of whom you speak. The Church will not tolerate such broad views and you can be imprisoned and persecuted. You would be barred from trade in most of the western kingdoms if your views become too widely known. Such universality is not in the concept of the times. Besides, you are literally denying the divinity of Christ and the Pope. Those are heinous crimes and strike at the fundamentals of our beliefs. I am a tolerant man, but I believe in the certainty of God and Christ. I am a good practicing Catholic and for me the Pope is God's true vicar on earth. What he says is my law and I am bound to obey his every command and admonition. I have a new born son in my house for whom I have great ambitions. I shall prepare his world as best I can to assure him of a successful future."

"I realize that I do indeed speak at odds with the Church of the west," replied the merchant, "but I am careful where I speak and in front of whom I speak. I have lived these many years without conflict and shall continue to do so. You are a good man, sir, and have always been fair and honest with me. It is not only the west that will not tolerate my ideas. The Greeks, although much broader minded than most Europeans, will not go so far as to intimate that the Son of God is not divine. However, they have changed their Pope and Metropolitan into a political figurehead and he is appointed or removed at the whim of the ruler of the nation. The Jews and Turks take issue with me at times because I will not proclaim their faith as mine, although with them I have less differences. All people pray to God when they go into battle or face extreme circumstances, so there must be a fundamental idea existing that a supreme power beyond our understanding exists for everyone. Certainly something motivates this world. Something gives life and takes it away. The roll of the oceans is fearsome and the force of the winds is awful to behold, yet I have known more peace riding the ocean or facing the winds than I have ever found in any place of worship and I have attended them all. I have repeatedly gone to synagogues, mosques and churches of the Christians and have found them to be pleasant and basically in agreement with each other. Yet I have heard priests of all faiths thunder against other beliefs and other peoples. It frightens me to think that men of God wish to murder or conquer by the sword. I believe that anyone must fight for existence and fight against encroachment, but I believe this is a matter for governments and men, not one of the interpreter of faith. But let us change the subject – you say you have a son? Congratulations, may he be blessed beyond all men. A person is lucky to have children and a son is special. Do you have plans for him or have you decided to wait and see how his talents will indicated? I realize that I am more than a question box," laughed the Levantine, "but a son excites me. I have many by my wives and I have great plans for all of them. My greatest wish at the moment is that they will grow in good health, have some intelligence and bring me happiness by being successful in business and bring me many grandchildren to sustain me in my old age." He laughed loudly.

"Yes I have plans for him," said Gilbert Becket, laughing with his visitor, "he will be trained in the Church, and in business. My family are business people or people who serve in the government. His mother's people are farmers. She brought a small but substantial dowry that has been set aside for his future. I would like him to study at Oxford, the new universities abroad, particularly the one in France and be able to be versatile. The law is a very desirable profession to have to go with a business or Church career. I have many relatives here in London town and some small influence, so if I live long enough, I may perhaps get him launched here in the city. How does he look? Strangely enough he looks slender, dark of complexion with brown eyes. Is it not strange what with his mother and me both being blonde and short, that he would already appear to be slender and dark?" queried my master.

"Not necessarily so, my friend," said the merchant quietly. "Despite what many people may believe, there has been a great interchange between the east and west for centuries and the ancestry of most people is a blend of all persons. The people of southern Europe have filtered north as long as time has existed. You know yourself that in the region from where your wife comes, she has many relatives that are slender, of dark complexions, and southern ancestry. Now, me, I think that dark people with black, black hair are the most handsome people on earth," laughed the visitor.

"You are right, so correct," said Gilbert Becket swiftly, "I have not thought beyond my Norman ancestry. I have accepted the fact that my children would be fair and stocky so completely that I have been blinded to true matters."

"Does the wife do well?" inquired the visitor.

"Well enough, but not as well as I expected," and here a worried look creased Gilbert Becket's brow, "you know I have daughters and my wife had no trouble at their birth but this one has been different. She has not felt well at all and tends to droop at times. However, the babe is only a few weeks old and I pray that she will mend as time goes on."

"I do so hope that myself," the merchant spoke with earnestness, "I shall send him a gift when I return to my ship and have sorted out something suitable."

"It is not necessary," Becket assured him, "you were more than generous with my daughters and even if you are a friend of long standing I would not have my job or our friendship compromised with an accusation of favoritism. Simony in the church is an accepted thing even if the Cistercian monks do preach and advise against it. This attitude extends to all phases of life and a person so jeopardized by such an accusation stands to lose all that he has gained. I have seen some brutal sequestering of lands and savings by the king's officials when an individual became embroiled in charges of dishonesty."

"You worry too much, my old friend," soothed the merchant, "I would do nothing that would cause any trouble for you. We have been friends too long for something like that to happen. It is of no consequence for friends to exchange gifts at the birth of children. It is the practice of granting special privileges and favors at the expense that caused differences among men. I would never demand that. I prefer fairness in my business dealings and attempt at all times to separate it from my private life. This simony you speak of, disillusions me with your church. I realize that the selling of money profiting schemes is universal. Grants must be made for concessions but the idea of God's work being utilized for such purposes is repugnant."

"I agree. Consequently I am most careful to see that my personal priest is free from such sin," said Becket positively, "and there is a new crusader, Bernard of Clairvaux, who is attracting worldwide attention by exposing such ills. His work will expose more than just simony, I fear, and reform can be a dreadful thing. Many innocent people can be hurt or ruined for life. That is why that if a movement for general reform both in the secular and temporal world does arise, I want to be in the clear with my honesty unquestioned. I am not so worried as I wish to make sure that myself and none of my family, and that includes my or my wife's relatives here in England are unaware of the great priest's sermons. I will accept your gift in all graciousness and I will promise that my son will grow to know the generous giver. I have never given your children anything of good faith, chiefly because I have never known when one was born."

"Thank you for your kind intentions," laughed the Levantine, "I am a wanderer, thus I must appreciate the stable people like you who stay in one place and provide people like me with a haven of rest and refuge from the crushing world of commerce and travel when we come to land. Rover that I am, I relish visits such as this. Your home is one of the most restful I have ever known. In cold climates such as this, my spirit withers if I am exposed to the elements. A brisk walk is fine and a short stay in the north is good for reinvigoration but I could never survive in this climate. I don't want to survive in this climate. I am a southerner. I love the warm, hot sunshine, the desert air and the cool, dry evenings. I love to eat outside, sleep outside and to know that I can arise and travel without fear of too drastic a change in the weather. My life, strangely enough, is governed by the relative stability of the weather of my home. And as for my children! Ha! You could never gift my children. I have too many. At times I must prolong my stay at home in order to bring peace among my wives and inventory my children. You monogamous westerners with your ideas of one woman whom you, in many cases wind up hating, after you become bored with her, and cannot get free of her, would never, never understand the delightful variety of more than one wife and the joy it brings to a man to have young love in his house at all times."

"No I would never understand that," returned Becket, "I observed these manners while on the Crusade, but I would get just as weary of supporting all these people and trying to please so many people that I'm afraid I would not make a good husband and father. My mind does not comprehend the management and requirements of such a large household and so many personalities involved. No, no, I fear I could never find happiness under such circumstances."

"I would slit one woman's throat if I had to live with her all the time," the merchant smiled with shrewdness, "she would become so boring to me that I cannot even contemplate the thought. I am a born itinerant. At home, I wander from house to house seeking different entertainment. My first wife is becoming somewhat of a shrew, she is getting too fat, she is almost past the childbearing stage and although we have had many children, only two live and they are girls. That is to her everlasting shame. I shall turn her into a housekeeper and nurse for my younger children when I return home, it is best for her, then she will not expect love from me and will free me for the younger ones."

"How many do you have?" asked Becket.

"Six at the present," smiled the Levantine, "I believe I have taken two since I saw you last, and I plan to add two more to my harem if I can find enough eunuchs to staff my home."

"Do all the wives have children?" Becket's interest was visible.

"Unfortunately the number two and three wives do not, or perhaps it is fortunate. The fourth, fifth and sixth women are proving to be prolific. The two barren women devote themselves to nursing the others so they stay busy and useful, else they would have to go. I cannot afford unproductiveness in my household. They are good fieldworkers also. Their gardens are very fine but they tend to use too much water if they are not cautioned from time to time."

"The idea of being a eunuch is repulsive to me," said Becket with some heat.

"It is to me also," agreed the merchant, "but one cannot have active males in a feminine household, especially when one has to be absent from home as much as I. It is a bad practice, but very practical. Seldom will you find a eunuch objecting with his condition. He is generally a child of slaves and is emasculated at a very early age, so he knows no difference. Most of them are very strong, have effeminate characteristics and are, in general, very loyal. No large house is complete without a good managing male and in the absence of the lord of the house, the men are indispensable. Quite often, as in my house, eunuchs handle all the finances, the management of the estate and in many cases, discipline of the women and children. I could not provide an existence for so many people if there was not some way to have adequate male and female management. It is very satisfactory for me and most reassuring to know that in my absence my children and wives and lands are relatively secure. With the incursions of the Crusaders, though, we must be ever more vigilant, because they, like you, do not understand. Many of them are most rapacious and they are superior at looting. I shall perhaps have to curtail my traveling and stay at home more in order to safeguard my own. I too, like you, wish to provide security for my family and protection, also. The future of my sons and daughters is rapidly approaching me, so my visits may be more and more infrequent. I hope they do not cease. I know I shall be very discontented if I am confined to such a small area as my estates. Yet if I must, I will accept the kismet and attempt to insure the security of what I have."

"It is sad to contemplate the loss of your visits. Although I have many visitors, yours is one of the most welcome. You bring a breath of the land of sunshine with you and also the news of the conditions of that area are welcome. It will be to my advantage to advise that shipments of assistance be stepped up to the Holy Land. That means more contact with the slippery Venetians and Genoans. They can be most disagreeable. I understand they are very demanding on taking government cargo to our Crusaders and that they tax those poor people before they will land any material. It is sad that this country does not have sufficient vessels to handle this problem." Gilbert Becket shook his head.

"It would be good," replied the Levantine, "I too, cannot deal with the Italians. I must watch closely when I am at sea that they do not board my ship and enslave me and my crew. Fortunately, we are fighters who do not care for slavery, thus we have been able to repel any boarding crews that have attacked us so far. And they will demand stiff payments to land in any ports they control. The Greeks are the easiest to deal with because they have no ambition to rule the world. I must be going, my good friend. The hour grows late. It is almost dark and I must see to my ship before my men disperse. If I do not see you again before I sail, I wish you all the happiness there is."

"The visit has been most enjoyable," Gilbert Becket returned as he arose. "I will see you to the door and have some servants attend you to the ship. Son of Wat, "he ordered me, "run to the stables and tell three of the men to report to the front entrance immediately. Tell them also to bring stout sticks as they are to go to the docks. As you well know, the streets are not safe after nightfall," Becket explained to the visitor, looking meaningfully at the flashing raiment that swirled as the man walked.

"I visit too many places to go abroad like this, and I never go unattended," the Levantine explained. He clapped his hands and three men materialized from the shadows of the entry way. One held a coarse nondescript cloak that completely enveloped his master.

As I ran to give the men the master's message, I knew they would grumble at having to leave their warm quarters and go into the cold wet streets. Most of them were scared of the evil spirits that could be found in the fog and they were even more so afraid of the footpads and impressers for the navy. "I must get a name for myself, I thought. I cannot go forever without a name. Son of Wat was nothing except for the merest identification. Even dogs, cats and horses had names." I did not ponder long because the house was cold away from the fire and I felt very, very sleepy. I hoped the master would need me much longer. Without visitors or something to hear things could be very slow. The women were locked away in their quarters. The girls were very boring when they were about. The cook and the servants only found chores for me or else they cuffed me for the slightest thing. Sleep by the warm fire, curled up on a ledge just above the dogs was what I wanted most.

When I got back to the fire, the master was standing in the room conversing quietly with the visitor as the men silently stood in the shadows. Almost at once, the men came around from the stables and with a small wave, all departed.

"Go tell the cook to send me some hot wine, then go to bed. You must be very tired."

I did as I was told and brought the wine back shortly. The master seated himself on the shadowed side of the fireside with the wine cup in his hands. I went to the opposite side and crawled upon a ledge. I did not envy my brothers and sisters huddled in the damp straw at home. I remember nothing more of that day. I was awakened before day break by a maid who was sweeping up the ashes and rekindling the fire. The dogs were gone and the house was very, very quiet and cold.

"You've got to get out of my way," the woman snapped. "The master is about and in a hurry to get to his office."

I ran down to the hall to the kitchen where cook was frying a huge amount of bacon. I easily broke off a chunk of bread, dipped it into the hot grease and lifted a half raw slice of meat to my mouth. I ran off to the stables savoring part of the bread and meat, being careful to save some for my father, who I knew would be hungry even if he had just eaten the thin gruel that my mother had prepared. My father was a kind and considerate man and he let me lean against his legs while he ate. He never scolded us and shoved us aside as my mother often did.

CHAPTER 3

The boy, Thomas grew apace. I somehow gradually, in addition to my other chores, became to be his companion. My father did not hold to my becoming a personal servant because he said that it did not have much security. It depended on the whims and fancies of too many things and too many people. He was determined that I should learn the arts of the ostler and I soon became adept at handling horses. I loved the animals and feeding and grooming them was a pleasure. Working saddle leather into intricate forms and inserting brass and ornaments into the leather was not what I liked. I liked to rub the horses until they shone and I liked to see them in warm comfortable stables, sleek and restless from good food and good grooming.

My master, strictly forbad us to ride the horses as they were for his constant use and chiefly baggage animals. They had to have exercise though, and he reluctantly allowed me to do the work. No other male servant seemed to care for the job, and I accepted with alacrity. The most pleasant part of the day if the horses were not to be used was to mount one and ride him over the fields outside the city. I became adept at riding. More so than many children of my age because it was largely unsupervised. Certainly other servants and their children envied me and I could only ride when the daylight was at the full and I could not ride far from the city's edge. My father never failed to remind me that poor people's children never rode horses and should a brigand attempt to take the animals, I could expect very little in the way of justice. I was heedless to any caution except that I never gave anyone a ride or conversed with anyone. I never took the horses home. Only armed travelers, nobles with guards or the king rode in that part of London. Even they were not safe from having spoiled vegetables thrown at them or attempts made to deprive them of clothing or valuables.

After I began to exercise the horses regularly, the days were the same as drinking heady wine. Whether it rained, snowed or the sun shone made no difference. I exulted in just being on horseback galloping across the soft moors and downs, occasionally taking a hedge or ditch in my desire to master the art of riding a horse in a commendable manner. I loved to ride alone and I made every attempt to let the other exercisers and riders stay by themselves. It mattered not that the warhorses and racers looked down their noses at my stolid, unexcitable mounts. I was as well as the best in the city and I knew it.

By the time Thomas Becket was five years old he had attached himself to me in such a manner that it was hard to avoid him and go anywhere, including home. I still had not settled on a name but was coming close to using the old Saxon name of Egbert and I was slowly encouraging him to call me that. The family hardly noticed it in the Becket household. I did not dare mention it to my parents, because it would be unseemly. They would give me a name when I was old enough to go into the world which would be a few years yet. I would not let Thomas go riding with me and he whined so much about it, until the mistress suggested that I not ride until the youngster was able to do so also. This meant that I would be in and around the house all the time because I was required still to run and fetch and help in the stables. Only the common sense of my father and the steadiness of Gilbert Becket kept me from rebelling.

"My son," my father would say in that soft musical unhurried voice of his, "never tempt the fates or rebel against your good fortune. Do not do things that are forbidden and you will find in time that is forbidden you." (Oh, when I think on these pithy sayings of my long dead father! I catch myself still saying them to my poor dead Thomas also. And the Lord knows, I said them to him enough while he was living!)

"But sire, I am tired of nursing the little boy all the time. I am tired of running here and there for the mistress. Some of the servants are forever calling me to fetch this and that and I eternally shovel manure from the stables or groom the horses in some fashion!"

"It is busy that you should be and then you will not have the time to think on devilment. You will not have time to shirk or think of ways of shirking. And I am not pleased at your attitude at home. You must never show disrespect for your mother. Never let me hear you talk back to her or fail to do her bidding in your very best manner. It is difficult enough on mothers to rear children and maintain a home. She must be respected and loved and obeyed. Evil or mean thoughts of or toward one's mother is to invite eternal shame and sin on one's soul."

"But she screams at me and tells me that I think I am better than the rest of the family and that I am fat while the others are thin and hungry. And father, she smells when I get near her. She does not wash often enough."

"Your mother has had enough trials already to kill any other woman. She lost five babies in a row before you were born and she still has four at home that must still be reared. I shall place them in good positions as soon as I am able, then she will have more relief to rest and save her strength. As for washing, if you were not in this particular home, neither would you be washed. I only wash myself because the master expects it of me and provides toweling to dry myself on. I hate for him to see the cloths clean all the time! There is hardly sufficient water to cook with and wash the few clothes that we wear. There is none for the luxury of bathing your skin. The men here in the stables never wash, yet you never seem to find them exceptional."

"Oh yes I do. I do not go near them if it is possible. They smell worse than the dogs in the house, but mother smells worse than any! Do you realize, father, that Mistress Becket requires me to wash from my elbows to my hands, from my knees to my feet and my neck and face twice a week? Even if I find that to be too much although I admit I wash my hands more often, because I have learned to like clean hands when I eat."

"Well, it's a changing world and I don't know what things are coming to," sighed my father, evidently wishing to close this conversation for fear of what I would say at home. "You have stayed here so much and known peace for so long that it would be difficult to ask you to change or to keep you at home to help your mother."

"Help my mother?" I gasped. It had never occurred to me that mother needed anything. She had never demanded that I stay at home and the idea was repugnant to me that I should have to stay in the hovel other than just nights when my father insisted that I go and stay with the family. I must admit that I got awfully tired at times chasing Thomas and the other children of the Becket household and I really fretted when Mistress Becket and all the servants combined converged on me to run this chore or that chore. Washing produce or taking a knife and skinning the hair from meat from the pot was equally irksome. I was forever demanding that cook or Mistress Becket, who generally did the purchases from vendors who came to the door, demand that the groceries be presented in a better and cleaner fashion. Quite often, they would look at me as if I was a little daft because such things were not the custom and therefore not expected.

They did not have to do the washing and cleaning. It was always me or some scullery maid, or more often both.

Messir Becket came into the stables while father and I were discussing the home situation.

"Do we keep him from home too much, Wat?" he queried my father.

"No sire," my father firmly replied, "there are many at home. It is just that I feel he must be reminded that there is a home and that his responsibilities lie in both places. I am happy for him here and that he can be so lucky as to get such a good situation."

"He is apt and able and little Thomas loves him dearly. So does my dame. He is very useful to his household and even I find pleasure knowing that he is about because he runs endless errands for me when he is about. I am beginning to understand your Saxon attitude about loving home and family. It seems that it lies in the Norman blood to go forever about and look for new lands to conquer and new peoples to subject. I fear I am becoming English," he smiled, "because I am becoming fanatically attached to London and my placid way of life."

"I hold it my bounden duty to love and protect my family," returned my father with dignity. "We are poor but we can be proud, love our masters, king and country and still be the better for it. Besides, the Holy Church teaches that it is honorable to honor they father and mother. He has no grandfathers or grandmothers to have to visit, so I fear, he must learn to love and respect his mother and father. It reminds me of the perilous days of King William Rufus," my father said, "when neither kith nor kin were safe from the rapacious Normans. People were slaughtered for no reason other than they offended the king while on tour when they failed to all come forth and kneel to the ground."

"Those were bad times," agreed Gilbert Becket, "and although I was not here all the time, I have heard much about the senseless cruelties and the bestiality of that less than noble ruler. But did you know, Wat, that in the Holy Land, the lesser folk care little for children once they are able to steal and fend for themselves?"

"Many who have been on Crusades tell me that people die very early over there from many diseases, and that children are about in significant numbers who do not know of parents and homes. I wonder how they manage." My poor simple father who had always held us closely to him was at a loss to understand a society that left children in an unaccountable and unmanageable estate.

"I never could understand it," Messir Becket said scratching his head, "but we always had hordes of children who attached themselves to us, yearning for food and love. There were many very young girls who had babies and did not know how to care for them. I am sure this was a result of careless relations to the ever ready soldier and the children's desire for food. Hunger at times knows no rationality and we did leave the fields and stock in sadly depleted conditions wherever we went. We had to live off the land and it was perilous at times, especially in the land of the accursed Greeks. It finally came to us forcing the granaries and stock pens of smaller towns and villages. I preached constantly that it would be wiser to take only what we needed and leave something ere we wished to return that way again. There were many who felt the same way as I did, but generally such attitudes fell on deaf ears. The soldiers and particularly the camp followers, destroyed what they could not carry. Things got very, very bad when the Greeks started scorching the earth before us and poisoning the wells and turning out their armies to repel us when we needed food. Many weak and hungry children, women and old men fertilized the plains of Greece and the Holy Land with their unshriven, emaciated bodies. At first, we were careless about the dead and in many cases, left them to be despoiled by the birds and animals.

Unfortunately, they became tallies to the Turks and the Greeks who could tell the condition of our armies, by the number of the fallen. After that, all dead were buried and carefully marched over and over their graves, the army left no telltale signs of weakness."

"Sounds horrible," shuddered my father, "to be buried in unhallowed ground and unshriven. The movement to join the holy orders and fight the infidel was strong in me at one time. I am now glad that I did not go. Why you could not get to Purgatory if you were not given unction at death." My father was appalled. I was too, and horror showed on the faces of the servants of the stable and the hangars on who were ever there to listen and visit. Whatever we might do or say, we were devout members and believers in the Church and its benefits. All of us simply wanted to go to Heaven when we died, and the functions of the priest were as essential as eating and breathing while we lived. To die and be buried without notice was condemning our souls to eternal damnation. It was unthinkable. The stable buzzed with angry and distressed sounds. Many vowed that they were strongly tempted to take up monasticism, thus ensuring their orderly progress into acceptable eternity.

"Your lad has been defiling me to let him ride the horses, master," my father said diffidently.

Gilbert Becket smiled. "Does he harass you or beg?"

"No, even at the tender age of six, he is too clever for that. He is uncommon smart and almost too beautiful to be a boy. His mind and language are most pleasing to me and I fear that in a moment of weakness I will yield and displease you."

"That is his way in the house," Becket smiled ruefully, "and with me also. I continually must watch myself not to yield too suddenly or too much. I find his countenance pleasing, but it befuddles me from where comes his pale complexion and aquiline features. He is clever in his presentation of his desires and I have never known him to lose his temper when he does not gain his wishes. However, I am beginning to realize that he comes back at a later time and presents his case all over again and usually gets what he wants. If he did not gain my favor so willingly, I would be more alert to saying no or giving him a deferred judgment."

"That is the way he handles me also," said my father. "I cannot be ill tempered with him because he never arouses my hostility or my ire. I feel that perhaps with my son here that he can perhaps begin to ride one of the gentler mounts."

"I feel so too," Becket agreed readily, "he must begin to learn some of the necessities of life and not be cloistered with his mother and the girls too much."

"He is tall enough to pass for an older age," my father said, "and that will help him somewhat."

"Agreed," said Messir Becket.

I listened to this conversation avidly. I was beginning to become most irritated in being confined to the houses too much. My growing charge was wishing more and more for activity and becoming more and more demanding that I allow him to participate in my activities. This I let him do, except the servants would not let him run errands. As the son of the master, they would not or could not bring themselves to order him around or assign him any menial tasks. Madam Becket was relying much more than I thought proper on her growing daughters to run and fetch for her.

My own family was becoming a problem. My younger brother had to be taken into the stables. His mind ran to gardening, horses and roaming the streets. Already he was a gifted petty thief which pleased my mother and horrified my father. He had forced my brother to come with him to work but our population explosion was becoming of concern. Then too, my brother, like me had no given name so there were two sons of Wat around and it was at times perplexing and confusing. I had quietly determined that on my twelfth birthday which would not be far off, that I would become

Egbert Watson and so have my name registered. My brother
was equally determined that he would have a name also and
we spent some anxious moments deciding what it would be.
He loved the name Edward so we decided it would be that if
the law allowed. If not, then he would be Arthur or Eggleston.
My father was disturbed at this.

"You put yourselves above your station, even if the law
does allow first names to be given to everyone," he cautioned
us.

"I am an Englishman and proud of it," I said to him
loftily, "and if our Norman conquerors can come to our
country and impose their customs on us, this is one that we
should readily adopt. Mother thinks that the girls should have
names, also."

"I did not think you agreed with your mother on
anything," father said to me.

"I can't agree with her much, but on this I do."

"Have you decided on names for the girls? Three are a
lot of thinking."

"Yes," I returned quickly, "actually three names are not
many since there are so many to choose from. We think Sarah,
Margaret and Matilda would be good names."

"Take care," warned my father, "those are common
names among ladies of royalty and gentry."

"But also among the commoners of Anglo-Saxon
ancestry," was my rejoinder. "Madam Becket has already
looked into it for me and we stand on firm ground and in no
respects do we flout the law or pretend. I can't stand pretense,
but I have an intense desire for identification and have had
this desire since the day young Thomas was born. It was so
satisfying to know that the babe had a name! He would not
forever have to be called son of Gilbert or Becket. However,
the relatives have pretensions since they are Normans and
identified with the Conqueror and insist on attaching the
continental fashion of 'a' to his name as if he came from a

great house. Me, I choose to ignore it, and if he is to become a true Englishman the 'a' must go."

"So now you go and change the actions of your betters," my father said sarcastically, "perhaps I let you stay in the big house too much."

"Father, you know I hate pretense, but these are changing and momentous times. Even if we cannot rise above our station, we can be individuals."

My brother all this time had stood by and been mute.

"Why did you not support me?" I stormed at him after we were out of earshot of father.

"It would not have been wise," he answered earnestly and softly. "Father plans to apprentice me to the house of Freteval next door and thereby I shall gain my freedom. As you know they have a huge stable, many country estates and require large staffs. In that way I can do my work by the days and be free to roam the streets at night."

"What are you saying?" I asked him incredulously. "You know that father has never let us out at night and you know perfectly well that brigands are heartless with children and that impressment gangs are forever looking for young and healthy cabin boys. You could disappear and never come home."

"You forget that you only have been home at nights since you were five," he said tartly, "where were you when you were free? And before you get on with your tirade, let me remind you that you grow more like father every day. Demanding, supervising, training, seeing that I become competent. Also you forget that I have had some time of my own all my life. Mother welcomed us getting out of the house and out from under her feet. I know the neighborhood well and have been able to survive on the streets for a few years already."

"Do you mean you associate with the wandering ruffians of the streets and deal in thieving and street traffic?" I asked aghast.

"I find the wharves and houses of great merchandise to be most exciting and challenging," he answered me, "are you simple enough to believe that we have existed all this time on father's starvation wages and the skimpy rations you have brought home? If father were not so severe, mother and the girls could have been wearing bits of finery all along. As it is, I have been able to procure enough meat and vegetables so that we haven't starved. Do you not think we would be whey faced and skinny like the other half starved people in this place if we had existed on the meager provender that has been furnished? You are simpler than I thought, brother. You have been too long protected by the sanctity of the Becket household. Mother and I have always agreed to that."

My being discussed by the family without my knowledge was a new and fascinating challenge to me. I admit I had always been a bit stiff necked with them, but now I found it embarrassing to know that they were not as doltish as I had presumed. I looked at my brother in a new light and with new found respect. I could see that he was not undernourished and that his thighs and wrists were beginning to thicken from much hard labor. His hands were calloused where I had always tried to keep mine soft and presentable.

"I go to take up my new position tomorrow," he said matter of factly. "You will not tell father of our conversation will you? Oh Egbert," he exclaimed excitedly and as you can see, we were bandying first names around readily, "life can be challenging here in London town and in England. I have pimped you know," again with some small pride in his voice and I registered horror, "oh it's not so bad when you come to think on it. The sailors are a jolly lot and not too particular about their women after they've been on a long voyage. The foreigners are the best because they will accept the diseased and old ones in their desire for a little friendliness and consideration in a strange land. And the undesirable women are very grateful and reward me generously when I bring them customers who are not too choosy."

I was speechless. Here I, who prided myself in leading a blameless life, who actually dreaded the streets after dark and would have accepted slavery as readily as pimping and thievery or as cabin boy on a naval vessel, found myself with an accomplished brother who was younger than I! His casual statements rang in my ears. And to think that my father was so careful to see that we were properly reared! I was right in being distrustful of my mother. She was too lenient and grasping. Her pride was little and her desires to deceive were too strong.

"Where has mother been all this time?" I demanded. "Did she not see that you were close about?"

"Egbert, let us look the truth in the face," he stated earnestly, "mother is somewhat of a slattern. "Now hold on," he said rapidly seeing that I was going to defend my mother. "You are not the one to be so pious. I readily admit that our father married beneath his station or his steadfastness and honesty. But she is our mother and I for one love her dearly. But she cares little for cleanliness and less about how her children are reared. The zest of life has left our mother if she ever had any. She must have been meanly reared and she means to continue in the same manner. You know yourself that she holds in contempt the rearing you have had in the house of Becket. She would prefer that you had been kept strictly in the stables or allowed to roam the streets as I have and bring home something more than honest wages."

CHAPTER 4

I stared at my brother as if he were a stranger whom I had never seen before. I jumped up in my consternation and rapidly paced the stable floor although I was not thinking. I was too stunned. The lure of this conversation did not entice me. It was too far beyond my imagination to conceive of what I heard. To leave home surreptiously! Where would I go? Not me, I could hear from my insides, not me, I am too afraid.

I sat down still stunned by these revelations. Such knowledge would kill my father I was sure, and a scandal would cause us to be dismissed from this generous house with which we were connected. Already they had spoken for Sarah to enter it because some of the servants were getting old and infirm and I was rebelling against the errand running. The Beckets had seen to it that Wat and his family were not meanly treated by life. Scandal or imprisonment would mean the end of this orderly and peaceful existence. Edward must have read the indecision and my confusion in my face.

"You will not tell father of my thoughts," he begged, "I don't wish to leave home just yet nor do I wish to leave my family alone. Remember Egbert, the sea is a fascinating place. People sail because they like to. Not all are impressed into sailing. I find sailors fascinating, and their tales are the best listening I know. The continent is one place I plan to see many times and the Holy Land is another. I would like to sail to these places because I dislike walking. However, if I must, I will join a Crusading expedition. I, being radically of different mind than yours, wish to travel and see things and people. I might be base born but I'm not ostler born. I may never be able to rise above my station, but I shall not follow in my father's footsteps. If I get the opportunity, I shall settle in some far distant land and attempt to mingle my blood with that of a well born maid and thus someday be reckoned with as one of high estate."

"Your ambition is unbelievable," I gasped to him, "imagine a common Saxon, illiterate, living under the occupation of the Normans speaking as if he were nobility or a great man of letters or repute. Where did you learn such foreign thoughts and how could you understand them at so early an age?"

"From the sailors at the wharves. I can jabber and make myself understood in many languages. I have a small treasure trove of coins and small objects that must be of some value. I do not intend to reveal their hiding place, so do not press me to do so. They are my gateway to freedom if I ever need them. As far as the press gangs, they don't bother me. It is easy to elude them or to resist them if you know the technique. Threats of retaliation are the best method. Many of them are impressed themselves if they realize that retribution might come home to them someday. The children of the streets are not above vengeance nor are they to be trusted just to be children. I have seen some very mature people who are younger than I. I mean to learn that maturity and the new job will give me the opportunity. I do not fear the dark streets. They are the safest place in London if you have a secure place to return to after you become tired. To sleep in them, is dangerous I admit. In fact, you court certain disaster more from the wandering dogs and odd people than from the weather or the law. I have worked the streets at night since I was six. It's easy to enter our house or leave it since the family are such heavy sleepers. With the exception of mother of course. She has let me in more times than I can count and will continue to do so I am sure. It will not be safe anymore though, since I plan to spend a great deal of time at the mansion next door. I am sure that I can arrange it so that my employers can use me in the evenings."

It had finally begun to penetrate my mind that there was some more independence in my family other than mine. I could not imagine where the wild ideas of my brother could come from. My mother and father were relatively placid people who accepted life as they found it. I truly did not see the possibility of rising above the station of ostler or footman in a great and noble family. This to me was the highest of ambition. To deliberately join a ship and sail to foreign lands! And moreover, to live there if one found it compatible and challenging. The ideas were so new and novel to me that I had to sit down and accept them slowly. That my brother could be so quick witted and accept the seamier side of life so complacently was unbelievable. I could easily envision him as a seagoing wayfarer such as the Levantine that I remember so clearly from the age of five. Or the very solid, slow thinking Flemings who sold the fine woolens. Or the unbelievable tall Danes who were frightening in their size and ferocity. The oily, capricious Genoese who drove such hard bargains with my master. All these and many more foreigners had been coming to the house all these years and I had made it a point to be necessary to the master so I could be present and see these strange and fascinating people. I had seen many and learned much. But the ledge by the fireplace was growing too small and the fleas from the dogs bit more ferociously. Besides, the young Thomas was allowed to stay up later and later. He was so bright and affable that all of us were spoiling him terribly by granting his wishes especially if he became persistent. But to wish to sail with these people and leave England perhaps never to return and be drowned or become a slave in a foreign country or a free man in a faraway place among strangers was repugnant. And as far as being on the streets after dark deliberately to outwit the brigands, the watch or impressment gangs was beyond my ken. I had so ingrained my habits and thoughts that it was difficult to conceive of such wildness.

"Do not stare at me as if you are seeing me for the first time," my brother said surily, "if you would stop to realize it, you are rapidly becoming the servant of the youngster in the household. Further, you are too big to be running around in a smock. So am I as for that matter. If we are not able to procure men's clothing without too much suspicion on the part of father and mother, I shall be forced to go into my savings and purchase some."

I looked down at my grubby knees and bare splayed feet. I felt a chill going up my bare legs. My flesh shrunk visibly. I wanted to hide my shame and nakedness. I was not a little boy anymore. I blushed to think of my unconscious nudity before my mother and sister when I slept at home and before the servants as they came in to light the fires in the big house. I was a heavy sleeper, always having to be aroused. I hated my brother for an instance. He was forcing me to flee my innocence and making me become a man. I was not ready, yet here he stood, legs apart, arms akimbo searching my face avidly for an emotion that might become visible. It began to rain. For the first time in my life I felt the damp chill up to my buttocks and although I wanted to urinate badly, I would have died before I would have done so in front of my brother or any other person for that matter. I felt that I could not force myself from some place of concealment until leggings or a long robe of some sort was furnished me. I was shocked to find myself agreeing in my mind with my brother. I would gladly steal if there was no other way to conceal my nakedness.

"What think you, elder brother?" he queried me as I stood lost in shame and conscious nakedness. "You will not tell father of this, will you?" he asked anxiously, "Because if you do, I shall be forced to run away and I don't wish to do that."

"Be quiet, let me think," I snapped at him. I had never before been under such stress and strain. Here I was, the superior knowledgeable member of the family being forced by the formerly unacknowledged younger brother to become aware of the pressing facts of life. We stood silently as I began to gnaw my nails in my nervousness. They were not overly clean since we had been busy in the stables this morning and the meat and vegetables had been particularly annoying with excessive foreign matter on them. An early noon meal had been ordered by the master because some Irish and Welsh merchant men were coming home with him and I had anticipated greatly hearing these brawny and loud men talk of mountains, fens and clan wars. They would also tell of new ships abuilding and whether the king's mercenaries had raided their villages. I would miss this meeting because I would not appear at this meeting even if the master were to beat me. My mulish, stubborn Saxon mind was made up and death would be preferable to being the object of ridicule because of my nakedness. No one had ever mentioned it before, why should they now? My reasoning knew no bounds. I could hear them all laughing and making lewd jests at my expense. The humiliation would be too great. I must get busy and convince my father that my brother and I must be clothed properly. It would not be easy. Perhaps I could appeal to him through his pride and the necessities of health. It was raw, cold and wet and my ankles and knees were the perpetual blue I habitually acquired in unseasonable weather. It had always been of concern to my father but my mother was indifferent to it saying that the human race had endured through much worse torment.

"I must convince father that the clothing is necessary." I told my brother slowly because my reasoning was not sound or firm although my resolve was a burning flame. "It won't be easy," I cautioned him further, "and what about mother. Do you think she will agree?"

"She will if she does not have to wash them," my brother answered indifferently. I looked at him askance.

"That is the second time that you have made a crass remark about our mother. What has she done that you are so against her?"

"Nothing. I love her. But remember that I have been at home all this time. I have seen and lived in that dirty place all these years. Why she wouldn't even bother to wipe our noses when we had colds."

"You sound as if you had lived there for many, many years and I remember well that you are a bare eleven years old if that much."

"One matures rapidly in this world and don't forget that you are only a mere eleven months older than I. Even if you and I are young, there were five before us. Our mother and father are old people. If not in years in looks."

Silently I agreed with him. Father was already complaining of the cold and aching joints and at times I could swear he shuffled. I was in no mood to concede much to this knowledgeable brother of mine. I still smarted from the consciousness of my dress or state of undress as the case may be.

"If I get the old man to agree that we must have clothes, can you produce them?" I asked Edward.

"Easily," he answered.

"They must be worn clothes and not too elaborate, else he will suspicion that they have been stolen," I warned him.

"They will be the coarsest of hose and shoes," he replied loftily. "When I get next door and he can't check on my every move, I shall wear better ones. Egbert," he said earnestly, "we are old enough and big enough to make our own way. Why don't we just sit down with father and get him to agree to let us do so."

Again I was amazed. I did not want to leave home so soon. I would probably never leave if I were not forced to do so. I couldn't conceive of such revolutionary ideas. To be in rebellion of my father was something that had never occurred to me. I knew in my heart that I would rebel if he did not let me cover my legs.

Father was most conciliatory. He was even slightly amused at my concern. "In my day," he mused, "youngsters never thought of such things. What would you affect, young sir, a robe or stockings?"

"Stockings," I replied without hesitation.

"You know that you must bind them around your waist and legs. You must also wear shoes. Poor people cannot afford many of those things. Your mother had only had one pair of shoes in her life and she only wears them in the winter. These clothes will be very hot and the shoes will hurt your feet. How will you run?"

"I'll manage," I returned quickly.

"I will also," echoed my brother. I don't think my father heard him. He gave me a very small amount of small coins. They didn't look sufficient to me. I looked at him.

"Come," my brother tugged at my sleeve. When we had gotten out of earshot of father he whispered softly into my ear. I quickly left and begged Mistress Becket to take leave of the house to go and get some clothes in the meanwhile, attempting clumsily to cover my knees. She laughed and readily agreed.

"Come with me," my brother said and took me back of the house where we lived. "Stay here," he said, "I will be back directly." It only took a few minutes for him to return with a small bundle. I was wordless as he unrolled two pair of the cheapest pair of hose with adequate withings and two pair of shoes. I put them on. After I had wrapped my waist and legs, I still did not feel secure at the waist.

"You stole these," I turned on my brother accusingly. He merely shrugged his shoulders and stretched. It was obvious that he was accustomed to wearing his clothes because they were already stained and torn slightly. I was too carried away with possession at the moment. We went swaggering into my mother. For the first time in a long time, she smiled.

"I don't feel easy in them," I told her, "I fear they might fall."

"I can remedy that easily enough," my mother smiled and forthwith she lifted my smock and punched four holes in the waistband then tied additional small strips in them and crossed my shoulders with the narrow bands. I admired her and for once in my life, I loved my mother. She smiled gently when I hugged her wrinkled and dirty neck. When I returned to the stables my father looked his approval. In the big house the servants laughed at me but Mistress Becket was pleased.

"I vow, son of Wat," she said, "those coverings do become you well. Now that I think on't Messir Becket has some old and worn hosen around the house and I shall have the seamstress alter them so that they may be worn." I almost burst my heart in gratitude. I was sure that I was the only poor boy in London town who had more than one pair of leggings! There could not have been much old clothing in that house because the stable and male servants had been wearing Gilbert Becket's castoffs as far back as I could remember. The new clothing set my head afire for my next project. After the supper dishes had been cleared from the table and the Beckets were talking while watching the children play before the fire I knew I must speak even if it displeased them. I had not needed to stay tonight because my new clothes had raised my status both in the eyes of the master and mistress as well as the servants. I had always despised running after the little girls but Master Thomas was demanding more and more of my time. I set my determination and approached the cleared table and pulled my forelock. This got Master Becket's attention.

"I must needs speak to you, sire, on private matters."

"Speak my son," he said as they both smiled at my new found youth and maturity.

"I must beg a boon. My family, the children that is, wish to have given names and I beg your assistance in getting them registered."

"Why son of Wat, the stableman!" Mistress Becket said sternly. "No peasant has a given name. He carries the name of his father proudly."

I looked from her to the master ready to lose my dignity and manhood and burst into tears. The excitement of the day and the adjustment to the new clothing had taxed me beyond the point of endurance.

"No my bonnie Rohan, you are wrong," sire Becket corrected her gently, "They are beginning more and more to register given names for themselves."

I sank to the floor in relief and let the tears flow copiously. I could have kicked myself for crying in front of them, yet I couldn't stop myself. The children stopped playing and watched me curiously. The two elder Becket girls were tall and fair bidding to become comely. Thomas ran over to me and put his arms around my shoulders and looked at his parents questioningly. Thomas was ever a sweet and sensitive child and his rage would mount when he would find the servants or his sisters cheating at games.

"Oh boy," Mistress Becket spoke to me peevishly, "I did not mean to hurt your feelings. Nothing is this serious." She smiled at me sweetly and the tenderness on her face for her son was her undoing. It gave me courage to pursue this matter to the end. I looked at Messir Becket with longing in my eyes.

"Run and fetch me pen and ink and sand," he spoke to me kindly. "We'll make this a family affair."

I truly sped on that errand and breathlessly stood before him. He listed the names I gave him and carefully folded the paper and placed it in his purse.

"Give no more thought to the matter," he said kindly, "tomorrow one of the clerks will make this a matter of the official record."

Madam Becket had been silent all the while. "Do you mean to tell me, Gilbert Becket, that the most common of all people in the Empire are taking first names?"

"No not all, only the ones who live in the cities and those that hear about it," he answered her.

"I have not heard of such from the continent," she said.

"It has ever been the custom for educated and upper classes to take given names," Becket explained to her, "and the Englishman has always been somewhat different. He has shown more desire to be independent and has sought for individual identification ever since the conquest. This has been noted by all the Norman officials. Many of the gentry discourage or outright resist such new fangled notions, but I for one feel that it should be encouraged. King Henry does not object but some of his Norman counselors do so violently. All my clerks, whether Norman or English have first names."

"I don't seriously object," said Mistress Becket, "it is just that the idea is so new that I must become accustomed to it. Come here Egbert, son of Wat," she said in a sudden excess of affection. I went to her and she placed her arm around my waist, giving me a healthy squeeze.

"I am proud for you," she said gaily, "you are so near a son to me."

"It is Egbert Watson, dear mistress," I corrected her gently as tears streamed down my face.

"La, so it is," she agreed at once, "Egbert Watson, how nice is the sound."

I hated myself for the ease of my tears in front of these kind people for by now the children were dancing around singing my name in chorus. I stood in embarrassed silence and surveyed the commotion I had caused. I did not understand all that the adults seemed to understand but there was within me a desire to be identified. I could still muster a weak argument against being just a first name from somewhere. Many people, having been reared from the places of their birth had forgotten their origins and were almost restless. They adopted names of their professions or those of their masters lest they lose all their identity in society.

CHAPTER 5

"We will all be Englishmen," yelled Thomas and was abashed as I at what he had said because it was an expression that was meaningless.

"Yes, we shall all be Englishmen," agreed his father as he patted the boy on the head. "You will be educated in English schools in English ways, and God grant that you will love this island as I have learned to love it."

"He will sleep with me from now on," Thomas spoke stoutly taking advantage of the great love that his mother and father had for him.

"How now, little man," said his father attempted sternness, "do you propose to take over the household and issue the orders?"

"Oh father, I did not mean to anger you," he said abashedly and scuff the floor with his toe, "it's just that I am getting too big to sleep with you and mother when I get scared and I dislike girl servants around me all the time!"

"It appears that the males of this household are all getting ideas at the same time. I think I like the females around me," sniffed Mistress Becket.

"Oh mama," young Thomas said as he ran to her hugging her, "I will never leave you because I love you best of all."

One could see her face melt as she looked lovingly at her son. The girls, aping their more aggressive brother, ran to the mother and vowed their undying love, then using far more judgment than did their brother, ran to their father and smothered him with hugs and kisses. Becket responded to this by cuddling them both and giving them small coins to buy ribbons for their hair. Their squeals almost pierced my eardrums. It was altogether a scene to remember and in later days of stress and strain, I longed for the peace and order and unbounded love that was in this house that night.

"I think it not too bad that Thomas have a manservant," said Master Becket.

"Perhaps it is best," agreed the mother, "but he is not yet six years of age. Egbert Watson," she looked at me to see how my new name would fit. I stood straight and tall as if I was before a queen. "Go and fetch bedding and make yourself a pallet on the floor of the young master's room. It will be your place of abode from now on."

I did quickly as I was bid and by the time that I had finished, young Thomas joined me and we were told to go to sleep. I found the floor to be hard and cold. No harder than the fireplace and perhaps not as warm, but softer than the cottage floor where my father and mother stayed and warmer than the straw and pitiful rags with which we made do for cover. I hoped the fleas and other bugs would not be too bad as I drifted off into blissful sleep not dreaming of the demands of my new duties nor the storm that would arise from my family on my almost complete break from my home.

When I arose and reported to the kitchen there was little to do so I went to the stables and started to help clean up and feed the animals. In addition to the horses, Master Becket kept cows, sheep, goats, and swine. These had to be driven to the fields each day and returned. There were several witless men around whose duties it was to see that no harm came to the domestic animals and get the milk from the goats and cows each day. Butter and cheese were processed directly in the big house under the eye of a very severe cook. All helped in feeding the animals, sweeping out the stables and doing the general chores. For these duties, these people were given their food and clothing and twice yearly at Michaelmas and Eastertide, gold pieces to spend as they wished. Messir Becket would have found it to his advantage to pay these people and let them purchase their way through life, but such was not the custom between gentry and peasants. Nonetheless, his provender payments must have been enormous even if he did serve the coarsest of fare. In addition to this, the men were issued grain for bread and meat occasionally for their families. Vegetables were grown by the individuals in the family plot near the house or on the edge of London town.

I told my father of what had transpired in the big house the evening before. He looked downcast and angry.

"Does this mean that you leave my house forever?" I will not have that. I do not yield my children without my permission even if I am poor and lowly. I am a freeborn Englishman and I will flee to the forests before I will yield to Norman slavery."

I was dumbstruck. My father, who was always the mildest of men and who had always allowed me the wildest of latitudes was taking exactly the opposite attitude I had anticipated. I felt in my heart to be over elated at the great opportunity that was being granted to me and was nonplussed at his anger and distress.

"But father," I told him, "I thought you would be pleased with these arrangements. Just think, I will not have to be fed nor housed. I will see you every day and I'm sure I will be allowed to go home whenever I wish in the daytime. It isn't far and I can run over there at any time you desire."

"It is not that at all, it is a matter of principle," my father said gruffly, "do not press my young man. Tonight I shall stay and settle this matter between myself and the master. Say no more for I must think this out."

"This depressed me because I could see my father objecting to this arrangement and I would be assigned to the stables permanently or put out of the big house to seek other employment. The thought of adjusting to someone else or running the streets, terrified me.

"Father," I said to him, "I am not the same as Edward. I care not to leave you so soon and I fear the streets and the very thoughts of going into new employment terrifies me. I have saved every copper I have ever received, except for those with which I bought my clothes," I added hastily lest he quiz me on the rapid acquisition of my apparel, "I am not venturesome. I love security and the knowledge of what tomorrow will bring."

"I know that, my son," father said gently, "I do not fear that we will lose Edward soon (How quickly we adapt to new ways! I thought, 'already he is calling us by our given names and us not sure that they are registered yet!') because he has forever been more independent than any of the children. Your mother encourages him by not asking where he has been and letting him stay from the house much too long. But I don't intend to have my house dissembled so early. It will be good, I admit, not to have so many mouths to feed and it should ease your mother's burdens but still and all, a man must have a part in decisions of such great import. Leave me now," he ordered me, "I must think and decide."

I slowly found my way to the big house. Exercising the horses would be out for me today and I regretted that. One of my greatest thrills was to make those gentle animals gallop if it was possible over the greensward through the grazing animals and poultry. I found things to be very routine. Thomas ran to me eagerly to play some game with him and I did so grudgingly. As I was taking my noon meal, the mistress sent for me.

"Egbert Watson," she said to me, rolling the unfamiliar name on her tongue, "you have entered into a new role. You are to stay with Master Thomas day and night, wherever you might go or he might go unless we give you permission to do otherwise. He is your charge and his welfare is placed in your hands. You will be relieved of your other duties and will be only responsible to me or your master for assignments."

"Thank you madam," I said as I touched my forelock, "but I will sorely miss exercising the horses. That has been one of the great pleasures of my humble life."

"You will still exercise the horses," she said to me, "only Thomas will accompany you from now on. It is time he learned to ride and to learn to do manly things. He will help in cleaning the stables, also and will learn to milk."

My mouth hung open as I stared at her. "Oh fiddle," she stormed at me, "although my son is city bred he shall learn of how other people do things. I would not have him grow up without knowledge. Mayhap evil times will fall on him and a man can always live if he has knowledge of horses. Take him now and start teaching him."

Young Thomas showed an amazing ability in riding and I had to restrain him from jumping and galloping to his harm. He was not so sure that he would like to milk and I could see the distaste in his eyes when it came to shoveling manure. However, he did not shirk and for a six year old, he acquitted himself admirably. I cannot recall when he failed to report to me wherever we were to go for his morning ride, rub the horses down when we returned and feed them and often join me in the shoveling manure, for the rest of his life. A most amazing child if ever I knew one. It was obvious on this day as we happily came back from the ride to see that life was to be glorious if father did not upset the plans. We had seen Edward with some animals next door, but he rode under the careful and contentious eye of some older groom who carped, cuffed and gave orders incessantly. It was a large party and I had never bothered to realize that the house next door must be enormous to accommodate such a large body of retainers, but they did not have other animals than horses. Edward did not seem to mind that he was ordered about and responded well to instructions. Later in the day he came over to tell father that his duties were onerous and many and in order to learn them well he would have to sleep in the stables for a while. Father reluctantly agreed and Edward and I both could see that he was suspicious.

"You had best stay in and do as you have said you would," I cautioned him, "because if father becomes overly suspicious he will either terminate your employment or set a groom to watch over you."

"I know, I know," Edward said angrily as he gritted his teeth in frustration, "if I had enough money to suit my needs, I would run away to sea. Ah, how I could be gentry so easily!"

"Bide your time," I pleaded with him, "you are still nothing but a puling babe. There is plenty of years ahead to get what you want."

"I am almost in my twelfth year," he said as he pulled himself up to his greatest height. He was almost as tall as I.

"I will rack those streets, brother," he said to me, "not as a brigand or footpad's helper, he quickly assured me, "but as an independent agent. I must needs take only money or objects that are quickly convertible because father would catch me for sure if I cannot hide what I own. Oh, don't worry for me," he said, "I know almost all the wenches, night men and buyers. They are not too secretive when they know you. I must be careful of the law and those bullies who will take everything if they know you have something. I do not want trouble or a reputation. I will be best off as a normal everyday peasant. I will see you on the mornings I am allowed to exercise the animals or in the early evenings when the chores are done. Never fear, I shall always be in contact. I don't intend to go home any more than is absolutely necessary."

He stared thoughtfully when I told him I had made practically the same decision.

"Poor father!" he said compassionately, "losing us at the same time. I am sure he is glad to see us get started in life because we must have been an awesome burden, but he is so affectionate and so watchful! Mother will be glad because her burdens will be lessened with fewer to cook for and to clean after, not that she ever outdid herself. I will be glad to see the girls grow off and leave that dirty hovel."

"Now aren't the gamey ones," I laughed, "standing here and deciding who goes where and when."

"I am deadly serious," Edward looked at me meaningfully.

"I too," I agreed with him soberly.

The scene when Master Becket arrived home was painful. There were guests that night, Osbert Huitdeniers and some merchants from Italy so my father had to hurriedly say his piece. He would not do so until Madam Becket was present which made her irritable since she had to leave her toilette. The conference was held in the kitchen since it and the eating hall were the only rooms that were heated. The foyer while large enough, was too cold for the guests to talk and wait or for us to talk in. Although there was no snow, the fog was damp and the whole house was chilly except where fires were going. My father came rapidly to the point. The Becket's were profuse in their apologies and assurances.

"You must forgive me Wat," said Becket earnestly, "it was a simple oversight not to consult you on so grave a matter. The press of affairs and your being with me so long made me forgetful. Too, Egbert's being in the house, has made me associate him with my own children. For some reason, I felt he would keep you informed of the activities in the house and that you agreed to all we have done."

"My sons are not tattlers, my lord," said my father proudly, "nor are they encouraged to do so. It prides me that they confide in me, but I do not wish for them to gossip."

"A noble attribute, my good man," agreed Gilbert Becket.

"But you cannot underestimate freeborn Englishmen, my lord," my father said stoutly, "we do not yield our families easily."

"No one wishes you to yield your children," Mistress Becket assured my father, "why I love Egbert as dearly as I do my own children and I never intended to infer that we wished to separate families."

"No tis hideous," Gilbert said with alacrity, "there are too many homeless waifs in this town, already. I am forever opportuned by them for alms. God knows, my heart bleeds for the poor unfortunates. I do think what we have decided is best for your son and for us, if you agree."

"It is best, your lordship," my father grudgingly agreed, "and we will forever be in your debt. May I have leave to take him home with me tonight so I can confront his mother with the tidings?"

"Do so, by all means," Gilbert Becket quickly, "the sooner the matter is settled the better."

"Wat," intervened Mistress Becket, "Wat?"

"Yes m'lady?"

"I understand you have a young lady in your family who needs employment. I have need of a child to do errands since we are losing this one. Think you that she could be spared?"

"I do not know, madam, on that matter I must needs consult my wife. She is of great help around the house, but she does need training badly."

"Let me know on the morrow if she can be spared. I will give her a comfortable home and will train in manners and good service. The only thing," and here Mistress Becket paused and peered anxiously at my father, "she too must stay in the house since she is a girl child and there are so many things for her to learn, she cannot go homes of nights. Perhaps she will be allowed to visit every fortnight or so. Is that agreeable?"

A grimace of pain crossed my father's brow. "It sounds agreeable, Mistress, but as I say, I must consult my wife. If all is well, I shall bring her on the morrow or soon thereafter since this matter must be gotten used to."

"Very well," the Mistress agreed.

"Is there anything else, Wat?" Master Becket queried my father, "does all go well at the stables?"

"Aye sir, all goes well with the animals and poultry and that is all for me. I do thank you most graciously for attending me and I pray that I have not inconvenienced you," said my father.

"Not at all," said Gilbert Becket briskly, "but enough of this. "Rohan, are you ready to receive the guests?"

"What?" squealed Mistress Becket all aflutter, patting her hair, smoothing her clothes, "never, my toilette's not complete. Eeeee! I must go!" and she scurried from the room.

Thomas Becket roared and father smiled. "Well, Wat, I leave you to your problems. May you solve them as easily as this one has been solved."

"Good night, kind sir, I'm sure that all will be well when the sun rises."

Thomas and I had taken this in wordlessly. So had the cook and the rest of the female servants who had managed to stay in the shadows and listen. Tears came in Thomas' eyes.

"Come my son," said my father to me, "we must go and face your mother."

I felt sorry for my poor loving father. I knew my mother would not care but I could not deceive him or upset him by saying so.

"But I won't have anyone to sleep with," wailed Thomas. He looked all of his six years with shoulders huddled and tears streaming down his face.

"It will just be for the night," my father said to him kindly.

"But it is at night when I'm most afraid!"

"What a man like you, in this great house filled with servants, mother, father, sisters and dogs, you are afraid?"

"It is lonely and frightening in my room, besides Egbert has promised to stay with me forever," he said petulantly.

"You will survive," my father said shortly at this attitude. "Come, son we must be on our way. Footpads and the watch will be abroad shortly. Thomas ran from the room not looking back. I, dreading what I anticipated must follow, slowly followed my father to the door. I remembered just in time to run back, wait for cook to turn her head and snatched a part loaf of bread and some generous bacon slices. It would sweeten my mother to have fresh baked bread and meat. I knew it must be a relief from the boiled mush and turnips which she habitually ate with not a touch of meat to make the dish more nourishing. I remembered that Edward had given me a small amount of salt also. This was a treasure. If one was caught filching salt, the punishment was severe because of the scarcity of the seasoning. Father strode silently and briskly along taking care to watch for assailants or an overly vigilant watch. It was near to curfew but not quite. In our time, being abroad after night was serious business, both in the eyes of the law and in the interest of personal safety. Only the nobility or well to do and the night creatures used the streets. Also it was slops emptying time. As people finished their evening meal, all manner of refuse would come hurtling from doors and windows. At times, this danger, added to that of scavenger dogs and pigs, was more fearsome than meeting with humans.

Having gained the house, father took the two smallest girls on his knee and commenced to talk to my mother. Everyone had eaten but mother took the bread and meat and cut small pieces from them for my sisters. A great portion, too great a portion I thought, was reserved for herself. This food disappeared rapidly and until mother was completely finished and had her fill of warm water would she deign to listen to my father. Sarah was all eyes and ears. I wished to get her from this house soon. She showed the need for food and cleanliness. She was sallow, thin and dirty. Her hair had not been combed or washed in a long time. All the children freely scratched the lice in their heads and on their bodies. At nine, Sarah was too tall and too starved not to be allowed the good fortune that was being offered her.

"I don't know," mother simpered showing her rotting teeth, "she is of great help around the house. It has not been easy for me, you know."

"I do know, my good wife," father said sweetly. How he could possibly love my mother I could not understand. She never bathed and rarely ever washed her clothing. I could not remember seeing her more than comb her hair with her fingers nor could I remember her fingers ever being clean. I had gotten so it revolted me to think that I had to eat there. I would stuff myself at the Beckets so I could honestly say that I did not want the mush and turnips even if they did contain bits of port, hare or goose, which was seldom. Her teeth were beginning to rot and fall out and her complexion, clouded with smoke and dirt was positively gray. I know that Edward brought her finery such as stolen combs, laces and silks but she sold them as quickly as she could for sweets and ale. Not that mother was a drunkard which she was not for which I thanked the Lord. But she did love sweets and to get tipsy over much. I don't believe father ever knew. If he did, he was magnificent in ignoring it, because the simplest of fools she did not ever see any money. Morally, it never did occur to her to patrol the waterfront and sell her personal wares as did some of the sailor's wives in the neighborhood. Besides my father's supervision was too close for that. My paragon of a father! Steadfast, imbued with pride and family love, steadied us all with his even disposition and consistency.

My mother fondled the small bag of salt. She drooled some into the pot and all of the family, including my father gulped mightily. She had each of the children come up and place a minute amount in their palms that they might lick the savory. Salt was truly delectable. She carefully wrapped the remains and tucked it away in the cupboard.

"I don't know," my mother mused. This is the way she conversed with us. If she did not whine and complain of her ailments, she conversed indirectly. We had all learned, even the smallest child, to pay close attention to her, because she could become abusive if not listened to. More than once, she boxed our ears severely if she had to explain or repeat herself. "What with the two boys gone so soon, I fear to lose my girl children so early, yet it would be nice to know that Sarah be so well placed. She too, could bring home more food and learn to sew, then I could once in a while have a new bonnet or a new dress." She preened herself and hitched the sagging neck of the filthy dress that she had on to the point of decency.

"Yes, that could happen and you would have less to do with only two children in the house. Besides, they are eight and five are they not?" asked my father.

"I don't rightly know. So many came so quickly and so many died that I lost count of the ages," she said.

"So have I," my father ruefully scratched his head, "but if I reckon correctly, the two boys are close together, Sarah came after one was lost and these last two are close to Sarah. They are getting large!" My father affected astonishment, pinched the girls and they squealed delightedly and nestled closer to him. He obviously gloried in their closeness. He was ever the loving and kind man.

"But we can spare her for her betterment," whined my mother in that somnambulistic voice.

"If she is well placed, a suitable husband can be found for her," my father said matter of factly.

"Yes, that would be nice. I hope for her better things than I have known." She leered at my father in a threatening manner as if to challenge him to an argument.

"We all wish that for our children," my father agreed gently taking the sting from her words. All of us sat dumbly, thinking deep thoughts on the decisions to be made.

"Egbert is to stay in the big house from now on, to serve the young man of the house," my father told my mother. "He is to learn the duties of footman, equerry and the lord knows what else."

"It is good," said my mother indifferently, "he and Edward were ever dissatisfied here at home. They have looked elsewhere for parents and abodes since they were large enough to do so."

"They will come home from time to time and Sarah will only be home once every two weeks."

My mother began to cry silently. My father instantly came to her side and comforted. My two smaller sisters began to weep and tears came into Sarah's eyes. I could not feel this emotional wave so I took this opportunity to tell Sarah to busy herself and wash a bit.

"What are you whispering to her?" my mother hissed, sentiment forgotten and anger rising easily to the surface.

"Nothing other than she should bathe and comb her hair," I answered truthfully.

"So I've whelped a member of the gentry," she shrilled and snatched up the serving spoon to belabor me.

"No wife," my father ordered, "he meant no harm. They live differently than we do. The boy is right. She should not go amongst strangers without looking her best."

"You should know," she snarled, "tis bitter to see your children reject you."

"Now, now my sweet," cooed my father, "children are ever so. Do as your brother tells you, daughter," my father ordered. Sarah returned in a very short while not showing too much evidence of having used water.

"I guess I must show you how," I said resignedly. The two younger girls stared at me. When I thought on it, I could not remember having seen either one of them ever use the short supply of water that was in the hovel.

"It's hard to carry that water from the fount," my mother whined, "be sparing of it. We don't ever seem to have any."

"Just let it wait," I said wearily to my older sister but I shuddered inwardly to think of even the servants in the Becket household seeing her incredibly dirty feet and snarled hair. The morning came soon and I was anxious to be off. My mother began to wail and cry. To see her become emotional was incredible to me.

"Easy on, girl," my father sympathetically patted her shoulder. "It's not as if she was dead."

"Tis so," wept my mother, "'Tain't like the boys at all. A girl child is of some help to her mother. She won't never come back." She sobbed inconsolably. She was rather woebegone and I felt sorry for her. In her distraction she did not see me slip the distasteful gruel to my younger sisters who gobbled it greedily up. Mother subsided enough to let us depart. Poor Sarah! A big girl of nine left that house in her best clothes. They were rags at best. No shoes had ever been on her feet and the chilly cobblestones turned them blue before we had gone a short distance. I pitied her going through the thorough scrubbing and hair combing that Mistress Becket would demand.

CHAPTER 6

Things went well for the children of the Beckets and Wat for the next year. I saw Edward more than ever, because he seemed to be giving the horses of his stables exercise at the same time as we did. I, being the elder, allowed him and the young Thomas some measure of friendship which they never had while Edward was in the stables of Thomas' father. Thomas was tall for his age, very acute in his sensitiveness and was a match for Edward in the word game.

"Come, let us race these nags," Thomas would cry to Edward.

"No, absolutely not," I would storm at them. "Master Thomas, since these are the horses of your father and I am in charge of their care, I cannot forbid you their running, but since I am the older brother of Edward, I can forbid him, and caution you to take care."

They would grouse for some while, but Thomas would see someone from another house who he knew and he would ride with them in mild contests. I would take these opportunities to constantly remind Edward of his station in life and that groomsmen must keep their place. One word of malpractice that got back to his employers and he would be back in the stables with us. Fortunately, he had the common sense to see my arguments and never disobeyed me publicly. We had many things to talk about on those cold, dreary, foggy mornings as the multitudes of sheep, goats, geese and all manner of people milled around and about the greenery.

"Can you not tell that I am coming up in the world?" he asked me one day. I looked at him and noted that he had on a fine pair of Flemish woolen hose, a leather smock and new shoes.

"Where did you get those?" I demanded. I knew that he did not have the money for such finery. We were only given small amounts of money on special feast days and this was never enough other than to purchase the barest of necessities. I had spent my life savings on the worn clothing that he and I had purchased. Had not Master Becket had the extra pair of hose that he did not want, I would have worn my one pair out long ago, and been reduced again to the smock and the exhibition of my legs to my eternal shame. I was careful not to wear or tear my clothes.

"I'll get you some too," he parried my question.

"Oh no, no, don't," I pleaded with him. ""I could never pass the discerning eye of Mistress Becket. Once suspicions are aroused, you too, will get in trouble. I could use new shoes," I said ruefully as we surveyed the patched pieces of leather on my feet. "But I can't afford them and even father would be suspicious. I am surprised that he has not noticed you already."

"I always wear my old, ragged clothing home," he said solemnly. "A man must survive in this world by whatever means."

"Where did you get those clothes?" I demanded again.

"From a stunned footpad," he returned nonchalantly.

"From a what?" I shouted.

"Oh someone had laid him out with a stiff blow," he explained to me. "Since I knew he had stolen these clothes, I merely took them for myself."

"If he ever sees you or denounces you to the sheriff, you will be severely flogged or thrown into prison or hanged or all three," I gasped at the enormity of what he said.

"I will not," he returned. "It is common to take clothing from people if you cannot buy them. There are a thousand people in the city who wear clothes like this. Besides, that fellow can only come out at night and will not recognize me or the clothes. I am free of such folk in the safe daytime in a safe job such as this."

"Perhaps he is the same as you," I admonished him, "a decent work by day. A bounder by night."

Doubt began to cloud his features but he immediately brightened up.

"I'll take my changes," he laughed at me, "besides I plan to go to sea shortly. I have passed my twelfth birthday and I think I can pass muster."

I drew in a sharp breath and looked closely at my aggressive younger brother. Security and solid food had begun to show on his ample frame. Although he was not as tall as I, he was muscular and evidencing maturity. I looked at myself and saw a sallow, stringy fellow doomed to the life of an ostler and to be the servant of other men. My brother's eye had the defiant look of independence and his actions indicated more.

"Are you not happy where you are?" I asked him.

"Very," he said, "but I want more than this petty thieving to survive. I don't like cold and servitude and being bound to this stinking city. I must rove and see sunshine and free people and fight great battles and roam this wide world over. I will not be bound by hedges, the gentry and even my family. I hate all this!"

"What will you tell father?"

"Nothing, absolutely nothing, and neither will you. I will just walk out the stables one evening, go down to the wharfs, sign on an ocean going vessel and sail. That is all there is to it. No one can stop me. Whatever one says I can always escape people or confinement and I mean to be off!"

I was startled at this vehemence and weary of the suspense of his leaving. No, I wouldn't tell father although his preemptory attitude irked me. It would solve nothing to get embroiled in a futile family argument. I was reluctant to leave him but I had to.

"Come let us ride," I told him, "I must needs see to my charge. Your supervisor is calling to you."

We rode along companionably for a few yards then he veered his horse over to where his company was assembling. I went to fetch Thomas from a group of children his age who were pacing and yawing at their mounts bridles. I did not fear for them, because they all had escorts who anxiously supervised them. I extracted Thomas from the group and headed home. One of the grooms with whom I had a speaking acquaintance rode up beside me.

"That one is apt," he said, "He understands animals and the bidding of them. He is much more alert than any child in this group."

"Yes," I said dejectedly, "Yes. Would that my brother and I had the same opportunity."

"What say you?" queried my escort.

"Oh nothing," I returned, "I was agreeing with you. Yes, Thomas Becket is gifted with quick intelligence and an agreeable nature."

"He certainly is," agreed the man, "why, he obeys me faster than the boys from my own house. I could teach him much about horses and riding if he were under my tutelage."

"Why do you not ask his father to let you do so?"

"Who is his father?"

"The port-reeve of London."

"The port-reeve! Why that is only a burgher's position!"

"Yes," I quickly interposed, "but a fine house and a fine master. There are many worse people in London town."

"Oh I am sure there is," he too readily agreed with me, and I could see that both Thomas and I had fallen socially in his eye sight. "My master would never agree to such a thing," he too earnestly spoke, "I work for a Norman noble who hates Saxons except for the work they can do."

I looked closely at this man and realized that he was either lying or was proud to be associated with the nobility.

"Gilbert Becket is Norman also," I told him with severity, "there are many who come to his house of all ranks. He does not hate us and is extraordinarily kind."

"I could never rise in that house," he said superciliously, "I have ambition to become a footman or mayhap a groom to some higher house."

"Even if your employer hates your race?"

"Oh he does not hate us so badly when he is nor angry or in his cups. He can be kind in his brutal way and I have not been struck in a month."

"He strikes you?" I asked incredulously. I could not believe this. I who had been so gently reared by both a father and the Becket family. I had never had a voice raised to me or heard too many raised in anger other than my mother. I was appalled that this man actually seemed to enjoy such a tale.

"So to teach a burgher's son would be too low for you?"

"Yes. I am sorry I confused him with a Saxon. Now that I observe him closely he is Norman but I could never get my master's consent to teach him."

I turned my horse and took up the slack on the lead rein of the other two horses I had. 'Perhaps we are all better off than we know,' I thought. 'To associate with this lout, however much he might know about horses or anything else is demeaning.'

"Don't say anything about our conversation to anyone," he warned me.

"I shan't," I told him. I called Thomas who came instantly and we rode homeward. I could see in the distance Edward's group turning into the city streets. I rode silently, listening vaguely to Thomas' chatter of how he was going to begin training his horse to obey more rapidly. I had known and heard of people of the type that I had just met, but I had never talked to one. Saxon, and common ones at that, deserting their people in their ambition to rise. Perhaps Edward did know more than I realized. Thomas pulled me out of my musings.

"Edward Watson," he said brightly, "do you not think I can train this nag to jump and canter?"

"I doubt it," I cautioned him, "your father will never allow it since these are carriage horses. Besides, he will not wish for you to injure yourself or the horse. They are expensive and hard to come by."

"I shall ask him anyway," Thomas said stoutly, "I am getting bored just riding out and riding in. I think the horse is doing likewise. I think I am old enough to be able to train a horse and not affect his senses. Yes, I shall ask him anyway."

In the year that he had turned eight, he had also changed. He was showing litheness and great mental ability. Already he was teaching himself to read in Latin and was attempting to leave the French that was spoken chiefly in his household and master the English or Anglo-Saxon language. I had observed both the Master and Mistress watching him closely. I felt that great changes were not far off. I resisted his practicing his learning on me. I did badly want to learn to read and write my name but I was determined not to attempt some of the great books that were in the Becket home. They appeared too frightful. Besides, the parish priest said that it was a grievous sin to read something or anything without his approval. I did not intend to damn my soul to eternal hell fires because of a silly old book. I was satisfied to be competent in the supervision of my young charge and to do a good job with the horses.

Edward was not with the household's horses the next day. The chief groom wore a sour look. He was rarely with his group, so it was with surprise that I noticed him giving orders and at the same time beckoning us over. Thomas and I took our horses to where he sat his. He waited until his group had gone a discreet distance.

"Where is your rascally brother, son of Wat?" he growled at me. My heart beat wildly.

"I know not," I told him truthfully, "he is consigned to your care."

"Do you mean to tell me that he did not go home with you last evening?"

"I did not go home last evening, only my father. Edward only goes home seldom."

"Ed—Edw---Ed---what?" he demanded.

"Edward," I sat resolutely.

"So you too are giving out the names, he said sarcastically, "imagine a common Saxon peasant lifting himself up to the gentry by using names. Churls do better remembering where their station is, lest they either be imprisoned or exported over the seas. But no matter, where is your brother?"

"I know not," I earnestly tried to convince him.

"Well, he has broken his 'apprenticeship," he said sourly, "and if the law catches him, he will deserve what he will get."

Thomas and I both sat silently.

"Won't get much out of you two," and truculently he turned and shouted orders to the rest of his retinue to start exercising the animals. Thomas and I rode silently off and as soon as I felt we were safe from watching eyes, put the animals to a gallop. The horses were reluctant to return so soon, but I felt that father should know as soon as possible. We slowed the horses to a walk as we entered the streets.

"I admire him," said Thomas diffidently.

"I don't," I snapped, "He is a fool and an idiot. There is no telling where the wild boy is at this moment. He could be on a ship, in jail or dead on the streets."

"I hadn't thought of that," said the youngster riding by my side, "I can just see him riding down the Thames to the sea and out in the open with the sunshine and salt air all around."

"If he is lucky enough to be on the sea he is probably in some foul galley learning how to cook or scrubbing a deck. His lot could be slavery or worse if his ship is captured. No doubt he is enjoying himself and thinking how stupid we are."

"Why have you not run away, Egbert Watson?" asked the young boy.

"I am happy with my lot," I told him, "roving is not for me. I like security and peace and quiet. I am satisfied with what the good Lord has given me."

We rode into the stables and I began to call for my father. He came at one with a scowl on his brow.

"Edward's gone," I said simply.

He sat down heavily as if he had been clubbed.

"Get up, you lazy lout," the head groomsman ordered immediately.

"Leave be, Harold," my father implored him, "I have just had bad news. Seems as if my youngest son has run away." Father covered his face with his hands and slumped his shoulders. Tears streamed through his fingers.

"Sorry to hear such Wat," sympathized the ostler, "but I can't give you much time. The mistress wants the carriage today and we will have to go as footmen or outriders, I don't know which."

Father's shoulders heaved.

"I don't know what else you could have expected old man," said Harold, "you let the boys have such fine airs. Hose before fifteen years of age. And first names! Ay, 'tis bitter to see so little appreciation in these new and modern times. And usuns under the yoke of the invader – but a good house we are lucky to be assigned to," he said hastily rolling his eyes at Thomas to see if he had noticed the criticism. If Thomas heard, he gave no notice. All the Norman were becoming accustomed to Anglo-Saxon detestation and since they had no intention of leaving the country they had conquered, they were becoming immune in being angered by remarks.

"I will go home with you father," I said as I sat down and put my arms around his shoulders,

"I don't believe I can face your mother alone," father agreed.

"But Egbert, you can't go tonight!" wailed Thomas, "I didn't bring up the horses training last night and without you there, father won't listen to me."

"We can settle it another day," I said as I went to him. Tears were in his eyes. I did not realize how attached I had become to this sensitive and alert youngster. I was too worried about Edward to take time with him at this moment, and he went running to the big house, disappointment registering in every step.

"Here's what your brother left," one of the loutish stablemen from next door said to me while standing in the door of the feed stall. I took the rather large bundle quickly and sat on it hoping that father would not see.

"Thank you," I said wearily to the stableman because at the moment I had forgotten his name. He raised his hand and left. I looked around to see that the men were busy and quickly concealed the bundle under the straw of a feedbox praying that cleaning would not take place that day. I left father to go to the big house because I feared that Mistress

Becket would not give me permission to go and I also wanted to tell Sarah.

My sister was tall and sluggish not exhibiting the quickness generally found in my family. She wore a nondescript gown of faded gray but she was reasonably clean and her hair was combed. There were no shoes on her feet. I felt that Sarah would never be ambitious for betterment because she had my mother's temperament. However, she was competent and did not have to be reinstructed once she understood what to do. She had refused to learn to read and write but she could sew a reasonably fine seam and cleaned adequately. This was the extent of her knowledge. She rarely came to the stables to see father. It was usually when my father sent for her and at no other times. After she got over her homesickness, and became accustomed to sleeping in a warm house and eating a variety of food, she seemed to lose all interest in her old home and relatives. My father said it had caused my mother many a tear.

CHAPTER 7

"Edward's gone," I said to my mother without elaboration.

"Well, it's no more than we expected," she said to me laconically, however, her glistening eyes and shortness of breath betrayed interest and excitement. "Where do you think he's off to? Normandy? Cathay? Venice? The end of the world? Do you think he might get on one of those ships and sail over the edge of the water and fall into nowhere?"

"I have no idea," I said dispiritedly. I knew she had not the slightest idea of the names she was calling off. She had heard them while serving at the Becket table, but they meant nothing to her more than pretty and unusual sounds.

"When do you intend to go home?" I asked her.

"I do not know," she said indifferently, "but not now, I don't like to see people upset, besides I must help cook tonight and also help at table. There will be important guests. I've been ordered to wash myself especially well and I'm getting one of the older girl's dresses!" Here she showed excitement which was unusual for her phlegmatic nature.

"I did not know that there would be extras for supper," I said frowning. Since I had become so closely attached to Thomas I had begun to miss many things as being near to help when important guests came. I could not help but feel envious and interested. My curiosity had surely been aroused and was being developed in this interesting place. I had allowed myself to unconsciously slip into a state of anticipation just to see and hear strange accents and see strange faces.

"Yes, there will be many," Sarah told me, "because the mistress has ordered the coach to go shopping herself. They must be churchmen because she plans to have a variety of fish dishes. I don't know what dress I will get from what girl, brother, but since we are of a size, it won't matter, just having a dress will be the thing!"

"Does a dress matter so much more than your brother, sister?"

"I never did know Edward well. He stayed from home so much, both day and night and never had any time for us. Then when he came here he was only there after I went to bed so I saw him ever and when he went next door he has never even been back to say hello to me. He would only wave to me when I shouted to him from a window. I need a dress brother, this is all that I've ever had to wear and it is important to want new clothes!"

"Well, so be't," I gave up. It would never do for both of us to ask off on a night of importance. Even if Mistress Becket was a most understanding soul she would never tolerate a shortage of help when they were most needed. About this time, Mistress Becket came hurriedly into the room and gave Sarah a dress.

"Oh thank you Mistress," Sarah said as she went down on her knees.

"La child," Mistress Becket said dismissing her, "'tis an old one that Mary has outgrown and 'tis only right that females have clothes. Mind you to have it fitted nicely for tonight." Mistress Becket's brightness fairly gleamed.

"Egbert," she turned on me, "I must go out and I shall take the girls. I will not take Thomas so mind him well. Take him to the mall and let him play. Ooooooh, it is late and I must be off. Children! Children! The coach is at the door, Come, we must be off!" She straightened her bonnet and tightened her gloves. The girls came pell mell, laughing and giggling at something. They did not even look at Sarah or me. The house was very quiet and Sarah preened with the new dress held up to her. It was a brown wool trimmed with pink laces. She oohed and aahed without realizing I was there. I slumped my shoulders in hopelessness. Father would have to face mother alone tonight. I had failed to ask the mistress for permission to go home.

"It's just as well," said my father resignedly, "I shall leave as soon as possible the sooner it's over the better."

I was on the mall when I remembered the package. I have even forgot to look to see if it was molested! After letting Thomas run himself out and spending as much time as possible, I hastened to the big house with him tagging at my heels. It was just prior to early dusk when we got there and we slipped into the house without fuss. Immediately Mistress Becket started calling for us. We ran to see what she wanted.

"Thomas, your father will be here directly with the visitors. Egbert, take him and scrub his hands and ears well and do so for yourself. I want you presentable tonight." Sarah was at her heels dressed most becomingly in brown wool but still shoeless. The dress almost swept the floor so it was not too noticeable until I saw the Becket sisters admiring new satin slippers then my sister appeared naked. We hastened to do the mistress' bidding and I made Thomas change into clean stockings even if he protested that the ones he had worn were only slightly soiled. I put on my clean clothes and pacified him somewhat, although my shoes were in a sadly disreputable state. Not that this was uncommon. Poor people rarely if ever, had shoes at any type, so some were better than none but I did so long for good shoes. Not necessarily out of pride but because my feet were getting tender and becoming accustomed to being covered. A person had to experience our cold, wet English winters to appreciate covering of any kind. The worst case of being uncomfortable is to be cold and damp and not able to get warm. I believe this is worse than hunger. A person can get accustomed to being hungry, but chill and damp are inescapable.

The Becket house was in an unusual state of upset due to the visitors. Mistress Becket had all the rosaries out and every one displayed them prominently. The holy relics that the master had preserved from the Crusades were in the center of the table. There was much veneration and the house was in a state of being subdued even if things were at a high pitch of expectancy. Cook did not grumble and the maids scurried quietly but efficiently from minor task to minor task.

I do not think I had ever seen the dining table so well appointed. Clean wooden trenchers and spoons were evenly distributed. Fresh rushes covered the floor completely. The dogs had been driven from the house. Flowers were stuck in anything that would hold them and incense floated from many containers. The main hall was dusted repeatedly and the clean bed linens were checked repeatedly by Mistress Becket herself. The master had withdrawn himself to a quite part of the house and was being shaved with particular care, something he never did other than twice a week. His most elegant clothes were laid out. I remember them well because his tunic was of red velvet and his hose were of the deepest brown. His modest yellow leather shoes had a modish cut and I envied them. They would never wear out because he wore them only on special occasions. He would not wear a cap or hat tonight, but would wear his beautiful hand embroidered vest. This was a new garment to be seen in England at this time, worn by men who had been to the land of the infidel. It was short and rounded and completely covered by intricate needlework. It was said to be a garment very popular with the people in the Holy Land. The master's underclothes were all of the finest linen.

"These must be churchmen visiting tonight," the cook told me as I sopped the grease from the pots with bread. For once she did not forbid me to eat.

"I do not know," I answered, my jaws puffing out full of warm bread and rich gravy. "No one has said who it will be, but the best of wines have been pulled from the cellar and the main hall is as clean as it will ever be. I have been given no duties. I wanted to go with my father badly tonight, but I wouldn't dare to ask to leave. I have scrubbed Master Thomas as best I could."

"It would be good to know for whom I am cooking," grumbled cook. "One of these days I shall walk from this house and seek employment in some establishment that tells me things."

I knew cook's threats to be in the merest flimsy. She had been rescued from a life of drunkenness and abandonment. The master had gone to prison and stood for her good behavior if she was released. The other servants said she had been a bad woman but the mistress kept her on the strictest religious regimen in the house. Being very religious, cook had responded well. Although she used wines liberally in her dishes, I had never known her to turn up an unfinished bottle nor to allow anyone else to do so. She drank only beer with her meals and at times only water but her nature was perpetually sour and discontented. I know her feet hurt her because of her great weight but she never complained of them. They were huge feet, I thought, as I looked at her moving slowly about checking this pot and that roast. Large splayed calloused feet that were as flat as they could be and about as dirty as anything that could be found. Cook was not married, and had no children. Of this she complained from time to time.

"I am not past the age of child bearing," she would say and toss her head gaily when she was in a jocular mood, "and

I don't think I am uncomely and I am a lot of woman for some deserving man!"

No one would ever say anything when she was in one of these moods only the kitchen scullions or the maids would titter. This would inflame her instantly.

"So you don't believe me, you scurvy sluts," she would storm, "at least I keep my honor and don't bed with every mongrel that walks the streets."

This would silence the even more audacious girls, except some of the saucier ones who would toss their heads and remove themselves from the reach of her huge arms and the serving spoon that she usually had. If Mistress Becket heard of this through a chambermaid or one of her own children she would berate cook gently but soundly.

"Such language is uncalled for and unseemly," she would state calmly but with deadly seriousness, "this house is clean and godly. There is not call to befoul it with licentious and coarse language. I will not have it so."

Cook would apologize profusely and in all sincerity promise not to fill the air with oaths, although she might lose her temper before the mistress got fully out of earshot. She actually brought an air of normalcy to the Becket household because away from it, especially in the stables and on the commons, the language of men particularly and the trulls that they shouted at as they passed, was most obscene.

"Yes, I must work for people who confide in me," snarled cook.

"It is most unusual for them not to tell us who is coming," I agreed, "and instruct us on how to conduct ourselves in the presence of visitors."

"Well, I am cooking pork and have leavened the bread. I have put the best table wine and port that we have in the house out to cool and the mistress has blessed the kitchen a million times, so it has to be churchmen. Of a special breed also I would say." With this, cook went to the back door to check the wine ledge that stood closed securely in the cold storage pantry. Anticipation was beginning to grip me although I knew I would see little of these people. Sarah would do the running and fetching, the serving maids would do the placing of dishes as well as the removal of them and the pouring of wines under the direction of the master and mistress. Our house did not have a butler or major domo which we sorely needed at times. The children had been fed separately as was the custom and the servants had had their meals, so all was in readiness as darkness fell for the anticipated guests to arrive momentarily.

They had to arrive shortly because it was not safe on the streets after dark. No man in his sane mind would venture out unless he knew how to survive in the jungle of street walkers, prowlers and thieves. Well to do people traveled in large groups with large retinues of servants but unaccompanied people went to their destinations before dark and spent the night with their hosts. Proper servants and courting youngsters would take to the stables or gardens behind secure, closed walls. As darkness fell, each house in London town became a barricaded enclave that closed the world out. Poor people, barred the doors and windows to the intruders as well as the night air and went to bed. It was a great occasion to lean out of one's window after dark and watch the great torch lighted processions of the wealthy if any went abroad.

"Ware, 'ware!" the outriders or lead footmen would cry to the almost empty streets and the great coaches or sedan chairs would slowly negotiate the tortuous turns and the piles of refuse that made the streets and directions hazardous. The lurid light from the torches would make the travelers appear as if they were from another world as they would go from one island of fog and darkness into pools of light.

All sounds in the house suddenly stilled. One could not hear from the street to the kitchen but the noises in the house were excellent indicators of affairs. The immediate quite indicated that the great knockers on the front doors had resounded and the anticipation was over. Cook began to feverishly check the food once again to see that all was in order. The serving girls appeared almost magically and cook began to set the chilled wine bottles on their trays. I darted up the back stairs to see if my charge was still presentable. He was sitting before the street window of our bedroom wrapped in bedding and staring out the window. Only one taper was burning. I went over to the window wordlessly. The two of us had too many times watched proceedings from that window to care to indulge in conversation. I too looked out the window. A great fog was settling and the vision was badly obscured.

"I saw them," Thomas told me matter of factly, "they were not impressive since all they had were three men servants and those were not heavily armed."

"God does not need arms," I answered him as I too looked out the window thinking of my brother and my poor woebegone father. I saw a shadow scurry along the street and I wondered if it was Edward returning from a disastrous encounter. I prayed it were so. We never heard from Edward again.

"I would that we could play," Thomas said crossly.

"Nay," I told him quickly lest he charge me and begin the rough and tumble that was almost a nightly occurrence. "You will ruin your clothes and be unacceptable when we are called to the great room."

"I know, I know," he said as he stood up, dropped his wrappings and kicked a pillow across the room. "Me thinks it is unusually chilly this eve."

"It is that," I agreed with him. "Let us go down to the kitchen and talk to the light bearers. Perhaps we will find who our visitors are."

His eyes lit up and wordlessly we bounded from the room. Me following him as always with the servant and the master. The kitchen was warm and redolent with odors of gravies, meats, savories, sweat, and warm bread. Garlic, cloves, and peppers were especially strong. Cook had done an especially good job with the meats as I could see. The huge carved hams were somewhat smelly but she had artfully concealed the odors with a thick crust of syrups and spices. The fresh boiled tongues and the baked geese and fish appeared delectable.

"Are they not serving?" I asked as I eyed the three men in the corner eating from high piled trenchers. Their knives flashed as they carved bread to put with the dripping meats.

"Yes they serve," said cook, "but the guests linger over the chilled wine and hot soup. Ah, here come the wenches. Mayhap we will get on with the meal."

She showed the girl the great salmon on their platters and instructed them to come back rapidly for the ham and goose before they got cold.

"I thought they were only having fish," I looked at her inquiringly.

"My master has ever bade me have other food," she said positively, "What with so many mouths to feed in this house, there is never enough. Those gluttonous girls and stable and garden hands will never be filled. Neither will those yawning caverns in the corner."

I had forgotten the visitors but Thomas and the girls had not. The maids cast shrewd glances in the corner as they began to come and go rapidly. I slipped into the shadows behind my young master and listened.

"I am Thomas Becket," he said proudly.

"We can tell, young master," one of the men said with a mouthful of food.

"Where are you from?" he queried them.

"Merton Priory in Surrey," he answered matter of factly.

They had finished eating and Thomas and I stood there in our uncertainty. We had never heard of the place and we waited for further information but it was not forthcoming. The men stood and yawned mightily.

"It has been a long and hard day," the leader said, "and I fear it will be a long and hard morrow. I wonder where we sleep."

"In the stables as you are accustomed to," the cook said testily.

"But it is cold and the horses make much noise," protested the man.

"Did you not bring bedding?" she asked.

"Very little," he answered her.

"Do you not sleep in stables where you live?"

"Yes."

"Then off to them, you lout," she said stoutly. The man smiled and ordered the other two to follow him.

The evening dragged on. The girls scurried to and from the kitchen and at last began to clean the used dishes from the table. I was sleepy and Thomas was nodding. We were summoned to the great hall. I was peevish and went slowly. Little did I know that events were to set in motion that once they started would hurry us along to great eminence and great tragedy.

CHAPTER 8

The hall was warm and smelled of food and wine. The fireplace roared and the smoke was somewhat heavy. Sweat glistened on the faces of the men. Mistress Becket, the only female present, dabbed delicately at her face and neck from time to time. The mulled wine was steaming in the great silver bowl in the center of the table and in the silver cups of the guests. What with the absence of the ever sniffing dogs and the elegant linen on the table, things were princely and very, very charming. The guests turned to face us. They were churchmen, beyond doubt, because one of them was a tonsured monk. All were thin but warmly dressed.

"Come here my son," Gilbert Becket beckoned to Thomas. The lad went and stood before him. "These are our guests and your future mentors. This is Father Alais, Father Gervais, and Father Odo from Merton Priory, Surrey."

Thomas pulled his forelock to them and made a deep bow.

"And do you fancy an education my son?" Father Alais spoke to him gently.

"I've never thought on it, father," answered Thomas.

"How old did you say he was, Gilbert Becket?" the priest asked of my master.

"Eight almost nine, and of a good mind, ever questing about for the answer to things," answered the burgher.

"All things are known to God, but little to man," said Father Alais.

"Amen," all said in unison.

"My son, we have it our minds to send you to the school of these good fathers," Gilbert Becket smiled at Thomas.

'School! I thought incredulously. An Augustinian school at that. Was my young master destined for the Church?' I was so confused that I failed to hear the soft voices at the table.

"What does he know now?" asked the priest.

"How to ride a horse, course the hounds and his prayers," Gilbert Becket told him readily, "although he has never assisted at mass, I feel he is capable and ready to do so."

"That is well," answered the priest, "because although we teach, our first duty is to God and the Church. Perhaps we have here a capable mind that can dedicate itself willingly to that which is proper and noble."

"I feel sure of that," Gilbert Becket said assuredly.

"Is he immediately available for the training?" asked Father Alais.

"I feel sure of it," Becket answered, "although I have not prepared him for leaving home. I was not sure that he would be accepted and I did not wish to upset him or have him anticipate that which he cannot have."

"A wise decision," agreed the priest.

Mistress Becket had begun to sniffle quietly.

"How now, madam," the priest said turning to her, "do you not wish it so?"

"I do so wish with all my heart, father," she quavered, "but I find it hard to see my son depart my house."

"Do you not agree that training and dedication to God and the Church are the highest aims of man on this earth?" the priest persisted.

"I agree most heartily, father," she whispered, "it is indeed an honor and a distinction to see the Lord's will be done."

"Amen," they all intoned. Mistress Becket was a most pious woman. Although quiet, efficient, and capable, she demanded the utmost reverence throughout her house. Prayers were said promptly. Church was attended regularly by all and generous gifts were made to the confessors and holy men of London town. She never failed to tithe and attributed the good fortune of the house of Becket to the supervision she received from Heaven. All her house had had catechism and were communionized under her strict supervision. No person could come near her without vouchsafing for their religious qualifications. Although inclined to be too gentle, she was adamant about all attending church and she would call roll to see that all attended. She was ever doing novenas for the Crusaders, for afflicted persons and for her far away relatives.

"Doubt not my wife's piety, good father," Gilbert Becket smiled fondly at his buxom and comely blond wife," she attends us all as any good shepherd his flock. Religious education is not neglected in this house down to and including the lowest scullion and stable hand.

"That is good to hear and I bless her and her household for it," said Father Alais.

I wondered what they had been talking of before we entered. Politics or business probably, because this information should have been revealed long before now. I was still dumbfounded and so was Thomas. What was to become of me? Would I return to the stables forever and lose my good standing in this warm and wonderful household? Where was Sarah and the other maids? All activity in the great hall had stopped as if frozen. Not a sound was to be heard in this usually noisy and busy house full of love and warmth and freedom. I found out later that cook had taken over the supervision of the female help and had bundled them all off to bed. She herself took over cleaning up the hall, even if she did have to arise in the early morning to start preparation of the days' food. I did not know that the entry into school or preparation for the priesthood involved such delicate negotiations.

"I will see that Merton Priory gets its just dues of my income and benefits," Gilbert Becket assured the father, "I have saved money for this occasion and goods which I will send back with you. I have several founts, some plate and a beautiful crucifix that will grace any chapel well."

"That is good, very good," beamed Father Alais, "although people do not realize it, maintenance of God's house must be done and the more acceptable it is to God the greater the graces."

"What specifically, besides religion, will my son be taught?" asked the master.

"Latin for a certainty, the figuring that is common to the day, the history of England and the Conquest, political problems of the day and we are attempting the new English although it is extremely difficult to establish a vocabulary. It would be much easier to teach only Latin and French, but we seek to satisfy the needs of the times."

"That is good, good," agreed Master Becket, "this new language confounds us all."

"Norman French is spoken in this house as you can see," stated Mistress Becket, "not that we would have it so, but the servants speak their native tongue and it has proved difficult to learn. I do know enough to shop, interview servants, and find my way around London town. The children are bilingual. They speak French, English and combine them both with ease. It is not hard once you attempt to adapt yourself."

"I suppose not," mused the priest, "only French and Latin are spoken by us now, but we shall try. We feel that the

Greek thought boarders on heresy, so the pupils are warned of its dangers. So also do we not emphasize the insidious thinking of the Muhammeds that is coming out of Spain and Sicily. It shocks me to see the oriental sinfulness of dress and living manners that have been brought back from Byzantium and the Holy Land. Why, even the servants to the Crusaders swear and attempt to leave God due to the treacherous teachings of the infidel! Woe to them, I cry, God will not turn his face to them in their adversity if they choose to leave him for a foreign and alien luxuriousness. To rescue the birthplace of Christ is one thing, but to absorb and adopt the facile and softening influences of godless people surely secures damnation for the careless souls.

'I hope Thomas does not choose the priesthood,' I thought to myself that it would be very uncomfortable to have the cold and merciless eyes of a churchman on you at all times. I felt I must put my mind to employment in some other house or to some guild, because the severity of religion was not for me. I felt that I worshipped adequately and properly. I could never sustain constant admonition and fear of my damnation. If the Crusade had softened Messir Becket, all was to the good, because he had been nothing ever more than steady, gentle, and kind. There was nothing austere in this man or his family. They were wealthy and assured of their station. They rubbed shoulders easily with the natives and their own Norman kind. All were treated equally and with kindness. I would not wish to serve under a harsh master. My independence would get me into endless trouble. Edward was too forward and thoughtful even for this house and he must needs seek release and freedom elsewhere and by other methods. No, I did not wish for the regimen of the Church to be brought to this house.

"Does he come to us alone and unattended?" the priest asked.

"No he will bring his man who stands yonder by the fireplace, one Egbert Watson, who is a good guide and steady influence on my son's activities. Come forward, my boy," called the master.

"A Norman child! A servant in the home! This is new to my experience," remarked the priest. All three of them strained forward to look at me as if I were some caged animal on exhibit.

"This is nor Norman child," Mistress Becket, "he is a native bred Anglo-Saxon. His father is one of our ostlers. That was his sister who ran and fetched for us at meal time."

"But with two names! That is uncommon with the islanders," aid the priest with intensity.

"These are uncommon people, father," said Gilbert Becket with emphasis, "They are intelligent, shrewd, industrious and loyal. This one," and he put his arm around my waist drawing me close to him, "is like unto my own son. He has been with us for many a year and we grieve to part with him as we do our own. He will regret to leave us, eh my boy?"

For an instant I loved this well fed, apple cheeked Norman almost as much as I did my father. Truly he had been kind and patient and although seemingly distant and careless of me, I realized that I was very near to him having spent so many nights in his presence.

"Yes sire," I said softly, "I will hate to leave this happy house and my family but I will do as you direct. I would not be parted from my charge unless it is your desire."

Thomas ran around to me and encircled my waist with his arm and looked up adoringly. This was his way. Ever winning, ever pleasing. This suddenness of news had us both stunned but if we were not to be separated, we could make the way of each other easier.

"Do you see father?" Becket spoke musingly, "the native born are truly the salt of the earth and surely the bulwark of this island. I must admire their independence of spirit and their desire to express themselves."

"I could not spare them," said Mistress Becket, "I would not feel that this house would be complete without some of Wat's progeny under my roof."

"I am astounded," said Father Alais, "a feeling of kinship between Normans and the Angles. To think that Merton Priory will have a free thinking native under its roof!"

"Will we be required to teach this peasant?" Father Odo asked.

"Are you not of peasant stock albeit from across the water?" asked Father Alais severely of the questioner.

"Yes father, I stand rebuked for my forwardness and ill manners," the shaved monk bowed his head.

"Consider it so," commanded Father Alais.

"No, I cannot ask that you educate young Watson here," said my master, "and as for two names that can be easily explained. This child has been reared in this house so he accepts that everyone will have two names. Further, I petitioned the courts to grant given names to all his family. His mother and father refused to so, but all their children bear the double mark. Perhaps our Norman influence is beginning to take hold. I believe he has a younger brother who has been apprenticed as ostler to the esteemed house next door. Is not that so, Egbert?"

"He has run away, sire," I spoke with tears in my eyes.

"Run away?" Becket reared back, "I did not know that. No one told me of this. I have noticed that the little Sarah has been somewhat downcast but I laid that to her being homesick to Mistress Becket's remarks that the child was of somber mien.

"He has been gone for some time now," I told him, "and we have never heard.

"Why did he run away?" he asked me, "were they not kind to him? It is a larger establishment than mine, but it is a fine place with kind people."

"They were kind to him, sire," I explained, "but he said he must have his independence and know himself. He was not willing to accept his station in life and figured to better himself in some far away land."

"My word," gasped Gilbert Becket, "do you see father what a breed of man comes from this island? Although defeated by the Conqueror, by arms, they are never conquered in the spirit. It makes me proud if I am to be a citizen of this kingdom to have my son a native born Londoner and Englishman!"

"'Tis passing strange, it surely is," breathed the priest and he and his fellow leaned forward to gaze at me. It was uncomfortable. Thomas and I stood straight and tall, brothers now by nationality, and gazed back at the churchmen.

"I fear we are all tired," Gilbert Becket said simply, "I know these youngsters are. If you are through good fathers, we will see you to your beds."

Mistress Becket was nodding. Poor soul, she had been everywhere, both in the city and in the house, all at one time and I'm sure that she was tired past caring.

"Yes, we are tired," Father Alais said leaning back, "I can see now that my fellow travelers would welcome some rest. We would be up on the morrow and be on our way at the break of day. We have other homes to visit, both here in London, and in the countryside."

"Be gone, young varlets," cried the master and gave us both a playful shove, "sleep well with the cheering news you have received this night."

I wondered to myself why people must always bring tidings of great import by night and expect a body to sleep after the excitement. As I left the room, I saw Mistress Becket stand drowsily and heard Father Alais ask.

"Do you not have servants to see us to our rooms?"

"Not in this house," replied Master Becket, "I do not have that many. Besides, I require much industry from them and they are very tired at the end of each day. They have been a bed many hours. Your food will be prepared on time, even though cook will come in and clean after you have left."

"You Normans have almost become English," smiled Father Alais, "what with your native industriousness and their steadfastness, I believe I have glimpsed the changing times this even."

"I am not aware of any new innovations, but if this is one, I welcome it," replied Gilbert Becket with alacrity.

"I am not sleepy," said Thomas crossly as we entered the freezing bedroom, "this news has me much upset."

I was not sleepy either, but not over the news as I was over my forthcoming interview with my father. That would be painful.

"Neither am I sleepy," I spoke to Thomas, "and although the news is exciting it is not really unexpected. You are overdue to begin and you know it."

"I am not prepared," said Thomas from under the covers. We had both dashed for our sleeping places. He in his upraised bed amid goose down mattresses and clean silken sheets and me to my pallet of goose feathered mattresses on animal skins. My covers were of stuffed finely woven wool the same as Thomas'. Mistress Becket said they were just as cheap and that she could not sleep with the thoughts of her house servants being cold. In a moment my bed was warm and comfortable as I'm sure was my young masters. The master and mistress and guests would find their beds warmed by wrapped bricks left under the covers to rest their feet against. I cannot remember if Thomas said anything to me or not. I can only recall that I was groggy for sleep the next morning as I was shaken by a chambermaid. It was and always has been thus with me. I prefer to stay up late and sleep late.

I left Thomas abed as I often did, because I knew that Master and Mistress Becket would not tolerate laziness. I dashed down to the warm kitchen in time to see the sleep ridden attendants of the churchmen come and sit down to bread, ham, fish and hot water. The chambermaids were scurrying back and forth from kitchen to great hall. Some were carrying large basins and ewers of warm water, which meant that the guests were performing ablutions at the table. We would not be allowed in this room this morning as we would not know the final decisions of Thomas' and my departure until the Master or the Mistress told us. I decided to go to the stables and see my father. He was already hard at work.

CHAPTER 9

As much as I reveled in the luxurious living in the big
house, I still liked to come to the stables, if nothing more to be
near my father for whom I had a warm and secure
attachment. He was a stolid, unemotional man with hair
seldom combed or cut. His fingernails were never free from
dirt and his beard ever needed a trim which he could seldom
afford. My father seldom spoke, exhibiting his woefully rotten
teeth, but when he did speak, his words were of great comfort
to me. I loved and respected my father who made the most of
his miserable lot in life.

"There are priests at the big house, father," I told him
simply.

"I know," he answered without emotion, "gossip
travels fast in these quarters. I knew something was amiss
when you or Sarah did not come last evening."

"They came to discuss Thomas' education."

"It is time. The lad is getting tall and mettlesome."

"I am to go where he goes."

"'Tis ever as in these changing times. The servant must
needs go with the master. Where will it be to?"

"Merton Priory in Surrey."

"Well, 'tis not far and you will be able to come home at
times."

"No, the distance is not frightening but I fear the stay
will be for great lengths of times."

"One cannot get educated if one stays in the road all the time, son," my father admonished me.

"But I will receive very little of any education offered," I told him.

"Whatever you get will be more than you will get if you stay here. I will not say no to your going. It would not matter whether I said anything or not. Really, I wish for you to go. It will be good to get whatever education you can. I do not wish to lose you so early, but since Edward has run off to sea so precipitately, this will perhaps steady you, and you will at least stay near home."

"Yes, I will stay near home as long as I live," I told him positively, "and I do feel that they will let me learn to read and write my name. I do not feel that I have the capacity for a scholar so I would be wise to learn a trade such as yours, at least then I can always find employment."

"That is so," father readily agreed, "Will you be taking the horses out to exercise? If not I will assign the duty to one of the grooms if the master groom agrees."

"I do not know," I scratched my head reflectively, "things are in such a stir up there, I am sure not one will be settled by the time the master leaves for his office."

"Well, if I don't hear from you in about an hour, I will have them on their way."

"How are the visitors' animals?" I asked him.

"They travel on sumpter mules," he said and all of them have been fed and rubbed down, "here come the men now."

"The retainers are a poor lot," I remarked sourly.

The men slung well stuffed sacks across the rumps of the mules and without saying goodbye or anything else, silently took the halter ropes and led the animals around to the front of the house. The head groom stood in front of the stables with his hands on his hips and a sour look on his face.

"Norman priests with their Norman dogs," he growled. "God grant that few of them ever come here."

"Our master is a Norman," my father said.

"At least he is becoming Englishized," returned the groomsman, Osbert by name. "Furthermore he bothers us little and stays well away from the stables most of the time because he has learned that natives are every bit as intelligent and capable as are any of the scum imported from over the seas."

My father nor I answered him as he turned grumblingly back to his work. This was morning for contemplation and the thinking of long thoughts that come with parting. Of the lingering ache that remains inside at the parting of loved ones forever. Of the things unsaid and the things undone, of the fellowship between two people who love and understand each other.

"What will mother say?" I asked father when all were out of earshot.

"Very little, if anything, except to remark that you are rising in this world and will have little time for your kin. She will also put in the eternal remark about your turning your back on your raising and will never know your kith and kin."

I knew this to be so and it bothered me little.

"She will be glad," father mused, "to be relieved of the responsibility of your being looked after. Your mother's health is not good and her attitude is such as to not be concerned with things that do not concern her. I shall put your sisters in good homes as soon as possible. They are growing tall without training. Wildness in females is bad, because neighborhood lechers look for uncared for girl children early. Since I cannot stay home all the time and I fear your mother is not too careful of the children's associations, I shall put them under the care of responsible people as soon as I can find a position for them."

"I have never cared for where we live father," I told him truthfully. "The dirt, squalor and filthy people with even more filthy minds is not enjoyable to me. I tire of the eternal swearing and drinking and closeness of unwashed bodies all the times."

"I had not thought of it as being so," he said absentmindedly, "it is the safest part of the city and the house is dry and I manage to keep food in it, even some little salt and seasonings."

"Yes, yes," I agreed with him hurriedly. "You are a good man and mother is a good mother, but you can see that Edward and Sarah and I have left early. Perhaps you have been too good. We are all ambitious to see beyond where we have lived."

"Perhaps I should have taken to drink and stayed near the house more," he smiled gently. "Perhaps I should have beat you and made you work for money or apprenticed you to a wine maker and told you to steal all you could. I could change, you know, and then I would not work at all."

"Oh not that," I said horrified. About this time there was a commotion in the stable and a howl from one of the idiot grooms.

"Wat," roared Osbert, "come supervise this melon head before I split it for him." Sarah came flying from the big house. She threw her arms around my father. He kissed her tenderly on the top of her head.

"I cannot stay, father. We are needed at the big house to clean after the visitors. I came down to tell you good morning, and to tell Egbert that young Thomas arises and the mistress wants him at once," she clung to father fiercely. This was the more surprising because she only barely acknowledged me at the big house and never spoke of going home. In fact, I had become worried about her great silences and about her indifference to me.

"I must be going, father, let someone else take the horses. I might as well begin to get accustomed to the fact that someone else will be taking my place for this duty. Come Sarah," I spoke to my sister. She silently left my father and followed about three paces from me not saying one word. When we entered the kitchen I immediately took a chunk of bread and started dipping it in hot crease and gravy. Sarah did the same. She had not become used to eating hot food or all she wished to eat, so she generally ate as much as I did. She went so far as to go to the table where the priests' retainers had eaten, and wrung the partially eaten drumstick from the carcass of the goose. With bread in one hand and meat in the other she went toward the great hall. Cook looked lovingly after her.

"Takes a heap to fill that girl child. I swear I will never get her filled out decent. She's all skin and bones and so quiet. Children like her please me. Here boy," and she rapped my knuckles with a stirring ladle, "can't you ever get enough? I've been stuffing you all these years. You've got to quit eating so much or you'll founder!"

"That's what horses do," I told her with my mouth full and a leathern cup of table wine in my hand.

"Also pigs and Michaelmas geese," she said hotly, "and don't you let that cup get out of this kitchen."

"I never have lost anything around here yet," I said with asperity, "won't I ever be trusted to leave things where I find them?"

"You'd drink from anything and leave it anywhere," she said with finality. This was one of my bad habits. I loved wine and if any was left from dinner, especially after guests, nothing gave me more pleasure than to drink chilled wine from the silver goblets the master used. The only thing that complicated this was that Master Thomas loved luxury more than I thought was becoming and he insisted that left over wines be preserved from him. He would not drink from leather unless he thought he displeased his father or mother by being ostentatious. So I was reverting more and more to table vintage and resorting to ever more sly tricks to get the good drink. I drained the cup, sat it down carefully making sure that cook observed me from her pot stirrings and went to the great room. The master was leaving for his office. The mistress, the Becket daughters and Thomas were having their breakfast. I regretted eating so greedily in the kitchen because this was a good breakfast. I was so busy looking until I hardly heard the master leave.

The Becket family was sitting to fresh pears and grapes, kidney pie, kippered herring, tea, wine and hot bread. This was a table that was seldom seen in this affluent house. The fruit must have arrived by boat from over the seas. There was even salt and sweet syrups on this table! Mistress Becket stood up and ordered the table cleared except for what the children were eating. She herself took the exotic condiments to the storage cabinets and put them under lock and key. Thomas was dawdling with his food which made me fretful with him because I knew we would not get to take the horses out this day. As I watched him delicately peel grapes I thought to myself that this was one who had an unwarranted love and taste for sumptuousness.

I knew then that this was my charge. That I would have to care for him and keep him from harm if I could. This olive colored, dark haired changeling, that was mixed in with the blonde stoutness of Norman and Anglo-Saxon. I resolved on that morning never to be parted from him if at all possible, because in our togetherness, lay our salvation. He would always be the master, I would be the servant.

The time came on us to leave the big house before we were ready. Thomas cried a lot when we would discuss it, not wishing to leave that dark, comfortable womb of a place where he was cherished and catered to at every whim. But leave we did, not without a rather distressing scene in my home.

My mother, strangely enough, did not want me to leave.

"Better he were dead or never had been born," she wept, "first it was Edward now this one. When I think on the pain of their birth it might be better if I had never had them. It is the duty of children to remain and care for the old parents. What will be our future? To be sent to the almshouse, no doubt, because our selfish children choose to abandon us." She wracked and sobbed before the smoldering fire while the two smaller girls sobbed with her.

We had never seen either of our grandparents on our mother's or father's side. They had died early, so our father said. His brothers and sisters lived somewhere on a manor and my mother's relatives were right here in London, although there was never any visiting. Father said his home was too far away to visit and that the times were too unsafe for peasants to get permission to travel the countryside. He said that mother's relatives here in London were all thieves, prostitutes, and drunks. Whether this was so, or not, I never knew because we did not see them. I was not even curious about any of my relatives. As far as I was concerned, they just didn't exist. None ever came to our home while I was there but I felt sure that someone came, because tonight, for the first time that I could remember, there was a hint of gin in the room. Mother was too excitable. I could see revulsion in my father's face when he got near her.

"Now Godewine," he cautioned her, "do not fret so before the children. He will not be going forever. We will know where he is. He must needs be trained to make a living for himself and you yourself know that there is little for him in the ostler's trade."

"You have done well enough," she shouted at me, "look at your father. He has maintained his dignity, clothes and fed us all without tearing about the countryside and wishing to consort with priests and his betters."

I said nothing. Neither did my father and my sisters. We were dumfounded. Mother had never talked like this in all the time that we had ever known her. In fact, she had never done anything except whine, wear her rags as poorly as she could and stay dirty.

"Where have you been, that you would hear of such things?" demanded father.

"Oh one hears things on the streets and I associate with people who know," she smirked, "I just don't sit here in the house all the day long."

"Perhaps I'd best stay home some days," father said testily, "I too would like to know these interesting and knowledgeable people."

"I'm not locked behind bars, you know," mother said with spirit, "and people do talk. All does not go on in the big houses. The common people listen and say what they think."

"That will be the downfall of this country," father said with asperity, "wagging tongues spreading untruths broadcast like the rains foment senseless revolutions and actions for which people do not hold themselves to account for. Perhaps the gin mills do much for such dispersion. I did not know we could afford such things in this house."

"Anyone can get alcoholic drinks, father," I told him positively, "you just work too hard and do not realize that people are forever moving around and looking for things to do. Have you not noticed the rash of drinking houses here in London town, especially along the waterfront?"

"I only go to the waterfront on special occasions. Between my work and the rearing of a family and food, I cannot say that I am particularly interested in these things of evil."

"Well, they are there, and an awful lot of people go to them," I said.

"Why don't you go once in a while?" mother asked me with a scornful glance, "instead of mealy mouthing all the people with money and something to give you, it would be better if you stood on your own two feet, earned a living, and brought money home to your mother and father."

"He is but a child and is forbidden to frequent such places," father stormed at her losing his temper.

"He is a useless, biggity toady to the infernal, damned Normans," mother returned, her eyes flashing.

"He does what is required of him well," father said firmly, "I will hear no more of this talk in my house."

"In your house?" mother laughed wildly, "what house? A moldy vermin-infested hut that is always damp and dark. Oh, Wat," she began to cry, "Edward is gone. Sarah is gone. Now this one leaves. Where are my children?"

"I thought you wanted them out working and making their way," father said to her perplexedly.

"It is a relief not to have to cook and clean for them," mother said dispiritedly, "but it is hard to lose them, especially to this hateful, occupying, grasping Norman from over the seas who ride us down in the streets and treat Englishmen as if they were dirt."

"One must live the life that one finds on earth," father cautioned her, "such loose talk will get us in trouble with the law."

"Trouble is all I know," mother whined.

"Stir up the fire, Egbert," father ordered, "we have had enough of this talk for one day. We will have some hot water before we go to bed. I will be glad to see the summer come on. There is too much cold, fog and rain in the winter."

"Careful with the water," mother said, "there is not much in the house. I get tired carrying and fetching water but I guess the rain barrels are full. It has rained enough today."

I shuddered at the thoughts of using rain water. Some days there was a green scum on the top of the barrels attesting to the fact that they were seldom scrubbed or emptied. The fire caught readily and I put a small pot of water on the hook.

"Don't be so wasteful with the peat," mother snapped, "if you are so accustomed to riches I will keep you home for a day and let you dig and fetch fuel."

"Why must you be so testy with the boy?" father turned to my mother.

"Because he enters this house as if he was condescending to lower himself to come to us. You have turned this child, Wat. He will never be content to stay here anymore, nor will he ever feel at ease in the house where he was born. It angers me that one of my own could feel so superior. Those are Norman ways and I do abominate them!"

The water was hot but the smoke was filling the small, dark room. I went to the door and gulped fresh air. The drizzle had set in and it was very dark and fearsome. I had determined to leave this house forever when the opportunity presented itself. I figured to wait until my parents had gone to bed but that appeared to be forever. It sickened me to see my mother under the influence of gin because it surely brought out the worst in her. Father must move the girls out of here as soon as possible. They were unspeakably dirty. Their hair had not been combed in a week. If I so much as said a word tonight, it would set mother off and I hated to part forever with bad words between us. I did not want to go through the emotional turmoil of saying goodbye. Mother would either dissolve into tears or berate me for leaving. It would be best just to slip out and leave and never come back.

"I would like to go for a walk," I said.

"One does not go out on a night like this," said father, "the diseases of the night air will bring you down."

"Footpads and revelers don't seem to suffer," I told him.

"They wind up dead, with heads cracked or in gaol," father spoke impatiently. My mother's intransigence and my restlessness were beginning to affect him.

"I yield," I said resignedly. I was more determined than ever to leave this hovel just as soon as I could. Mother had taken a stool and was sitting in a smoky corner of the fireplace. Her clothes were unspeakably filthy; her face was raddled and her gray hair sprayed around her grimy face. Father had gone to put the younger children to bed. He had given them some of the food that I had brought. That dirty, straw strewn, dark, airless room! I wondered now how we had survived, sleeping on the cold damp straw. The feather mattress and warmth of the Becket house beckoned me. I would wait until all had settled down and then I would leave. When I returned to the fireplace, father silently handed me a broken crack of warm water. We could not afford leathern cups as did other well off peasants. We only had the leftovers that we had scrounged from the scrap heaps. The warmth was good but warm wine would have been better. At least it would have put us to sleep.

In no time at all, the house was still with restless people turning and twisting to avoid the lice that infested them and to stay warm under the pitiful coverings that my father provided. I went to the door, undid the latch and left without a sound. It was pitch black in the streets and pouring rain. I made my way safely to the Becket stables and sleep was not prevalent there. The grooms had pulled in some women from the rainy streets and the straw in the loft rustled and crackled amidst the giggles and groaning of struggling men and women. I found myself a corner, far from the activity and drifted off to sleep, dreaming of being with Edward, walking in clean dry sand in a warm sun in a faraway land across the seas.

CHAPTER 10

The journey to Surrey was but a three day journey but it was tiresome. The master, mistress, the two Becket girls, armed retainers and various servants went with us. Father would not go, fearing to leave mother alone overnight. The countryside was warm and dreamy as it ever is in the late summer. The trees were in full leaf and flowers bloomed everywhere. Dust would trail us at times but it was not at all bad, since the winter and spring had been so long and dreary. Mornings were the sweetest times of all when the dew glistened on the grass and the birds lifted their voices in wondrous roundelays. We traveled through glen and glade, slowly and peacefully. There were no signs of robbers but watch was kept at all times, particularly when we skirted castles or went through deeply wooded areas. Peasants were lolling along the wayside, resting before the harvest and kine stood knee deep in lush grass endlessly eating.

Since no one was provided with horses except the women, the master, and two knights, walking was the chief feature of the trip. One would be so tired at night, that the evening meal became a chore. The master and his retainers would be jolly, but feeding the baggage animals and erecting tents and serving the food was tedious when one was so tired that the feet seemed as leaden as weights. Conversations between Thomas and his parents were long.

"You will only come home once a year," the master told his son, "since the distance is great and travel is difficult."

"I know father," Thomas said manfully, "I shall be diligent and attentive and shall look forward to coming home, when I can."

Mistress Becket wept softly. "Do not cry, mother," he said to her, "it is time for me to get started in this world." Tears would have flowed from his eyes for a bit and from mine also.

"Yes son," Gilbert Becket said stoutly, "everyone hates to see their young leave their roofs, but the world demands that we accomplish something on this earth, and with times as they are, an education is necessary. The Church has many places in its hierarchy both spiritual and lay where employment is good and steady. It is for this and the glory of God that we do for you what we can. Do you think you can stay at the monastery for this long time?"

"Yes father, I can stay," he replied, his boyish face all seriousness. 'I too will stay, whether I like such or not,' I thought to myself. This monastery bit might not be too pleasant for me, but there will be other servants of other students and of the monks so things will not go too badly.

"When we arrive on the morrow, I hope the parting will not be too tearful," Gilbert Becket sighed," 'Tis ever hard for a man to see children and womenfolk cry and not be sad. What can one do to assuage tears? There is no remedy that I know of."

"I know I shall cry," Mistress Becket said. "I cry now and will cry then and possibly for many days in the future. I shall miss my male nestling even though I know it is for the best. It is never easy for a mother to part from her children." She hugged Thomas to her.

I could only stand in the background hopefully hoping that there would be a kind word of remembrance for me since there had been so little when I left my parents. Mistress Becket came over and embraced me.

"You are now a young man, Egbert Watson, take care of my son, I charge you."

"I will, madam, believe me. I will look after him as best I can." I drew myself up to my best height which was a bit more than my short mistress.

"My," she murmured, "my how you've grown! I did not realize it. I hope you grow some more and develop into a fine broth of a man. The stronger the better and perhaps we will betroth you to a fine peasant girl who you can love and care for."

I grew fiery as if I had been burned badly by the sun. I liked girls but not that much. To be so near one as marriage was too new an idea to contemplate. I shrunk from her. She and the master laughed merrily.

"Not so soon, silly," she twitted me, "it will be many years before you can take on that responsibility. But when the time comes, I shall see that you are properly cared for."

My obvious relief was shameful. I was not prepared to take a young girl and care for her as well as Thomas.

"Leave be, mother," Master Becket said gently, "you have teased him enough. He will die of embarrassment!" They laughed some more and the campfire that night was merry as the flames flickered across the hobbled horses and the gently swaying tent tops. I sat blissfully and gazed at my master and mistress in adoration, realizing that these were my true family who had always been gentle and kind with me and giving lavish attention to my needs. I would miss this kind, ebullient couple who drank so deeply of the good cup of life. I would miss truly the great house with its exotic visitors, solid comforts and excellent food. I had learned to love the comforts of life and even now wondered if I would be able to ever have a feather mattress to sleep on again.

"It grows late," said Master Becket, "we must to bed. If we arise early, we should reach our destination after the middle of the day."

"I shall be glad," remarked Mistress Becket as she surveyed her dusty clothes, "I don't believe that there will ever be enough water to cleanse me and if there is, then I shall need even more to cleanse my clothes. And...my daughters! They are dusty from head to foot. The good fathers of Merton Priory have never seen such a washing as I will have!"

"Come, sweeting, rest before you charge into the monastery and cleanse the monks from their very rooms," laughed the master.

"I shall not leave that place until every article is well washed," she asserted stoutly, "including the two boys. I will leave them to someone else to see that their bodies are clean. I am afraid that men are lax in such matters. It never hurt a body to be well scrubbed once in a while."

"I agree with you pet," he said to her very gently as he led her to their tent. Thomas and I looked at each other, at our smoke and dirt begrimed faces and clothes. What a humiliation! To have to submit to a washing before we had established relationships with the other people of the Priory! I could hear the maids and grooms whispering that they would avoid this somehow. They would not wash if they could help it and some of them smelled as if they had never submitted to water in their lives. We did sight the monastery long before the noon hour and all other time was spent in watchful expectancy. We arrived at their gates about the middle of the afternoon and were received hospitably by the monks. All except the master's immediate family were consigned to the stables. I resented this bitterly but I'm sure the good fathers never dreamed of sleeping servants in quarters with their masters. The females, yes, the males never.

The master and mistress settled in for a week's rest and religious meditation. And washing. Mistress Becket did not rest until the lowest of the servants stood before her scrubbed red with sand and water. There was much grumbling about this. The grooms swore that such action would give them a grave disorder but they did look better with the accumulation of a lifetime of sweat and grime removed from their leathery skins. All clothing was scrubbed and it was laughable to see sinful men attempting to hide under the adequate garb of the monks. The Becket household was never so clean. Food was another matter.

The monks ate pitifully. There was little or no meat. What there was of it was doled out carefully, generally being boiled to pieces and mixed in with the wheat which appeared to be their principal diet along with fruits and cheese. I could see a long stretch of monotony ahead for me and it was not a pleasant view. I resented sleeping in the stables and most of all I resent the enforced separation from the master's family. After all, was I not almost one of them? I shared equally in Master Thomas' fortunes, why should I not share in some of the amenities of life? Thomas told me later of my trials and tribulations. During my resentment and adjusting to the routine of the monastery, the week sped by. I was astounded to be called in before dawn of a morning to bid my master and mistress goodbye. We all wept copiously. I can still see them in my mind's eye as they rode off into the rosy sunrise even if it has been two kings and many lifetimes ago.

Thomas told me this of my misery. Master Gilbert approached the abbot about my welfare.

"His welfare will be seen to, rest assured, good sir," the priest said.

"But will he be near my son?" queried the sheriff, "please to remember that he has been reared in my house almost the same as a child of my own. He is unfamiliar with living without the confines of an abode."

"It is not the custom to accept a servant," he was told frostily, "but the exception has been made in respect to your son. There are no facilities nor provisions for servants in the Priory. He must needs sleep in the stable but you can see for yourself that they are adequate. The cells for the servants and ostlers there are as gracious as ours. All live the rigors and contemplative life. There are no exceptions. We cannot have non-instructive people among the students. As you can see, there are many servants and many students as well as young monks and priests. Both will have adequate companionship and supervision. Do not fear, Master Becket, these young men will grow well and prosper."

"As you say father," Gilbert Becket spoke softly. We all took our tearful farewells. I wished fervently to be with the returnees because I was missing most cook's bread dipped in hot grease. Here, I had already found that all food was either baked or boiled and only enough food to sustain body and soul. Other than the cook's helpers, no one was allowed in the kitchens and filching extra food and wine were out of the question since the cellerar was a monk held to strict account by his superiors. The regimen of accountability was respectable but not loveable nor livable. Further, we began to either wear monk's attire or the cape that was being introduced as standard peasant's wear over our shirts. Shoes were not even considered for servants, but I insisted on mine and was ever bedeviled for this custom.

The years passed swiftly by at this school. It was one continuation of prayers, lessons and retreats. Thomas did well in his studies and became proficient in Latin and the new English. He was not of the turn of mind to be bookish though, and I fear he was somewhat of a disappointment to his good parents. We shared many things including clinging to each other regardless of whom we met. We were never the closest of friends but many of the things we shared in common were things that close friends never did. Such as the matter of riding.

This was a serious matter at this monastery. They only kept mules and these did need exercise as horses did. Nevertheless, Thomas would come to the stables and we would lead forth animals and gallop as best we could around the countryside. The chief groom was amazingly tolerant of us so we had some sport together. Also, he would sneak me food from the pantry from time to time, but it was always fowl of some kind that was either roasted or boiled. I longed desperately for pork or beef. I almost rejected the diet of bread, suet and vegetables.

I got awfully tired of schools and lessons. Thomas got to where he could do his Latin and English very well. He would make me listen as he recited his lessons in rote. I learned the prayers of mass very well and the plainsong did get very pleasing as I caught on to the nuances of the voice and began to understand the words. I did not wish to go to school and the monks made no attempt to teach the servants. We had to go to mass, yes, but it was unthinkable that the lower classes should want to learn to read and write. Thomas did teach me to write my name very plainly and I was proud of this accomplishment even if the other servants did say ugly things to me about this. They often accused me of putting on airs.

We brought our bedding from the big house and the cover made the straw in the stables livable for me. Thomas said he slept on hard cots in the monastery but they did let him keep his cover. We both had bugs from time to time because the good fathers were not as meticulous about cleanliness as was Mistress Becket. I really learned about sex at the monastery also. The fathers were very lax in their supervision of the servants and never came to the quarters after dark. Furthermore, they believed since they had all males, that the men were naturally good. They were very, very bad. As night would fall, the maids from the countryside would come and stay until females had to go home.

"It's free I am, this evening," they would sing out as they entered the building.

"'Tis best you are," a servant would answer as he came to claim a girl.

There was great promiscuity here. The girls were taken one by one by any man who stepped forth. They were stout, hairy women who smelled of sweat and manure as strongly as any man. Their raucous voices while tumbling in the hay, were hideous. And I do not say this because I reject dirty women or that I am above such things, but they were really too much to stomach after having been reared in the Becket house. The days that all ate onions and drank too much wine were particularly revolting. I marveled that the supervising fathers did not object to the strong and raw smells that hung over the buildings. I will never forget the early evenings in that school because the men and women made them memorable with their coarseness and lack of care. Privacy was unknown to this group and they did not particularly seem to care. Religion or their vows in church meant little to any of them. I was not too young not to appreciate the females, but their forwardness and their body odors repelled me. It would do no good to discuss this with Thomas because he was too young to understand. My days and nights were miserable at times because the men would say anything since they were not under the watchful eyes of their supervisors. My only relief was to escape whenever I could.

But the years passed swiftly. We managed to get to London at least once yearly. Mistress Becket and her daughters would cry over us, and the master would be exceptionally kind. I could swear my mother hated me. She hardly even spoke and she frankly stated that there was no room in the house for me. I stayed in the stables with father or in the house with Thomas. He was ever kind and interested in my welfare. Sarah was distant and had become very tall over the years. My little sisters at home were planning to go into service as soon as they could. All in all, everything went quietly for all and I could see little change in the lives of those I knew best.

The second year at the Priory was interesting in that King Henry's son was lost at sea and all London was astir about the succession. Mother quietly laid down one day and died. Father was shaken by this and lapsed into a state of apathy. He was forced to put my sisters in an orphanage. Had I not had my obligations to Thomas I would have stayed at the big house and helped him. I could not do this. My sisters were put out to work and I never heard from them again.

In our sixth year at the Merton School we received word that Thomas' mother had died. When we got to London, we found the master in almost the same state of apathy as had been my father, who had somewhat recovered, thank the good Lord. Money had been specifically set aside for Thomas' education and my sister and his sisters had been placed in a convent. Sarah caught some kind of fever while we were home and died almost overnight. Only my father and I were left alone with the Becket family, or what remained as the active part of it. My father to serve a master who began to fail noticeably, and I to link my destiny with the young Thomas.

A cousin of the Becket's, Osbert Huitdeniers, the sheriff of London and an enterprising businessman, took over the management of the remaining Becket business. He appeared to be as kind as the master and mistress had been, but we saw him very little. Messir informed us that in accordance with the old master's plans, we would be sent to Oxford as soon as arrangements could be made, where Thomas would be trained in business and law as a clerk. I was told that I would accompany Thomas as his personal servant, doing whatever needed to be done as befits a young man whose station in life is in the upper middle class.

CHAPTER 11

This was Thomas' fifteenth year and my twentieth. I had not grown tall, but I was stout. The typical Saxon which did little to keep the Normans from saying ugly things to me from time to time when I asserted myself. I felt that I had done a remarkable job of freeing myself from prejudice because the Priory was a hotbed of hatred. The servants there were forever cursing and demeaning anything Norman and were intriguing always to be foment rebellion. They were too cowardly to reveal themselves to the priests and monks whom they particularly hated, even though they worked for them, but the vilest of language was never too expressive for them in their hatred for their overlords. I could tell that the Huitdeniers looked on me the same as they would a piece of furniture or one of their cattle.

Thomas was another matter. He was already tall, very athletic and had a most winsome character. He utterly charmed his uncle and the family, and consistently got anything he wanted. His black hair, big, expressive eyes and olive complexion won him friends immediately wherever he went. Entering Oxford was evidently no problem for him because he found us quarters and made his entry on the same day that we arrived. The quarters were in a cellar and very, very damp, but we could cook and be to ourselves.

I hated the place because I was alone so much, so I roamed the streets and learned what Edward had already told me. There was much activity during the day and there was much that could be readily stolen. I could not bring myself to do this, but I was fascinated when I saw students and urchins of the street, grab and run. The days were too long and the nights even longer, so I would go and stay in the stables of Thomas' guardians whenever I wished. Although I did not have access to the big house, the food served to the servants was adequate and much, much better than the cold bread, cheese and wine that Thomas and I ate so many times rather than try to cook or to have to clean afterwards. Thomas never questioned my comings or goings. He did not seem to care if I was with him or not. My jealousy of his studies and student friends knew no bounds.

"I shall leave this place and never return," I would grumble, "perhaps I would be better off working in the country on a farm or off on the high seas. This life in this cellar is boring to the extreme. I have so little to do!"

"Oh, Egbert," he would look up from a book or say as he was leaving for a visit or street roaming, "you know I couldn't do without you. I'm sorry if I have so little for you to do, but bide awhile, there will come a day when you will be busy every minute. Why don't you read? Or I shall recite today's philosophical dissertations to you. In that way I can learn as well as teach."

"Don't try to stuff my brain with your university ideas," I would warn him half in fright, "you know that Abelard has been consigned to the lowest regions of Hell and trafficking with him is to the eternal damnation of your soul. You were told that over and over in the school at Merton. The very mention of his name or his blasphemies are injurious to your changes of going to Heaven."

"Oh, the Devil," he would laugh, "Abelard was not blasphemous. He was merely trying to chase some of this ossified thinking from our narrow minds. I don't necessarily agree with him, but he has some good ideas that lend themselves to thinking and debate. If people like him didn't exist, life would be boring to the extreme. How can we ever determine the nature of divinity if we do not at least hear what others have to say."

"Hush my good master," I would pray to him, "do not defile me. If you do so, I must needs spend my life on my knees before the cross attempting to cleanse myself of the heresy of just listening to you. Leave your arguments at the school or take them with you to the tavern. I am much happier not knowing of this foreign thought. It is not English bred not the product of an Englishman's mind. It is certainly against the teachings of the church, because the good Saint Bernard has said so repeatedly." I would cross myself repeatedly, hoping to ward off the curse that I was sure that would be visited on us any instant.

"I respect the good Saint and all the teachings of religion," Thomas would tell me merrily, "but I must needs know. I wish to probe, question and determine for myself that which is right and that which is wrong. I do not consider myself as being heretical or sacrilegious by discussing discrepancies in the bible or the teachings of the clergy. It is stimulating to hear them challenged. If I were smart enough to have original ideas, perhaps I would take them to task myself. Surely there is something to the Muslim ideas or so many of them would not believe. They do believe in one God you know. They also have written much on the concept of God. And the Eastern Church must be very strong to have so many believers in that part of the world. And what of the Holy Roman Empire? The Germans make and unmake Popes! So many faiths and so many beliefs must indicate that there is much to be learned about religion and why men differ over essentially the same central idea. I must learn and learn and learn."

My head would reel when he started one of his discourses.

"Please," I would beg of him, "do not utter such blasphemies in the house. You compromise my soul. Keep them for your fellows. It is not so bad to say such things in taverns and places that are not the House of God. But I can only see that you blaspheme and in your actions you carry me with you. Why send both of us to the nether regions? I am happy with what the priests tell me and I do not wish to have my soul jeopardized. It hurts my head to think on what you say. I stay confused from time to time and when I find myself thinking on such things, I hie me to the nearest church to cleanse my mind. I am too simple to unravel such complicated matters and my head reels from your arguments. You do me much harm when you subject me to your ideas because they make me doubt my faith. To doubt for me, is fatal, and I fear my prayers will not be heard. I spend my money and time working for candles for the souls of my relatives. Since I have been here with you I fear that I should burn candles for myself."

He would laugh merrily.

"Never fear, Egbert, I will never place you in awkward positions with the church or with other people. What I say here is for your benefit and to exercise my mind and reasoning. You can't stop the world old man, and the more you find out, the happier you will be. Just think my father was lucky enough to go on a Crusade and he learned many things. He told me often of them. He found good people from here to the Holy Land. He liked it over there. He found the Muslims to be the most tolerant of people. They wanted you to become one, yes, but they did not insist on it. They respected Jesus as a prophet and they worshipped the same God that we do. And you know that they are the descendants of Abraham. It says so in the Bible. You have heard it many times in sermons. Why then, should we disbelieve what the Arabian philosophers have to say? They have sent us our numbering system, they have shown us that there are many good ways to live, and it is a passion with Crusaders to stay in the Holy Land once they are there. How can you see so much wrong with this talk?"

"That is not what I object to," I told him firmly, "it is the questioning of the faith and speaking irreligiously of the teachings of the church. All these new fangled ideas of angels dancing on a pinhead and such are not fit subjects for men to dwell on. Such matters belong with the priests and the teachers of the church."

"That is not so," he objected, "all matters of learning belong to all people. Man was put here on earth to increase his learning, else there would be no schools to teach religion, law and such like. We would go back to our caves and remain beasts which many of us still are. We close the caves of our minds and live in perpetual darkness of thought. I find this strange, too, that with all humanity exchanging ideas, that people can remain so insular and unaffected by people with whom they associate everyday. It appears that something would have some effect on them or especially their thinking. It mystifies me that if people do not wish to hear, they can actually ignore affairs that daily surround them and show no curiosity for the strange or questionable. They accept what someone else says the same as sheep do the shepherd and follow obediently wherever they are led whether it be to their downfall or to their glory. I could never do that. I must know why. Behind each act or thought there is a process that brings the person to such an act or thought and unless he can adequately explain such, I can only be skeptical and place my own reasoning on an equal plane. That is not so strange, when you think on it. Each person has a mind available for his use and all he has to do is exercise it to question what he sees and hears. I feel it is rather sinful to close one's mind to reality and refuse to improve himself as best he can. If he comes into collision with unproved statements, then he should challenge such. It never hurt anyone to challenge, albeit there are many who are so singular in their thoughts that they resent being challenged. I feel in some respects that the good Saint Bernard just couldn't cope with Abelard's revolutionary ideas and he refused to allow him to be heard. All men should be heard. I disagree with the church on this. All men should be heard. If one does not accept their ideas, then all one has to do is reject them. All men must be heard."

"You make sense and you do not make sense," I moaned, "and you end up confusing me so badly that I curse this University and all that it embodies. The Lord will visit his vengefulness on this wicked center of rebellion and wipe it from the face of the earth. I do so hope that I am not here when it happens. I wish I had never been near this wicked place."

Thomas laughed heartily at me more than once.

"Oh free yourself from such gloomy thoughts. One doesn't have too many miracles in this enlightened day and age. Destruction is always at the hand of man as a rule. Earthquake and lightening or a storm yes, maybe, but man always manages to survive. So do these cursed lice!" he scratched vigorously, "but fear not, you will never witness the destruction or blessing of a heavenly act, Egbert Watson, you are too practical. You wouldn't believe such if you saw it."

"It is time your cousin took you from this accursed place," I spoke to him stoutly, "you should be put to work and kept busy. The life of a scholar is not for you and I fear you will never be happy in the church because of your reckless nature."

"Have I not acquitted myself well here?" he asked me severely, because he was ever sensitive about his accomplishments, "do not my companions speak well of me? Does not my cousin say that my teachers send him commendable reports on my achievements? What else have you for me to do? I realize that I am not of the brilliant turn of mind as some of my friends are, and I do not wish to be so, but I can hold my own with the best of them and you know it, because you have been here and heard me."

"Yes, I agree that you have a very facile turn of mind. It is your blessing for which you should be eternally grateful, but you need more. Something practical to test your ability to survive. You have ever been to school, and have been protected, so you do not know who it is to look after yourself. 'Tis a hard way, fending for oneself. Not at all like having everything provided for by a thoughtful parent."

"I shall be ready when the times arrive for me to go it alone," he said confidently, "never you fear, little Thomas will be able to care for himself. And for your information and edification, I shall go to Paris after this term to complete my education. I will not be prepared for this cruel world until I have mastered the French language."

"More school!" I stormed, "Across the sea! In a foreign land, and among people who do not talk as we do and eat all those fiendish dishes that we do not know of. You will run out of patrons and money someday Thomas, and will have to beg on the streets for employment. It has been an eternity at school. I like not this part of the city, these roistering, broiling students, their coarse jests and ways. Neither do I like the food that we can afford. It sickens me to see young people founder on too much wine and indulge in morals that would sicken a dog. My bedding is so vermin ridden that I must find some way to cleanse it, but I see so little sun here, that I fear things will be worse instead of better."

"Oh, stop your complaining," Thomas snapped at me, "this is Thursday. The day after tomorrow we will go to Sir Richer's and rest awhile from the taxing labors of my studies. We will not go to France until the summer. You will get your sunshine there and in plenty, battling for food and quarters. Meanwhile, I must be off. A party awaits me at the Swan. Here," he tossed me some cappers as he was over what to do, "go and find yourself a skinful of wine and forget our cares.

Do not wait up for me as I shall leave the group only when we have exhausted tomorrow's lectures."

He left singing, wearing a finely turned leather tunic and amber colored cut velvet stockings. He favored wine colored shoes above all else and a hat to match. The hat perpetually had a jaunty feather in it, setting him apart from his fellows. When he did wear a robe, it was of the finest Flemish woolen, usually black or amber. My Thomas lacked not in the taste to dress and he was always given ample money to do so. The thoughts of going out and indulging in wine did not appeal to me so I secured the money in my pouch and saved it against the day when it would be needed for more important things. My saved money always bought us a hot fresh meat pasty whenever Thomas ran short and he was reluctant to send for more. I dwelled on the visit to Baron Laigle's estate. I always enjoyed these visits, because there was food in plenty, many handsome and curvaceous maids around, and I was not treated so much as a servant as a true manservant to a gentleman of rank.

Sir Richer Laigle was one of those substantial Normans who held his possessions in a lordly manner with little or no friction with the crown. He had a castle of true baronial proportions and a retinue of retainers of knights and servants which would have served a person of much higher rank. He was obedient to his king and was thus favored by good King Henry when it came to awards of trade and lands forfeited to the crown. He had vast flocks of sheep, swine, kine and horses. His husbandry was fabulous. He was indifferent to people as a general rule, but he was fastidious and a hard taskmaster when it came to accounting for his herds and money. His wealth was solidly accepted and he was generous. Especially with Thomas. He had been a friend of the Becket family as far back as time permitted to trace friendships and he always gave us free run of his estates. He welcomed Thomas to his banquet table, taught him the art of falconry and hunting to the hounds. Thomas was one of the best bowmen in England and after a hunt, the quarry he brought down was the pride of the hunting group. In this house, Thomas learned to be discerning of wines, entertainment and in general, the life of a nobleman. We went to Sir Richer's as freely as we would have gone to the Becket home. Messir Osbert's home in London was nice, but it was a city home confined to the narrow sunless streets. Thus a visit to the Laigle's was doubly welcome. I was allowed to ride a good horse and be with Thomas on his outings. I looked forward to a few weeks visit to the Laigle holdings.

Sir Richer was a huge man. Dark, saturnine but most pleasant and thorough with his training of the young noblemen who were in his house for tutelage in the ways of knighthood. Joustings were almost a daily occurrence with the master personally conducting inspecting the equipage of his charges. He was harsh with a lax warrior to be and his punishment could be severe. He readily and cheerfully furnished Thomas with armor and accoutrements and was delighted when Thomas proved to be one of the better of his pupils.

CHAPTER 12

The young trainees would have to gear themselves up in the afternoon after a hard morning hunting and report to the tournament field. Sir Richer would pair them off as opponents and set them to their work.

"Charge!" he would scream in a voice that would fair burst your ears at a hundred paces and two young men would race toward each other with blunted spears. The clangor and rattle could be heard for miles.

"Wield that sword, swing that mace as if you mean it!" he would roar to a lagging student. "I would not send you back to your father as the same puling infant that you were when you came to me. Into the fray! Convince me that you are capable of defending yourself and the king. Lower away! Fight! Fight! Do not turn, do not weaken, keep the eye on the opponent, strike him where it hurts the most. Batter that shield, command your horse, be alert. Fight! Fight!"

The tournament field was serious business and when the jousting was done, Sir Richer and his more experienced knights who had been helping him supervise would lecture the novices on their shortcomings. Many hours would be spent on reviewing mistakes and increasing knowledge on the art of warfare. After these sessions all would change horses and go their separate ways. If hunting was done, Thomas always managed to insert himself in the part because he was addicted to the bird and bow. He always acquitted himself in both hunting and fighting although he was very slender and had to yield weight to the other lads in training and he also had to yield in honors of the blood. Thomas soon learned it was not meant for a merchant's son to attempt to gain social equality with those children of knights or to the manor born. If this discrimination ever weighed on him he never voiced an opinion to me. He ever looked forward to visiting at Sir Richer's. When at table, he was able to find a place at the salt line. Never above or below and in his shrewd decisions the knight favored him mightily.

"Serve the middle of the table with good cuts of meat and plenty of bread and wine," he would order the servants, "I would not have food passed to them from other parts." I had become adept in receiving the food and seeing to that my young master was afforded first servings. He always got the top of the wine jug, never the drags. After the meal, the fire would be hotted up and if music was not provided we often saw mimes, juggling acts, trained bears or listened to a wandering troubadour. The Welsh singers were the most enjoyable and any were in the neighborhood, they all knew they were welcome at Sir Richer's table. Thomas always managed to be at Sir Richer's elbow during these times. Never was he obtrusive or forward but near to seat of influence, always able to turn a pretty phrase or to insert some wit into a dragging conversation. He was in many cases, Sir Richer's pride. Often you could see them in conversation, the tall knight's huge arm around the slender shoulders, talking animatedly.

"Woulds't be a priest, Thomas?" the knight would inquire.

"No, not that, sir, not clerk I don't think. It has been the way in my family to be merchants. I feel that business is my calling, however the Church is very enticing if I can qualify for a good position within."

"It is a good and honorable profession and for the glory of God," Sir Richer said piously.

"I am not austere by nature, sir," the young Thomas said humbly, I prefer the more worldly aspects of life. It becomes me to like good clothing, wine and food. I like stimulating conversation on many things, so I feel that I should position myself where life flows vigorously and the riches are easily accumulated."

"Strange," the knight looked at him with respect, "coming from an orphaned merchant's son. There must be some knightly or royal blood in your veins because I do not believe that you are vainglorious and I have never seen evidence that you are proud or greedy. Ambitious yes, but not to the point of being obnoxious. I have observed your management of the young people in my household and you appear to make the cruder, better born young man your inferiors. They accept such and I have had not complaints that you are officious or unbecoming in your manners. I cannot believe that you are base born, yet you have no claims to blood lines or titles. Your tastes are far beyond your years and your perception will carry you far. This is not time for common people, unless they curry the king's favor, to rise high in England and I do not believe you have connections that will bring you to the attention of the royal house. I myself could never do that, although I am one of the king's councilors for this district."

"No, I have none of that," young Thomas answered pensively, "but I have a brain, a quick ability to learn and am observant. I attempt to profit from what I see in others. It is the only way for me who must succeed on his own merit."

"Yes, that is they way," agreed Sir Richer, "and you do well. You are a natural born horseman, fighter and diplomat. These are the main requirements for success. If you can enter into a thriving business, attract the attention of the Church and the King, you will go far. I believe this to be so. Destiny is with you at the tender age of sixteen. I hope that I am doing my part towards contributing to your success. This is the responsibility of those who can do so. One must help others to rise and discharge their responsibility to society. It makes for a better world to open the ranks to upcoming youngsters. Each generation should succeed better than its predecessor. The world can always accommodate success."

"It is my prayer that such is so," Thomas said meekly.

"It is so," returned Sir Richer authoritatively. "I hear from some of the other youngsters that you hie yourself to Paris in the near future to further your education."

"Yes sire, in these days of Normans ruling the country, one must needs know French if he is to work for the government. There are many, many people in this country who do not speak English. My father spoke it brokenly, my mother never mastered the tongue of French or English well. I learned more English than French because of my schools. The person who is not accomplished in the language of the Normans is one who will be saddled with his lack. My kind cousin has told me that father provided for me before he died. It is a small remittance, but my servant and I can make do. We will survive and in small style," he laughed.

"You are remarkable in that you are so adaptable. It is a trait that can hinder or help. Chameleons survive by it, but I fear at times they might suffer but only overly so. If your needs become desperate and your guardian does not respond adequately, send me word and I shall see that you do not need. I can always find a small remittance somewhere in the house if no where else than in the good wife's small hoard." He laughed heartily. Thomas smiled.

"I trust that I will never need it," Thomas said gratefully, "but if I do, rest assured I will ask. A little bread, wine and cheese can sustain me, and garrets are plentiful in France so I've heard. I must needs get through the thick head of my man servant that he too will have to learn the language of the country if we are to survive. The common Anglo-Saxon can be stubborn about many things and I fear at the moment, it is fashionable with them to resist the occupation. Especially taxes, levies of manpower and travel to the continent. Mine will go with me I am sure, but he will take some convincing."

"Whack him briskly about the head and between the shoulders and he will obey readily," said Sir Richer. I bristled at this. I would never resign myself to being beaten even in jest. I would go to sea first.

"I could never strike Egbert Watson," Thomas told the knight earnestly, "he has been in my house as far back as I can remember. He is more my flesh and blood than he is a servant. Then, too, he might whack me back," he laughed merrily, "it would be hard to distinguish who might get the worst of such a bout. I cannot think of beating him. It is beyond my imagination."

"What, you have a servant who has a surname and a given name?" Sir Richer asked in disbelief, "is he of some ancient lineage that he is allowed to break convention and follow our style for names?"

"No, sir, my father was lenient with his servants and the children of Wat wanted identification, so they went and registered for names. It was very simple and I believe it will become common here in this island. These are strong, independent folk who will someday blend in with their conquerors and will again rule their country."

"You speak as a seer which is unusual in one so young," Sir Richer said earnestly, "one can be too kind to conquered peoples and they will rise up and rebel. That is ever the way when people are educated and allowed to express themselves too freely. It is the nature of man to cast of yokes of their rulers even if anarchy results. I personally advocate harsher measures to keep the ruling elements among those that are capable. It bodes ill when common folk with no training assume too much freedom."

"Not so," defended Thomas, "true it is that kings should rule by their very rights, but intelligent people, from whatever walk of life should advise and say what is good for the populace. They know, because they have been there and can express the will of the majority. A king is no stronger than his nation and can always be deposed of or assassinated."

"You speak treason," warned the knight, "the king and the nobility would never allow that. I myself would not tolerate these oafish peasants have a say so in the administration of my estates. They are not truly good supervisors. No, it is wrong to allow the commoner too much freedom."

I thought to myself, 'you noble bastard, you and your kind will be the cause of rebellion in this country. It is small wonder that we hate the Normans with their superior ideas of grinding a man down beneath the yoke of servitude. The day will come when you will be thrown into the seas never to return.' But I could not hate this open minded uproarious man. He never did me an unkindness even if he never acknowledge that I existed except to peer interestingly at me from time to time. And I actually did not place much importance on these conversations because the days and nights were filled with pleasantries. By the time the fighting and hunting training were finished and the gear and clothing cleaned and stored, little time was left for eating and sleeping. There was not time for thinking. Life was too pleasant to waste one's time on futile thought. I dreaded the Paris ordeal but I was confident that Thomas and I would survive if given a decent chance. My short stays at the Huitdeniers had taught me that the streets were ripe for survival and one could always find safety in the warrens of humanity that filled the endless buildings of any city.

"I for one," Thomas told the nobleman, "will always make my home here in England. I am native born and find that it is my place to live. I have no desire to stay on the continent overlong and I intend to be in the midst of any changes that occur in this country. You know that King Henry is old and ailing and his daughter, the Lady of Matilda although connected to the thrones of Scotland and Wales, is continental bred. She has already laid Henry of Germany in his grave and is married to one of the most rapacious Normans that is alive. Although Fulk of Anjou can never legally rule this country, he can fight and insure that his wife rules so I can see a long overlordship by the house of the Conqueror. I will prepare myself to fit in the scheme of things. I wish to be accommodating both to the natives here and to the ruling house."

"You are wise beyond your years," the knight said admiringly.

"No, not necessarily," Thomas said airily exhibiting his embarrassing youthfulness, "I have learned from my father, my cousin, and you, sir. All the people I have ever known have been successful, accomplished and well endowed in life. Why should it not come natural to me to ape my mentors? I think you would find it more unusual to see me inefficient, unaware of my surroundings and indifferent to life. I have had the privilege of knowing very wise, very substantial people, and I find this type of life attractive. I am not one who would be shut of the cares or affairs of life. I wish to participate in whatever comes my way. I find myself at ease with commoner and ruler and I find life fascinating. I will not turn my back on people nor shall I rush out to meet them. Life to me is to be lived, not lost, not foolishly spent in criticism of others. There is room in the world for all and space enough for the lesser as well as the larger. I shall fit comfortably in the middle and profit from all that occurs."

"Perhaps I could learn from you," Sir Richer said smiling.

"No, sir, I have learned from you. I find you intelligent, open minded, tolerant, considerate and devoted to improvement. You are an ample tutor, sir, and I am indebted to you for your teaching."

"Fie, boy, I do no more than is my duty," the great man said bashfully.

"Then that is my desire," Thomas said simply. "I wish to find it my duty to work in my best capacity and to uplift whom ever comes into contact with me."

"As you know, I have continental holdings, also, as do most of the Norman gentry. You know where my castle is in the Vexin near Pontuilly. You must come there when you are in Paris and get refreshed. You must not abandon your training because fighting is a way with this world and the fighter survives."

"How well I know, sir," the young man said with emotion, "I fear it will ever be this way. How stand you on the succession?"

"It is Matilda's, by God," the knight swore angrily, but for her despicable attitude toward her subjects, she would make a good ruler. She is tough and tempered for the queenship if she would just learn reason and humility. She knows her father will die shortly, and she is being groomed for leadership, but her intransigent nature will cost her dear, I'm afraid. She is Norman to the core and she feels that all her subjects should bow without a murmur. Some of her people are her near relatives and the desire for a throne can be great. The house of Blois is large on the continent and here in the island. They are ambitious to a fault and would not be averse to poisoning her wine or slitting her throat. I believe both peoples on each side of the channel would rise in revolt if she tried to place her husband on the throne beside her. She has an infant son for whom she could establish a regency if she could contain the conflicts that are bound to arise. The males in Blois will demand succession as opposed to a female and they will fight for it or stoop to any method to secure the crown. I know them well and I fear them. They are a cruel, ambitious family intent on strengthening their continental possessions at the expense of the Conqueror's heritage. If that woman were not such an insufferable termagent!" Sir Richer said bitterly, "she has the knowledge and the support of the people and the Church if she does not alienate them. Why couldn't the king have had more sons so that this thing could be resolved without bloodshed? I intend to secure my affairs and ride this thing out if possible and avoid the conflict. I have made one Crusade and wish to make another. If things become too perilous here, I plan to take my family and establish myself in one of the Frankish kingdoms beyond the sea."

"I thought you were rooted firmly in this soil with no yearning to go abroad," said Thomas disappointed.

"I do, I do," said the knight earnestly, "but I wish to spend my declining years in peace and tranquility. If I must be poor, I will be so where it is warm and my care will be lessened. This climate is not kind to the elderly. Have you ever noticed that we have very few old people around here, Thomas? There are so few that they do not constitute a problem as to their care. Cold, damp and rainy wealthy takes its toll among the infirm and the weak and many die horrible deaths of the chills and fevers. No, if I become ill, I wish at least to be warm."

"Egbert's brother Edward said almost the same thing," Thomas said.

"I can never become accustomed to a peasant having two names," Sir Richer said kindly, "but if it is a sign of the times, so be it."

"Sir, I must be making my plans to enter the Paris University," Thomas spoke to his benefactor, "so I must needs to say goodbye now and leave early on the morrow. I must talk at length with my guardian and secure passage to the continent."

"That will not be hard for a cousin of the sheriff of London," Sir Richer said ironically.

"No, it will not be hard," acquiesced Thomas, "but I plan to stay at least two years and finish my studying if possible. It is time for me to go to work and find out where I fit in life."

"That is so," agreed his host, "so remember that you are always welcome to my home wherever it might be and do not fail to come there whenever you have the need."

"You are more than kind, sir, and I thank you," tears sprang into Thomas' eyes.

"And you are also welcome, Egbert Watson," he said to me kindly, the stranger name hesitantly falling from his lips.

I bowed low and touched my forelock. "Thank you, your lordship, I am grateful."

We left the presence of the great man hurriedly and went to eat together in the kitchen, Thomas not wanting to ruin the fine effect of this conversation. One of the grooms was shaking my shoulder before I got to sleep good, telling me that it was cockcrow, and time to leave. We caught the pack train of a merchant and walked with it to London town. We were tired and dirty when we arrived but the house of the sheriff was warm and welcoming. The cook, delighted to see us back, sat us down to hot bread, vegetables, venison roast and cool wine. We ate until we were sated. Thomas said wearily that his cousin would have to wait for the morrow to see him. He went to a room, lay down, and was instantly asleep. I found the stables to be cozy and quite, these servants doing their wenching and drinking in pubs and inns, because the sheriff tolerated no laxity among his household. The returning carousers did annoy me, but I was far too tired to take umbrage. The day had been too tiring, and the morrow brewed fair and exciting even if I was terrified of vast expanses of water, ships and strange people.

CHAPTER 13

Paris, when we arrived, was a topsy turvy town. It had taken us many days of walking to reach the city and I only enjoyed the sunshine that we had occasionally on our journey. I did not like the peasants on the continent. They were surly, suspicious, and animal like. The food was plain but filled with onions, wine and various spices. The inns where we stayed were dirty and stunk of stale wine, sweaty bodies and horse dung. The vermin on the continent were particularly vicious and when one asked for water to bathe, the natives looked as if you were daft. The lack of hospitality, the fear of being taken into bondage by marauding knights, and the tales of viciousness by the highwaymen made me feel as if the journey was a bit perilous. We remained joined with large merchant trains or bands of students who seemed to be forever traveling over the countryside. Truly, here safety lay in numbers.

Thomas did not seem to mind the hazards of the road. He ate little, was gay and entertaining with whatever group we were connected, and seemed to find companionship in the high and low elements of society. He would quaff a cup of wine with the leading merchant of a caravan or share food with obviously professional beggars. I fear that in some cases we might have shared food with highwaymen and the thoughts made me doubt my own integrity and honesty. To take food from some poor person or hungry child did little to settle my mind. Thomas would scoff at me and enjoy whatever we had with little or no thought to its origin. We did not suffer on our overland journey because we did not attract the attention of any hostile elements that might be abroad.

The first thing to do in that teeming city was to find living quarters in the warrens of buildings where students dwelled. Every building that we looked at was filled. They were dark and tall and all were joined together by walls. Every entrance had an incredibly dirty man or woman who sat behind a wall and counted the people who went in or out and collected the rent if they could identify their boarders and make themselves understood. It was a great student game to stay in one of these houses and pay no rent but the concierges were tough and wise and it was a seldom person who escaped their accipitrine scrutiny.

We finally found two pallets in the English nation and they were no more than pallets of filthy straw. Our clothing had to be either worn or guarded because these people of our own nationality knew no morals or hesitation when it came to permanent borrowing. A person's valuables had to be secured by the concierge, thus almost always insuring rent collection. The rents were cheap, because we were bundled together in our rooms on the filthy straw like faggots. The rooms were airless and until one became accustomed to the odor, it was difficult to sleep or even breathe. Despite all these problems, there were, eternally, students who would huddle and discuss lessons, the instructors, politics, Paris, home, or just plain gossip or relate the age-old stories that are forever bandied about among boys.

The few candles or candle ends that were bought or stolen were shared mostly by the copiers of books. These intrepid and constant souls worked night and day to transcribe the lectures, then sell them to the highest bidders, who were often sons of noble or wealthy parents, and were either too lazy or too busy to take notes.

I could see very early that Thomas was one of those who would not provide himself with materials for study, and since I was responsible for his welfare, I must needs add this burden to the ones of providing us with food and clothing during our sojourn in this land of the very foreign people. I began to put my mind to just how far the meager income his father sent us could be stretched. It took snatching food from the market places and judicious cooking to keep us reasonably fed. How I was to pay for the lesson copying was something to ponder on. I insisted that the young master write his father of the problem and beg for an addition to his allowance. This he refused to do and he informed me that I must do the impossible and make ends meet.

"But I am an ostler," I informed him, "not a jack of all trades. I have never been trained in cooking and accounting or trading. Only stealing and caring for animals."

"Best you learn quickly," he smiled brilliantly at me, "we must live and that is your responsibility. Mine is to acquaint myself with the law and the language, because when I leave here I shall be qualified to work anywhere in the kingdom."

I knew I had lost the argument when he turned to a long-haired, dripping nosed Frenchman and they began to converse in an animated fashion. The only thing I could do was to sigh and put my mind to the resolution of the problems. I could have cheerfully kicked the visitor up the street, because it was obvious that he had not eaten for days and this one day the concierge had a full pot of cabbage and meat boiling for us. My portion would go down the gullet of this gluttonous scarecrow. I was determined to eat something even if I did risk the master's displeasure. I had bread and meat hidden away just in case he was too severe. Let the damned French look after themselves! I would look after me as I had always done.

The most entertaining things that happened to us while in France were the visits by our countrymen. When the wealthy or generous churchmen or noblemen came, they distributed largesse among everyone. Often by dint of a small lifting of coins here, a concealing of a scarf or unnoticed coat there, I could later sell the articles and we would eat to our hearts' content. The visitors would tell us of home. Of the exciting events that poor King Stephen would get himself into, or of the wars between the King and the Empress Matilda. There was evidently so much fighting, that there was considerable booty to be garnered from the defeated forces, because both the King and the Empress imported foreigners who brought great quantities of supplies with them from over the seas. I wanted to go home and fight in the wars and gain some fame but I couldn't even consider leaving my master. Young Thomas probably would have put me in jail if I left him.

We had hardly been in Paris a year when the sad tidings came that the Becket buildings had burned. All this serious news was depressing, so we took what little money we had and joined a caravan of merchants who were going to the coast. Thomas helped me beg and filch on this journey in order to conserve payment for the ship. His winning ways and charming manners often gained for him an invitation to an elegant supper with the wealthy merchants in their tents that were warmed by braziers. When I knew that he was fed, I felt a sense of relief. I could always join any group of servants around any fire and get food. And there was always some man's loose wench who could bring me a bite if I pinched her bottom effectively and promised to sit with her if her man went to bed early.

The weather was absolutely abominable that winter and the road to Witsand was a quagmire that hindered traffic and kept us cold and miserable most of the time. Since we were so poor, I persuaded Thomas to conceal his fine fur coat beneath a coarser one in order not to attract attention. Finally, we made the coast and here it was that the friendships that he made on the way benefited us. We were invited to board a vessel as guests of the merchants and we did not have to spend one penny for the voyage. I was seasick from the moment I put a foot on the vessel and Thomas had to nurse me all the way over. He was cheerful about it and chided me severely for being a weakling, yet he found time to take meals with our hosts and thus he earned our passage.

An official of the Huitdeniers' establishment, Messir Glanville Smythe, met us at the boat with the last of the Becket horses. It was such a relief not to have to walk the dreary roads, but walk them I would have done, just to be home in London. How I looked forward to that exciting and most wonderful of all cities!

To me Paris couldn't hold a candle to London for excitement. Thomas informed me that I was a foolish dolt and a churl not to appreciate the French capital. I didn't care what he said just so that I could put one foot in London town. I would never leave it again, except possibly for a short visit and I was determined never to leave England's shores under any conditions for anyone. Little did I realize when I made these vows of the unhappy days I was to face in Canterbury and on the continent!

"I can smell it, I can smell it," I raptured aloud.

"We can all smell it," Messir Smythe spoke to me evenly, "the sad odor of death, burning wood, and the stench of poverty."

"I can stand anything if I can just reach London town," I spoke carelessly.

"It is a sad house you return to," Smythe spoke heavily. "The spark of Becket has gone with the fire."

"What do you mean?" Thomas spoke spiritedly.

"Wait until you get there," Smythe returned heavily.

"I can care for myself," Thomas spoke with pride.

"And I can look after myself as well as you," I told them swelling my chest. 'If I can just get to that wonderful city,' I exulted to myself. 'Just turn me loose where there is plenty of employment and many of my kind. I can live! I can live! I won't be burdened with having to speak some hideous foreign tongue and if I have to steal it will be from honest, cursing Englishmen of my kind! God, let me get there! Oh, just let me get there!

I couldn't help a small twinge of conscience when I thought of my moralizing to my long lost brother. I was as accomplished a reviver as he had ever been and I found that it didn't bother me one small bit.

"Well, it won't be long," Smythe said pulling a long face. My heart quickened in anticipation.

"Tell me what to expect," Thomas commanded him.

"The presence of your father in the business is missed, naturally," Smythe said, "but the loss of the buildings is the difficult part. I fear your fortune will never be put together again. I warn you that you perhaps must needs sell the big house and seek smaller and less expensive accommodations. The garden and animals are of great cost."

"Oh come now," Thomas remonstrated with him, "it can't be all that bad, I'm sure."

"Yes it is young sire," Smythe spoke heatedly, "you cannot afford to heat the big house, you cannot afford food for these continuously eating animals. You will find it hard put to feed your people, few that they are. None of your people have said that they wish to leave your house unless it is absolutely necessary, because it is their home, also. Besides, I'm not sure that they can leave voluntarily under the law."

"I will give them their freedom and they know it," he spoke seriously, "all they have to do is to ask."

"I know, I know," Smythe spoke impatiently as if to a small child. "But who would care for the property? You? Ha! You who has never been required to lift a finger even in your own good. I have not been retainer to members of your family all these years not to know their history. You have always been the handsome child of light, the pride of the relatives. You will do well to retain servants for yourself. Do not become obligated to do that for which you yourself can do."

"I am trained and able to work in the law if nothing more," Thomas spoke firmly, "and there are many things I can do if I set my mind. One of the things I can do, and that is to earn enough to care for myself and support my house. No, my people and I are not leaving the big house. I would not be happy elsewhere. I will let the animals go. I will place all servants in other positions if necessary. Egbert can become a personal servant if the occasion arises. The house might be shut down, temporarily, but I will never let it go."

I stared at this confident, handsome young man who had never been anything more to us than a pampered, dashing youth who had been given anything he had ever desired. This was a stranger to me, because to my knowledge, he had never lifted anything heavier than a pen or a ball.

"We have many relatives and friends in this city," he said, "and they can do as much for me as my father has done for them in times past. I can still take orders if I must, and enter the church, although that is the least thing that appeals to me at the moment. I have not played in and around my father's business for nothing. I can write a fine hand and keep tallies. Further, I speak French, Anglo-Saxon, and Latin. Surely, I can be of some use to many people. Any of the great counting houses or trading places can use my talents. I am sure the work will be boring but I can always make light of it as I can always go to Pevensey where I know Sir Richer will make me welcome as he always has. No, we will keep the house and I shall support it. I am confident that my father was too wise to have left me totally destitute. So, we can manage until we decide what is the best thing to do."

Smythe and I continued staring at this beautiful, luminous face that was speaking so ponderously and authoritatively. I was so deep in my fascination that I missed the excitement of entering the city proper. We are already a hundred yards within the slush, garbage ridden street before I got over my amazement. I had never conceived that the young master was so mature. I guess I had made the common mistake as had the others. Thomas had matured while I watched and I had not realized it. The man that rode with us was no longer the dependent school boy, spoiled and pampered by every one who came near his magic spell. I forgot to exult in my entrance into my native city. My interest in my new master was greater. Despite this, as I began to really look around, it all began to come back to me.

"Look, look," I cried, "it is beginning to snow and tomorrow we can enjoy the winter pleasures!"

"That is a peculiar attitude," Thomas laughed at me jeeringly, "I can remember just a few days ago, you were cursing the French snow and praying to get warm."

"You can't make me sad," I laughed at him, straining to restrain myself from jumping from the horse and dashing off through this heavenly city.

"I'm glad I'm back," I shouted drunkenly and waved my hands in the air in delight.

"Careful," Smythe warned me, "the watch will take you to jail for drunkenness.

"They don't arrest you for being happy in London town," I shouted.

"Careful," Thomas laughed and covered his ears.

I could see that my enthusiasm was beginning to infect him. Smythe even smiled and some of his severity and gloom seemed to lift from his shoulders. We let the horses canter. Thomas and I would have let our horses gallop except the city did not allow it due to the congestion and danger to the citizens who walked. We did move as swiftly as we dared, and the candlelight that came from the big house was almost unbearable in its beauty.

"Go on, go on," Smythe growled pleasantly. He took the reins of the horses as Thomas and I dashed for the door. I diplomatically let Thomas enter first and by the time I reached the great room, the master, my father, and cook were waiting for me with open arms, while Thomas roasted himself before the great roaring fire, sipping some mulled wine that the onerous cook had so thoughtfully provided. Master Becket was obviously aged and infirm from so much tragedy while father was not much better. The air of Smythe's management under the supervision of the house of Huitdeniers prevailed. The cook pummeled me, held me off from her and tilted her head. Poor soul, she was trying to compensate for the loss of the mistress, the senility of the master, and the inability of my father to welcome us.

"I've got me a fine pair in these two," she said as she twinkled. Then she smiled wanly and sadly. I hugged her from sheer love and the joy of returning. I began to walk around the room and inhale great gulps of the familiar air, while cook put her apron to her eyes and left for the kitchen. I went over to the fire and stretched. It was good to feel small and warm again and yearn for hot meat pie and a warm pile of skins. It felt that I could sleep a year if I was not disturbed. I turned to find Thomas and Smythe in deep conversation. Thomas was weeping unrestrainedly. The sadness descended. Smythe had had the horses fed and bedded and now he peered around the room with familiarity. I went over and stood beside him. It had finally come to me again that I would not this night, see the mistress' cheerful face nor would I hear the girls, neither Thomas nor my sisters, squealing in the back rooms. I could have also cried but I did not.

Cook, her face red from weeping, brought in a great mutton pie, dripping with gravy, and filled with great rolled dumplings. My father went to the kitchen and brought a jug of table wine. Despite our sadness, Thomas and I wolfed the hot food down. Truly, there is no dish on earth as good as hot mutton pie filled with fat dumplings and delicious herbs. Smythe watched us wonderingly. Thomas turned to him.

"Both of us are going to work immediately," he told him.

"Don't be hasty," Smythe cautioned, "I did not mean to frighten you unduly on the way over here. You are not yet so poor that mistakes have to be made. There is an adequate amount to sustain you temporarily. You are not totally destitute. Your cousin asked me to inform you of this. You can sustain for awhile. Your father's investments and rentals are sufficient for the moment. True, there is no capital to recoup the fire losses, and until you know more about business matters, it would not be wise to attempt it. With so few to support, you should not be overhasty. As you know, Messir Huitdeniers is very successful and wishes to purchase the business property and the Becket good will. The sale of that should keep your father, the ostler, and the cook in a smaller house. The animals will still have to go. Your cousin knows you can work. He thinks it would be good if you would stay at home and rest for awhile. He feels you should take the time to review your situation thoroughly. There is truly more employment here than there are employees. People are being imported into the city daily to do work that is necessary for which there is no available labor. All this he has told me to tell you at the appropriate time to put your mind at ease."

Thomas sat back. He was never the hearty eater that I was. I took the horn ladle and began to methodically scrape the pan of the last vestiges of gravy and pastry. The taste of good home cooking drove me beyond the realm of discretion.

"You will become ill, if you don't stop stuffing," my father cautioned me.

"I shall enjoy it," I smiled gaily at him as I wiped the drippings from my face with my sleeve.

"Let the man be," Thomas cautioned gently, "we have been long from home. We need to eat, rest and in general get fattened up. Do you wish to know what I have accomplished?" he indulgently asked the master who smiled benignly but with no understanding.

"My French is of the best. I feel that I know the law sufficiently to be a merchant and someday I intend to go into business for myself."

"It is good to know the law," Smythe said, "had there not been financial reverses your cousin would have sent you to Bologna for training in canon law. The unsettled conditions demands that a man be trained in all fields. There is a dire shortage of clerks who know law and foreign languages. Your cousin has great need of you and he will also hire your man. It is a time when young people can rise to dizzying heights of success. London has become the paradise for trade."

My heart swelled to hear his words.

CHAPTER 14

Everyone sat in the great room in silence. I was excited over the thought of entering the business world and being allowed to work for a wage. To earn money on my own had been an impossible dream. The master and my father sat very still. Thomas and I grouped ourselves around Smythe.

"Watson is an ostler and that is his place," Smythe began. There is a great demand for keepers and trainers of animals. The pay is good and it would not be fair to have him disappointed. For all the free and easy changes in social status, it is not wise to reach too far above one's station."

"He will not reach too high," Thomas spoke firmly, somewhat reminiscently of the master, "it is good to have more than one string to one's bow. A man who can read, write, and count will make a better ostler and can work in the royal stables if he wishes. Egbert is my man to the death and I shall pleasure in his success."

"I don't know about that," father scratched his head in confusion, "it's not good, this business of a man rising above his station. There is something in the disorder of things that comes from this."

"Nonsense old man," Thomas laughed, "times change, and the wise man changes with them. We are at the age and stage where we can work eighteen hours a day, and I intend to, to build the family's fortunes again. We are of the young people of the town. We are qualified to provide for ourselves, and this world exists to serve the young. Stand aside, and let the next generation have its say."

Smythe looked at this wise and sagacious young man in admiration. It was obvious that a good report would reach Master Huitdeniers.

"I feel that we shall yield to young master," he said softly. You are mature, wise, and competent."

"Thank you my good man," Thomas said kindly, "may you ever think so."

The fire had died down in the fireplace and a chill was beginning to creep over the room. Cook had cleared the table and the dogs were sleeping soundly. I began to nod as did the master, my father, Smythe, and cook. Thomas stood.

"It grows late," he announced.

"Your beds are in their usual places," cook told us, "I hope you sleep soundly.

Goodnight was said all around as father led the old master to a bed in the warm room. Thomas and I went rapidly to our freezing rooms. As sleepy as I was, I could not rid myself of the exciting prospect of employment.

"Do you really think it will be easy for me to find gainful employment?" I asked him.

"I should think so," he said quickly as he burrowed into the soft skins.

I wanted to talk more but I realized that Thomas was snoring gently. The thought of tomorrow was so exciting that I wanted to jump up and race around the house. I could swear that I was still thinking this when cook came in and ordered us from the bed.

"I am still sleepy," complained Thomas.

"But it is ten of the clock," cook said firmly.

"It is?" we chorused together as we sat up and stared at the daylight streaming in through the drapes that cook was drawing to one side.

"Yes, it is, and good people have been up and about these many hours."

"Dear sweet, the same old cook," Thomas said as he sat up and looked at her. "Do you know, woman, I love you. Are you available for marriage?"

"Go on with you, you daft, ever silly, idjit," cook beamed.

"I'm serious," Thomas protested, "I am so glad to be home, that I feel you would make a perfect wife."

"I too," I chorused, "two men should make any woman happy."

"Oh shut your mouths, you two geese."

"I'm coming out," Thomas shouted as he threw back the covers.

"EEEEEEEEEE," squealed cook as she fled from the room.

"That's rather silly," I remarked to him. "She has seen you ever since you were born."

"One should never attempt to fathom the female mind," he said absently as he stood up, shivered, and stretched.

I could not wait for this slow poke. He would take a long time to dress, comb his hair and prepare to make a public appearance. He did not care to be seen unless he was flawlessly dressed. With me it was little matter. I raced down to the kitchen. He didn't hear me.

There was a beautiful roast on the spit and vegetables were boiling in the pots. Gravy bubbled in a flat pan over the coals and the very air in the kitchen was redolent of garlic, pepper, clove and hot bread. I could have inhaled these odors and died a happy man. I went over, sliced myself a huge hunk of bread, went over to the gravy and ladled generously. Then I cut myself a hunk of half-done meat, poured myself a leathern cup of wine and proceeded to dine as I turned before the kitchen fire.

"Ever the glutton, who cannot wait for others," cook scolded gently, "will you never stop to learn gentle manners? Go into the big room while I prepare the young master's tray. I would have done as much for you if you had let me." She spoke in an aggrieved tone.

I stood with my mouth hanging slack. Had I risen so far in the world that a cook would prepare and serve my food? I went silently into the great hall and by the time I saw the dogs my spirits were up again. They were so fat and lazy that they would only wag their tails. They didn't even beg for food. It was obvious that they were spoiled outrageously. The fire felt good. Thomas came in slowly and he literally walked in an aureole of light. He had on brand spanking new clothes. His thin, aquiline face was almost ruddy, his brown eyes glowing, and his light brown hair brushed to a turn. Truly he was almost too beautiful to be human. His new clothes were yellow. His hose were of the softest wool and the surcoat was the most beautiful shade of cut yellow velvet that I had ever seen. The matching silk shirt was filled with flowing full cut yellow silk that swirled around his wrists and forearms. The shoes were boots that came to the mid-calf and they fitted him like a glove. He had put on his heavy gold necklace with the emerald and it glittered like green fire.

Again, I stared. He looked like a living flower placed in this glowing huge house. His brilliance made the snow seem pale.

"How do you like it?" he asked, turning.

"Those are the most beautiful clothes I have ever seen," I told him in a reverential whisper.

"Where are yours?" he asked me.

"Where are what?"

"Your new clothes. You know that father would not buy me a new outfit unless he bought something for you. Are you sure there were no clothes near your bed?"

"I didn't look," I admitted sheepishly. I knew full well that there were no new things for me. Why should there be? My clothing was adequate, albeit they were impossibly filthy. I had intended on wearing some rags and stay within the house for a few days while my clothes were being washed.

"Go see," Thomas commanded me imperiously.

Cook had entered with his food and she put it on the table. She stood expectantly while he came to the table to eat. I went to my bed and there lying in a neat pile were my new clothes! I could have sworn that they had been put there after I had left the room although I admit that I had not looked. Even if I was almost twenty five years old, I could have cried. The clothes were of good wool and matched throughout. There was even new undergarments of linen.

I slipped on my new hose and they felt creamy against my legs. The tunic was a golden color to match the hose. The coat was of durable leather, but generously cut and handsomely sewn. The shoes were tanned leather and came up to my mid-calf as did Thomas'. I felt positively elegant. I walked to the window and aired my feelings. I wanted to shout loud enough for the roof tops to tremble. I had to go to the great room and show off my finery. Father was there.

"A new lord has arrived in this house," he said gruffly but affectionately.

"A new lord indeed," sniffed cook as she cleared the table, "the young master is sure to spoil that one. The idea, dressing as his betters and him an ostler's son!"

"Turn, let me see how they fit," Thomas said as he turned to cook. "You must be careful whom you criticize, madam, anyone can rise to high places in the government left by the Conqueror. Soon it will not be unnatural to see men of capacity serving where they are needed. If only we could rid the country of that usurper, Stephen of Blois! And send from this country those vicious, marauding mercenaries! The land will never know security and peace until we have a rightful heir on the throne. It's a pity that the Empress could not win over him and put all the recalcitrants to death."

My father put his finger to his lips.

"Careful what you say, young master. London is Stephen's city. You make treasonable statements. It is best that good citizens do not participate in politics."

"Your new clothes are fabulous," Thomas told me as he observed my turning. He turned to the master.

"A person must participate in his government or it will never be better. I learned in Paris that a healthy discussion is good to clear one's mind. Some students there could discuss the argument between the great Abelard and the monk Bernard of Clairvoux. It is a pity that England does not have a University. I fear we will never become a country of any repute unless we have some centers of learning where our young people can go and debate the great issues."

"Nevertheless, it is treason to criticize the king."

"Someone must be against him. He cannot control the barons, much less a small insignificant citizen like me," Thomas said haughtily.

"Careful, my young master," I said to him, "you are not in Paris arguing with your favorite pedagogue."

"It does not matter where one is," he said earnestly, "all know that Stephen of Blois gained the throne illegally. It is a pity that there is not a law that would insure the succession. Until one is written, we can only pray and yearn for the peace that the old people tell us we had under the good King Henry. In the meantime," he said seriously, "I would have the horses saddled Egbert. We are going to Merton."

"Today?" Cook asked him incredulously, "why you've hardly arrived."

"I feel that I must see the fathers immediately. With swift horses we can be back by early dark."

"What will the fathers say to unannounced arrivals?" cook queried him.

"The fathers understand me," Thomas lordly replied.

"Get your warmest clothes," he informed me, "it looks as if it will snow heavily."

I hurried to the bedroom and put on my oldest and worst clothes. I was not going to ruin the best I had ever had. I had an inkling that my new master was emerging and I wanted to fit into his every wish. I anticipated going to the priory since the trip would offer me the opportunity to see the changes in the city. Also, I welcomed the opportunity to visit with my old friends, the servants of the fathers.

"I must return to Messir Huitdeniers," Smythe informed Thomas. "Can I tell him you will see him soon?"

"Yes," Thomas spoke warmly, "I will see him within a few days. In the meantime, continue to manage my father's establishment."

"Goodbye, young sire," Smythe said as he bowed out.

There were no great changes in the city. It was still odoriferous. The streets were still piled so high with garbage that the horses had to go around them. Cries of 'Ware!' kept us aware as we threaded the mazes. At the cities edge, we broke into a gallop and the spires of the priory appears as if by magic.

"I hope we have not driven the horses too hard," Thomas said as he dismounted. They were blowing rather hard.

"See that they are properly cared for," he instructed me, "although we saw no robbers or highwaymen on the way over, they might accost us on the way back. I intend to fight as well as run."

Again, I stood aghast and stared at him. This was not the student I had brought home. He had never used his ornamental dagger even in jest, now he spoke of using it very casually.

"I will return before long," he spoke off handedly, "the holy fathers do not believe in retaining people. Besides, I did not come to spend the night. Be sure to see that the horses are dried, rested, and fed lightly."

I could hardly believe my ears. I thought I knew everything there was to know about this slender, dapper fellow, but evidently, I knew nothing. In days past, it had taken the master and a large entourage almost a full day to make this journey. Here, we had taken less than two hours. Either London had grown considerably or we had run the horses harder than I had expected. The horses were not overly tired but I was disgruntled because I felt that I could not visit as leisurely as I pleased. As I went into the stables, several old Anglo-Saxon friends came forward to greet me.

"How are things old friends?" I tried to appear jolly and bright.

"They will be good when the day comes that the cursed Stephen, his Flemish wolves and the more cursed Normans have been banished or buried overseas," said Burl the miller's son.

"Aye, let the good Lord send that day soon," chimed in Tanock, the swineherd's son.

I winced because I was not sure that they were not talking of my master and I smiled as cheerily as I knew how.

"Is all this country talks about is politics?" I asked them.

"Nothing is left to talk about except Burl is going to become a father," laughed Tanock, his dirty yellow teeth seeming to fill his face through his filthy, straggly beard.

"How fine," I said to Burl who was hanging his head, "we had not heard that you were married."

"I'm not," Burl protested angrily, "and what's more I haven't seen that slut of an Alice in six months. She is just trying to find some fool who will give her latest bastard a legal name.

I looked questioningly at Tanock.

"He done clumb the leg of one milking girl once too often," roared Tanock, "and her daddy and mother and the fathers have caught him. He's tagged this time and he can't get away from it."

Burl looked as if he was about to cry.

"I went with that cow, sure, but who hasn't? Any man with two legs that can walk to her and lie down is sure of love. I went, more than once, but so did a lot of others. I can remember one night when there was five of us there. I am not the father of this one and she and God above knows it. She's had two already, and no one has had to marry her. She just thinks she is getting old and her parents want her to get off their hands. I don't know why though, she works like a horse and she is strong as a man. Lord, she would beat me to death. I can't marry her, and if people keep talking, I'll run away over the seas and never come back," he declared breathlessly.

"Listen to the hero run," chortled Tanock, "why it has only been a few nights ago when he was bragging about his private stuff that was so free. He practically lived over there."

"Maybe I did brag some, and maybe I did stay over there two much at first, but I haven't been near that woman for six months, and the men have never stopped," Burl said defensively.

"They have now that the word is out that she is to be married to you," grinned Tanock.

"Now Tanock, you stop that talk. If you say it enough to enough people, they'll believe you," warned Burl, "why only this morning, Father Joel talked to me and to Harald, the other tanner's son. I told him it wasn't me and I wasn't ready to marry a ready-made family. I'll pick my own wife, unless my father or mother can find me a suitable girl who is clean and virginal. I will not have a woman whose reputation is that of the community whore. I don't care who says I will!" The poor man practically wept in his defiance. I stood quietly by and listened as hard as I could but I couldn't grasp the gist of their bucolic chortling. As a rule, country people and poor people are the most courteous people in the country. These bumpkins were not being rude to me, but they were delving deeply into humor and excluding me from it.

CHAPTER 15

"What and who are you two talking about," I yelled.

"We're talking about Alice, the milkmaid, daughter to the baker of Sir Oswald's. The gal who has been sleeping with every man and animal in the country and who has just found out that she is pregnant. She has already had two children who her parents eagerly took because they were boys, but they have decided that they don't want any more and they have already decided that their daughter should be married. The father had slipped around and found out at least a dozen men who know her and he has told the fathers and Sir Oswald. As soon as it is decided who is the best one, Sir Oswald is going to take his retainers and go after a husband for the wench. He has already made his vows before the Holy Virgin, so he means business. Poor Burl, poor, poor, Burl!" Tanock smiled evilly.

"Well, I won't stay here as long as the roads are open," said Burl stoutly, "I will escape into the forest if I have to and become a robber and if I do, yours will be the first throat I will cut, Tanock. I'd do it now, except I've got enough trouble as it is, but I'll leave England before I'll be saddled with that awful woman."

"Funny, you didn't fuss about the saddling before," Tanock jeered.

"That was a different kind," said Burl resignedly and he turned to me, "excuse us for being rude. We are glad to see you visit us, are you hungry?"

"A little bit," I admitted, "I have been in France for a year and I still haven't got enough of this good home food to satisfy me."

Instantly they were alert.

"Where have you been?"

"To Paris, my master went there to study the law."

"Is not Paris where the hated Normans and Flemings come from?" asked Tanock suspiciously.

"No, the Normans and Flemings are not French. They do not have the same rulers." I explained.

"Is it not over the sea?" asked Tanock.

"Humph! Anything from that direction is a Norman to me," said Tanock angrily. "Who is your master? Is he not Norman?"

"I don't think so," I answered him, "he is a former student here, Thomas Becket, and was born in London."

"I don't remember him," said Tanock scratching his head.

"I don't either," said Burl, "but that is no matter. Here we stand here, while this man, a friend of ours, is hungry. We are not being very kind or inhospitable. Wait here, friend, I will only be a moment." Burl left in a trot.

"I don't remember a pupil by the name of Becket," said Tanock worrying the matter as a dog would gnaw a bone, "and it is getting so bad that one cannot tell a Norman from a native. Damn them, they come faster and faster, and gobble up the land and the money and rule in the harshest fashion. I curse the name of the Conqueror every day that I breathe. I hope he burns in Hell!"

"That is sinful and you can burn for wishing it. Besides, it is treasonable to speak in such a manner," I spoke to him severely.

"I take care to speak only to friends," he leered at me wickedly, "and any food who would report me would not live long."

I shuddered at the wicked knife he was sharpening on his shoe sole.

"I may be a conquered Saxon," he said positively, "but I don't worship with the Catholics. I have the old gods to look after me. I am also a man born to breathe English air and I'll give my life before I let someone take it from me."

"Are serfs and villains allowed to talk like this in the employ of the Church?" I asked him my unbelieving ears refusing to hear what I heard.

"No, they are not," he said, "but I have never yielded to the Norman bastards, and even if my lord did rent me out to the fathers, he did not rent my ability to think, nor my will to fight if I can find a leader who will chase the thieves and murderers into the sea."

Burl returned with a smoking meat pie, a cruet of clabbered whey and a small beaded jug of sweet wine.

"The fathers in the kitchen say to eat heartily. They can understand why a returned Englishman can be hungry. They say if you want more, there is bread and cheese and fruit."

"Thank you, thank you ever so kindly," I said, sitting down and beginning to stuff my mouth with hot pie and drinking deeply of the soured milk.

"What did you do in that – that – place?" Tanock asked.

"Do you mean Paris?"

He nodded affirmatively. I did the best I could to explain a student's life, but they shook their heads in incomprehension.

"I don't have the slightest idea of what you are talking," said Burl losing interest.

"Me either," said Tanock, "but what does this Becket's father do?"

"I don't understand what he does," I said lying, "I am only a servant, and thanked the guiding hand that made me wear my dirty and soiled clothing, "but he is in some sort of business."

"Never heard of him," said Tanock dismissing the subject, "but he would almost have to be Norman, because those dirty toads wouldn't let a decent Saxon be prosperous."

I let the matter drop as best I could and began to ask of mutual friends but the subject again centered on Burl's problems.

"Them's nasty people," he said disgustedly, "as many as twelve sleep on the floor in the same room and they don't wash, or hide their feelings. I don't like them."

"Is that where you got to know the hussy, so well?" Tanock sneered, "in a packed bedroom with her brothers, sisters, parents, and brats?"

"We took to the hayricks and meadows, I'll have you to know," Burl said proudly, "I'm private in my dealings with females. I don't run in public like some I know." He glared at Tanock.

I stood up.

"Thank you for the food," I said, "I want to see old Oss and a few others. I'll see you fellows again in a little while."

"Not Burl, you won't," he'll be deep in the wild forest or over the sea calling himself a Norman or Fleming," laughed Tanock.

It was a relief to get away from that tense atmosphere. It was evident that the Saxons were far from tamed and that they were spoiling for a fight. I found the old gardener, Oss, in a corner of the potting shed with a warm fire going. He was glad to see me.

"Sit down, sit down," he insisted. "Here. Here. Near to the bench." He instructed me rapidly as he flung a worn, white piece of linen over the bench and began to rummage in a cupboard. He placed cheese, apples, and pears on the table. I stared at them.

"Eat, eat," he said, "I grow the fruit and we make the cheese in the springhouse. The cheese is sweet and tart, so are the apples. The pears are mellow and good. Eat, eat," he insisted, "We cannot have you leave, hungry."

"But I have eaten," I protested, "too much already."

"There is always room for cheese and fruit," he chuckled and bustled, "the crops were especially good this year and for that I am grateful. The fathers and their servants will eat well all the winter if they can avoid politics."

I spread my cloak to dry and began to eat. I was filled to surfeit.

"Is it all that anyone can talk of, this politics?" I asked him.

"Aye my son, the reign of Stephen is grievous, grievous, and bringing the country to ruin, even the religious are not safe."

"I have been over the seas with my master," I explained to him but he did not seem to hear as he cleared the table.

"Did you not like the food?" he asked solicitously.

"It was magnificent," I told him, "but I must hurry. The master will be calling. We must be back in London town before dark."

"Take care and come again," he waved cheerfully and seemed to dismiss me.

I crossed swiftly to the main house of the monastery to see if I could find my master. A monk told me that he was probably in the basement chapel. I went there and found him with two fathers praying. I knelt in reverence, although I was not a practicing Christian. I still had a great deal of faith in the old gods and the old ways. I did go to the services when required, but that did not mean that I was a believer. The three men rose and I did also. My master went to the statue of Saint Swithun and lit a candle then turned to the fathers.

"Thank you my good fathers," he said in beautifully modulated Latin, "you have been most kind. I shall never forget Merton in my prayers. I pray all the time that you will prosper in grace. You are so wonderful and kind."

"Thank you, thank you, son, and come to visit me again, soon. May the good saints care for you and guide your footsteps ever in the way of the blessed Christ.

"Thank you father," he said and knelt to kiss the ring on the extended finger, "goodbye."

We left at once from the basement and proceeded up the stairs to the main hall, leaving the fathers in deep conversation. Thomas went over and picked up his cloak and clasped it around his neck. Beneath the cloak were two Norman broadswords. He took one and looped its retaining belt around his waist. The other he proffered to me. I stood and gaped at it. I thought we were tall, but these ungainly instruments would dangle from our waists and scrape the ground.

"Take it and put it on," Thomas commanded in an authoritative voice. I did as I was told and began clumsily to bind it to me. He impatiently began to help me and finally I felt secure.

"Go and get the horses," he said.

I must have looked piteous.

"Oh, alright, I will come with you," he said impatiently and after we had cleared the house and were almost to the stables he turned to me.

"These are what I came for. I acquired them when I was here. The fathers merely kept them until I called for them."

"Are they not Norman fighting swords?" I asked him, already envisioning the stable hand's reaction.

"They are fighting swords for fighting men. If a brigand or a highwayman wishes to attack, let him do so at his peril," he said as he swung the sword wickedly. It sang in the heavy, wet air. He replaced the huge, heavy weapon jauntily.

It took all my composure and strength to clear the dragging tip from the ground.

"Don't drag your weapon, you peasant," he spoke to me sharply, "remember, that instrument may save your life."

"I don't know how to use it," I said timidly.

"You don't have to know how to use it," he said acidly, "just release it from its scabbard, hold it with both hands and swing away. Any man with good sense will run from an armed scared man sooner than he will face a trained fighter. Be careful, if we have to fight. Don't hit me."

"An armed servant is subject to punishment, master," I said quaveringly.

"You are armed under my supervision which suspends all the rules for being armed. If I say fight, you fight. And I say, if we are set upon, fight for your very life, and mine too." He spoke with authority.

The reaction at the stable was worse than I had envisioned. The cold air became colder and all of the stable hands stood mutely staring.

"They are damned Norman," hissed Tanoak, "They are armed as Normans!"

"What did you say, churl?" demanded Thomas, "I heard you, you fractious Saxon. I am not Norman any more than you. I was born in London. These instruments for fighting, I acquired when I was a pupil here at Merton, but no matter," he clapped his hands loudly, "fetch the horses, we must be off!"

They all ran furtively and began to saddle the horses. I went to help them. They shied away from me as if I was a leper.

"Go from here," hissed Burl, "there will soon be a riot, and you will have to kill Tanock."

Thomas mounted easily. I could not do so with the unfamiliar weight at my beltline. Thomas grabbed the nervous horse's bridle while Burl ran to help me onto the horse. Once aboard, I sat nervously.

"I may come to London town for help," he whispered to me.

"I will do all I can, "I answered.

My master began to canter his mount away from the stables. A light snow began to fall. I felt that that damned sword would pull me from my saddle. I looked back to see Tanock thrust his thumb upwards in the age old contemptuous gesture. My master held back for me.

"Can you not wear a sword?" he asked.

"I cannot, neither do I desire to," I gasped.

"Stop," he ordered.

We dismounted. He took the sword from around my waist.

"I can see one reason it is uncomfortable," he said disgustedly, "you are ever the glutton and that gut is well stuffed. Never mind, take the sword and bind it to your saddle horn and to the bottom of the saddle on the left side. Don't foul the hilt because if you have to draw, do so swiftly."

That I could do possibly. I could have never had freed it from my waist. I looked down at my offending paunch.

"I am a servant, master," I told him, "not a fighter."

"You are also a thief and a gossip, also," he returned matter-of-factly, "and a damned spoiled one at that. I shall go into the world soon and you are my man. I will not desert you, neither will you desert me, because if you do, the penalty is death as you well know, so get the cowardness out of your system, and plan to fight if need be."

I said to myself, 'This is a crazy man, not the man the master and I have raised. This is a stranger to us all.'

The snow began to fall heavily as we entered the city and the darkness was beginning to settle fast. We could travel rapidly because the streets were clear of people and footpads had not begun to circulate. We were forced into a side street once when a great and arrogant bishop rode by with his large armed retinue. The stables were warm and inviting and father was waiting. Thomas gave him his horse and went to the house without saying a word. I stayed to help father grain and rub the horses down. These three precious animals, all that was left of a previously sumptuous stable, echoed in the empty building.

"Our new lord is a changeling," I told my father laconically.

"It is ever so with masters," my father explained patiently, "you are no longer an infant. In fact, I shall start looking for you a wife. Your sisters and Master Thomas's are brides of Christ, and your brother is lost, so it is up to you to carry on the family name of Watson."

"So you have adapted it too, I see," I said mildly sarcastically.

"I change with the times. I take great pride that we have a surname. It separates us from the common serf."

"And makes us more like the Normans."

"Perhaps, perhaps, but if that is good, so be it."

"Are there not enough cousins in the male line old enough to be married who can propagate the name?" I asked him.

"I don't know. I was separated very early in life from my parents and if I have brothers or sisters, I know it not," my father said sadly.

"I will think on it," I told him kindly, "in the meantime, before you and the master make any decisions, remember I have nothing of material value to take to a wedding, except the travel and ideas I have acquired. I will not wed a country maid with warts on her chin or who stinks of the cowpen. I must accumulate something of value before I can contract for a wife."

"The master, although he had little, will provide for you," my father said confidently, "it is his duty under the law, and whatever he might let go, provisions for your marriage will not be abandoned."

"Let us go to the big house and eat," I said to him as I placed around his shoulders which I noticed where beginning to get round. I also noticed with sadness that his hair was snowy white. Funny, I thought it was a sandy brown, and I should have noticed any change when I returned. Father was growing old.

"I still have a few green years left," I assured him, "and I will be near for a while. I am anxious to wear my new clothing, and get these washed."

"Give them to cook in the morning and she will have the launderer to clean them," he said.

"Good, good," I said. "Since the death of the mistress I cannot get accustomed to the cook doing the house."

"She does not do all that much," my father said, "she has a daily char in to clean and a scullery maid for the kitchen. Other chores are done by me or a man who I supervise. With every one being adults, it is easy to manage."

"I am glad," I said, "because the young master and I plan to be home for a good while. That is until you and the old master decide that you will be foistered on some unsuspecting female."

"We will forebear," my father assured me, "no one is in a hurry for drastic changes."

As we entered the kitchen, we went to the servants table to eat with myself and the scullery maid serving. Cook had kept the girl to stay in the house for a few nights until the house could get adjusted to our arrival. We let the gentry dine alone and I went to bed early in order to get rested for a wearying day on the morrow, if need be.

CHAPTER 16

The next few months proved wearying indeed. The young master was listless and unhappy, and we all watched him anxiously. He had to make a decision on his future, but the old master refused to hurry him. He would counsel, but not cajole or encourage. He was determined that his son would make a wise choice all on his own and no one would guide him in this matter. We practically lived in the office of Huitdeniers, because the remnants of the old master's business was conducted there. Huitdeniers had eagerly gathered in the good will and clients of Master Becket and had given the old man ample office space and had employed his clerks.

One had to see Osbert Huitdeniers to believe him. He was a vast man. Not huge, but vast. His stature was not large, nor was he fat. He was wide of shoulder, big of hands and feet, and endowed with boundless energy and a consuming desire to be the richest man in the kingdom. He was not frugal in dress nor food. Neither was he vulgar or auspicious. He was always clean shaven, clothes spotlessly clean, and given over to grays and whites in his dress. The whiteness of his linen intrigued Thomas and he immediately gave the young man two spotlessly white linen shirts that had collars that came to the chin and tight sleeves that clasped at the wrists.

Huitdeniers was enamored of the beautiful Thomas and gloried in his yellow outfit.

"Anyone who would dress in that manner besides you, dear cousin," he would say, "would be laughed out of the city. You look perfectly groomed, and I might say a fashion setter if you are not careful. When and if you make a decision to go to work, I hope it will be with me. I am in desperate need of one who can write well who is multilingual. I will put you in the front office to receive visitors and represent me to my clients."

"I am flattered sir," replied Thomas with pleasure.

"Don't be," said Osbert confidently, "you are yourself and your qualifications are excellent. You will be of great value to anyone by whom you are employed. Have you thought of the Church? Outside of the royal household, the Church is the greatest and broadest road to success. It is difficult to be employed by either, but if you are, there is nothing to bar your progress."

"Perhaps your business is the best for me," Thomas told him. "I am not sure that I can serve the King, because my sympathies are against irregular succession to the throne. King Henry the First brought us peace and security and prosperity. This one has brought nothing but anarchy and ruin."

"Times are truly unsettled," said Osbert, "and I am as you are, anxious to see a lawful ruler on the throne, but take care in this city, because it is for the house of Blois."

"So I have heard," said Thomas reflectively. "I wonder why that is."

"Because of the arrogance of the Empress," said Osbert firmly. "I could not support her cause. She came to this country and the city welcomed her in style. A holiday was declared and she held court at Westminister. She absolutely refused to see her common citizens or let them see her and she recognized no one in England except those of Norman lineage, and here chiefly, only the house the Conqueror or of Anjou. This outraged the citizenry and they pelted her train with rotten fruit and vegetables. She had few people to see her sail when she fled from Stephen's forces. I could never support an unreasonable woman for the throne."

"She sounds impossible," Thomas mused, "I wonder why one who was reared to rule would show so little consideration for her people. She must have found London distasteful and possibly provincial after Germany and Normandy."

"Whatever she found, she lost," Osbert said finally. "London is England. Whoever holds the hearts of the London citizenry holds the heart of this island. We are proud of our city and every successful person does what he can to beautify it and make it better. We will not have a ruler who has no sympathy for us whether they be born to the purple or no."

"What of her son by her last husband?" Thomas asked.

"She has several sons and at present, none of them appear to have the strength to rule. Besides, England will not serve a foreigner. The house of Anjou is more than foreign. It is Norman. A more detestable heir could not be found. The throne will go back to one of the earlier royal lines unless another invader appears who can conquer Stephen and the whole kingdom."

"God forbid," Thomas said earnestly, "in the short while that I have returned, I can see that something must be done to bring peace. England cries for it."

"That she does," Osbert said rising as a clerk beckoned him to the front office.

"I will make a decision, shortly," Thomas assured his cousin, "and I can almost state with confidence that I should like to work for you in any capacity."

"God bless you for saying that," said Osbert, "no wonder your father is so inordinately proud of you. A son who can say the right thing at the right time, is a miracle. I have no male heirs and as much as I love my daughters, the female is not suited to this business."

We left as the kind man left the room. He actually filled the doorway as he swung his wide shoulders into the front office to interview a client. The next morning was bright and shiny and a hint of spring was in the air. The snow and chill and not completely gone, but everything was soggy and wet and bits of green were peeping through. The birds had begun to sing in the wee hours of the breaking dawn and it was refreshing to see the streets in all their ugliness free of some of the dirty rotted snow. The horses even pranced a little in the nippy but greening air.

"We will not ride again," said Thomas, "to work, that is. We must needs hire footmen as does father, because the horses are too much bother to tether in the city."

I silently agreed with him, but I really did not wish to walk this morning, because I had on my new clothes and I did not want them soiled any sooner than was necessary. I knew my master was planning to impress his cousin this day. He kept his cloak wrapped tightly to him and only black boots and black stockings showed. He would not wear shoes that did not match his clothing, so consequently, he had at least two changes of clothing that were the color of his shoes. He had gray shoes, black shoes, and the new golden boots. He did not soil or wear his clothes out as I did. Since I had not seen him dress, I too was curious to see how he was dressed this morning. His black gloves gave no indication of what was beneath his cloak. Only the ugly Norman broadsword extruded. I had cajoled him out of making me wear or carry that fearsome weapon. The most dangerous thing in England was a servant armed without a coat of mail and not in the train of other fighting men of some great baron. People not only sneered at one's pretensions, but also wanted to see if one could fight. I was not a fighter as I had remonstrated with my master. My mind leaned to peace and conciliation. He did make me wear a large, serviceable dagger that we had found in one of the cupboards of the big house that had been left there by some long gone and forgotten visitor. It looked mean and wicked but I doubt seriously if I could have wielded it. I bound it to me as inconspicuously as possible and prayed we would never see it use.

We put our horses in the courtyard with those of the master of the trading house and proceeded to report to work. Osbert was in the outer room obviously waiting for us.

"Come in, come in," he said warmly. Thomas unhurriedly ungloved his hands, removed his cloak and left us speechless. He was a vision of simple black and white. His mother's green amulet on its golden chain gleamed with green fire against the contrasting background. The black hat perched atop his head with the inevitable pheasant feather, made him appear tall and very noble. Osbert exhaled loudly.

"By god," he wheezed," I almost went to my knees in fear that my visitor was royal."

"It is one of the few articles of clothing I possess," said Thomas simply. "I cannot afford many, so I must choose carefully."

"You not only choose carefully," replied his cousin fingering the beautifully fitting surcoat of slashed velvet, "but you choose well. It is one of the most stunning outfits I have ever seen. Perhaps more spectacular than the yellow.

"Thank you," Thomas said humbly, "but I believe I came here to work, not to parade clothes. I must beg you to employ my servant. He is able and can do almost anything he is bid. I cannot let him stay idle all day and he can work for his keep. I can give you my assurance that he is reliable and is a man of many talents, one of which is gossip. He is the best news gatherer and news spreader in the whole of London town."

"What is he good for?" the cousin asked.

"He is an excellent horse tender and cook."

"Good, we can always use an extra man with the visitor's horses and baggage. My chief ostler has complained for these past six months because of the shortage of help, but isn't he rather overdressed for the work required?"

"Oh, that," Thomas said, "father gave us both new clothes because we have just returned from Paris and he wanted to make a good impression. He has his work clothes with him. I require that he stay clean and keep his hair clipped and clean shaven."

"Fine, fine," the cousin rubbed his hands, "he can be used in many ways besides with the horses. It has been my lucky day. I agree that you did not come here to be a fashion plate but the clothes are beautiful. Imagine a burgher's son in cut velvet and Spanish boots!"

"It costs no more to buy a few beautiful clothes and care for them than it does to buy many cheap ones and ruin them with filth and carelessness," smiled the tall, handsome youngster.

"How old are you, young man?" Osbert asked Thomas.

"Almost one and twenty," he returned quickly.

"Old enough, old enough," said his cousin, "come, we will start to work. You," and he turned to me, "report to the stable and tell Will my ostler to show you around. Tell him you are to observe for a few days and you are to be familiar with the sleeping quarters of the guests."

"Yes, sire," I bent a knee and pulled my forelock. This commanding man was impressive, both in size and manner. I quickly departed into the rear courtyard.

"Do you accommodate guests, here?" Thomas asked the older man as they went into the vast warehouse where clerks were busy posting ledgers, rearranging goods for receiving and shipping, and a small group of local buyers stood waiting for Master Huitdeniers to come and approve of the contractual arrangements they had made with his warehouse manager.

"When my guests come to me, I bed'em, feed'em, and charge'em," smiled Osbert, "the important ones, I put into the large hostels in the city, the very important ones, I put up at my home. Their lackeys and the lesser of my clients can find sleeping arrangements right here for a fee of course. They are safe, well-guarded and I boast of one of the finest inns in the city. You will be pleased to eat there, because we feature the freshest viands in London town. I insist that my trulls and serving men be reasonably clean which is more that most of the innkeepers of the city do."

"A most impressive establishment," said Thomas admiringly.

"It takes that to be successful. Your father taught me everything I know, and saw me on the road to success, safely. I am delighted and honored to do as much and more if I can, for his son."

Thomas was introduced to many of the minions in the vast organization of his cousin even to and including the managers of the inn and the hostel and some captains of the ships who supplied Osbert with his overseas goods. One of the things that we had not realized was that Master Huitdeniers occupied one of the most advantageous locations in this vast commercial complex on the great river Thomas. Although the entrance to his establishment was a hundred yards from the waterfront, he owned his own wharves and had a private street leading to his storage and inn complex. Visitors could eat and sleep in the sound and sight of that fabulous river and goods could be shipped up the river or through the city easily. Mule and human trains were coming and going constantly from the land side while boats were constantly being loaded or unloaded at the wharf.

Thomas was impressed with the vastness of the establishment and the establishment was impressed with my young master. He was a ray of sunlight flashing among the duller workers, interviewing this client, arranging sales of these goods, and checking his ledgers to see that a profitable margin of payment was coming to his cousin. We had not been employed a month when customers who returned were asking for my master to conduct their business. He was noticed by everyone and as far as I could ascertain, he had no enemies. He was proud, yet humble, well dressed, but not ostentatious, and as alert as any businessman in Christendom. His facility of languages gave him a tremendous advantage. Although every man in the establishment could speak English which was rapidly becoming a bastardized version of Anglo-Saxon, Norman French, and antiquated Latin, and every man could understand vulgar French and common Latin. He did not necessarily write them or read them.

The man who could read and write and make good figures was at a premium. Thomas was one of these. His hand writing and figure making was superior to most of the experienced people who worked for his cousin, and he developed the intricacies of trade with amazing speed. His spectacularly beautiful features and his ever present effervescent personality made him easily the most popular of all employers. The common and rude people who did the menial work felt if they could stand near him, they would somehow be blessed. I could swear the serving maids in the taverns and inns would have raped him publicly if he would cooperate. He did not hesitate to reveal his repulsion to the female advances, but he was ever kind and understanding to all people regardless of their station in life.

Our first year in the office of Huitdeniers passed uneventfully and rapidly. I rather enjoyed my work and my master matured rapidly and grew more beautiful. His manner became more winning if that was possible, and the old master positively glowed in the reflection of his only son. The old master was a very sick man. Although alert and always wise in counsel, he could hardly move about the house at times. There was nothing visible that we could see wrong with him and the surgeons and leeches admitted that they could do nothing for his condition. Cook and my father hovered over him and he received the best of care and the finest of prepared food. Thomas and I made more than enough, because Huitdeniers paid us liberally, so the household expenses were never a problem. Thomas indentured two scullery maids to cook and an ostler to my father, because he planned to set the big house up again as it had been in our young days. We had looked and speculated on new horses, furniture and repairs for all the buildings. But the old master failed more than ever. One day we went home to find that he had died peacefully in his sleep. Cook was in shock and father had to be cajoled from his depression. Thomas turned all the servants over to his cousin for employment and we took rooms in the inn.

We loved the waterfront. I loved being near my father who was beginning to show his age. I defended him fiercely against the barbs and unkindness of the stable hands and warehousemen and got him established in the rear of the stables with a dry and comfortable room. It was a good and richly rewarding life despite our many sadnesses.

I noticed that Thomas became moody when I went in to see that his clothing and room was aired and cleaned daily as he required. I was still his personal man and I did not forget my duties. In fact, it was becoming more and more evident that I would have to give up my other work and work only for him. He wanted his food preparation supervised by me. He even insisted that cook, old as she was, and beginning to fail as did the old master, prepare and arrange all his dishes. He began to eat more and more in his rooms, as he became dissatisfied with the vulgarity and odors that permeated the dining halls of the inn.

He was yielded to at every turn. His slightest whim was immediately obeyed. No one told the staff to obey him. He commanded it, and it was obvious that the new man in the trading establishment would be Thomas Becket. Already Osbert Huitdeniers was talking of expanding and opening a brand new counting house devoted only to the banking of

money which his cousin would be in sole charge. Between
father and my master, I was kept busy. He traded the horses
from the old house and acquired a handsome stallion that was
almost a destrier for himself. He trained this horse to paw, bite
and kick. I acquired a magnificent gelding of sixteen hands in
height that could hold his own in any fight or race. We had
two snow white mules to bear our luggage if we wished to
travel. Thomas had reestablished his warm relations with Sir
Richer de Aquila and he thought nothing of telling me to
saddle and pack and we would ride out to Pevensey castle for
a few days. While there, he would train in the arts of war,
hawking, and hunting. Thomas could wield that awful
Norman broadsword as well as could the Norman noble. His
falcons were the swiftest in the mews and he could ride as
swiftly to the hunting kill of the falcon or the hounds as could
the swiftest trained huntsman. He took great delight in
besting Sir Richer or his guests at the lists. His tilting lance
was gaily beribboned with many awards he garnered in the
contests.

CHAPTER 17

My master could dally with the best of the young swains with the attractive young ladies who were constantly about the castle. He was adapt with the lute and dulcimer and the songs that came out of southern Aquitaine were stirring and told of love unrequited and encouraged hot blooded romance even in the most temperate of English youths. He learned one very positive thing while making calf eyes at the maidens. This was that few children of burgher origin aspired to the hand of a woman of noble blood.

For a man of Thomas Becket's slender build, he was physically amazing. He could make his broadsword sing and he held his lance in the best approved manner. He unhorsed many more than unhorsed him. The ladies of the Pevensey household and their visitors to the castle boldly importuned him to wear their favors and it was many a serving maid's favors whom I enjoyed. I saw many of them who I would have gladly married, but he clearly and firmly forbad me to become committed. I could not marry until he did or without his permission, so I enjoyed my pleasures as I found them among the highborn ladies' serving maids. He had corrected my grammar so much in all the languages that he spoke, until I could easily pass for an upper class commoner. He even made me learn to read and write in a rudimentary form which was no mean accomplishment. Had it been anyone other than he, I would not have gone to the trouble. He was persistent and firm and I yielded as the easiest way to avoid trouble. It paid off when we visited Pevensey. I could enjoy the run of the female quarters of the servants after dark, because of my language facility. Had I been offered the opportunity, I would have freely chosen this great castle with its easy going supervision as my second home.

Sir Richer and Osbert joshed my master because he would not choose a bride. Both men could have found him maids that were fair and with good inheritances, possibly titles. He consistently pled with them to let him be that he was still young and still needed experience. His usual competence in debate prevailed and he was allowed to enjoy life unmolested.

One day he called me and told me to wash my face and hands and dine with him. He sat at a large table in the corner of the inn where sunlight fell. His translucent skin and golden clothes made him appear unreal in the shaft of sunlight. The cool warm days of summer was on us, and I was as eager to be abroad as he and I hoped we were going to Pevensey or some other estate and ride and play for a few days. My table was immediately behind his so we could converse easily. We had hardly been seated, when Sir Richer and his entire family of retainers, wife and children entered the inn. It was too small for so many, so the chamberlain of Sir Richer's ordered the inn master to set up tables in the courtyard.

Thomas rose to greet his friend and we were puzzled to see the seriousness of the lord's countenance. He seated himself at Thomas's table, ordered his man to stand behind him until he was served, then he could sit with me, and directed Lady L'Aigle to take the children and her personal servants to sit in another part of the room. The other retainers were cleared from the inn. It was so vast a group of people that they overflowed the facilities and spilled into other eating places. The two men settled down to serious conversation.

"I have been ordered from my estates by King
Stephen," said Sir Richer, "in order that William Fitz Stephen
can have a modern, well-built castle. I have supported the
Empress and now that one of her sons, Prince Henry has
become of fighting size, I will support him against the upstart
house of Blois."

"Prince William, not Prince Henry, excuse me,"
Thomas said quickly, "Sir William is a bastard and cannot
own property as would a legal member of the royal house or
any established house for that matter."

"He has been legitimized and wishes property near the
city," Sir Richer said, "and I was selected to yield. I cannot
contest the decision because the king's armies would demolish
me in a matter of days. I have removed my movable property
already to Normandy and my household departs today. The
ships are anchored at the wharf and they will sail with the
tide. I will stay here in London for a few days if you will
permit me, and close out my business connections concerning
Pevensey. I will live on my estates in Normandy which are
more generous than these and I intend to lead the van of the
fighting forces of the House of Anjou when the young Henry
is prepared to campaign. That house will rule England
someday. I do not believe that King Stephen can possibly
secure a legitimate succession to the throne for his son
Eustace. He has already sequestered his daughter Mary as the
Abbess of Rumsey Nunnery so she will not attract attention,
nor enter into the question of the succession."

"I did not know all this," said Thomas, "I have been
busy working for my cousin, but I too favor the house of
Anjou, although I know little of the Empress' children."

"There are many of them," Sir Richer, "but only Henry
seems to have the ability and desire to wrest the throne from
his dastardly cousin."

I looked around nervously. So did Itha, the baron's
henchman, whom I knew very well. This was most treasonous

talk. In fact, we all would be executed if this conversation was overheard. Low born men, such as I was, would be beheaded without trial, just because we were the servants of these men. I wanted to find an excuse to be elsewhere until this conversation was ended.

"I will be on the side of anyone who will bring us peace," said Thomas, "and bring back security to the countryside. There are too many war parties abroad and it is unsafe to pass almost any castle, especially if a baron has a great number of retainers who like to fight. It is unsafe for unarmed citizens to travel the countryside and that is a national disgrace."

They ate in companionable silence and we served in fear and trepidation. I was hoping they would eat quickly and go to see the Lady L'Aigle off to her ship. But Sir Richer had not done with the subject.

"Will you not go with me, dear Thomas?" he asked, "to where it is safe and serene. I will do all I can to get you introduced to the court of the Empress and you then can fight for the Anjous."

"I am sorry, but I cannot," the young man said truly regretful, "I am gainfully employed by my cousin who could not spare me to leave without sufficient notice. He has been kind and I feel loyalty to him for helping me when I needed it. I must serve him for a few years at least. I will come over to see you though, if I am welcome, and you will be returning to England from time to time to see after your interests, so we will not lose touch. Perhaps someday, when I own a castle and have money, I can have you to visit me, as you have so kindly done in the past. I will forever be in your debt for your great consideration and past kindnesses."

"It has always been mine and the madam's pleasure to host you at Pevensey," Sir Richer assured him, "and I would have gladly have employed you, except you and that other half of yours you call a servant, did not wish to leave the city."

"I could not leave my ailing father," Thomas said quietly. "The unexpected death of my mother and the dispersal of the family was a sore blow. I am not over it yet. I am pleased that my sisters are cared for. It is one great worry off my shoulders."

"I am sure it is," said Sir Richer sincerely, "but we would have taken them and reared them as our own as I offered, but they are in the best of places. The Church looks after its own, and it is the safest place on earth for unwed, untrained maids. It is an honor to dedicate one's life to Christ. I only hope I have a daughter or a son who will do the same."

The mistress rose and came to us with her brood of children and servants. She was a lovely, tall woman, fair skinned, black haired with great dignity.

"Hello, our darling Thomas," she smiled sweetly, "I presume that Sir Richer has said the goodbyes. We must sail soon, you know. Normandy is my home, and I am eagerly looking forward to be safely settled among mine and Richer's relatives. Will you not come with us? It will be a happy life."

Thomas rose, bowed low, kissed the lady's proffered hand fervently.

"Would that I could, my lady, I will miss you so. I must needs stay and play my part in this game of life. Perhaps though, we may meet again, either here in England or in Normandy."

"I hope we will never return to England," Lady L'Aigle said rapidly, "it has never been, and never will be home to me."

"I am sorry, my lady," said Thomas, "you have provided me with magnificent entertainment in Pevensey. It has been a part of the happiest times of my life."

"It is my function in life to provide my husband and his guests with the best possible home, besides we loved you as one of our own. I do not mean to criticize this country, it is just that I am a Norman bred, and I love security. The security of my relatives and my husbands. You see, I am the favorite in-law in the L'Aigle family. It is a position to be envied. I get the best of everything." She laughed infectiously. We all smiled at her obvious enjoyment at returning to her native land.

"I can sympathize with you," said Thomas, "I and my servant were overjoyed when we returned from Paris. We love England just as passionately as you love Normandy."

"It is not a sentiment that I am ashamed of," she said to him.

"Nor I," he returned quietly.

The group fell silent. The odors of the abandoned food rose around us in the warm perfumed air of the early English summer. It was raining gently outside. One could hear the servants rustling around outside seeking protection from the deluge that came from the shower.

"Gervase!" Sir Richer shouted.

"Yes sire," the chamberlain appeared as if by magic in the doorway.

"Marshal the group, we leave for the ships immediately."

"They are ready sire," he said with authority.

"After you, my lady," said Sir Richer, and we all bowed as the regal Alexis L'Aigle swept past us.

"I will join you in a few minutes, my lord," Thomas told Sir Richer. "Your departure has been so totally unexpected, I am not prepared to travel. As soon as my horse is saddled, and a garment fetched, I will ride with you a ways."

"Ever the considerate saintly child," Sir Richer said as he patted Thomas on the cheek, lovingly. Thomas turned to me.

"Go!" he spoke sternly as I fled. I was not too happy having to plod uncovered in the rain. It seemed as if we had to go out when I had my good clothes on. I would not have time to change and would have to chance getting my clothes soiled with mud and mire. I dashed to the quarters to get the rain repellant garments, and as I was hurrying back, I remembered the cursed swords. I got the masters, but deliberately left mine as I always did when I could find the excuse. I laid the cloak and sword on his dining table. All the servants in the end found convenient excuses to leave the room. They were like me, the sight of a fighting weapon was not for them, and its very presence suggested conflict. They wished to be elsewhere.

"If you will dress yourself," I told him, "I can get the horses that much sooner."

"Good thinking," he agreed with me as he began to strap on the bulky, unwieldy Norman sword unconcernedly.

He was standing detachedly in the entrance of the courtyard as I came around with the horses. It was now pouring rain and I knew our ride would be steamy and muddy. We caught up with the train just as they were arriving at the boats which were only a little way from where we ate. It was somewhat foolish to ride this short distance, but my young master would do no less than did the highest nobleman in the kingdom. Despite the driving rain and the splashing mud, we went down to the quay to see Sir Richer and his family off in style. Sir Richer divided his family among the six boats required to take them over the channel. All males of the family line went separately, regardless of age or size. In this manner, in case of shipwreck an heir to the estate would be assured of living. The loading went rapidly and efficiently, the chamberlain having everything in order and every servant or attendant of the great baron knew his place and duty. Sir Richer was severing all English connections except those of business. He was angry and bitter at the house of Blois and vowed to fight them if and when an heir to the throne arose.

We went back to the inn and business as usual, except there was never anything usual in the life of Thomas Becket.

CHAPTER 18

We had hardly arrived within our quarters, when a messenger rapped on the door and urged Thomas to come to the office immediately. I had to follow him because my curiosity was getting the best of me even if I did not have the stables cleaned completely from my clothing. I had been too busy wiping my master's clothes and boots to do justice to myself. We hurried through the connecting tunnels and emerged in the great, spice smelling warehouse. When we came to the receiving room, there were two monks waiting for us. They were damp and muddy and shifted from foot to foot. When they and the young master identified themselves, he would hear no word from them until I had led them to quarters in the inn and acquired clean robes for them to wear.

We always kept spare robes for lower churchmen to wear while their wet ones were dried. Except for the higher orders, no traveling friar or monk carried with him anything except the clothes on this back. Our weather was often disagreeable and especially so in the spring. This one was no different, consequently, no churchman came to us in a comfortable state of clothing. It was so routine, that I turned these men over to a servant, who led them to their quarters and provided them with dry habits and shoes while he took their clothing and shoes and dried them by the kitchen fires. My master would not let the men speak until they had drunk freely of the hot mulled wine, warmed themselves before the great roaring fire in the tavern dining room and tasted the warm bread and cheese from the kitchen. They sat back contentedly and looked him over appreciatively.

"We are from the Archbishop of Canterbury," Friar Justin opened the conversation.

"From where?" my master asked stupidly. Even he was non-plussed.

"From Canterbury. The master has heard nothing but good from you, and he is ever on the alert for talented and aggressive young people. He wishes you to come to Canterbury for an interview with the intention of entering his house of learning and accepting a position within the Church."

We could hardly believe our ears. Nothing was further from our minds than entering the Church! My master motioned me to him.

"Go fetch cousin Osbert," he commanded me, "tell him it is of the utmost importance. We will talk no more until he returns."

"Are you obligated in some manner to Messir Huitdeniers?" asked the second of the two, Friar Biddle.

"No, except he is in a manner of benefactor," spoke Thomas seriously. "He has befriended me and given me a position of some importance. Since my father and mother are dead, he is the relative closest to me and I would not want to consider anything that would take me away from the business unless he were present. He will make no decisions regarding my future, but I hope he will offer me counsel and advice which I value highly. He will come at my summons because he fancies himself my official parent. He is a most unusual and intelligent man and you will benefit by the acquaintance. Canterbury! That holy place! I have never conceived that I would ever enter it except to hear a sermon from the most reverend Archbishop."

"Few are chosen. Many are found wanting," murmured Justin. "It is a rare and distinguished privilege to serve God and receive training in the great house of Canterbury."

"I realize full well the awesome responsibility of making a choice," said Thomas earnestly, "I hope my dear and respected cousin will give me guidance and good judgment."

Osbert arrived at the table, panting. I followed as close as I dared. My mind was in a confused whirl. Would we enter the Church, the greatest of all chosen professions? Would my master take orders and would I become a monk or friar or remain a servant? Would we be fortunate to serve God as all men aspired to do? I could hardly contain myself, although I wanted to ask a million questions. I was the good and dutiful servant, standing as still as I could, motioning for the tavern servants to serve more wine and food. No one took the slightest notice of my agitation. Master Huitdeniers stared at the visitors.

"Please repeat your offer," he said, "I am not sure that I have heard alright."

"It is not great legal matter," Justin smiled gently at him, "it is merely an offer to join the great Archbishop's house at Canterbury. He has heard so many good reports from your young protégé that he feels young Becket is qualified and able to train under him."

"The great Archbishop has heard of us?" Huitdeniers spoke awesomely.

"Yes," said Justin firmly, "after all, you are a leading merchant in London and hold the position of port reeve as did Thomas' father. You have always been fair with people, you enjoy a reputation for fair dealings, and you have always contributed generously to the Church. Why would he not hear of good men? It is his job as vicar of God's kingdom in England to know of the good people."

"I can hardly realize it," Huitdeniers said drinking deeply of the hot wine and apparently not testing it. He never drank during business hours, regardless of the occasion. His philosophy was that drinking and business were incompatible, but today he was so shaken he was breaking his own rules.

"Well, you must," said Justin firmly, "your house is becoming known throughout the land, and this fine young man with the challenging personality and the ability to please and interest all who come to do business with you is becoming famous also. Further, anyone who is friendly with the L'Aigle family, is known throughout England because they have a reputation of integrity that few can match. They fought honorably and courageously beside the Conqueror, thus they are a family to be reckoned with."

"I never knew," said Huitdeniers dazedly, "Sir Richer was so kind and unassuming and the Lady has never made any demands on me."

"Oh, they did not recommend young Thomas to the Archbishop," Justin corrected him, "he has been mentioned by every merchant who travels. He was especially recommended by Masters Eustace of Bologna and Lester of Rouen."

"They are some of my best and most reliable customers," said Huitdeniers.

"And some of the Archbishop's greatest and most reliable friends," returned Justin equably. "Any recommendation that they make to him, he usually weighs carefully and follows."

"Will you come?" Justin turned to the silent Thomas. The other monk Biddle gazed on him fondly as was the custom of all who saw this youth in his blazing yellow. Thomas sat silent, still unable to assimilate this startling news.

"It is too early for the young man to make a decision," Huitdeniers said, "Let us not rush him. He is still young and must be given ample time to think."

Thomas looked at his patron gratefully.

"I can see why he would defer to you," Justin said gently, "you are a wise and thoughtful man."

"Although he is of legal age," Huitdeniers return introspectively, "my cousin asked me to counsel him if he asked for it. I shall do so to the best of my ability."

"It is the honorable and respectable way to treat people," said Justin, "would that all men did so."

"The weather will clear soon," Huitdeniers went to the door and looked at the rain that had dwindled into a fine, soaking mist, "stay the night with us. Let Thomas show you London. Let us think. The Archbishop would rather we make a correct decision, I am sure."

"Yes, that he would," Justin told him. "We will stay, although we have probably seen more of London, than you," he smiled, "after all, we come here to assess the conduct of the churches, abbeys, convents, and monasteries. We have been in the city many, many times. We will go and visit some of the places and see how they are treating their parishioners and how they hold their services. Let Thomas stay here with you and you two talk things over. We nor the Archbishop did not anticipate that our visit would be so unsettling."

"It is not unsettling, let me beg of you to understand," said Huitdeniers, "it is just that it is so sudden. We do not take our religion lightly, and entering the Church is not a matter that one is afforded every day. I just wish to be assured that my young cousin realizes the grave undertaking before he decides. Service to God is the greatest service. We will be honored if he finds he is strong enough to perform the Lord's will."

"We will go," said Justin as the two monks rose as a man, "we will return and spend the night with you if you will be so kind. Tomorrow is not too early to make your decision."

"You are most kind and considerate," Huitdeniers stood and bowed to the men as they made their way to their rooms to change clothing.

"Go and have the horses saddled," Huitdeniers orders me. "Come, Thomas," and he put his arm about the shoulders of the stunned young man, "let us go and conclude the remainder of the days business. The foreman can dismiss the workers. We will go to my house and acquaint Mistress Huitdeniers with the fact that she must feed guests this evening. We can talk better there. I wish you to look over your business with care. I feel you will never return to it, although if you choose to leave it, I wish you to know that you may always return and the inheritance here is yours."

"Thank you, my lord and master," said Thomas humbly.

"Neither of those," Huitdeniers corrected him, "just an old and doting old man who is determined to provide you with the best life has to offer if it is possible."

They went their separate ways. Thomas to the front office to see if any customers were dissatisfied or wanted waiting on, Osbert to the warehouse and counting rooms to see that orders were filled, goods received, and that the money was being tallied in the proper manner. The rain had temporarily halted visitors, so all was put in order for the day with ease. When I announced that the horses were ready, they were also. We rode through the greening city streets. London was decking herself out for the summer in all her finery. Although dirty piles of snow lay here and there, the return of spring was inevitable. Surely this was the most beautiful city in the world at this time of the year. The greens that peeped through the water and wind was there to smell and almost to feel. I wanted to dawdle and enjoy the balm but my masters hurried the horses so I had to pay attention that I did not get splashed. Having to watch and be alert spoiled the day.

When we arrived at the big house of the Huitdeniers, we hurried inside. I enjoyed the momentary luxury of letting another servant care for the horses. I had to stop and savor the moment despite the obvious agitation of Thomas and his cousin Osbert. They communicated their unease to the mistress of the house and she began to give orders to the servants in a hurried manner.

"My land, Osbert," she upbraided her husband, "the house is a mess! If I had just had one little inkling that guests were expected, I would have done a little cleaning! And, oh dear! Churchmen! Oh my! My good gray and white gown is not presentable but I must wear it. I've told you many times husband, I do not have the proper clothes to wear. The dressmakers of this provincial city just have no taste. Everything they make looks exactly like everyone else. They have no style!" She stopped to gasp as she polished the table top to a new sheen and directed the small maids as they strewed fresh rushes around where the guests would sit. The cook came in to get the menu straight while her tiring maid was directed to clean and freshen the garments that she would wear tonight. We all smiled at her distress. Her husband kissed her lightly and lovingly on the cheek.

"My dear, my dear, it is only humble monks coming to visit. They are most undemanding and humble. Anything you serve or any way you dress will please them. They wish to talk to us about Thomas entering the house of the Archbishop of Canterbury for training."

"Thomas? Leaving?" the distracted woman stopped and placed her hand to her cheek. "Why, he's only come to us and I enjoy caring for him. He is the child I never had. To Canterbury!" She drew in a breath. "To Canterbury! My, I've never heard or known anyone who has been that fortunate. To sit at the feet of the great Theobald and hear the Lord's words from those eminent lips. But to leave us, why he can't do that," she whirled on Thomas, "you are not unhappy with us are you? We've done nothing to make you not like us have we? We love you, you know. It will grieve me to see you leave after so short a stay. But to go and know the great Theobald!" She finally stopped, realizing the enormity of it all.

"My dear," Huitdeniers held her gently to him, "your visitors will be here in a few minutes. I asked them to come as soon as they finished their business."

"Coming here? Now? Oh, Osbert," she wailed, "I am not prepared. I look a fright. EEEEeeeeeeeeee." She squealed as she rapidly made her exit calling excitedly for the servants to follow to her dressing room.

Osbert sat down and smiled.

"She is ever this way. That is why I love her so. For me to come home, is to find excitement. It is so different than the office, and she is really a warm and loving creature. She needs me to protect her, and as you can see, she keeps an immaculate house. She is a dear one, is my wife. And wait until you see what cook puts on the table! I don't know what it is, but it will be a delicacy."

Thomas sat down dejectedly. I decided to go and investigate the kitchen because I was feeling hungry and cook might as well that she was feeding no ordinary servant. I would go to Canterbury if my master did, and besides I had just left the horses in care of a servant and had walked off as would any gentleman. I hope I left that man with the proper impression. If cook was a good lady, I might just find some special highborn priest who might say a few special prayers for her dead and even might put in a few good words for her. The kitchen was straight ahead and it smelled too good to be true. I entered hesitantly lest she eject me before I could state my case. I couldn't help but hear Huitdeniers and my master before I could enter the kitchen.

"Thomas, we are not ignoring you or the seriousness of this visit. It is just that a lady's looks before strangers is of the utmost importance," explained Huitdeniers.

"So I can see," said my master tiredly, "it is just as well. I am so dazed that I cannot make up my mind just what to say or do. I am very happy in your employ and you and the mistress have taken the place of my departed mother and father. I wish to rise in the world, but the Church! It is the last place that I would have voluntarily chosen. Perhaps it has chosen me. Do you think so cousin?" he asked worriedly.

"It is hard for me to say," returned the merchant scratching his head, "I am not one who knows the Church well. I am awed that so great a personage as the Archbishop would notice so humble a house as mine. I am not sure that I am willing to let you go, yet I too, wish to see you rise to the heights to which I feel you are capable. There is the element of greatness in you Thomas. Everyone can see it. Perhaps this is the call for you to follow. Perhaps this is your destiny. I cannot advise you. As the mistress has said, we love you. You are our child that we never had. You will leave a void that cannot be filled. We have enjoyed the sunshine that you have brought to us. Memories of your stay with us will remain with me until my death. I feel as if I might not have done all for you that I could have. I feel remiss, somehow."

"Do not feel so, cousin. I have been very happy in your house. It has suited me to perfection. That is why I am so hesitant in making a decision. Where else will I find such happiness? Who can provide me with such happy surroundings? I have enjoyed complete freedom, including choosing my own sleeping quarters down at the tavern. This has been my home by choice and you have been all that a person could possibly hope for. I am afraid that I will be unhappy when I leave."

"Do not do so, then," said the merchant stoutly, "you do not have to leave unless you specifically desire to do so. I am sure that not even the great Archbishop would force you against your will."

"I feel that I should go and honor the great man's request for an interview," Thomas told his cousin, "but I will retain my reservations and decisions until after I have thought much on it."

"Spoken as it should be," said Huitdeniers emphatically, "that is the way it should be. Let us be up and about to make our ablutions. We can discuss this thing in full when the good fathers arrive. My, the kitchen odors are delicious, are they not?"

"They are that," Thomas inhaled deeply, "I shall see that I do justice to cook's skill. I am so hungry, I do hope the visitors will not delay!"

"Have you ever known traveling churchmen to let food spoil or grow cold?" laughed Huitdeniers as he stretched and began to leave the room.

I did not hear my master's rejoinder as I just had to go and taste the savories that I smelled. Cook was most civil when I told her of our prospects at Canterbury. She was kind and very prayerful.

"I hope you will pray to the precious Virgin and the generous Saint Swithin for me," she implored as she poured me some of the Huitdeniers' vintage wine, and placed generous slices of venison roast before me.

"We are not there yet," I cautioned her, "but if we do go, and I am worthy, I will remember everyone in my prayers, especially if I am privileged to worship in the presence of the great Archbishop."

"May Heaven grant your wishes, my soul would rest easy if I knew that someone was interceding for me with the supervision of the most reverend Theobald present," she intoned as if she were actually at prayer. Juice from the well-turned squabs ran down my chin. They were fabulously basted plentifully with garlic sauce that was well salted. Truly cook was earning her way to Heaven if I lived to get under the tutelage of the Archbishop of Canterbury and learned to live and pray in the true Christian manner. Our conversation stopped abruptly as the mistress stood in the doorway.

She was well turned out in muted grays and whites. Her hair was completely covered by her modified turban and her wimple held her face muscles perfectly in place. She had found time to wash her face and hands because they were very clean. She had pinched her cheeks and lips unmercifully because the imported oriental paint glowed red and gave her the appearance of being lustfully healthy. It was nice to see clean hands and a clean face. I was sure that above her wrists and below her neck she was as gray as were cook's and mine. With only one bath a year, she was wise to keep her exposed portions soft and white. They contrasted sharply with my muddy dusty skin and cook's smoked hair and soot lined wrinkles.

"We will begin to serve at once," the mistress announced to cook and she surveyed the three serving maids who had lined up for inspection. They were at least not so wrinkled and repellently dirty that they could not work in the dining room but they were a sadly sagging lot. Their splayed feet could not be concealed by the cheap shoes and stockings they wore. The hems of their dresses were incredibly soiled and their body odors were at times redolent of hay and manure because they not only cleaned and served but they also helped the gardener in the kitchen garden. I know for a fact that this particular group tumbled in the stable garrets nightly with whomever they took a fancy. Osbert Huitdeniers had a very satisfied staff of groomsmen and villains because this trio of females with bad teeth and stout bodies were more than his small staff could handle. The competition was keen for men among the many maids of London. Most of the times they did not wait for marriage to begin living with men who chose them. This group would be married within the year. They were already eighteen or twenty so the weddings would be arranged between the mistress and the representatives of the families. It was only due to the goodness of the Huitdeniers that they had been lucky that their house servants were not with children. Cook began to serve up the food in the platters and the girls began their procession to the dining table. The old wine servant, a man who was well past fifty, followed them with the wine vessels.

I followed the procession and took my place silently by great fire with the dogs. The room was very cheerful. Great sconces were flaring from their emplacements on the walls and the roaring fire chased the chill of the settling dark that was gently falling outside. The rain was coming down steadily as the thoroughly drenched windows attested. It was good to be inside dry and warm. The visitors looked dry and satisfied. They fell to eating after the briefest of thanks.

CHAPTER 19

The servants began to clear the table and everyone sat back to enjoy the exotic fruits and hot wine that were left on the table. The monks had truly been good trenchermen. They had cleared the platters and stripped the bones of any shreds of meat which showed that they were well trained in good table manners. The master had committed the epitome of gracious hosting, when the maids brought individual bowls of hot water scented with orange rinds in which the guests could dip their hands and wipe their greasy faces on the huge linen napkins that were provided them. These courtesies were normally reserved for the richest and noblest houses, but this forward thinking London merchant had learned from everything he heard, and he provided his guests with the very best of everything. Why shouldn't he? He had the choice of every product that came to his trading house so he could choose and keep anything that was desirable.

As well as the guests had eaten, the mistress and Thomas had barely touched their food. She because she was very conscious and proud of her svelte figure and he because it did not become him except to taste only the choicest and best tasting meats and seasoned vegetables. He loved foreign fruits and delicately flavored cheeses and often he would turn with disgust from half baked bread or mutton floating in grease. He did this night, nibble at the brownest of the venison roast which the master insisted that he taste and he did eat half a squab because they were delicately stewed in wine, milk and nutmeg. His ascetic face glowed in the soft flickering light of the scones. His brown hair gave his features a halo effect and his long, white tapering hands were of the most delicate of ivory tints.

"The food was marvelously cooked and flavored," Justin spoke softly, "I cannot recall when I have eaten better, even in the house of the King. I must get your cook's recipes, mistress, for surely she is one of the best in all England."

Osbert Huitdeniers straightened and sat very tall from this flattery and the mistress hung her head and blushed prettily from embarrassment.

"She is diligent and faithful," Huitdeniers state simply, "but it is my wife who teaches her and supervises my house in the most perfect manner," He looked lovingly at the obviously flattered woman who sat at the middle of the table.

"I do no more than is my duty," the mistress said softly, "really it is easy. My husband provides me with every necessity of life. He is constantly bringing home new foods from the lands over the seas for me to experiment with. You should see some of the dishes I serve him!" she laughed merrily. "Have some of this, my lords," she suggested as the maids came in with flat wooden platters piled high with candied fruits.

"They are delicious," Justin smacked his lips, "I am full to overflowing, but this is unbelievable. What on earth is it?"

"Fruit covered with syrup made from sugar. It is flavored with saffron powdered lime blossoms and crushed almonds. All come from lands that I cannot pronounce," laughed the mistress, "these are mine and cook's specialty. We delight in seeing our visitor's reactions to them. The servants will not touch this. They are convinced that a foreigner's curse is on this food."

"Perhaps they are a bit unusual," Justin agreed, "but they are delicious and the flavor haunts my palate. It is little wonder that gossip has it that the Flemish and London burghers are the best and most exotically fed people in the world!"

"We live on that that is provided by our industry," said Huitdeniers modestly.

"It is a good living," returned the monk, then he turned to Thomas, "and what of you young man, have you learned well from this worldly cousin of yours?"

"I have done my best to be an apt pupil, father," Thomas said simply and the good man's face beamed.

"Are we decided that he will go with us?" Justin asked the merchant and his wife.

"It must be his decision," Huitdeniers answered heavily, "Thomas is a man full grown who has enjoyed advantages beyond that of the normal merchant's son. He has been educated well and his education has been varied. He is qualified to speak for himself. We love him dearly as he well knows, but he is his own master."

"Well, Thomas?" the monk turned and looked him full in the face.

"It will not be a commitment, to go and see the great and venerable Archbishop? You see," and he set in to explain, "I was educated in my early years by the good Augustinian fathers at Merton in Surrey, but then I went to Paris. I have learned to love good food, fine clothing, and to enjoy varied friends. I wonder if I am qualified to meet the great man's rigid requirements as a student in his house."

"You will qualify, never fear," Friar Justin assured him, "he would not have sent for you, had there been any serious doubts in his mind or had you not had the highest and most reliable recommendations."

"I want to go badly," said Thomas hesitatingly, "it is only natural for a man to want to rise in the world. But the beginning with the Archbishop of Canterbury! That is soaring high on the first leap. The fall could be severe and disastrous."

"Be brave, attempt it," advised the monk, "it will not be too serious if you are not accepted. You can always return to London and begin again in your cousin's establishment I am sure or in any good mercantile shop in the city. It will not be the end of the world or of your life," laughed the monk.

"I guess not," mused Thomas, "I would chiefly surer a bruised ego. I can always survive that."

"Then it is decided?"

"I presume so," said Thomas definitely as he looked at his cousin whose tearful wife sat near him. "I must make a decision. I can no longer stand at the crossroads of life. I can only hope and pray that I am the man the Archbishop thinks I am. I will never know until I go."

"It grows late," said Friar Justin, "shall we being our journey to Canterbury tomorrow?"

"No, no," Thomas said quickly, "I am not physically prepared. My clothing needs attention. I must close out my end of my cousin's business. I must tell my friends where I am going. This is not a trip to a monastery for me as yet, I must not leave without making adequate preparations."

"How long will it take you to arrive? I must know so I can give the Archbishop a definite date."

"Say one week from now," Thomas spoke to him masterfully, "my manservant and I can get there well enough. We made the trip to Paris and back without mishap. We can surely get to Canterbury easily enough. I will not bring horses. We will hire on to caravans."

"I am sure you can fend for yourself," said the monk hastily. "A week it will be and you can depend on it, the Archbishop will be expecting you. Now we must to bed. My compatriot nods and yawns. We will be up with the daybreak and will say goodnight and goodbye, now. Mistress Huitdeniers you are a magnificent hostess. We are grateful for your care and hospitality."

"Will you not stay for breakfast?" the mistress asked.

"We cannot," answered Justin, "we still have a few chapels and churches to visit. We will depart your house at dawn and begin our rounds. We cannot stay long in any place. London is so large that it takes a longer period to inspect. We must return to Canterbury ere long, or the Archbishop will send for us. He is a true caretaker of souls as well as church business." He smiled.

"I will have cook to make you up some cold meat sandwiches," Mistress Huitdeniers started for the kitchen.

"No, no, you must not," said Justin hastily, "already you have been too kind. We have caused you a great inconvenience. We will eat with some of the churchmen where we go. Bless you my child, you are so kind."

"Thank you father," said the good lady proudly, "the busboy will light you to your rooms. I hope you find them comfortable."

"Thank you," returned Justin and raised his hands in benediction as we all knelt.

They left the room quietly enough and we dispersed because we felt talked out and were bone tired from the day's suspense. Our room was almost identical with the one we used to have in the Becket house and the furs were as comfortable. I wondered if the great house of the Archbishop would be as well run. I regretted leaving London. Why we had just returned! Only to leave again. This wonderful city of my dreams and desires. I felt I would never be able to settle here. I would be a world wanderer only returning to my love as the winds of chance allowed me. They were calling us to breakfast before I was hardly asleep. We came into the big room to find the master at the table alone. He welcomed us heartily. Thomas went to the table, I to the stables to see about the horses and then to dine with the kitchen servants. We left for the warehouse shortly after eating. The streets were alive with sweepers, vendors and people going to work. The wonderful odors of smoked bacon and hot bread filled the air. It was truly the city of which any man could be happy.

"I am looking forward to going to the Archbishop, cousin," Thomas spoke as he looked vacantly over the busy town.

"I cannot blame you," answered the merchant, "nothing can be better than serving the Lord. If you do not choose to do so, then the training will always stand you in good stead. I do not believe my business will fail, in fact, it seems to get better. I can only pray that that fool king will not involve us in any wars or bring down an interdict on us. His absolute failure to control the affairs of the nation and his antagonizing the Church dignitaries will be some day come to disaster. Those are things that the Englishman must plan against. I would love to see peace and prosperity come to our land. I am tired of plots and counter plots. I am tired of uncertainty and anarchy. We have a weak man as a leader and the alternative of that foolish arrogant woman is worse. All England can pray for is a successor to this madman who will bring law and order."

"I am sure the Archbishop has ideas," said Thomas, "as the first advisor to the crown and primate of all England, he must know more than anyone what we face. It will be interesting to be in the center of things and to observe at first hand what is happening. Who knows, I may get to go to court, if as nothing more than a handler of the horses or writing pens!" he laughed, "I may replace Egbert."

"Go if you are given the opportunity, however you may serve," said Huitdeniers earnestly, "and return from time to time and tell us what you see."

"I will do that," said Thomas, "well, here we are at the house of business, cousin. I will be about my business. Egbert," he called to me, "get about, secure us a place with some train going to Canterbury, then come to see me. I have much for you to do. Also send my tailor to me. I must needs have a new costume. These are getting rather seedy looking."

"I stand to pay for it," Huitdeniers, "whatever the cost. Pick your materials from my shelves and be sure to let me see you before you leave dressed as you will appear before the Holy Father. I think I checked in a consignment of new Spanish boots. I'm sure that a pair can be altered to fit your princely foot." He smiled gently.

"Thank you cousin," Thomas said simply.

I was lucky. There was a train of two hundred and fifty mules leaving for Sandwich the port past Canterbury within the next two days. It would take us three days to reach the cathedral, so we must needs hurry. The tailor grumbled, but he left for the counting house at once. All went well and before I realized it, we were ready to go. Osbert had given Thomas a large leather trunk to hold his personal articles. He let me store my meager belongings with his. Our departure was drawing near and frankly, since I had to go, I was looking forward to it in the sense that I dreaded it and yet I was for some strange reason, anticipating a change.

The trip was heavenly. The caravan we were in was slow, carrying much native produce of hides, feathers, linen, and processed wood that makes bows for which our country was famous. The caravan had to go by Canterbury, because most of the produce came from the lands of Canterbury and the Archbishop often wished to view his business transactions in person. He liked to talk to his employees and look to their state of morale, their health, and hear from the attitude of holiness within the countryside. There were also returning monks and servants of his and knights who were going to do their stints of service to the Archbishop who was their suzerain. It was a moderately high keyed group of people bound together with the common bond of loyalty to the Church and the ruling ecclesiastic.

"How is the Archbishop's house conducted?" Thomas asked one Wolfram de Nevers, a local knight from an estate located somewhere in Kent.

"I have enjoyed it these many years," he said confidently. I peered at him closely. He could not have been more than twenty two years of age.

"I have been knighted since I was sixteen," he explained, "and every year I do from fifteen to forty five days service. I am a small landholder and I welcome the change to mingle with the young people of the great household. Besides, we play games, have tournaments, study a great deal, learn how to live nobly, and once in a great while, we get to make a progress with the Archbishop or someone in the household. You know, his brother is Archdeacon of Canterbury and makes many trips throughout his diocese and he is a kind man who lets many people travel with him. I have seen much of the countryside and have had a few tiffs with some local knights who fancied themselves fighters. And there are many people who visit Canterbury. Bishops are constantly coming and going and people in their trains are always ready to exchange news and sit over a cup of wine. It is an enjoyable place."

"I do hope so," sighed Thomas, "I am leaving good employment with a good future if I am accepted in his house. I am leaving London."

"Oh it is not far," said Wolfram, "London is really only a few days journey at the best, and if it keeps growing, it will grow right up to the doors of the cathedral. Besides, I am interested and impressed. You said you were going to join his household?"

"I don't mean just that," Thomas said hurriedly, "I have been asked to come for an interview."

"This is something," Wolfram looked at him wonderingly and earnestly, "many are interviewed but few are chosen but most of the applicants come to the great man. I have never heard of one being sent for. That must surely mean that he intends to accept you. You are one lucky man."

"I hope, I do hope so," Thomas said seriously, "I had never even remotely conceived of being fortunate enough to even get in a bishop's employ and the Archbishop of Canterbury and York are so far beyond my conception, I still find it hard to believe."

"And you come armed?" asked the young man in his boundless curiosity, "and you," he turned to me, "are you going to enter the house also?"

"He is my man and lifelong companion," said Thomas defensively, "where I go, he goes, where I stay, he stays. I will not stay anywhere without him."

"A young lord with his personal batman," said Wolfram impressed and unable to conceive it.

"No," said Thomas emphatically, "I am only the son of an honest Burgher. Fortunate, yes, to have had so indulgent a father, and so loving a mother. I have always felt the charge to keep the family together. His father is in the employ of a cousin who treats him the same as my father did. His sisters are in convents the same as are my sisters. He is my family, nothing more. He is not with me for my glorification. We are one and the same, inseparable, because there is no need to be. We are self-sufficient men and we can fend for ourselves. Either can and will support the other. We are the same as brothers."

"How fascinating," said the knight, "but I guess there are many like you in England."

"I do not know," Thomas said honestly, "I have never truly thought about it and this is the first time it has ever been discussed in this matter. The monks of Merton kept him when I was there. We went to Paris together and now we are going to Canterbury. If the Archbishop cannot employ him, I will not stay. It is as simple as that."

"He will employ him, never fear," Wolfram hastened to assure my master, "another man is always welcomed in that busy place. There is never enough help to tend the gardens, horses, and house."

"That makes me feel better," Thomas said with relief and I felt secure about our immediate future for the first time.

"I'll tell you what," Wolfram said, "the merchant who I am traveling with feeds me well for protecting his property. In fact, with a little persuasion, I am sure he will tolerate me a guest or two. Why do you not come and sup with me this even? It will of course, be meager fare as is ever the case of travelers. We will stop near no inns tonight, since we will arrive at Canterbury shortly after daybreak, so I fear the wine will be sour and the meat mouldy and very salty, but it will be hot and filling. We can eat in my tent which will be muddy but dry. I carry it on the one sumpter mule that I own and I possess stools. We can sit and talk around a small brazier if I can get some coals from the fire. Your man is welcome."

"Thank you, we accept," Thomas said cheerfully, "in fact, Egbert can go with you and set up the tent and get us some heat. He is a magician at producing the unproduceable."

"That would be fine," said Wolfram delightedly, "I have only one man servant who is not too inventive. Come with me, he ordered. We are joining the advance party who is preparing the food. I can see that nightfall will approach rapidly and it will surely begin to rain before long."

It was the simplest thing in the world to set up the tent. I even managed to acquire some bedding so we could sleep there. We had not anticipated sleeping on the road. Had we not been invited to eat, we would have ridden on to Canterbury after nightfall and sought quarters in an inn. Getting coals was especially easy, and the tent was warm and cheery in no time. A well placed sconce flared cheerily and even if the old goat, Notte, Wolfram's servant did complain constantly about being away from home all the time, he was efficient and we had comfortable quarters in a very little while. Wolfram was right. It began to rain in steadily increasing sheets. In a way this was favorable because I sent Notte to get our portion of the food which left me free to expand the menu. I warned him that my master only ate the best bread that was well browned and well done. No doughy centers and not char. Also I told him there would be trouble if he returned without good meat. No sinews, blood, or raw portions, and definitely no outer fatty stuff that was fed to servants. Only the juicy, lean centers. I told him also to get good wine, nothing that was sour or had dregs in it.

It was easy to procure a pile of boiled eggs here, a pinch of pepper and salt there. A little nutmeg would make the meat taste better and candied fruit heavily dusted with sugar would make an adequate desert in the field. When we finished laying the table with the wooden trenchers and the condiments scattered about, it was fairly decent and smelled as a proper dining hall should. I constantly kicked the stinking skulking dogs from the door. There always seemed to be a surplus of dogs in any English establishment whether it was permanent or not.

"This is not possible," sniffed Wolfram unbelievingly, "it smells so good in here!"

"All things are possible if you have an accomplished thief in your company," said Notte primly.

"Bless him whoever he is," Wolfram said innocently as he seated himself at the table.

"I agree," my master joined in warmly, "it is a good day to enjoy hot food."

I asked permission to be excused. I had met a very friendly cook in one of the merchant's company. He was going to serve roast duckling with stuffing. I had not had any in a long time and my taste was at the moment for sage. I joined the cooking crew quietly, tasting here and there and before I knew it I was full and quite content to return to serve my master. I entered the tent as quietly as I could, the grass serving as a wet, cushiony silencer. I went to our pack and removed the leathern cups and served the eaters wine that they did not know existed. They must have been miserable trying to drink from the same bottle. Notte did not seem to realize that I had again introduced his master to another nicety of life.

"Do you carry that sword everywhere you go?" asked Wolfram.

"Everywhere," answered Thomas, "and my servant carries his knife and hatchet. He fears to combat. Says he is a servant, not a fighter."

"My master speaks true," I said proudly, "and he is most proficient with the lance, that sword and the short bow. His ability with the mace is to be feared. I only serve that he might succeed."

"An admirable attitude," said Wolfram, "every one to his talent, and everyone in his place."

I resented this for my master because it was my eternal hope that he would rise to fame and glory. He was a man destined to do great and high things. I did not care to see him categorized by a mere rural knight who knew nothing except to fight and work under the direction of another. Thomas Becket would someday know no master I felt sure, and I wanted to be there to share his glory and independence. Certainly he would never settle for a mere clerical position with anyone or some obscure ecclesiastical assignment where his quick mind and great natural abilities would be wasted. Better to go back to the counting house and the appreciation of the Huitdeniers.

"I am unsettled with anticipation of my interview with the Archbishop," Thomas said beginning again the conversation that I was thoroughly sick and tired of. We had left London, apparently forever to live there permanently, and I was resigned to making the most of our future.

"It will be easy, I assure you," Wolfram spoke with confidence, "of course, I have never been truly with the great man since I work under the direction of his military captain, but I have sat at his table, and he seems to be uncommonly kind. He never raises his voice in anger and he is always instructing his bishops and young charges. I would be eager and expectant if I were lucky enough to be chosen and I would try to please. You have, as I can see, nothing to fear."

"I do hope that it goes successfully," my young master rubbed his hands together against the dampening chill. "It would be most disappointing if I did not succeed."

"You will, you will," Wolfram clapped him heartily on the back, "I have never before known anyone in so short a time who I like so well. You could charm the eyelids from a chicken if you put your mind to it."

We all laughed at this ancient rural joke. Wolfram looked at me questioningly. Notte busied himself about the tent ignoring the conversation. I realized quickly that a servant did not mix with his masters except in private and I put my mind to arranging the beds. I wondered where I was to sleep. It was obvious that this country knight with his provincial ideas of protocol would not abide me to sleep in the same room as he. Little did he know that my master had slept together for the past few nights, not only for warmth and companionship but for the fact that I would not have to worry with two beds in the inns. If Thomas gave it any thought, he did not let on to me. I went and found the servants tents and they were crowded and stinking with the odors of unwashed bodies and onions. I knew I would spend a miserable night here but I resigned myself. The ground was all soiled and trampled with muddy feet. I could detect a few of the grosser men who were well into their wine cups and they leered even at the men. Perhaps my knife or hatchet would stand me well tonight. I made a show of my defenses, but some of the coarser louts leered the more. After staking out a sleeping place, I returned to the tent to help Notte clear things away.

"I am tired from worry and my head aches," Thomas said ending any conversation.

Wolfram silently went and turned back his bedding, crawled beneath the covers, muddy boots and all, and appeared to fall asleep instantly. Notte silently started his departure.

"Bring the light when you come, please," he whispered it might burn down and catch fire.

"I will," I told him, "but first I must attend my master."

I removed his boots and he fell into the bed.

"Clean them, please, Egbert," he said to me, "I am too tired to care for my clothing. Tomorrow I will wear the black. See that is ready."

"Yes master," I said reluctantly because I dreaded leaving this warm, relatively dry area for that foul smelling muddy hovel. There was nothing to do except shrug, resign myself to my fate, clean the boots, and try to get some much needed sleep.

I was up before the dawn, glad to be out of that awful place and warm before a fire even if it was out in the open. The servants of the merchants looked much more appealing when they were busy. It took no time at all to secure my bedding, shake out the master's costume and go into his tent with a brazier smoking with coals. He and the knight sat up instantly as Notte placed a sconce in its place. Breakfast was a silent meal consisting of hot hard boiled eggs, limp bacon, cold bread, and hot water. My master dressed quickly. I straightened his wrinkles, patted him lovingly on the bottom and the shoulders to make him stand tall. I brushed his lustrous hair as he combed it vigorously. The knight and his servant gaped at us through their matted tangles of hair. I hung the golden chain with the jewel around his neck and placed his cap with the jaunty feather on his head. He was truly a child of light and beautiful in that drab tent as contrasted by the rumpled and uncombed countrymen.

"You will be successful, I swear it," Wolfram said excitedly, "I have never seen anyone look as well as you. That costume is better looking than is the yellow."

"I hope the Archbishop feels as you do," he smiled gently as he carelessly and jauntily placed his fur cape on his shoulders. He truly had the regal air of one born to the purple and he was impressing his countrymen as he ever did.

"Thank you for your kindness," he said to the astonished knight, "my servant and I will precede the train. We must be going if we are to do so. We shall see you after things are settled, if things fall that way."

"Yes, yes, I will make the effort to see you," Wolfram said effusively, "my lord, it will be an honor to acknowledge your acquaintance."

"Never my lord," Thomas said severely, "I explained to you that I am low born with neither fortune nor title. I am no more than the commonest born man in the country."

"Your looks belie your birth," Wolfram said seriously.

"Thank you, thank you again," Thomas said shaking the knight's hand. He gave Notte a loving pat on the cheek. They looked as if they had been suddenly blessed.

He made our thanks to the busy merchants who were conversing and supervising the train in its arrangements. They too had to please the Archbishop's supervisors and prepare for some shrewd trading at the coast. They said goodbye negligently and we left the still standing train as the first rays of the sun broke over the horizon. Here we strode into the gold and glory of a new rising day with the mist rising, the clouds cleared, the eaglet in his flashing commanding costume of black and white trailed by his one pack mule and drab little sparrow.

CHAPTER 20

We approached the door with great fear and trepidation.

"Take the mule to the stables," Thomas ordered me as I stood and stared with a lack of comprehension, "see that he is rubbed down well and fed. We might need him in case our departure is rapid. Clean my clothes and get everything set aright, including a good airing of bedding. Find out where the concentrations of food are and be prepared to secure some in haste. You will hear from me sooner than you expect if things do not go well. We will catch the next caravan returning to London." He turned and looked at me.

"Why do you stand there?" he asked.

"But," I stammered, "you do not wish me to attend you? You cannot go alone. You have never been without me."

"I am a man full grown," he said to me as he straightened to his full six feet, "I must learn to go alone. We both have things to do that must be done. I am frightened and you would give me assurance, but I will face this interview alone. Go, go," he pushed me purposefully, "join me in the hall if you wish, but have everything in readiness as you do so."

I left for the stables, crestfallen and determined to hurry, lest he suffer from my absence. The servants in the dining hall told me every detail of my master's entrance. He came before the door and announced himself to the footman in a loud and commanding voice. He was led into the dining hall immediately.

"But this is not where the Archbishop is," he instructed the servant.

"You are wrong, young sire," he was answered, "Archbishop Theobald rises early and sits on his dias in this room for hours. He requires that everyone attend early mass and eat breakfast where he can see them and speak to them if he wishes. He interviews servants, fighting men, bishops, and visitors as he sits and nibbles and drinks. It is his main meal of the day. From now on he abstains until the morrow. His saintliness feeds him. If he is to see you, it will be here, this morning. Wait and be seated. He has important visitors talking to him at the moment. It is Bishop Henry of Winchester, the King's brother, the Legantine for England."

"Is not the Archbishop the Papal Legantine?" Thomas asked the knowledgeable steward.

"Not in this confused government," the man answered looking about him carefully," the King gave the Archbishopric of Theobald but rewarded his angry brother with the Legantine Commission. It is probably this division of power that they are discussing. The Archbishop refuses to yield his position as first advisor to the brown. It makes no difference to our vacillating King. He tries to please everyone and ends up pleasing no one."

"Who tells a servant these things?" Thomas asked him sharply.

"No one, young sire," the man said humbly, "I speak the common gossip of the Archbishop's court."

"Careful with your tongue and criticism," Thomas cautioned him, "the King's agents will have your head and the Archbishop will suffer exile if you are overheard. I am new here, and I wish an auspicious beginning not that of a slanderous, loose tongued bearer of trashy news."

"I beg your pardon, young master," the servant looked at his evilly. I know these things because a hall sweeper whom I came to know very well, told me these things. He swore he stood near them out of fascination of my master's looks and hear every word that was said. He was impressed both by the looks and demeanor of the young Becket.

"Announce me to your master," he ordered the footman imperiously, "I shall see him now, regardless of who is here."

"You should sit quietly, eat, and let the great man see you and beckon you to his throne," the man cautioned.

"Do as you are ordered," Thomas commanded, "for your information, I have eaten. I can care for myself. I do not this day choose to sit quietly, announce me, varlet, or else I will beat you publicly with the flat of my sword."

"Arms are not worn in the presence of the Archbishop except on travels or in the field of battle. They are expressly forbidden in the dining hall," the man spoke stoutly.

Thoroughly angered, Thomas drew his sword but I arrested his hand and the weapon was never raised.

"What are you doing here," he asked me stupidly.

"The mule is being cared for and our clothes are being cleaned, I swear it," I said hastily, "this great house has servants for every specialty."

There was no further conversation because Thomas' actions had attracted the attention of the Archbishop. As large and as noisy as the hall was with the busy servants, eating and talking people, they all stopped, stared at the Archbishop, then turned to stare at us. The venerable man motioned us to come forward. We stood there in a stupor. He with his hands hanging limply at his side, me behind him with my hand on the knife and the hatchet suspended by my side. The prelate imperiously beckoned us and the servant to him. The bishop and his advisors bowed before their lord and found themselves placed at the table and began to eat. The sun was steaming through the clerestories and the hall was alight with fresh air and the sunny atmosphere. We slowly moved the entire length of the dining room being critically inspected by what appeared to be young students who clustered together.

"Baillehache!" hissed one of them venomously.

Thomas ignored him but I stared. He was a skinny, sallow young man in his late twenties with sandy hair and aquiline nose that gave him an accipitrine look. His pale blue eyes expressed unconcealed contempt. I wondered who this belligerent person might be. If the Archbishop's house was unfriendly, we might wish we were back in London before nightfall. We came before the raised dias and I was stricken with a nameless fear. My knees gave way and I knelt with clasped hands where I was.

"Bless you, my son," the man said gently, "you may approach."

I timidly crawled forward on my knees and kissed the extended ring and raised my eyes to the kind and smiling face. He waved me away.

"Go and find yourself a place at the servant's table," he commanded me and eat and drink. I backed to the nearest table and shoved a staring lout over. A servant plopped a hot bowl of the greasiest gruel and the hardest loaf of bread that I have ever seen. He poured me a leathern cup of the foulest smelling whey in the entire land of England. I pretended to eat under the watchful eye of the Archbishop.

"Who approaches Theobald?" he asked the servant.

"Thomas a Becket, London born, sire," my master knelt.

"Did I not see arms raised in my dining hall?" he again asked the servant.

"You did sire," the servant answered maliciously.

"I became angry for which I humbly beg your pardon sire," Thomas stuttered slightly. It was a heart rending performance. The Archbishop's face melted into a glow of loving understanding. I wanted to go forward and kick that smirking and detestable steward. Thomas affected people this way on first sight.

"You are forgiven," intoned the Archbishop, "rise and face me. No, better yet, bring a stool and sit at my feet. We will talk. Fetch the stool, you dolt," he spoke curtly to the gaping servant who had escorted us forward, "can you not see that this young man is nervous and unstrung? Everyone is entitled to one mistake. He has committed his and is forgiven. Is there no charity in this house of God? Go! Fetch! Leave us! Assume your position," he said softly, "you are a good and dutiful servant even if you do become overly masterful at times. Thank you," he said very kindly as the flustered servant placed a foot at the feet of the sitting man. Thomas sank to the stool after kissing the ring. His beautiful cut velvet hat of black with the jaunty pheasant feather sank like a resting bird beside his shining boots that he had managed somehow to get reasonably clean. I wanted badly to rush up, straighten his clothing, polish his shoes, pat his hair in place and reassure him. For the first time the hatchet and knife felt comforting.

The Archbishop clapped his hands impatiently.

"Bring food to this man," he ordered as he turned to Thomas.

"I am not hungry, your reverence," my master said, "I have eaten."

"You can eat what they serve you, I assure you. Besides, young men are always hungry. Food gives the courage."

A servant brought a low folding table and others brought bread, cheese, fruit, and hot water scented with lime blossoms. His bread was beautifully browned in small cakes, his cheese looked aged and mellow, the fruit beautiful small pears and polished grapes and apples. The hot water smelled heavenly. He afterwards told me never to serve him nothing in the morning except hot water with lime blossoms floating on the top. Thomas nibbled delicately on the delicacies. He was obviously nervous. Sweat stood on his forehead although the throne was very distant from the roaring fire that warmed the chilly hall.

"Do you wish to serve in my house?" the old man asked.

"Very much so, my lord," Thomas answered, "it would be a privilege and an honor, if I am worthy. I seriously have doubts that I have the ability to meet your rigid requirements."

"You can be trained to meet requirements if you possess the necessary intelligence. I will be glad to accept you, but I will not yield my requirements. They must be met at all times, both those of conduct and progress in study. For whence is the origin of your family?"

"My father originated in Thierceville in Normandy," Thomas told him proudly, "I am of Norman descent but English bred."

"Ah, you are one of the Beckets of Little Brook. I remember the name. I too am from near that place," the Archbishop smiled, "it is comforting to know that there are other people in England who come from the land of my birth. Good, good, good."

"I am still seriously doubtful as to my ability to compete in your house, my lord," Thomas spoke seriously.

"Take a few days to think it over," the Archbishop, "my servants will provide you with accommodations. I am very busy as you will see. You must excuse me, people are becoming impatient to approach me. I will contact you later." The Archbishop waved another group of clerks to his dias and began busily to sign a mass of papers while listening to the accounts of his stewards among which were the merchants who we had traveled with. There was nothing to do except leave which Thomas, followed closely by me, did. He retrieved his sword from the disgruntled doorman who directed us to the dormitories. We were met there by six of the students who slept in common quarters.

"Ah, the gay blade with the servant who has a hatchet," a yellow haired, pale arrogant young man stepped forward to bar our progress, while the servant who was leading us, stopped in perplexity.

"Who are you?" demanded Thomas, "step aside or you will feel the flat of my sword, you English upstart."

"I am Roger Pont l'Eveque, the senior student of the Archbishop. What I say goes among the students which you will soon learn. We tolerate no insults from new comers. Put aside the sword and step forward. I will teach you a lesson swiftly."

"I do not put my weapon aside for nor Roger of an Bridge," Thomas told him haughtily.

"No fighting here, no fighting here," quickly interposed the servant who was our guide. "Seneschal, seneschal!" he called loudly and the sound of rapidly approaching steps caused everyone to turn and look. The man who approached us carried the mace of authority and even the students stepped back and regarded him carefully.

"What goes on here?" he demanded severely.

"He has threatened to do me bodily harm here in the house of the master," Roger quickly explained.

"Is this so?" the seneschal demanded of Thomas.

"Yes, but not until after he forced me to it, "Thomas said stoutly.

"We have no altercations here," the seneschal said, "I have the unquestioned authority from the Archbishop to conduct the discipline and no stranger can enter with a belligerent attitude. You are dismissed. You can only return on the express permission of the Archbishop. I will not inform him that I have sent you hence. You must manage your own affairs until you have officially entered the household."

"But the Archbishop told me himself to lodge here until our interview can be completed," Thomas said angrily.

"You cannot control your temper, I see," said the seneschal with dignity, "go. Go. I will brook no arguments."

"What goes on?" a kindly man was approaching followed by a priest and a servant.

"The Archbishop seems to have acquired a rebel, your grace," the seneschal told him, "already he quarrels with permanent members of the school."

"This is not an auspicious beginning," the Archdeacon turned to Thomas, "and the seneschal is the final authority in discipline. Come with me to my house and we will see if we can intercede with my brother. I am Walter, Archdeacon of Canterbury, brother to Theobald."

"Thank you, my lord," Thomas said humbly as we followed this kindly man from the room. When we arrived at the house of the Archdeacon we were shown to a small room and told to meditate on our sins and our future.

"Not here a full day and already we are in trouble," Thomas said in tears, "I would leave this moment if I dared but I feel deep within me that my future is here. If I can just get a grip on myself and ignore the detractors!" He kicked our pack angrily.

"I have business elsewhere," I told him. I wanted to see to the mules and also get a message to the Huitdeniers that we might return sooner than expected. I was careful to see that my master's clothes were brushed and cleaned carefully. The yellow and the white suites were beautiful. We got a summons to attend the Archbishop at the evening meal on the day following my master's dismissal. I say "we" because I was determined if our future was to be determined, I was going to be in attendance. I wanted no one to tell me of this conversation.

"I have intervened with my brother," Walter smiled at Thomas, "he understand this small altercation, but I warn you, he is a stickler for discipline even if he will smile as you young ruffians tear the buildings apart stone by stone in your boisterousness."

"I will do my best to do penance," Thomas said sincerely, "I truly hope to convince him that I deserve a second chance."

Thomas and the Archdeacon approached the throne without summons. Roger was already there standing as insolently as he dared, but it was obvious that he had had a severe lecture. My master fell on his knees with bowed head and kissed the extended ring.

"I beg forgiveness, my lord for an ungovernable display of temper. It will not happen again," Thomas stuttered.

"Good, good," the old man smiled, "and Roger here has suffered from the same illness. You are both forgiven and will do a small penance assigned by the Archdeacon. I want no quarrelling in my house. You two young men will sit and sup together in my presence."

I could see my master tense. When he hated, he hated which was one thing that he rarely did. The personal friction between these two people was plain for all to see but they sat together while I retired into the shadows against the wall and gnawed at a gristly bone and a hunk of bread that I had snatched from a platter that was being returned to the kitchen.

"You will stay in Walter's house for a few days," the Archbishop instructed Thomas, "my seneschal has been instructed that you will be dismissed no more without my express permission. Have you decided to try your future with me?"

"I expressed grave doubts as to my worthiness, your worship," Thomas said, "now you can see why I am hesitant. I am perhaps too much with the world, yet. I will not yield to unprovoked insults and I will not bend to someone who attacks me unjustly."

"I agree with you wholeheartedly. Roger will not provoke you any more without cause, but he has proved himself to be a superior student and he is the senior member of my erudite, so you must yield to his instructions and leadership."

"That I will gladly do," Thomas said warmly.

"Then you accept my offer to stay with us and train?"

"Yes my lord," Thomas said eagerly and numbly, "I feel that I am especially blessed this day."

"The matter is closed, both of your difficulty and your acceptance. You are dismissed. Relax and eat your food. Enjoy the company of your cohort. Call on me at breakfast time three days from now. I wish only to hear good reports of you from my brother."

Thomas began to eat while that dastardly Roger sat there with a satisfied smirk on his face and looked contemptuously at my humbled master. After he had finished eating, the Archdeacon stepped forward and tapped him on the shoulder.

"Come," he said, "we will retire from this atmosphere of hostility," and he looked at Roger meaningfully who hastily dropped his eyes, "stay from my house, Roger, and 'ware that you too can be dismissed. If this happens, you will find no friendliness in me. I disapprove of what you have done. Perhaps you could stand a lesson in cooperation and humbleness."

"He will be taught," Theobald broke off his conversation and turned to his brother, "I will personally see to it myself."

"Goodnight, your grace," Walter bowed low to his brother. Thomas and I did likewise. We went silently to our new sleeping quarters. We had hardly acquainted ourselves with our new surroundings when my master entered the great house of learning. I had by now found the stables and kitchen quarters to be friendly and charming with many new and kind people. I could be happy here.

CHAPTER 21

The rapid development of affection by the Archbishop for Thomas Becket buzzed throughout England and eventually reached the ears of King Stephen. Everyone wondered who this marvel was who could captivate the somewhat cynical and evaluative prelate. I saw little of my master except when the Archbishop would go on progress. There were always conferences with other church people and councils of State where I was forbidden the presence of high ranking dignitaries. The Archbishop refused to be separated from his protégé. Thomas slept in a small apartment just beyond the old man's door and was ever at his beck and call. The Archbishop would see no one or go anywhere without my master in attendance. It was not even noticed that Thomas had a chair in the shadow of the dias in the dining and receiving hall. He wore his stunning white clothes frequently because the Archbishop preferred them.

The Archbishop rewarded my master with income from several small churches and since he never forgot anyone, I was always provided for with small change. I bought my own clothes now, and could, if I wished, travel and pay for my lodging. I even toyed with the idea of purchasing my own horse and train him to my desires. The only thing that kept me from doing so was the fear of people wishing to attack me for appearing as a rich person. It still did not befit a common servant to own property and I had to be most careful with my spending money. I could arouse serious suspicion if I was not careful. It seemed as if we had hardly settled into the routine of the Archbishop's household when my master sent for me.

"Get yourself a waterproof cover and buy some new clothes," he informed me matter of factly, "we have been here over a year and I have finally convinced the good father that I must needs go to the University of Bologna to study canon law. The Church suffers for lack of trained attorneys and I am not needed here so badly that I cannot be spared for a while. I shall purchase some horses for us within the week and I wish you to train them and also train the pack mule to follow the horses. Prepare to take for me cooking utensils, and adequate sleeping accommodations should we be on the road for some time without a decent inn in which to sleep. And do not bother me without due consideration because I will be busy having my clothes fitted. I do not intend to go as a poor student. I have good provisions and adequate funds. I will not live in the scurvy quarters of students but in a villa with its courtyard and stables. You will be busy for once and you had best learn some Italian. It will come in handy for the required purchases."

"But master," I wailed, "it is almost summertime, the best part of the year. The garden is beginning to mature and I have many interests in Canterbury."

"I thought London was your chosen place for a home," he said sarcastically.

"It is, but London is far away, and my interests are near me," I answered him uncertainly, "when do we leave?"

"Within the month. I wish to be ready for the fall term," he answered.

I will ill. Positively ill. Everything I had organized was humming. My garden, my rooms, my girls. All was in perfect order for a delightful life and here I was, preparing against my will, to leave for the detested continent, to stay as long as the good Lord willed. There was one consolation. We would not be hungry, neither would we be forced to live in verminous quarters with uncounted numbers of squirming, canting students.

"I wonder what I have done to deserve this," I muttered.

"Do what?" he countered sharply, "we have not traveled for some while and you know well that I am determined to achieve success in this world. When I combine the knowledge of canon law with civil law and the experience I have gained in administration, I should be of value to someone, if no one except myself!"

"You wish to leave this house that you have set in order?" I asked appealing to his vanity.

"This house is always and has always been in order," he answered readily, "the great Archbishop sees to that. However, I have made some small improvements."

He spoke true. He had all the servants waiting on him to the exclusion of the other students and even to the Archbishop himself at times. Roger Pont l'Eveque was effectively tethered and control even if he did not lose his malicious tongue and his constant attempts to maneuver Thomas into embarrassing situations. My master had completely reorganized the order of the day for the students. He had convinced the Archbishop that everything must be accomplished at a certain time in a routine manner. After arising, all went to mass, then breakfast, then classes of instruction in mathematics, logic, canon law, civil law, rhetoric, church discipline, philosophy and disputation in that order. Students were free on Sundays and could have one afternoon a week off for their own pursuits. Otherwise, they were in the classroom, serving in the local churches, or studying their lessons. They were monitored at all times. They met curfew at eight o'clock in the evening. Three nights a week, they had a seminar under a visiting church dignitary or a famous scholar who happened to be in England at that time.

They were allowed to discuss the issues of the day either ecclesiastical or secular.

Thomas managed all this in addition to his studies. He was a strict master. He managed to know of all the visiting teachers or scholars and he scheduled them to meet with the students. It was at this time that he met the good Robert of Melun and induced his indulgent master to sponsor Robert in establishing a school in London.

"And you wish to leave all this?" I asked him.

"It is not a case of for wishing, you dunderhead," he scowled, "it is a necessity. This place will be cared for. I have charged Roger to maintain order and see that the school progresses."

"You have charged Roger?" I asked, drawing a breath.

"Oh I have not done so personally," Thomas said indifferently, "the Archbishop did that for me. You know, I could never get that stone head to rise above his intransigency. However it had been done, it is accomplished. I will not lose control, even though I be absent a year or two."

"A year or two," I wailed again, real tears springing to my eyes, "a year or two? Do we leave England forever? All my women will be married and I have spent so much time and money on them! A year or two! We will be strangers when we return. It will be Paris all over again.

"It will not be that," my master snapped at me, "stop that caterwauling and come with me. You distract me from my purpose. If you persist in your mewling I shall leave you here to the mercy of the first master to whom I can rent your services. I will let you stay in England, if you prefer, but it will be as a bond servant to the highest bidder. And what is this talk of women? You know that you cannot marry without my permission and that I surely will not give until I approve of the maid and her family."

"I have no thought of marriage," I said hastily, "and I do not wish to be separated from you. It is just that I hate leaving England so soon. Contracting me out to a new master would be serfdom. That I could not survive."

"You speak true," he smiled at me, "you fat, sluggish, impertinent son of an ostler. Just don't forget that I am the master of your destiny. If needs be, I'll have you gelded so there will be no desire for women. Come to think of it, I could use a nice fat eunuch to sleep near me on cold nights. Then I would have no fear of attack and would stay warm. Think on it, dunderhead, think on it."

"Whatever is your slightest wish, is my most urgent command master," I almost groveled. The idea of being a eunuch was severe enough to give thought on suicide. Who would like to live a sexless life? The eunuchs I had known, and they were common in the houses of the noblemen, were fat, sloppy, men who looked like over fed women. I do believe they squatted when they went behind the bushes. It was a repellant idea. I scrutinized my master closely as he strode to his appointment.

Tailors were waiting in a small room within the house. Thomas went over to examine the bolts of cloth they had brought with them. He selected some durable gray linen and some rust colored velvet. For me he threw out some dull green woolens.

"Make me some silk shirts to go with these garments," he ordered. I would have them with a reach that goes to the wrists. It gets hot in Italy and wool becomes uncomfortable. Make them in mulberry colors and in lemon. I wish them to be cut so that they will fit nicely through the crotch. The collars should be of the exact height of the outer cloak. I will interchange them with my woolen outer garments. I wish the sleeves of my outer cloak to sweep the ground." The tailor stared at him.

"At whom are you staring, varlet?" demanded my master.

"I beg your forgiveness, sire," he answered, "I have never made clothes such as this."

"It will not be difficult," said Thomas, "be sure that I am measured exactly. Make me a gray hat and a rust hat to match the garments. Acquire only the largest and most perfect pheasant feathers."

"They will be expensive," the tailor cautioned his softly, and no one wears silk except the nobility."

"Have I ever quibbled with you about prices?" he demanded, "and for your information, I will wear silk if I choose. As long as I pay, what business is it of your? You are a mere, common tradesman. I did not hire you for advice or criticism. Take the goods and get out of my sight. Return with the finished product within the week and see that there are no rough seams or any flaw that I can criticize."

The tailor bowed silently out.

"You rise above your station master," I warned him, "it is not seemly for a commoner to benefit himself above his betters. Already you dress better than anyone. Five changes of clothing! It is unheard of!"

"This is my day for unasked for advice from servants," he said wearily, "I plan to discard my older clothes. They are thread bare and beyond hope if that is any of your affair. Now come with me and have a pair of serviceable boots fitted and keep the mouth shut. When I call for an accounting and say that I am ready, you had best not be full of excuses, but answers that please me."

The boot maker stood silently behind his spread leathers.

"It is a pitifully small assortment," Thomas said in a manner most hateful, and the boot maker shriveled. "I will take a pair, colored a dull gray and one of soft calfskin that has been buffed to the color of beechnut leaves after the frost. I wish my gray boots to come midway of the calf and the brown ones to come to my knee in the front and mid-calf in the back.

Make my servant here a pair of unfinished, durable cowhide that will wear for a long time."

For the second time within a few minutes, my master had dumfounded me. The tailor stood there stupidly.

"What is wrong with you two?" he fairly screamed, "am I to spend my life explaining to stupid louts who cannot comprehend simple language?"

We stood mute.

"Draw me some pictures, you Saxon swine," he ordered the boot maker, "do you not have charcoal with which you fit the foot? Give it to me, "he snatched the marking chalk from the extended fingers of the poor misunderstanding tanner, "here, like this, and like this," he quickly sketched his desires, "is it so difficult to cut leather just a bit differently from that which you have seen all your limited life?"

The boot maker smiled in comprehension as he reviewed the crude sketches.

"That I can do," he crowed delightedly, "excuse me master, but it is just that I have never made shoes such as this even for bishops or princes. It will be delightful to please you. I will enjoy the experience of making something new and different. I assure you that they will be of the finest and softest leathers with the finest seams. I will even line them with a durable and soft velvet. May I have your permission of displaying them and duplicating them if my customers so desire?"

"Thank you for understanding me," Thomas said sincerely to tradesman, "you have my permission to do anything you wish with my ideas. Please have the shoes ready within ten days so that I can see that they fit and do not pinch."

"They will be ready sire," promised the boot maker, "I myself will personally fit them to your foot. I will not send them by an assistant. All England will speak of the elegance of the boots made by Sil the Shoemaker."

"All Italy and France perhaps, and other countries too," my master spoke kindly, "I plan to go abroad and study. They will be well advertised."

"Thank you, gracious one," the shoemaker bowed low and left. He was immediately followed by an ironworker who presented my master with the most wicked, pointed poniard that I had ever seen. Its' handle was wound with silver thread and inset with some of my master's mother's pearls. The blade fascinated me. It was short, beveled and very sharp. The workman held up a hair pulled from his head and sliced the hair neatly over and over again.

"Made in the fines Damascene manner that I learned in the Holy Land," he said simply.

"It pleases me," Thomas said simply as he tucked it in his waistband and paid the supplier who bowed deeply and left.

"First a sword, now a wicked sinful dagger," I said sarcastically.

"Yes," he laughed, his good humor restored by the understanding and promises of the boot maker, "I will be a walking arsenal. Woe until the dimwitted highwaymen who dare to attack Thomas Becket! If I don't get them with the broadsword, the dagger will suffice. I travel as a gentleman now, no longer as a begging, skulking student. If you were smart," he turned to me, "you would be about, seeking good caravan connections for us to travel with. You are a servant of person of consequence, so get about your business. I am tired of doing the thinking for both of us all of the time."

I strode from the room in a towering rage. If I had not left, I would have struck this arrogant worldling. He was turning into a person whom I did not know. The clinking coins in my pockets soothed my feelings somewhat.

CHAPTER 22

We disembarked from Sandwich, the port of the Archbishop, in horrible weather. Although it was unseasonably warm, the rain came in floods and the channel was very, very choppy. I was ill from the time I put my foot on the boat until we landed in Calais. I had had the foresight to pay a sailor to see to the horses and the mule, so I enjoyed my illness, because I felt that I would surely die at times. I did not see my master all the trip because I was too busy trying to survive.

The land trip to Bologna was dull and uneventful. We traveled in full caravan which had adequate fighters to discourage any one who wished to attack. The route was far enough from the sea to dodge the landed sea pirates and not far enough inland to tempt the marauding landowners and brigands. Our safe conduct passes carried us through Anjou, Main, Aquitaine, the Alps, the Kingdom of the Lombards and on to Bologna without mishap. Since Bologna at this time was under the control of the Papacy but desired by the Lombards and the emperor of the Holy Roman Empire, we were careful not to become identified with any of the warring armies. The people in these areas were suspicious of anyone and quite willing to swear fealty and loyalty to any conqueror. They especially distrusted students. My master had been taken with the romantic atmosphere of the Crusades that prevailed and our progress through Aquitaine, the land of the troubadours impressed him very much. He bought himself a loosely swinging cape, said he was going to style his hair as did the singers and he practices on the lute constantly.

The land of the Latins or the Italians as they were beginning to be called, was interesting. They made much wine and cooked dishes that had different spices and dishes that we were accustomed to. It interested us to sample the stranger foods and appreciate the fabulously beautiful women of this strange country. The University was no different from any other except that the students controlled it. They elected governors among themselves who consulted with the bishops who ran the school. If an instructor was very unpopular, he was removed by student pressure and if the administration adopted unacceptable practices, the students, after meeting with their representatives, could force a change. But they rioted, drank uncontrollably and smashed property and raped women with abandon. Quite often, there would be pitched battles with the authorities of the towns between the younger and more ferocious students. Heads would get cracked but we seldom had a death.

Bologna had some interesting people. Bernard of Clairveaux wrote to the most fabulous of the University's teachers, Gratian, and my master attended every meeting Gratian had, whether it was in the classroom, in a tavern, or on the street. This great man could teach and explain. We also saw the fiery and eloquent Peter Abelard and his co-equal, Arnold of Brescia. These rebels were constantly on the move, because their ideas were unacceptable to the established authorities and the law, whether ecclesiastical or clerical, was constantly against them. Thomas Becket would come in after attending the school with a chattering group of his contemporaries and they would argue points of church creed or discipline for hours. They would also eat quantities of cheese, fruit and wine.

We had a sunny apartment as my master had directed me to acquire. It was big and spacious and separated from our landlord. It was seldom that we received complaints because I did my best to supervise the servants in a peaceful and purposeful manner. Our servants seemed a happy lot. The cook was fat and jolly. The little cleaning maids went about singing and the groom and gardener reported to me faithfully. We always had fresh fruit and vegetables for the table. It was easy to procure lemons and oranges and bananas, those exotic tropical fruits because the trade of the south trafficked through the teeming city of Bologna on its way to Milan. Quite often a pope would come to Ravenna to take up residence and we enjoyed meeting people who traveled in the court. It was one of these bands who roved far wide, and any scholars who might be in the good father's contingent, came to Bologna to hear the lectures if they could, that my master met one of his future friends for life, John of Salisbury. John was a witty, learned man who was a scribe in the Papal Secretariat. He knew many people and had read almost every book that had been written. He spoke or read or understood many languages and was at ease in any country.

My master and John were particularly fond of a young lecturer, one Vacarius. He had the promise, so they said, of becoming a noted jurist, because he spent all his time reading and interpreting canon law.

"He had convinced me that the Church supersedes the State," John said earnestly to my master as they sat in a sunny spot of the courtyard. He was visiting us on one of his infrequent visits to the University.

"He had done as much for me also," Thomas agreed with him seriously, "I shall always be convinced that God supersedes man and his vicars on earth should administer the law."

"There is room for them to live side by side," John said, and the Holy Roman Empire is a good living example. It would be much easier for the Holy Father at Rome if the Germans could understand that. These Germans are stupid in their insistence that they dominate the Empire and the pope. They are wrong. I hear that they follow the theory of the Eastern Church of the Greeks which everyone knows is ridden to the earth with heresy. A king is seldom a good priest and there is no reason for the secular and ecclesiastical law to be in conflict. Everything should yield, in the end, to the representative of God. What higher power can there be than our Maker?"

"Agreed, agreed," my master said solemnly, "and not diverting from the subject, how do you like this flowered shirt of orange and purple?"

"It fascinated me," John stared at it, "it seems afire with color and I don't believe I know the fabric."

"It is damask from the Holy Land," Thomas explained, "Woven in a fashion learned from the peoples in far away Cathay."

"Why that is at the end of the earth," John exclaimed, "if you go beyond that, you will fall off into the endless waters. I have looked on the maps. There is no place to go if one jumps from that land. Let me feel it," he said examining it closer holding an edge between the tips of his thumb and forefinger.

"I could never afford it," he sighed, "besides it rivals the clothes of the Supreme Father."

"It is not expensive," Thomas said arrogantly, "I feel that a man can have what he can buy and it is nobody's business."

I thought to myself, 'he is arrogant and is due for a fall someday.'

"Ah yes, your theory stands well with any man," John agreed, "but in practice, it can bring much trouble. You survive with your unbelievable raiment because of your great personality and personal beauty. Few people look as well as you do, Thomas Becket, and fewer still enjoy the favors of the Archbishop of Canterbury who is one of the most influential men in Christendom."

"I appreciate my good fortune," my master returned modestly, "but say, my good friend, you are in luck, Vacarius and Gratian debate the issue of the Trinity tomorrow. They will contrast it with Arianism. Permission has been secured to do so from the present resident Bishop who feels it will be good for students to see the fallacies and weaknesses of the Arian philosophy. It will be good, I tell you. We will take a launch packed by my people, because I feel that the debate may extend into the night. I plan to furnish the speakers with adequate food stuff to keep up their strength. It will be conducted before a select few so there will be adequate room for all. Come, I beg of you. It will be delightful."

"I will be grateful," John said with alacrity, "this is an opportunity that one should not miss."

"Good, then you will lodge with me tonight. We have roast fowl, squabs stewed in goat's milk, and venison roast on the menu."

"It sounds like good, solid English fare," John said laughingly.

"It may sound like it, but wait until you taste it. What the cook does with herbs such as mushrooms, anchovies, and celery is unbelievable. She goes light on the garlic but is free with salt. Altogether delightful. Egbert," he turned to me, "please to tell the kitchen that we will dine especially early in order to get a good night's rest. We should be in the lecture hall at daybreak. Prepare for us also, hot water in leathern bottles, along with warm bread and cheese. We will eat in the morning as we listen."

"What about mass?" asked John.

"We may be forced to miss it tomorrow morning," Thomas told him lightly, "I am here to get an education. The student must attend when the master lectures. I go to church when I can. If you wish, we can get up at about three o'clock in the morning and be sleepy and dead tired all day. In that way, we can attend church, if it pleases you. There are small chapels and great cathedrals near the University, and if there is a break in the debate, you can always run out and attend a service of some kind."

"We will not get up early," smiled John, "but this must never get to the Papal Court," he explained, "or I would be severely disciplined. I will manage to get to church some way."

The meal was delightful as usual. I served them in the corner of the court, near the wall, where we could hear the noises of the street, and observe through a grilled placed in the wall, the passersby. They went to bed early, I stayed in the stables for a while with the young lady of my choice. I could get up with the master and see him and his guest off to school then go back to sleep. He did not need a guard in this safe school city.

Winter in Bologna that year was especially severe. We were hard put to stay warm against the cold mountain winds that would sweep down unannounced bringing huge amounts of snow or driving sleet that cleared the streets. I longed for England and the most temperate winters. Besides, these people did not enjoy the winter. They would huddle in drafty halls or the churches and never go out. I missed the winter sports and the roistering, warm taverns of my country. I longed for spring and warmth. John came to visit us as the spring began to arrive. The pope had to go to Milan for a conference, and he gave his clerk permission to come to see us.

"I go from here to Auxierre in a few weeks," Thomas told him as they sat warming their hands over a brazier and sipping hot wine, "my year abroad is almost up, but I have managed to wangle permission from the Archbishop to go to that school and at least get exposed to the learning there, if only for a little while.

"You are so fortunate," murmured John in admiration.

"I am in complete agreement," Thomas said humbly, "I fully intend to return to Canterbury and justify this great expense that my good lord has allowed me. I will be the true and diligent servant."

'How exciting,' I thought to myself. I had noticed the unusual activity of messengers about the house, but had never seriously concerned myself with their coming and going. 'My master wishes to return to England of his own volition! Oh, what I would do to hasten him!'

"I will see you there, someday," John promised, "I am in training and am gainfully employed by His Holiness, but there has been some discussion of my return to serve the Archbishop who has expressed an interest in me."

"How delightful," Thomas said warmly, "I will be a constant advocate for your return."

"I am not especially anxious to return until the succession is settled," John said, "There is constant turmoil in Rome about this issue. The Empress has a strong case going what with her vigorous son Henry being old enough and fighting for her. Bernard is on her side. The Archbishop of Canterbury is strangely neutral at the moment, so naturally Pope Eugenius the Third will not commit himself. Besides, we have our own troubles. The House of Hohenstaufen is strong and mettlesome. They talk of anti-popes. There is a young, warring prince up there, only a fourteen year old red-headed little snot, who is already making warlike noises and threatening gestures. If he succeeds to the throne, we are in serious trouble. The Pope is girding himself for the fight and he needs allies badly from the north. Stephen, as you know is not to be trusted, and with the House of Anjou in contention, an heir of that region is most undecided. We care fairly well depend on the House of Capet in France, but they are weak and poor. Louis cannot control his tempestuous wife, that Eleanor of Aquitaine. She holds lands much larger and richer than he, and she is a wicked high strung woman who conducts those scandalous courts of Love, where every no good singing wretch in Christendom goes to spin his life away in the sun in wine song. The Eastern Church has befuddled the Papacy with the way they have betrayed our people of the First crusade so the Pope views with distrust and dismay our attempt to gain the Holy Land. Some of our own Crusaders have proved rapacious and greedy. They have gone native and married infidels. The faith of Islam and the faith of Catholicism meet in that cursed place. The strong, greedy cities of Genoa, Pisa, and Venice keep affairs confused by their trafficking among enemies and allies alike. The pontiff is of the mind to lay an interdict on them to see if he can curb their offensive actions."

"My, that was impressive," Thomas spoke admiringly, "you know a lot about many places."

"One hears and knows many things at the seat of government," John explained seriously, "there is someone constantly coming and going. The responsibilities of the supervision of the world is large."

"Do you suppose you will come to England soon?" Thomas asked him, "Because I fear we will leave for Auxierre before you get up this way again."

"One cannot predict one's future," smiled John, "but I will not leave Rome until I am definitely in the employ of the Archbishop and peace comes to your country."

"That may be a long time," mused Thomas, "but in the mean time, take care, and perhaps we will meet again soon. If not, write me in care of Canterbury Cathedral and I will be faithful in answering."

"I will do that," said John. He departed early for Milan but we saw him sooner than we expected.

Our stay at Auxierre was uneventful and somewhat distasteful. The school was concentrated in among a group of farms and the peasants were very unfriendly, in fact they were hostile to the masters and the students. My master did not find the instruction to be too stimulating. There were no great teachers of note and there was seldom a riot or dispute on any matter. All was seriousness. Our quarters, the best we could find, were always a bit damp, receiving little sun and the servants were unimaginative and stupid. There were so few buildings for hire that we had to take what we could find. We were offered no choices. We left for England after staying there only about three months. It was high summer when we left the continent and England was at its fairest when we arrived. The Archbishop would not let my master leave him, so I went to London with some priests on mission to see my father and take news of Thomas' health to the Huitdeniers.

For some unexplained reason, things at the Archbishop's became dull. There was no excitement until the end of the year when master soundly thrashed Roger Pont l'Eveque for taunting him. Thomas was dismissed by Theobald in writing. Walter, the Archdeacon hurried to intercept us and personally conducted us to his house and gave us very comfortable quarters.

"I may not return," Thomas told him skeptically, "I am indebted to the great man, but this is twice he has sided with that insufferable wretch and twice I have been the sufferer. I have vowed to thrash Roger every day before breakfast if I can catch the coward."

"Do not speak so hastily and with such hostility," Walter cautioned him, "my brother is not angry with you. He is aggrieved. He misses you sorely. You are his life. He will discipline Roger, never fear. This will never happen again. He will send for you after a decent interval."

"I am strongly tempted to ride for London with all I possess and never look back. If I do not wish to work for my cousin, I am sure the King could use an able lawyer."

"Work for Stephen?" Walter asked incredulously, "my brother would never allow it. After all, he is the first advisor to the crown. The King would never employ anyone with whom the Archbishop disagreed or whom the Archbishop disapproved."

"All England knows the Archbishop and the King did not agree," returned Thomas pertinently, "perhaps he might take me just to annoy my lord."

"Commit no acts in haste," Walter cautioned him. "Take your servant and horses and some hounds and falcons from the mews and go to the Church forests and hunt for a few days. Let your nerves unwind and your ungovernable temper cool. Go and enjoy yourself. When you return, all will be right again. If my brother calls for you, I will send for you."

"Only once more will I return," Thomas said stoutly, "I will not be dismissed when I have been wronged. Seniority has no call for unfair treatment. I warn you, explain to the Archbishop that I will trounce Roger if he crosses me. I told him that before, and he apparently still believes that I will submit to that arrogant soul. I will not, I swear it. I will never yield to Roger Pont l'Eveque were he elected to the Papacy!"

"Ahhhhh," Walter and I drew in our breaths sharply, "speak not so loudly! If the servants hear and you are reported, the Church will discipline you!"

"I am not yet a churchman," Thomas reminded him, "and at the present I am not of the mind to take even minor orders."

"I must to bed," Walter rose hastily, "I have prayers to be said and many things to do. Good night." He retreated rapidly.

"Go to your stable, servant," he ordered me, "I sleep alone tonight. I will not have near me at this time, a sniveling cur who shies from the slightest gesture."

I shrugged my shoulders as impertinently as I could and left him without a word.

CHAPTER 23

We were called back to Canterbury by a command from the Archbishop in less than two weeks. The reunion of the old man and his favorite counselor was touching. Thomas sat on the dias to eat all his meals and the Archbishop had him to sit at his right hand at all the councils. The old man gave my master income from eight more churches and we were allowed to have our own eight room apartment in his vast mansion at Harrow. Again, we had been home for almost two years when we were sent on one of our most important journeys to Rome.

"I would have my power as legatine commissioner restored to me," Theobald said one day to Thomas, "do you think you could secure it?"

"I do not know," Thomas said, "I will have to research the title and see who is in the authority to award it."

"The Holy Father at Rome can award anything he pleases," the Archbishop answered testily, "he must be shown the wisdom of the selection. The House of Blois does not enjoy the best of reputations at the Holy See and I feel that Henry of Winchester will have a difficult time defending his appointment. After all, he has had it at the hand of King Stephen, whose position grows more and more precarious. I shall take you to the court where we will stay for three months and you can see for yourself."

This was most exciting. The King was staying at Winchester when we joined, but most of the official business was done in the field, because the Earls of Bridgenorth were in constant revolt. The army was ever on the move, and we after it. It became wearying to watch the army batter down a castle wall, only to be ordered to move to another that had been erected without the King's permission. The barons could not hope to overcome or resist the King's forces, and when they were defeated, they would come into the presence of the King on bended knee and pray forgiveness. The simple man would grant it and the vanquished would swagger from his presence and begin to plot again.

Stephen of Blois was too good looking to believe. In fact, he was effeminate in looks. His reddish brown hair was always curled and brushed to perfection, even when he rode to conquer a rebel. He insisted on having his hands spotlessly clean and his nails buffed constantly. He was careless of his clothes at times, and the spotted appearance of his hose and vests were in strange contrast to his fair skin, faultless hands, and limpid brown eyes that were so large and expressive that they reminded one of clear pools in a shaded glade. And his appearance was deceiving. He was so dilatory that he would make a promise or threat to one man and deny the promise or rescind his decision five minutes later. I believe this was one of the causes for his troubles. Even the commonest servant never knew whether the King would honor his word or not. It was not unusual to see his kitchen personnel receive severe canings from the chamberlains or seneschal for preparing a meal which they thought he had wished, only to find that this thoughts were for something else. Our visit to the court taught us to stay from that place if possible.

The King surrounded himself with the most detestable people a monarch could collect. His barons would countermand orders and attempt to execute people who failed to carry them out. He had as army commander, one William of Ypres, a Fleming who enjoyed persecuting Englishmen. His personal contingent of fighting men, brought expressly from Flanders, were all mongrels who looted, pillage, and raped without any thought of the misery that they visited on the countryside. Even if the peasants looked to the King for succor against the repressions of their lords, they would take up the flail, the cudgel, or any means of defense against the detestable foreigners who left a scorched earth wherever they appeared.

"I cannot remain with the court much longer, master," Thomas told the Archbishop one night at supper, "if I stay here I will attempt to kill these repugnant foreigners single handed. I cannot remember when I have seen so many people whom I dislike so intensely. If I could, I would gibbet them en masse. They are fostering more misery and fathering more bastards than any group in the entire kingdom. I could never like King Stephen. He has no thought of his people. I would welcome this House of Anjou even if it be foreign. The blood heir of King Henry the First must be better than this rabble. England cannot go down in its government! It is as low as it can get. It must go up!"

"How nice to hear you say such things," the Archbishop smiled and gazed fondly at my master, "it was a day of blessings and grace when you came to my house."

"You have not shown it in the case of Roger," my master said bitterly.

"Oh let bygones, be bygones," the Archbishop said blithely, "what I did was to teach you discipline. Seniority in the Church can never be ignored. Roger is a brilliant and sound clergyman. He learns swiftly and is steadfast. He is not my favorite person, but he is dependable and knowledgeable. The Church has need for many of his kind. It is a pity that he is of such a vindictive nature, but his efficiency far overreaches his shortcomings. He will not annoy you again.

You two are becoming men and will rise above such petty grievances."

"They are not petty with me," Thomas answered, "but," and he quickly smiled when he saw the frown of annoyance come to his masters' face, "I can let matters lie if I am not harassed beyond all reason. As you know, it is not my nature to carry nor hold a grudge. I do not deal in the negative. I am far happier when I am doing constructive work."

"Yes, you are," smiled the Archbishop delightedly and squeezed his protégé's hand, "my those are large calluses," he remarked in surprise as he forced Thomas' hands open to display the toughened interiors, "how did you come by these?"

"I practice constantly with the bow and arrow, the broadsword, and the shield. I am in perfect control of my destrier who, if you listen to the rumors, is the finest, strongest, and the most wicked at the court. He is as courageous as ever was born in a horse and he can trample a man or another horse in a twinkling. In fact, of the two of us, Le Lance is by far the more formidable. Have you not heard the gossip of the court that we are invincible?"

"I have heard the gossip," returned the Archbishop delightedly, "but it was only of the horse, not the master. I presumed that some strapping nobleman was merely at court having his pleasure."

"I am not one to boast, you reverence," Thomas said casually, "but I can fight and I know it. There are none in your house that will bait me now, including that group of Roger's sycophants. I will belt them good with my swinging sword or scare them half to death with my ferocious charger if I can catch them walking about the jousting grounds. That bunch of whining jackals are not worth one hoof of my horse. Further, I have a group of hounds that can course the fox with the best in all England and my stallion, Courier can run as swiftly as the wind."

"I am sure he can," smiled the Archbishop indulgently delighting in every word that my master spoke, "but it has almost been a year since I spoke to you of regaining my commission. Are you prepared?"

"Indeed, my master," Thomas bowed low, sweeping the forest green leather cockade from his head and letting the fabulously large pheasant feather trail negligently on the floor, "I have worked up the briefs of my case and the scribes are writing them out now. I will present them to you tonight at supper if it pleases you."

"What a pleasant surprise," said the delighted prelate clapping his hands in obvious pleasure, "surely I have the most beautiful and most intelligent man in all England to argue my case. The Lord blessed me when he sent me you, my shining child. What a fighting bishop you will make for me some day!"

"Thank you, my liege," Thomas said simply.

As we left the Archbishop's presence, my master instructed me to make plans to go to Rome.

"And hire plenty of servants," he commanded me. "I will take thirty five knights and adequate secretarial help. There will also be one hundred foot soldiers in the van. See that all is in readiness."

I sat stupidly on the ground where I was. This was the most astounding man I had ever known. No one had said anything about a train! How could he do so without permission? However, within the month all was in readiness and we disembarked from Dover to land at Witsand on the continent. How often I was to see these ports in the future! They would become our second homes because we should cross the channel so often, that my master finally acquired inns of his own in both places to insure adequate accommodations.

The trip to Rome was routine. Thomas Becket had so adequate a preparation that convincing the Pope and the Papal court was one of the easiest tasks that he ever undertook. We returned as legal messengers of His Holiness and with personal control of the Legantine award. King Stephen and Bishop Henry of Winchester, his brother, were furious. The King threatened the Archbishop of expulsion and furiously demanded the head of the man who had gone to Rome, but my master's name was carefully concealed so that he was never officially selected as being the culprit. We made many trips to select Kingdom in Rome. Each time my master won his presentations and each time the Archbishop grew in ecclesiastical power. The King had no alternative except to consult Theobald on every matter and not even the smallest parish was invested of a priest without the Archbishop's express and personal approval. The King, who had more on his hands than he could possibly control, finally yielded all ecclesiastical matters to Theobald without even asking for an accounting.

The years passed swiftly. The Anjous were constantly in England fighting here and fighting there. Young Prince Henry was becoming a household word. The Empress remained in Normandy most of the time, now. The King was beginning to age. The strain of his irregular rule was beginning to tell on him. Terrible castles grew about the land. Travel was hazardous because one never knew when a local lord would attack travelers for no provocation whatsoever. Even churchmen were not safe anymore. The mercenaries were the worst of all. They would forage the country for no reason and would strip a village of its valuables including those of the churches. They would often leave villages with no food for the winter and slaughter the livestock needlessly. The King was constantly besieged to remove this foreign element from England, but he turned a deaf ear to all entreaties. Rumors flew that the King was dying. That an invasion of the country was imminent. An invasion would be welcome from whatever country. Anything would have been better than the dreaded Flemish wolves prowling and destroying the countryside. King Stephen suffered a serious illness of the lungs and electrified the world by stating that he wanted his heir, Crown Prince, Eustace, crowned as his successor before he died.

King Stephen had his bastard son, William, safely installed with many lands, and married to an heiress of an old family. His news set all England agog. My master, at the direction of the Archbishop hurriedly left from Rome with a small band of attendants. On this trip we suffered. The time of the year was the summer. Roads were hot and dusty and clogged with travelers going almost anywhere and everywhere. One could see the results of the Crusades as oriental robes and turbans were common. The normally quiet province of Aquitaine was almost unsafe to travel in. Its heiress, the Queen of France, had just returned from the Holy Land as a Crusader. Her actions, while there, had scandalized all Christendom, and her husband, the Capetian Louis, was suing her for a divorce. We heard from many people that she had contemptuously dismissed her husband's charges of infidelity with the casual remark, 'One does not sin against a monk!' We were told also at an inn at Nice that Eleanor of Aquitaine had already had relations with Henry of Anjou and that the marriage was eminent if a divorce was granted by the Holy Father. We hoped this matter would not complicate our case.

The case of Louis and Eleanor was settled peacefully and divorce was granted on the grounds of consanguinity. This cynical manner of separating rulers titillated even the Holy Court. John of Salisbury had recently been appointed as First Secretary to His Holiness so our case was heard promptly. We were told to return to England and that the Pope would hear the case later at the Council of Tours which he intended to call in the autumn when the heat had abated. We traveled back and entered England as the poorest and most inconspicuous travelers because we had been warned that the King had ordered us jailed if we were apprehended. The Archbishop, upon hearing the report, ordered his staff to prepare to join the court where he planned to gain the King's permission to attend the proposed council. We were due for some disappointments and surprises on this visit.

The King adamantly and categorically refused the Archbishop's request.

"But my liege," the prelate argued, "it is my duty as the Father's representative in England to attend his councils. I never get to see him. Rome is too far for a person my age to travel. Would you deny me contact with my superior and yours?"

"He is my spiritual superior, not my secular one," the King said acidly, "I am England. He has not bothered to answer my suit about the succession, only that this asinine council will hear the case. It has ever been, and always will be, my policy to keep my ecclesiastical servants here with me. I disapprove their going abroad. They are needed here to comfort my people."

"But my liege lord," the Archbishop counseled, "will the Papacy rule in your favor with your chief pontiff absent?"

"It needs be they must," the King replied testily, "I cannot prove it, but I have a strong belief that you favor the House of Anjou for the kingship over Eustace. If I knew it to be the truth, I would have you executed for treason to the crown. I have permanently removed people for less. And that meddling crew of clerks that you have, will shortly feel the royal wrath. I hear that there is one among them who fancies himself noble and is also clever. Have I ever met this one, father? I cannot seem to recall his face or his name."

"There is no one in my house who acts without my express permission. There are no traitors to the crown in my establishment, I assure you, but as you well know, the Englishman is going to have political opinions. If you would stop that, you must remove all the tongues of your subjects."

"Curse them all," said the King angrily, "my answer is no to the council and anyone who risks my anger will be executed or expelled from the country."

"You risk an interdict or excommunication," Theobald warned him, "and possible national rebellion."

"I care not," the King said in his typical passionate carelessness, "if I cannot name my successor, what care I who gains the crown? You are dismissed from my presence old man. You have thoroughly upset me. Retire from the court of Canterbury and keep your own counsel lest you die for your cause."

We quickly left the court with the Archbishop in a high dudgeon.

"All is not lost your eminence," Thomas assured him, "we will get to Tours even it displease the King a thousand times. But you must be prepared to stay from England. I do not believe you will survive the King's anger."

"I care not a fig for this foolish man," Theobald said heatedly, "he is not King, only an usurper who cannot take advice from one who would be loyal if he were allowed to do so."

"Do not concern yourself about getting to the council master," Thomas said soothingly, "you will go. I only ask that you be prepared to depart without notice."

"I will be ready," Theobald said to him, "you make the preparations."

"So be it," Thomas said solemnly.

I did not see much of my master in the months following. He would dismiss me curtly if I tried to talk to him saying that he was too busy to deal in trivialities. He either stayed gone from the house or locked in conference with the Archbishop or surrounded by all the parchments of law that he could acquire. He read or traveled early and late. I always saw that food and dry raiment was kept ready and even took the opportunity to have him a new white woolen suit ordered with matching hat, gloves, belt and boots. It was completed by fine touches of purple that I directed the clothiers to edge the hat, gloves and boots. The tailor sewed on great ropes of woven ropes of silk on the cloaks that had just been introduced from Spain. This was the uniform my master would wear to astound the religious at Tours, I hoped. The tailor remembered to match the garments with a full short cape that I had forgotten. He had hemmed this with fine gold and silver thread. It was a magnificent garment that cost a small fortune and I prayed my master would see fit to wear it.

Our house and all England stooped to pause when it was announced that Henry of Anjou and Eleanor of Aquitaine had been married without due ceremony. Now here appeared a worthy successor to Stephen. His land holdings exceeded our small country and the people he ruled as a duke were many more than us. Eustace was a mere son of a pretender and national sentiment, as well as my master's, swung to this intrepid son of a great fighting house and who was a direct descendent of The Conqueror.

We really became frantic in our secret preparations to get to the Council of Tours without the Kind's knowledge. A fast stage of horses was set up to Sandwich, the Archbishop's port. Black waterproof garments were secured and a group of foolhardy sailors were hired only to sail across the channel and land us at Calais. The Archbishop announced that he was going to the coast to inspect the conditions of the churches in the area and possibly consecrate some new priests for vacant parishes. He only took me, my master, and three servants. We were allowed to take the minimum of equipment and would have to depend totally on the good services and loyalty of all the abbeys and convents on the route. We stayed in the

Sandwich area for six weeks and the King's agents left us to return to other duties.

When my master was assured that all suspicion was allayed, which was exactly seven days before the Council and we had received a letter from John of Salisbury that the Pope had arrived, Thomas announced that we would depart. The weather turned from sunny to beastly. It rained and blew and lightening played in the sky in a most ferocious manner. The sea was churning beyond belief. I refused to enter the boat that was rocking crazily while moored to the wharf. My master gave me a good shaking and forced me aboard. A chair had been procured for the Archbishop and he sat under what little protection was offered.

"Why should you be so afraid, if the Archbishop is not?" my master shouted at me angrily.

"He is one of God's elect," I answered back spitting sea spray from my mouth, "my soul is not shriven and I do not wish to drown."

"We have not time for praying," he shouted to me, "sit down before you fall overboard."

"Shall I put him to sleep?" a rough, swarthy asked my master as he raised a wicked looking club.

"If he persists in this caterwauling, yes," Thomas said curtly as he lurched to the side of the Archbishop and gathered in his law materials.

"Are you not afraid?" I asked the sailor. I was too terrified of the elements to fear this brute.

"I sail where I am paid to sail," he answered shortly, "now secure yourself, or I really will put you away for the voyage and perhaps for some time after."

This cold statement helped me to crawl to the mast and cling to it as did the other servants who also had tied the gear to it. They were all praying and that was comforting. The storm grew to a new fury as we entered the open waters and I was so sick that I became inured to the danger of drowning. It took all night to cross that channel and we beached as the day broke. When I saw the leaky condition of the boat, its small size, and the shredded sails, I could only lurch over the side into the gently swelling surf and crawl to dry land. Some monks were there to meet us with a small cart. They placed the Archbishop and the luggage in it and the rest of us staggered to a monastery that could be seen in the distance. After we were dry and fed, we began our journey to the Council aboard horses and mules, again using back lanes and traveling through the brush in order to avoid the King's agents whom the monks said were present, under the direction of the Bishop of Winchester, to prevent our attendance.

CHAPTER 24

The Council of Tours went smoothly enough although my master got in some heated arguments with the Bishop of Lisieux and the Bishop of Winchester. The Pope wished to know the lineage of Henry of Anjou while the Bishops who were the advocates of King Stephen presented a full dosier on Eustace.

"She is not a legally born heiress," the Bishop of Lisieux argued, "and by this I refer to the Empress Matilda, Henry's mother. Her mother was forced by his grandfather, Henry the First, from a convent without being properly dismissed, so the birth of her children is not regular."

"That is not so," my master returned heatedly, "I have the proof of the marriage and the recorded births of the children. Further, I have the permission of the reigning Pope of the time who certified the marriage as properly conducted with his blessing. Should Prince Henry gain the throne, he will have your bishopric for this."

"I only speak from very strong rumors," hastily said the Bishop, "they are so strong, there must be some verification."

"Can you certify this other than a true and legal document, your Holiness?" my master held some documents to the Pope who bent forward, took them, and motioned John to read them over his shoulder. The Pope looked at John.

"They are legal and in order," said John smiling, "the Archbishop of Canterbury would not stoop to forgery."

"So it is," said the pontiff emphatically, "you stand corrected and admonished, Arnulf of Lisieux."

"I yield, I yield," said the Bishop nervously.

"Your Highness," plead Henry of Winchester, "the cause of the Anjous is not good for England. The Empress could not secure the loyalty of the people at her father's death because she was not incapable of governing, but she had no clear mandate to rule as my brother has done."

"I know, my Bishop, that there is nothing but anarchy in England, and do not present it to me otherwise. Stephen of Blois has angered me by not allowing my subjects to visit me as they wished. Your own Archbishop, the chief of the priest of the land, had to steal to this Council like a thief in the night. I am of a mind to lay the country under interdict."

Everyone in the room drew a sharp audible breath and paled except my master and Theobald. They smiled shrewdly and primly.

"I do not mean to offend," the Bishop of Winchester fell to his knees, "neither did my brother, your Holiness."

"Beware that you do not," warned the Pope, "yet your brother could not find the time to attend me. He also refused my bishop's good conduct through unhappy England when I sent the palls to my Irish and Scottish canons. You must speak stronger and more certainly if I am to entertain favorable thoughts."

"I have become neutral," announced the Bishop of Lisieux to the assembly, "I have not been informed properly, therefore, I withdraw my advocacy for the House of Blois."

The Bishop of Winchester looked ill. He knew he had lost the case. Arguments were heard for three wearying days and the Pope raised his hand for silence on the morning of the fourth.

"I have come to a decision," he said, "I do not wish to hear further argument. I depart within the day for Rome. Eustace is denied my permission to be crowned King of England. There will be no succession approved by me or my office until the present King does penance and convinces me his house is the rightful heir. Go now, all of you. I have spoken. I will leave this quarrelsome place. This has been no Council, it has been a debating society, a tiring one too, but remember me to King Stephen. Disobedience to my decision brings immediate excommunication and interdict."

Everyone left quietly. Swift horses pounded from the courtyards and we knew that couriers were taking Stephen the news. While the Archbishop waited in apprehension, his fears were well founded. He was expelled from England. News came to us that Eustace, in his disappointment, was ravaging the hapless country with no one to apprehend him. We were very upset to hear that a madness of the bowels killed him. We concluded it must have been from eating and drinking without care. Also news reached us that a plague had swept London and that the Huitdeniers and my father had died of it.

Eustace's death brought the haughty and vacillating Stephen to his knees and we went home hurriedly, the Archbishop to the throne and Thomas and I to London to see about the catastrophe. All were dead and Thomas closed out his inheritance quickly. We returned to Canterbury posts haste because we felt we were needed there. And we were. Things were really in a turmoil. The King was totally distracted and distraught. He acted as a man who was bereft of his mind. The Archbishop, at Thomas' urging lost no time in arranging with the King's permission, a conference with the young Plantagenet who was campaigning in the north. At first the King was adamant.

"I will not leave my kingdom to the Normans," Stephen said irrationally.

"You will not be leaving it to anyone except the rightful heir my liege," the Archbishop argued, "it has long been the talk that you usurped the throne. Your dilatory tactics will leave the country leaderless. More damage will be done."

"What do you say, old man?" the King screamed, "Are you insinuating that I am a pretender who holds the throne by force?"

"Nay, my King," the Archbishop said soothingly, "but you have no heirs, except possibly your daughter. England would not accept King Henry's daughter, do you think your beloved Mary will fare any better? And do you not think William will be the first to suffer if you leave a legacy of hate and revenge?"

"There is always my brother Theobald in France," the King mused, "I can leave it to him, and in that manner, I can confound that bitch Matilda a bit longer."

"I will contest that action with every ounce of my strength," Theobald said stoutly, "your end will be one of the fire and the sword. The House of Blois will be hounded from the face of the earth. It will take a new generation of distant cousins to reestablish your name. Your kin are not strong enough to resist the onslaught of an outrages society. Remember, too, Henry of Anjou is the suzerain of Blois now that he has married. He can be expected to resist, and you know him to be a courageous fighter. This decision will be the ruin and the possible disappearance of your proud family. Think on it my liege, let me summons the young Prince. Acknowledge him as your successor. Leave England in peace."

"I wish I had never wished for this accursed throne. Perhaps I could find peace and my blessed Eustace would be alive. I yield," he said, raising wet eyes to the smiling, benign Archbishop, "I will send Eustace's wife and children to the continent where they can be reared in their ancestral home."

"That is good, my lord, the King," Theobald bowed, "I will schedule a meeting between you two within the week. It is April now. He will wish that the matter of succession has been settled."

The two gentlemen met at Windsor. It was obvious that the Plantagenet had come to fight if need be. His men were armed and hostile. The Archbishop was there with all the leading prelates of the realm, including the perfidious Bishop of Lisieux and the nervous Henry of Winchester. Rumor had it that Henry was amassing his wealth and goods on the continent and intended to resign his See. Arnulf of Lisieux quickly reminded the young Prince of his knowledge of affairs and immediately situated himself in the train of Normans, announcing that he would henceforth travel with the heir to the throne. No one really cared. Stephen sat regally and motioned the Archbishop and Henry to the dias. Theobald almost led Thomas by the hand as if fearing to lose him. Thomas had pen, ink, and paper.

"Who approaches my throne with you?" Stephen growled at the aging Archbishop.

"My chief clerk and confidante," the Archbishop said easily and carelessly, "I go nowhere or do anything without his presence and advice. I grow old and someone needs to be trained lest I suddenly fail."

"I have never seen him," the King said testily, "was he with you on that dastardly continental trip?"

"I do not recall, sire," the Archbishop, "but I hardly believe so. I seldom leave Canterbury without someone to direct it."

"I don't recall this rare bird of paradise, either," said the young Prince staring unabashedly at my master. He had on the white and I had brushed it to a fine sheen. The purple and gold were just the right colors to set off his rich, auburn hair that was done in troubadour style. He was truly the outstanding figure in all this collection of gaudily dressed ensemble. Beside him, the young, squatty, red-faced Prince with calloused and dirty hands with mustard yellow clothes stained from riding and being in the field was truly a dung fowl. He had a commanding presence though, and he did not speak a word of English although he seemed to understand readily. All conversation therefore was in French.

"My broom sedge plume is as fancy as his pheasant's feather," he said and held his hat aloft for all to see. Everyone laughed loudly. Meanwhile I had two clerks seated at a table from which I had removed two bishops who did not protest. I took the writing materials from my master.

"I like you," Henry said to my master, "come, let me talk with you a moment, while the Archbishop and the King converse. I am agreeable to anything they say as long as it is that I inherit the throne on the death of the King."

"God will that be so, my lord," Thomas said, "and God please will that the King not turn intractable at the last moment."

"He won't," Henry assured him, "I have enough good men here to insure peace and harmony and a willingness on the part of that usurping baster if I have to. Never fear, he will sign, under duress, if necessary. Although he is my suzerain for my English lands, I can still force him."

My master remained silent. The young man stepped back and ordered Thomas to turn around completely.

"You are the most beautiful thing that I have ever seen," declared the Prince impressively. No woman of my acquaintance has ever been turned out as well as you."

"Your terms are not very complementary, my lord," Thomas said with a little heat, "one does not compare a normal male with women."

"I apologize," said Henry quietly, "I meant no comparison nor insult. I speak in admiration. Would that I had someone near me such as you. Will you serve me if I become king?"

"That is not for me to say, your Highness," Thomas said flustered by the directness of this aggressive young man. I could have spoken for him. 'Yes, Yes!' I sang to myself. Imagine serving a king! I had never dreamed of such good fortune.

"Well, I will say if I ever sit on the throne. Until then, will you not fight with me and return home with me? Say yes," and the Prince gripped Thomas tightly by the hand. He looked surprised and turned Thomas' hand upward. "Why, I do believe you wear calluses on the insides of those elegant hands!" he exclaimed.

"You have a sword hand," Thomas said, "I fight with the broadside as well as any in your van."

"A fighting man who dresses to put a man to shame," said Henry.

"I spend my money as I please," said Thomas pleasantly, "I happen to like good food and fine clothing."

The Archbishop came to them smiling.

"He is ready," he told Henry, "give him a few minutes to contemplate and to yield. When he beckons, kneel to him. Oh, I see you two have met."

"Not met, sir," said Henry quickly, "but talked."

"This is my beloved, my sun, my first and most valuable assistant," Theobald said warmly, "without him I would not be able to do as I do. He advised me on all points of the law both canon and secular, he takes care of my correspondence and my appointments within the See. He traveled for me to Rome. He is the advocate who convinced Pope Eugenius that the house of Anjou was the rightful heir to the throne. He is slow to anger. He thinks no evil, fears no man, is not avaricious, and is completely knowledgeable and dependable in his advice. He is loyal to a fault with no pride whatsoever. He is my son or the one that I would have prayed for if I had been so fortunate. This is my child of light in whom I place all my earthly hopes."

The Prince stood non-plussed until one of his advisors tugged at his sleeve to let him know that the King would give him audience. The Prince and Archbishop went to the throne and sank to their knees.

"Let all men know," Stephen intoned, "that I hereby acknowledge Henry, Duke of Anjou and Aquitaine, Count of Normandy and Maine, son of the Empress Matilda, grandson of the illustrious Henry, is acknowledged my heir to the throne of England and all members of the House of Blois renounce their claims thereto."

The scribes wrote busily. Thomas supervised their spelling and wording. When they had finished, all dignitaries present signed.

"Now leave me," Stephen ordered nastily, "I am tired."

We all went our separate ways, intending to sleep beyond this town where the King might turn to treachery. The precious document was retained by Theobald and the guard was especially watchful that night.

CHAPTER 25

"He will surely come," said the Archbishop wearily, "I do not anymore have the strength to sustain the long arduous hours that is required to administrate a kingdom. Thank God for you my dear and indefatigable Thomas, you have literally served as a king for these three months. The Church is suffering, everything is suffering because there is not enough time to see to it all. If the Prince does not arrive shortly, I fear some usurper will arise and the anarchy that Stephen left us will be aggravated. Watch those accursed Flemings, son, and if some upstart baron begins to make martial moves, ride against him with every knight I and the Empress possess. Though only an Archdeacon, I empower you to fight for the future king and for the established Church."

"I will do that my lord," Thomas said as he sat sweat stained and weary. He had just come in from a two weeks tour of the coast to insure peace. I had not gone with him, since someone had to stay near and administrate his business.

Shortly after King Stephen acknowledged the succession, the Bishop of Rochester died and the Archbishop had appointed his brother to that position. Roger Pont l'Eveque, still the senior member of the household, was promoted to the Archdeaconry of Canterbury. John of Salisbury had joined our entourage within the week after the King's acknowledgement and this had proved a blessing because he took full charge of the Archbishop's correspondence which freed Thomas to assume more and more of the administrative load. With Walter gone to his seat of government, the burden was especially heavy. Before all had been secured in their new positions, word came that the Archbishop of York had died from being poisoned.

The wrath of the Archbishop fell on that diocese and despite their pleadings, he excommunicated over half of the chapter of the cathedral and expelled the rest. Some who convinced him of their innocence were transferred to other monasteries or churches overseas and forbidden never to set foot in England as long as they lived. Roger was sent quickly to keep control of the fluid situation and install new personnel. He showed shrewd insight and the Archbishop elevated him to the Chair of York. This backbiting, efficient man showed his intransigence again by insisting that he receive his official assignment from Theobald as legatine commissioner since Roger contended that the See of York was equal to that of Canterbury. The situation was so confused and pressing that the Archbishop yielded readily in order to avoid further delay and argument.

My master was appointed to the Archdeaconry and given six additional revenues from the rental of property and collections. This promotion brought him a yearly income of one hundred pounds in silver! My head swam when I attempted to compute the income. We now had a plethora of personal and official servants. The Archdeacon had a stable of the finest blooded horses in the land, including two superb destriers; a kennel that boasted the keenest and swiftest hounds of all description; and a mews that had falcons from all over the world. John of Salisbury had brought him one of the most magnificent peregrines from Rome that I had ever seen. I was now a major domo more than an ostler, and my duties were vast and many.

In August, King Stephen took to his bed with a broken heart at Winchester and died within three days after the onset of his illness.

"Send messages rapidly and plentiful urging Prince Henry to sail from Normandy," Theobald urged my master, "sign them yourself in the official capacity as my representative. Pray to him to come swiftly and immediately lest a pretender arise and he be faced with anarchy and rebellion."

The Prince dutifully answered each summons with polite replies that continental matters were pressing, and that he would come as soon as he could find relief. A convocation of churchmen and London governing officials was kept in a constant state of readiness for his arrival. Bonfire material was replenished from time to time to insure that the country would know that a King was newly at hand. Still he did not come. The time grew critical and matters throughout the land grew tense. Thomas directed the old King's justiciars to travel their itineraries swiftly and widely and administer justice so that legal matters would not accumulate. Those magnificent men, Richard di Luci and the Earl of Leicester, hired additional personnel to look into legal matters throughout the land. The Archbishop urged the Archbishop of York and all the other bishops not to allow their legal matters get out of control. Still the Prince did not come. The time for Michaelmas was approaching so much time was spent seeing that the Exchequer was in readiness to collect the taxes. Many lists were prepared of the active sheriffs, so an exact tallage could be conducted. My master was everywhere at once. He required a staff of thirty scribes and fifteen couriers to control the kingdom. The Archbishop's anxiety and age were beginning to show and a heavy cold incapacitated him for longer than three weeks.

"A sail, a sail!" A panting messenger ran into a conference between my master, the Archbishop, various bishops, and the justiciars. The meeting broke up without due ceremony, because any sail approaching Dover was reason to expect the royal entourage. This time it was the King and the Queen and an entourage of four hundred people, including the infant princes who were mere babes in arms. The King was unceremoniously conducted to London, amid thronged roads and through the congested London streets. The crowds were cheery and enthusiastic as ever crowds are when wine and beer flow freely. The bonfires glowed in a most engaging manner and broom sedge was in the hats or hands of everyone. The Prince was touched by this. He was crowned at Westminister on Christmas Day 1153.

"Who was responsible for my tumultuous welcome?" King Henry the Second asked the Archbishop as they sat in one of their many conferences.

"Thomas Becket, sire," Theobald said warmly, "in fact, he literally ran your kingdom for you. He supervised the administration, the law, and the collection of taxes. You have only to go and see him and the Bishop of Ely functioning at the Exchequer this moment, to see the most miraculous servant in all of your kingdom. I urge you to find a place in your government for this remarkable man. He is forty three years of age, fully matured in his mind, superbly trained in law and administration, and has full knowledge of the problems of the land. Remember also, it was he who so adequately represented your cause for the succession at Tours and at Rome. I would regret sorely losing him for myself, but I would gladly yield to see him utilized in his fullest capacity. He can supervise the kingdom as well as the Church. It would ease my mind to know that a reliable person is supporting you. I need a rest, your Highness. If Thomas Becket were placed in your cabinet, I could take a much needed rest."

"You are a good man," Henry said to the old churchman affectionately, "you have been my other self in my absence. Of course I will yield to any recommendation that you should make or any request that you would ask, however unreasonable. I must choose my cabinet at once. Whom do you have in mind for the various important positions?"

"Reaffirm my appointment of Nigel, Bishop of Ely, as your head of the Exchequer, Richard di Luci and the Earl of Leicester as your justiciars, the Bishops of Lisieux and Bayeux as your official advisors after me of course," the Archbishop smiled wanly, "and make Thomas Becket your chancellor."

"This Becket," the King questioned the Archbishop, "he is the gorgeously dressed man who was at the acknowledgement ceremony? If so, yes, I will have in my personal staff. Yes, I would see him now. Send for Thomas Becket," the King ordered his chamberlain, "instruct him that I would have attend me at once."

My master sent for me when the message arrived.

"Set out my green dress," he ordered, "at once. I must to the King's presence. Hurry!"

When we arrived, it was obvious that something had irritated the King.

"Why so long to obey my commands?" he barked at Thomas.

"I was in my working clothes, your majesty," he said modestly, "they were soiled and I did not deem it fit to enter your presence in unseemly attire."

The King smiled at the Archbishop, his anger dissipating instantly. It was not lost on anyone present that Thomas' elegant green was exactly the same color as the King's clothing except that there was a vast difference. The King inclined to be stout. His clothing was rumpled as if he had slept in them. His hair was uncombed and standing in all directions. His calloused hands were not clean and his short cut, paired fingernails were very dirty. He sat carelessly, yet in a kindly manner, in violent contrast to the cool, elegant, slender figure that stood before him, immaculately groomed with not a wrinkled or soiled spot showing. The face of the

Archbishop actually radiated his great joy at the sight of Thomas Becket. The cameo like face in which the great limpid brown eyes moved casually about completely captivated the King.

"Come near me," he ordered my master, "no don't kneel, you would soil your raiment." The King waved the churchmen who stood near him away.

"You are excused," he ordered all present and they stared at him in disbelief, "I am at home. I fear no man. I am the King of all my people, their servant, therefore I will be trusted and will hold private conferences with whom I please. I desire to talk with this man. Withdraw and do not come forward until you are so commanded. Thank you for your many kindnesses, father," he said gently to Theobald and rose hastily to help the Archbishop rise, "please return to Canterbury and take a long rest from your anxieties and arduous duties. I assure you I will make no decisions or promulgate any decrees without your prior advice. The kingdom will survive for a few weeks. We will do much better in our government if you can stay rested. We value your counsel above all. I will attend you. I desire that you completely recover from the strain of the past because are invaluable to my future."

"Bless you my son," the Archbishop said leaning heavily on his shoulder until servants could come to support him, "I am sure that the good God above sent you and my blessed Thomas to me. Especially to me and to England."

"The Angevin Empire, your Holiness," Henry corrected him gently, "I will rule on both sides the Channel with equal impartially. My servants will be servants of my entire kingdom. I want not provincial or divided sentiments about me."

"An, it is so good to talk to a man who knows what he is about," sighed the Archbishop, "and you so young! But I leave you in good hands with the fullest confidence that all will be well. It will be so good to take a long rest, free from the cares and responsibilities of directing a land so large and diverse. I feel confident that you can control the lawless bands of mercenaries and curb the wildest of the barons."

"If I cannot," smiled Henry, "I have an army that can. I will show temperance and mercy if I am allowed, but I do not intend to tolerate rebellion or disaffection. My fighting arm is at its best father, and I intend to rule my empire."

"It is good, it is good," said the Archbishop, "I leave you now, with your permission."

"Go," said the young monarch kindly, "and may God give you a safe and uneventful journey."

The King turned to Thomas as we all drew away and stood at a respectful distance.

"Go, all of you," he commanded sternly, "find employment. There is much to be done. Only my most personal servants are to stay and attend me. I would have wine served."

The high churchmen muttered as they departed the throne room while I moved over and integrated myself into the small staff of bearers who stayed with the King regardless of whatever he or anyone else said. I went forward with the wine bearers because I knew my master did not care for strong drink, except on a very rare occasion. He requested that I furnish him with a cool, dry wine that I carried everywhere he went.

"Do you not like your native wines?" the King asked.

"I am not one who indulges in alcohol, sire," Thomas answered quietly, "it stirs my blood uncommonly and upsets my digestion. I can partake in small measure from time to time but I do not crave it for a steady drink. Instead, I prefer flavored water if it is to be had. I also like my water boiled and in that manner, I suffer no evils of the blood."

"What a strange man and so beautiful," said the young King admiringly.

"Do you truly find me so, your majesty?" Thomas asked smiling gently, "I, too, find you most attractive."

"You will be my alter ego, I can feel the charisma already," Henry said firmly, "I intend to place you in my personal cabinet. You will be rarely from my presence. I warn you, I am tempestuous, given to choleric rages, and somewhat scurrilous in my desires. It will not be easy to serve Henry of Anjou. My turbulent heritage makes me difficult and my lusts are truly beastly. I glory in them and find my greatest relaxation in many women who are grateful and willing. I care not where they be highborn or of the stable, just as long as they are cooperative and high spirited."

"I am no ladies' man," Thomas spoke truthfully, "whoever I love, will be the only one. So far, the woman has not crossed my path to whom I can swear fidelity. Lasciviousness is repugnant to me as is most people who smell of unwashed bodies and foul breath."

"It is my delight," Henry smiled wickedly, "woman was made for man's delight, the more the merrier. The lower the taste, the more delightful the fruit. Do you not agree?"

"I would not know, your Highness," answered Becket, "I am not young as you well know. I have never known a woman. It has not been my desire. I'm afraid I will be a disappointment as a procurer. That is not my line. I love life with all its complexities and challenges. I am not emotional and am seldom attached deeply to people. Physical contact is another thing that is repulsive to me. I do allow my servant to wash my back but only because I cannot reach it."

"Baths?" Henry asked astounded, "you must be of oriental extraction. I have heard from the Crusaders, that the Arabs use flowing water overmuch. I would feel that they would catch their deaths of chills."

"I do not know of that," said Thomas, "it is bandied about from time to time that my mother was a Saracen, but that is not so. She was a small, husky, blonde Norman from

Thierceville near Rouen. Ever kind and considerate. My sisters are blonde as she was. My father, who was certainly the most French of all Frenchmen, had black or deep brown eyes."

"The color of your skin leads one to believe that you would have originated in the hot, foreign lands and the shape and color eyes only emphasize the fact," the young King said.

"Whatever is the case," laughed Thomas as they sipped their drinks in companionable conversation, "I am a true Norman of ordinary parents who were solid, honest, and indulgent."

"I wish I didn't know," the King said teasingly, "you are the only person whom I have ever known for whom I have held an affinity so quickly. I do not intend to lose you or yield you to some opportuning person."

"I do not wish to be lost or yielded," Thomas said gently, I too feel that I will be happy near you. It is my greatest desire to serve you."

"What position do you desire?" Henry asked him directly.

"That is not for me to say," Thomas said as he dropped his eyes, "I am not here to importune or ask for favors. It would be unseemly for me to unseat people with experience and records of loyalty to your family."

"Well said," Henry said admiringly clasping the long fingers of my master, "do not mistake my clasping your hand as an indication that anything is irregular in my affection for you. I am insecure. If I do not love, I tolerate no closeness. If I love, it is with all my being and physical contact with the one I love is the only proof I know. I shall always hold your hand and sit near you and damned be the man or woman who criticizes me. I will have them quartered and spitted before my personal attendance."

"You speak fierce," Thomas told him seriously.

"I live fierce," Henry said matter-of-factly, "and all who know me well stand back and show respect. Would you consider the position in my government as my chancellor, or is there another position you desire more?"

"I am not qualified to answer," said Thomas, "you have an excellent chief of the Exchequer, magnificent justiciars, and the finest of personal advisors. I hope I can fill the position to your satisfaction if I am chosen."

"Very well, we will the Bishop of Ely also function as my chancellor until you feel qualified, but only for a short while, mind you, he has much to do. I would that you quickly acquaint yourself with the chancellor's duties and in the meantime, work closely with the Baron di Luci in the areas of the law. The Earl can supervise the iters of the traveling justices, thus relieving di Luci and you to start the badly needed reforms of the courts. We have much to do quickly, my chancellor, but the law is to be one of the first areas to be corrected. Do you not agree?"

"Yes, your majesty," Thomas said.

"Stop calling me majesty in private," Henry commanded, "it saves time and besides I want to be the first person always in your life as you shall be in mine. We will not waste time on formalities. We shall be as brothers, only closer."

"It is good, sire," Thomas said as the two men sat with hands clasped together and quietly sipping their drinks and meditating.

Even the servants remarked at the tranquility of the scene and no one could recall when they had ever seen the young King sit as still and seem to enjoy it. The obvious rapport between these two augured well for the coming turbulent days of the settling of affairs in the turbulent kingdom.

CHAPTER 26

"I'm going to quit this life," I declared to Walter Map one day, "I've never given disloyalty to my master a thought before, but I am tired of this peregrinating life. We are never still. It is driving me crazy to pack and unpack all the time. The country is at peace and I never shall forget seeing that old buzzard, William of Ypres, hounded from the country along with his horrible mercenaries and all their bag and baggage. I should imagine that there are many weeping English born maids in Flanders today. That is their price for bedding with the abhorrent foreigners. Bad cess to them all, I say, and I must find a permanent resting place."

"I have it from good authority that the King had more unacknowledged children among the Flemings than many of the soldiery," Map returned flippantly, "he certainly has not established a reputation for continence. I regret that we cannot keep up with his amors. It would make good reading in my diary. I fear that Gerald of Wales is surpassing me in his recording the life of the court."

"I wouldn't know about that," I told him cautiously. My master had warned me that if any of the tales of the King reached these two that my penalty would be permanent expulsion from England. The King tolerated these two, because he would tolerate anyone if they did not offend him permanently, and for this he was universally loved. I was not about to get involved in Map's penchant for gossip about our royal master.

"We ride against the Welch soon," I sighed. "It appears that we ride against someone or somewhere all the livelong time. First it was against every baron in the land who owned a castle of which the King disapproved. Now it is to see if we can secure an inheritance for his brothers."

"What do you do and where do you and your master go when you leave the King's train for days at a time?" Walter asked me.

"We go and check the justiciars on their itineraries," I explained to him, "and as often as not, Thomas sits and hears cases, if the court load is especially heavy. We are forever on the go, but if you notice, he always returns to attend the Curia Regis."

"He is a free one in that area," Walter spoke in an interesting manner. He can sit or not as he pleases. And I hear that he can soften harsh judgments of the Curia or the justiciars. He is the keeper of the Great Seal, a baron of the Exchequer, the administrator of the Tower of London and numerous castles and manors, the Secretary of the State and Foreign Minister, the Controller of all vacant Church positions, as well as the personal confidante of the King. Is there anything he cannot do or docs not do?"

"I don't believe so," I said wearily, "I personally wish he would not do so much. The courtiers hate him for it and I know at times he gets despondent. I fear he will become ill. He is too old to attend a young king."

"He didn't look too old when the King took his coat the other day and gave it to the beggar. That was hilarious. That poor soul of an old man, walking through the snow and suffering. The sudden idea of the King to take the Chancellor's cloak and give it to the man surprised Becket, but when he saw that the King was serious he yielded with the best of grace."

"It was one of his nicer coats, ordered and finished for him especially from the Fur Guild in London. I expect it cost ten pounds. It would have been a wonderful cloak for me after he tired of it. But the tussle over the cloak was nothing. In private, he and the King play the same as two schoolboys. They wrestle all over the furniture, much to the disgust of the Queen and to the delight of the princes. They seem to have a lot of fun."

"Yes, and I hear that when you are in residence, the Chancellor is in charge of the rearing of the King's eldest, Prince Henry and about two dozen other children of nobility."

"My master cannot say no to anyone," I replied sulkily in spite of myself, "every day, we feed dozens of dignitaries, quite often the King himself, who if out hunting, will ride by and up to the very table. If he is thirsty he drinks form my master's cup, if he is hungry they share the same platter. The King never tells us when he is coming, neither can we order special food for him."

"Does he truly give the beggars and poor the leftover food and does he present every departing guest with a gift?"

"Yes," I said wearily, "the chamberlain is forever purchasing jewelry, gold cups, silver bowls, and the like. There is a room stacked to the ceiling with them. The supply seems endless."

"It must seem heavenly to live in unequaled splendor with no question of money," Walter said enviously.

"It is tiresome and galling," I told him shortly, "and what with this business of the King forever traveling, there is no rest ever for anyone."

"And did not the Chancellor design a special seal to mark the official correspondence?" Walter prattled on not listening to me at all.

"Yes, and the French King, the German King, the Pope, and the Norwegian King have adopted the idea as well as the

Dukes of Milan and Naples. It is easy now for the stupidest clerk to sort the mail by the signs of the seals."

We were interrupted by the sound of the King's voice. It was the middle of a cool autumnal afternoon and all the servants were busy preparing to travel. I prayed that the man would not decide to strike the tents and ride for distance before nightfall. I was willing to waylay my master and suggest that they go hunting or anything to divert the King from travel. The pompous Bishops of Lisienx, Bayeux, Chichester, York, and Rouen went by in train, followed by their personal hirelings. This was sizeable progress, more to the King's fashion than for war. The Chancellor had three hundred and fifty knights and two thousand foot soldiers who he was paying out of his pocket and who he fed at his own expense in this group.

"What ho, my Chancellor," called the King, "I know it is you. Stop and tarry awhile and say nothing to the one who loves you the most."

He walked fondly up to the Chancellor and fondly bussed him on the cheek while all other movement stopped. The Bishops watched silently.

"Why it is not a mortal man," the King teased, "it is a veritable peacock. What is this?" he roared.

"Only the clothes wear modestly," Thomas said even more teasingly.

"I'll be damned," said the King loudly.

Thomas stepped back and spread his cloak. I was amazed. Breaths were sibilant. He was truly arrayed this time. His cape, again in exaggerated troubadour style, was of purplish blue inside and sky blue on the outside. It rippled and glinted. His hose matched the outer portions of his cape and his doublet or surcoat was peerless. It was done in flower blossoms. In the centers were sewn cabochons, rubies, emeralds, and sapphires of enormous size. The petals were of pearls.

"It is unbelievable," exclaimed the King in awe. Here are more precious jewels than are in my and the queen's crown."

"Doubtless," said Thomas gravely.

"Is there more?" asked the King from force of habit.

"Yes," Thomas answered tonelessly. He slipped his cape over his right shoulder negligently and turned. Gasps were heard throughout the entire enclosure. The entire back of the jacket was sewn with seed pears from end to end. The bright blue that peeped through accented their number and brilliance.

"I don't believe it," whispered the King, "there are not that many stones and pearls in the world."

"This is only a few of them, master," said Thomas with a hint of laughter in his voice.

The king, realizing for the first time that he had created an audience whirled angrily.

"Begone, you lackeys, this is the royal enclosure. Only myself and my Chancellor are allowed in it. This spectacle is for royal eyes only. Clear out I say! Chamberlain, where are you," he screamed his face getting redder and redder. His face began to twitch so choleric has he become. The Chamberlain came scurrying forward. All people hurried from the King's sight.

"You varlet," roared the King taking a healthy kick at the cowering man, "it is your job to see that no one approaches me in my privacy!"

"I beg your forgiveness, sire, I thought you were resting. I was arranging for the travel tomorrow."

"That is not your job," he screamed, "I have others to do that. Your duties are to see that no one approaches me unless I give permission."

Thomas stepped casually forward and enveloped the King in his gorgeous new coat. I had stepped back into the shadows of our tent and Map had cowered with fear at the base of the ground. No one was safe from the royal wrath at this moment. Thomas whispered into Henry's ear and immediately the King smiled. They both threw back their heads and laughed then headed for the royal pavilion.

"You are forgiven," the King said absently to the cowering nervous servant, "but make sure that you follow us and see that we are not disturbed."

"He is a veritable maniac," Walter whispered, "I am going to seek safer shelter, my diary does not need filling this badly. I had no idea the royal enclosure was this dangerous. It is bad when bishops are dressed down in public."

"Stay where you are," I commanded him. I needed company now. This scene had unnerved me. If thy come here, I will seek permission from my master to go elsewhere. You are safer here than anywhere."

"Out there is safer," Walter declared, "at least I can get lost in their numbers. It will be seldom that I visit you in the future. Wait until I see Gerald! I wonder what the King and Thomas were talking of now?"

"Why don't you sneak up to the tent side and listen?" I asked maliciously.

He looked at me as if I were bereft of my senses and left quickly. I gathered up a clean set of silver goblets, some clean linen napkins, and a beaker of wine that I had cooling in swirling water. I knew what the King and my master were doing. I would never give Walter Map the pleasure of knowing. I knew also why the King was so insistent on keeping all doors closed and visitors out when he was in quarters. They were discussing the King's favorite sport – women. I announced myself to the steward who announced me and I was bidden to enter.

One has to see the royal tents on tour to believe them. They are not tents so one would know them. There were kitchen tents, receiving apartments, and sleeping quarters. What made things so miserable for me was that master's number and sizes of tents exceeded the Kings. They were enormous and a great deal of trouble. It took half the army to set up and strike the baggage of the ecclesiastics and leaders. As I wandered from one end of the vast royal tent to the other, which I deliberately did in order to hear as much as I could, I could not help but notice the dirty and somewhat inferior carpets and appointments, however the good taste of the Queen was, which they represented. The appointments were in pastel pinks, yellow, and greens, those favored by the southern Aquitanians, definitely not the positive reds, blues, and mauves favored by the English. The King cared little or nothing for his surroundings. He entered them with muddy or dirty clothes, on horseback, and with his dogs.

"I have the entire bevy back there, Thomas," he laughed, "all new local beauties. Shall I present them?"

"If you please, sire, but remember, my answer is no to any of them."

"As ever, as ever," said the King excitedly and clapped his hands. He did not notice or acknowledge my presence. To him I was not as important as a favorite dog. I was thoroughly shocked at what I saw. Twelve bodies with the skirts tied over their heads and their legs stockinged, slowly twirled before our eyes.

"I furnish the stockings," the King explained to the reclining Thomas, "these village people are as careless with their skins as I am with my hands. That is why I cover their legs because the sight of open sores revolts me. I give them the stockings, thus my stewards turn back dozens of applicants when I advertise for a bedding partner. Choose one, dear heart," he urged my master, "you like green. Take that one in the pale green hose. She is plump and tender. I will choose second after you."

"I do not choose, my liege lord," Thomas said with gentle finality because he had told me many times that the King respected his refusal of women and never pressed, although the King would never choose a woman until my master had seen her first. Thomas often said it was a wearying thing to constantly refuse the person whom he loved the most.

This was one of the reasons that Henry the Second was envied by all the European monarchs. He had a Chancellor who was faithful to him regardless of how violently they disagreed on policy or personnel and Thomas Becket had reputation through Christendom for chastity and incorruptibility. The King signaled for the girls to withdraw and told his steward carelessly that he would have the green legs tonight.

"Not tonight," he corrected himself hastily, "now. I am in such a state of anticipation that I cannot wait."

I poured the wine, bowed low, and left. They were sipping slowly as I returned to the tent to begin the wearisome task of final selections for packing.

CHAPTER 27

We campaigned ceaselessly against the Welsh or journeyed throughout the kingdom that year. It was continuum of packing, unpacking, or signing documents everywhere we went. I became thoroughly tired of supervising the securing of sand to dry the ink or seeing that adequate quills were on hand for writing. We often had to furnish the King's household since he very carelessly supervised his stewards. My master did all easily and without complaint. He constantly returned to his permanent abode and saw to the supervision of the noble children who had been placed in his house for training. He was strict with their manners and learning. He required that all students be taught to read and write as quickly as possible and that all attend him at meals. The honor students go to sit at his right and left during eating times and it was seldom that the boisterous young Prince Henry got to sit near him. The King had finally become weary of the road and promised to settle at Westminister for at least three months when word reached us that his father had died in Rouen.

The legalists of the court hastily departed for the funeral to represent the King who was too obligated to attend, and to see that his father's will was probated adequately. They returned to tell the King that his brother, Geoffrey of Anjou, was pleading for the Normandy possessions, which Geoffrey claimed that King Henry had agreed to before his father's death. The King publicly denied this agreement as such, so there was nothing to do but assemble an army to put down rebellion on the continent and to pacify the rebellious Anjou.

This was done handily but the city of Nantes received the brother which satisfied him somewhat. While on the continent, my master began negotiation for the marriage of Margaret, Princess of France, and the young Henry, heir to the throne of the Angevin Empire. We returned home to begin the preparations for an embassy to the Capetian capital. That was one journey to remember. It took six ships three days to ferry us across the channel. We looked like a veritable army on the move.

There were twenty wagons in the van pulled by the most perfect mules that France could offer. In these vans were gifts for the French King of costly furs, jewelry, and fine linens made in the country of England. There were two vans composed of casks which contained the fine wine made from corn in our country which the French were particularly addicted to. One van carried my master's chapel, one carried his kitchen utensils. Two hundred boys were dressed in hunter's green and marched along singing our national songs. Each wagon was guarded by a yeoman who was accompanied by fierce mastiffs because the French enjoyed a reputation of being notorious thieves. There is not accounting for the number of esquires and nobles who attended Thomas Becket just for the novelty of the trip, and all were accompanied by their personal servants. I counted sixty-five destriers that belonged to the nobility. The embassy covered a great length of the road, forcing ordinary travelers to the side. My master and some of his most intimate friends brought up the rear of this unbelievable entourage. He was dressed, as usual in cut velvet, the exterior being a purplish blue, while his pants, coat, and hat were of the lightest blue possible. Even the boots he wore today, were dyed to match the outside of his cape.

The French peasants stood agape as we passed, and the French King, being informed of the advancing army, hurried out and ordered all the Parisian vendors to furnish us with free food and drink. He did this in order to impress us with his largesse. My master, becoming apprised of this, sent his purchasing agents abroad and bought adequate food for his entire company, and in this manner, he astounded the French court.

Thomas absolutely overwhelmed the French King and the marriage was completed with the permission to take the infant girl to a castle on the border between Normandy and France where she could be reared in the proper manner by Robert of Newburgh and his good wife. Louis of France gave his daughter a magnificent portion of his northern possessions as her dowry. While journeying to the castle, the people of the countryside petitioned my master to ride them of a notorious local baron who was robbing and terrorizing the countryside. My master took his fighting men and easily subdued the recalcitrant and ordered Baron Newburgh to lock the highwayman in his dungeon for five years.

"He will be wiser, sadder, and older," laughed Thomas to Newburgh who was waneschal to all Normandy, "and I'm sure a bit less anxious to commit crimes for which he cannot defend himself."

We were surprised to find that the Norman people were unhappy with the tax that had been levied to secure young Henry's marriage. Some of the traveling English churchmen told us the same thing was true in England.

"I don't worry about such trifling matters," Thomas said to me testily one night as I was preparing him for bed, "we will be home in a few days and I will issue orders in the King's name to cease the grumbling lest reprisals follow to satisfy the discontented."

The next day, the Bishop of Mont-Saint-Michal, the monastery of Saint-Michael-in-Peril-of-the-Sea, visited us and informed my master that King Henry had given his assent and made arrangements for the marriage between Mary, the Abbess of Romsey, the daughter of King Stephen, and Matthew, the son of the Count of Bologna. My master was more than perturbed.

"This cannot be done," he stormed as he paces back and forth waiting for the ship's small boat to come to us so that we could be ferried to the ship, "it is against all ecclesiastical law. She is a dedicated daughter of Christ and her vows, unless she is declared unfit and incapable by a court of her peers, are confirmed and cannot be abrogated by any man. This is a violation of all that is secular and temporal. It will endanger the souls of all concerned. The King is wrong. He lets his desires to establish his family securely, override his better judgment. I must needs hurry and counsel him against such."

"I would feel it is too late for that," the Bishop said with finality, "the Pope's permission has been secured to unveil the nun and the banns have been published for three weeks as is required by law. The King has expressed his desire that the marriage take place immediately."

"Woe is me," Thomas said as he clutched his hair and stepped into the small craft, "row you sinners, row. Goodbye good Bishop," he said hastily, "I must needs be on my way to attempt to avert further disasters."

"You speak as if you commanded the kingdom," the Bishop spoke tartly."

"I do not," said Thomas resignedly, "but you speak as if you approved and abetted this action."

"I did," the Bishop spoke stoutly and with resolution.

"Your position is in jeopardy," Thomas warned him, "because if ever there arises a question as to your ability, I warn you, I will show you no mercy when it comes to your downgrading and removal from office."

"You are only a lowly layman," returned the Bishop hotly, "you are only in the lowest of minor orders. The Archdeaconry of Canterbury is yours because you were capable of mesmerizing the failing Archbishop. You conduct the King's worldly affairs, the Church will look after its own."

"I only ask you to beware," Thomas said offhandedly, "anyone connected with this affair is doomed to degradation and humiliation. God be with you," he raised his hand in farewell as the oarsmen bore us rapidly to the waiting ship.

"God grant you a safe journey," the Bishop called and he gave us his sign of benediction.

The ships were spread across the horizon. All would reach England safely within a few hours. Six of the ships of this fleet were my mater's own property and he paid for their maintenance and the salaries of the sailors out of his own income. I could clearly remember him offering the King the use of one of them when we sailed to subdue Geoffrey. The King remarked that it was a remarkably well disciplined crew who saw to his every comfort and made the crossing enjoyable. We landed just as the sun was setting and set out rapidly to locate the court. The King sent for my master immediately, stating that he was to eat, bathe, and sleep that night in his presence. The King evidently enjoyed seeing Thomas take a perfumed bath in hot water and putting on fine silks of many colors to sleep in. The next day was full of tension and quarrel.

"But sire, it is not so bad that they marry, as it is a violation of the vows made to the church. You know the law is that sacred oaths must not be broken. I know that the Pope has yielded to you and why should he not? You and Louis of France are his mainstays. Were it not for you two, he might perhaps be a wanderer on this earth. Everyone in Christendom knows that his income and security rests on your good will towards him. Only your strength and reputation as a warrior hold the German Emperor in check.

That is not the issue. I do not wish you to place your soul in jeopardy."

"Oh Thomas," the King said wearily as I spread a clean linen napkin on the table for two. I placed a new rose that still retained its morning dew in a silver vase no larger in diameter than my middle finger, in the middle of the table. I placed two clean wooden platters opposite each other and motioned the servants to bring forward the smoking food. There were smoking herring and bubbling kidneys to tempt my master's finicky appetite. I had ordered the cook to prepare small, hot, wheat cakes to eat with the meat. The fruit was fresh and polished and the cheese was pungent. The King sat down and began to wolf food unconcernedly. My master picked delicately at a portion of meat that I placed on his plate and smiled at me understandingly. The King horrified us all as he picked up the sweating wine pitcher and poured for himself. He could be guilty of gross manners when he wished. His advisors stood at a good distance in the corner of the hall. He could get very angry when anyone disturbed him in a conversation with my master. "I have broken no laws. I have done what I thought best. "True, I did not consult you on the matter, but you were on travel and it would have been next to impossible to have contacted you."

"I am not questioning your actions in the lawful sense," Thomas spoke to him smiling sweetly, "there is not ruler in all the world who knows the law better than you, and there is no legalist who can hold you a candle in administration or interpretation of the law, but sire, we live under the beneficence of God, and I take seriously promises made to our Maker. You have offended the Supreme Being as well as the Church. These matters cannot be taken lightly, since they override worldly matters. A nun cannot be unveiled to become a figure in state diplomacy. That is contrary to all that we believe and all that we teach our children and subjects."

"I have no intentions in violating my oaths to God," Henry said sullenly, "you can always manage to put me in a bad light. I am no ogre who contests the validity of oaths, but I must administer my kingdom as I see fit. You know we need other continental connections that are friendly to us other than those we possess."

"Did not the question of consanguinity arise?" Thomas asked him, "They are distant cousins, you know."

"It is not serious," Henry told him, "Matthew is a child by the Count's previous wife. They are only related on the male side and it is too distant to pursue."

"You tread on unsound ground, my lord," Thomas said, "I fear for you."

"Fear not," Henry said aroused to anger as he dashed the dregs from his wine cup in anger, "many of your church laws were made by men who really were not intelligent but survived because they were superior politicians. You nor anyone else can prove that they are the laws of God, therefore, I take the stand that what is made by man can be unmade by man, and I find a weak and greedy and ambitious Churchman to be the most pliable of all. A small threat accompanied by generous donations of money can subdue even the most hostile Churchman. Invariably, their greed overcomes their scruples, and fear of displacement from their high offices makes them most pliable."

"My king," Thomas said aghast, "you speak in a manner bordering on heresy. You have heard overmuch the teachings of Peter Abelard and Arnold of Brescia. Your cousin, the German Emperor speaks much in the same manner and one day the Papacy will wreak its vengeance on that stubborn and willful man."

"Frederick Barbarossa will also wreak his vengeance on that insipid, supine Pope if I do not support him," said Henry becoming more perturbed, "he is still a man who dreads the feel of hunger, confinement, and the lash. His effete body could scarcely survive the denial of the finest of garments, food, and bedding. I know men too well my beloved friend to sell them short. I appeal to their bases desires and they become mere putty in my hands. That is the strength of a ruler and I feel that my decision in this case is just as correct, just as justifiable, and in the interests of my kingdom as is Eugenious' about the crimes of the Barbarossa. It is only a question of interpretation. I will not contest the Bible or its Holy sayings," Henry assured my master quickly, "but I sure as I am born give any man's utterances Hell if I do not agree. Mary of Blois was not great shakes as a num. She was given the position as Abbess so the convent could milk Stephen of awards and money. I consider that a gross violation of what the Church stands for. If the Pope and the prelates of the Church can condone blatant nepotism, then my decisions of policy and polity are reasonably sound."

"I cannot win," Thomas smiled wearily, "you have said nothing of my success with the Capetian. It was not easy, yet it was much easier than I expected."

"My poor and opponent, honorable as he is, is a simple man," smiled Henry. He motioned a clerk to come forward with a sheaf of papers. "Here is my answer to your good work. In here, I think you will find ample reward."

"Your expression of appreciation is more than enough reward for me," Thomas told him sincerely.

"That's why I love you so," Henry bounded up nervously, "I must be up and about. There are mountains of correspondence waiting for you to review and sign. Do not bother me with it. Dispatch it all. And Thomas," he came to where my master was rising and kissed him full on the lips as would a child kiss his father, "do hurry with the work. I wish to hunt. We will ride far and wide, just the two of us with only enough retainers to see that we have shelter and food to eat. Hurry! It has been too long that I have been from you! I crave your company and conversation. "But remember," he frowned darkly, "no more weary talk of that silly little marriage that brings me so much security on my northern continental borders. It is done, my heart, and I will not undo it, not even for you whom I love so dearly. Would you have me pitch one of my epileptic fits for your benefit? I can easily, you know. I have been a good and diligent ruler in your absence and it would release many tensions for me to lie down, roll on the ground and chew on straw. In fact, I feel that a senseless rage might relieve the anxieties of my toadying courtiers in the corner. It would furnish them with entertainment for months to come. By the way, who are those men who write so busily? I can't recall their being court scribes. Are they yours? Do you conduct crown business at all times?"

"I might do so for the next few months, until I catch up," smiled Thomas, "but those are not official clerks of the kingdom. They are biographers and chroniclers of events. One is Walter Map and the other is Gerald of Wales. Both are skilled in the art of writing. They are gossipers, I fear, but they also are amazingly adept at recording people, things, and places. I sponsor them, my liege lord, because I feel that posterity might wish to look at you as you are. I would be remiss if I did not leave something of my great and wonderful king for future generations to see. After all, there is and will ever be, only one Henry, the Second of his line to rule England. Only one Anjou who rises above all, and only one great Plantagenet that all men must know about. I feel it is my responsibility to secure that image and leave records that all might see. You belong to history and the ages, my fabulous King."

Henry stood perplexed. This outrageous flattery was beyond him. He was profuse in rendering to his Chancellor, but he was suspicious when it was returned.

"If it was anyone else on God's green earth saying these maudlin things," he told Thomas hesitantly, "I would grab him by the throat and shake him until his teeth would rattle."

"However fulsome they might be, I mean them all," Thomas spoke to him smilingly, "I am your man and I will defend that right to the death. My every function in life is to glorify my master."

The King came to him and grabbed him passionately by the hand.

"You are too real to be unbelievable, but you leave me tongue tied, you silver tongued counselor. Best you hurry and mount your administrative accumulations. Else I will be forced to come and take you bodily with me. I am urgent that my kingdom be administered without pause, but I intensely desire to ride, ride, ride. My energies overwhelm me. I am called to the hunt. Hurry, dammit, hurry."

"It will be as you demand," Thomas bowed to him easily, "I will have screened the most urgent matters within the hour. My personal secretary is at this moment sorting the material, so I cannot sign with little or no trouble. Have your best and swiftest mounts saddled my lord, and unleash your trustiest hounds. We ride! All England will thunder to this chase."

"I am not letting those fat and wheezing Bishops go," the King whispered to him as he grinned wickedly, "only the hardiest common servants will attend us. It is not the day even for the nobility. There will be much grumbling but also much relief. Bring only a few of your best men. No high born people to weary us with demands for suitable accommodations when we bed for the night. This is yours and my hunt, Thomas, no one else's."

"It will be as you say, sweet King."

Henry left the hall hurriedly, beckoning his entire entourage to follow him. He would call on the Queen, check the royal children, and unceremoniously prepare to scourge the countryside looking for all and any game. Relays of fresh horses would be available and I already felt pity for my tired and aching rump that would feel the uneven rhythm of a bumping, tired horse. They would ride all the day, through rain and sunshine, and regardless of how tired as I might become, I must needs see that my masters' food was properly prepared, his clothing cleaned and dried, his body dried and warm, and his bed soft enough for sleeping. This was a delicate creature in my charge, and the responsibility for his health was an awesome task at times.

CHAPTER 28

The King became very annoyed at the constant rebellion on the continent and he became obsessed with the idea of conquering all the land south of Aquitaine and north of the Pyrennes. In this, he held that he could successfully contain the ambitions of the French King as well as obliterate what he termed a breeding ground for rebellion. His, the Queen's, and my masters' counsels were long.

"I tell you, it can and must be done. I must have Toulouse, that great city that controls the southern part of my kingdom," the King would begin the conversation.

"My former husband's present wife's sister is the wife of the Count of Toulouse. He is your suzerain," the Queen informed him.

"I know that," the King returned, "but I showed that silly man who was boss of the continent when he married the second time. He did not realize what it was to annoy me. I married his daughter to my son and secured her dowry which was a land mass six times the size of his petty little isle."

"That was a smart maneuver," agreed Queen Eleanor, "but the Frenchman is more alert to you, now. He has always hated you for marrying me, and not that you have five children by me, he dislikes you even more. I lay claim to Toulouse, because my father, Count Raymond of Toulouse and Aquitaine actually meant to leave me that city and its environs but my half-brother or uncle, as you would have it, moved in quickly at the news of father's death and invested the place. He is very strong in his position and possession is nine tenths of the law. It would take many years to acquire it through litigation, and even if you did, he would fight. I know him."

"You should, the King returned tartly, "is he not the famous uncle referred to in your divorce suit?"

"Would you reproach me with that that has no foundation in fact?" the Queen asked him in a hostile voice, "yes, if you insist on reviving dead issues, he was the one, but do not concern yourself my love. He wanted to sleep with me, badly, but he didn't. I've always been in control of any situation wherever I was, even with you. I could go to him now, if I chose. After all, it is still my land and there are many gallants awaiting the call to fight my cause."

"Oh, Eleanor, you were always the intemperate bitch," Henry said wearily, "no man, if you want to call those female looking freaks at your famous Court of Love, men, are waiting to fight for you. Sleep with you perhaps, but not fight. Why those funny looking feminine churls wouldn't fight a man, they would end up making love to him."

"There are many there who can take your measure whenever you are in the mood to try it," she flared back at him. "Don't anger me my lord, lest I flee this accursed wet island climate for the sunnier climes of my true home. It would not take much to prod me to leave."

"Dare you leave, you hellish cat, I will clip your claws by letting you reside in the Tower," he returned.

"You didn't speak to me in this manner when you wanted control of my inheritance," she said with tears in her eyes, "now, I feel that all you want of me is for a brood mare."

"You've served me well in that capacity," Henry admitted ruefully.

"I have not been adequate as I well know," Eleanor said with spirit, "I thought I was swapping a eunuch for a stud but evidently you are the type of stallion that must have more than one female in your pasture. I know of Rosamund de Clifford, my lord. I have interviewed her. Her type does not live long, neither do her bastards. What a mewling, sickening creature she is. Oh, I know, you see her as a tall, statuesque English beauty who is all peaches and cream, but I assure you before I left her, she was all curdled whey. Trying to remain the lady and looking stricken! What an act. Bedding was every rutting male who wanders near her bower. It wouldn't surprise me that she has slept with every lackey that you have so carelessly left to guard her precious reputation and beauty."

"How now, woman," Henry said astounded, "I know of your meddling, and I allowed it because you are a Queen and a woman. I have not tried overly to conceal her. But lay away woman, don't tamper with the royal prerogative. Why, I wouldn't even let my beloved Thomas enter into that realm. It is too warm and too personal."

"Your beloved Thomas, forsooth," swore Eleanor becoming really angry, "he is nothing more than a glorified pimp, serving a lascivious master who knows no bounds nor considerations. Your precious Thomas can go straight to hell, my King!"

"Now, now, good wife, mother of my daughters and sons," the King chucked her under the chin, "you are fascinating when you get your anger up. And you fascinate me. Careful, lest I bed you here in public. Then you would be shamed forever more."

"You would be surprised how little shame would come to me, you wicked bull, at least I know of one way I can conquer you," she lowered her eyes and gave him a lustful, inviting feline look, "tonight, I feel strong as a lioness. I could conquer the monster of Minos."

Both threw back their heads in unleashed animal fashion, hugely enjoying their joke, their anger forgotten and forgiven. Henry pulled Eleanor to him and gave her a wet, long lasting kiss.

"Do I kiss my mistress like that?" he asked as he leered at her.

"No you don't," she laughed at him, "if you did, she would have been dead a long time ago. I have let her live to get that boy of hers by you on the road to good health, then I shall take him to rear him with his other brothers and sisters, then that bitch will go to a lime covered grave. She is only good for fertilizer anyway, so good riddance to bad rubbish."

"Would you deny me variety and challenge, my Queen?" Henry asked as he tugged her yielding body closer to him.

"No," she answered, blowing on a nail and buffing it against her flowing garments and posturing alluringly with her hips, "not as long as you move fast enough that my long arm of jealousy cannot reach them. I do not have time to dislike dead females. Especially whores. And don't tell me that they aren't," she pouted at him as she placed her finger over his mouth to keep him from speaking. "No unmarried woman who willingly yields to a man is other than a whore. The Church has taught even you that much. I just consider myself the instrument of the Lord's when it comes eliminating women who threatened my supremacy with the great King Henry the Second of England. If all good wives followed my methods, there would be little adultery."

"What a funny theory for a supposedly Christian woman," Henry told her through pressed lips.

"But extremely practical," she said as she pressed closely to him and bit his ear lobe severely.

The King reared. Everyone stopped talking and stared. Eleanor swept her dress demurely aside and placed her hand on the King's arm.

"Let us eat my lords," she said loudly, "chamberlain, announce the meal. I council better on a full stomach."

She and the King led the assemblage from their council room to the dining hall. I thought this was a pity, because everyone was settled and ready to offer advice to the crown. The aged Archbishop was assisted by my master who had sat through all the preceding action and conversation without opening his mouth. The King seated the Queen on his left and Thomas on his right. He reached over with his hunting knife and speared the roast pig from my master's plate and rudely picked up the roast chicken from his and placed it on Thomas'. He was ever doing this. He explained often that the cooks gave my master the best cuts.

All ate silently. The scullions scurried back and forth filling trenchers, replacing exhausted meat platters and literally hurling great loaves of bread on the table at appointed intervals. After all had eaten their fill, the King excused the lesser men and the royal children. The servants quickly cleared the tables of food remnants and brought fresh cloths. My master particularly ordered that they do this. They also brought fresh washed drinking vessels for all. The King never would have done this. Neither would the Queen. They generally pushed the food away from them, cleared enough space to place their elbows and held their councils there and then. My master insisted on the ceremony of clearing the table and the laying of clean linen. Tonight he ordered that small warm orange scented bowls of water be placed before everyone and clean napkins furnished.

"I cannot abide the foul odors of stale greasy food," he explained to no one in particular, "if I could, I would bathe my hands and face after every meal."

"Bring a large bowl of warm water," ordered the King.

"Wash your master's hands and face," the King ordered me, "I'm sure you do it for him in private. Do so now. I will not sit idly by and have my Thomas unhappy."

I silently did as I was told. The Queen ordered her maid servants to do the same thing for her. The King picked his teeth with his hunting knife as he observed them. I rubbed my master's hands and face with a sweet smelling ointment brought from the East which I kept constantly on hand.

"Now that all is under control," the King said with finality and sat forward with a fresh cup of wine in his hand, "let us proceed with council."

"Hot up the fire," the Queen ordered the chamberlain, "I feel chill."

"Excuse me, madam," the King said solicitously, it is early June, but I forget your southern blood demands heat."

"Thank you, my lord," she said modestly.

"Gentlemen," the King began and all the barons and churchmen leaned forward to catch his every word. I intend to lay claim to my wife's inheritance of Toulouse with fire and sword if necessary. I will accept any suggestions from anyone on how this can be accomplished. I will tell you frankly, it is chiefly a matter of money. The country still smarts from the tax laid on for the recent royal marriage. The coffers are nearly empty but I must take what is legally mine."

No one said anything. All sat in deep contemplation. My master raised his head for attention.

"The only sensible way to get money for this matter is to tax. It is becoming more and more apparent that Englishmen do not like to leave their homes and fight. Especially during a long peaceful period such as this. They will almost be willing to pay any amount to avoid unnecessary military service. There is an old ancient tax called shield money or scutage that has not been levied in a long time. It is legal because kings before us have levied it periodically and there are no records that prove that there was discontent over its payment. This tax would suffice if --," he hesitated.

"If what, my bright and shining knight?" queried the King breathlessly, "I do believe you have hit on the answer to my problem. What a day!"

"If the old tax is doubled and everyone pays it," Thomas explained.

"To double it would bring in an enormous sum," explained the King wonderingly, "what a man, what a brain I possess," the King explained to all.

"What do you mean that all will pay?" asked Archbishop Theobald.

"Just what I say, your reverence," Thomas said levelly, "All, the Church included."

"What?" roared Gilbert Foliot, the Bishop of London, "the Church holds no fealty to the crown or anyone to pay for wars."

"The Church holds knights fees and services to the crown," Thomas said evenly, "the enormous lands and revenues were awarded to the Church from time to time by a King, surely it is not too much for a King to ask for an occasional return for his investment. This is not an unreasonable amount, and it will pay mercenaries to fight instead of uprooting hardworking, home loving Englishmen," he smiled wickedly, "who willingly pay taxes."

"It will be difficult to collect from the Church," Archbishop warned, "we are legally correct in our stand against fighting."

"It will not be difficult if the King elects to expel or incarcerate every recalcitrant Churchman," Thomas smiled gently at the old man, "the convents and monasteries cover our land the same as does the famous English dew. They are the majority owners, let them pay the majority prices."

"You traitor," bellowed Foliot, "this is the same as plunging a sword into the bowels of the mother Church."

"Not that vividly," Thomas answered him, "this will perhaps make the Church less fat and more hungry. It will not be so eager in the future to grasp at inheritances and unneeded property. It will free your people for saving souls and less from collecting money, which incidentally, leaves England and goes to Rome."

"Hear! Hear!" the King roared in glee as he pounded the table with his scepter for attention, "hear he, heed the council of my Chancellor. He has spoken as I would speak. His very words are my words and they will neither be disobeyed nor disputed. Di Luci! Leicester!" he roared, "step forward and get your instructions."

The barons came immediately before him and stood limply.

"It is your duty, as you well know, to get dispatches out to every sheriff in the land, instructing them to start collecting the scutage tax. Exempt no one. No one, do you understand? It will be Thomas' duty to enforce any difficult people you encounter. Do not tarry with delayed payments. Collect! Collect! I would have my treasury filled and audited by August. Turn over any reluctant payee to my Chancellor. He has full authority to render justice. Now be about yourselves my good men."

"The ever brilliant and resourceful Chancellor," Eleanor said wearily, "what would we do without him? I will tell you," she grabbed Henry's arm cruelly with her talon-like fingernails, "we can retire to the continent to our special little bowere and let this commoner be King! He is anyway."

"What do you mutter about, woman?" the distracted and pained King turned on her.

"If you would allow me to retire," she asked demurely, "I am tired and would prepare myself for bed."

"Go, go," the King waved at her abstractedly as she curtsied to him.

"I am sorry madam if I have offended in any manner," Thomas rose, clasped her hand and bowed low over it.

"You haven't offended, you necromancer, you never do," she smiled wearily, "but you always somehow manage to win. I have always thought it was left to a female to use guile and be wily, but with you, dear Chancellor, no one can compete especially for the favors of the King. I am married to him in name and in body, but you are married to him in heart and spirit. Be careful, do not anger me. If I thought you might at any time rival me to separate me forever from my lord, I would administer to you such a dose of foxglove that you would not awaken when Gabriel sounds his trumpet. I yield and I yield, when will it ever cease?"

"The King leads a happy life with you as his wife, I assure you," Thomas said sincerely.

"He leads a happy life with you as his man, I assure you also," she said a little bitingly.

"I do not mean to intrude, my lady Queen."

"I'm sure you don't, but you do a good job of entrancing him."

"I am his servant and do his orders."

"Yes you are, and yes you do, go and fight well, win for him Toulouse and I hope you win for yourself a nice, large well aimed spear right through your fashionable middle." She turned and left the hall before he could answer. John of Salisbury came up to his elbow.

"You do wrong my old friend," John said severely, "it is wrong to molest the Church."

"The Church is not being molested," Thomas spoke to him severely, "it is not wrong to ask them to pay some small return for all the years that they have accumulated."

"It is wrong, it is wrong," John said solemnly.

"It is wrong because it threatens your security," Thomas said sarcastically, "you have been reared and supported by the Church all your livelong life. If you had to get out in life and compete, you would be lost. Take care, John, do not wax too malicious. If you lose your income you will know true hunger because you cannot survive without Church income."

"What does this mewling clerk say?" demanded the King.

Thomas turned to the King smiling. Theobald moved up taking John firmly by the arm. Theobald smiled benignly on Thomas.

"Does he never do anything to anger you and the King?" John burst forth intemperately, "must everything that is said be said by him? Must all decisions in this great Empire be made by him? All people are infallible, you know. This tax is a great, great mistake. The people will rebel or be reduced to utter poverty. The Church will be reduced to its knees."

"No one can criticize my Chancellor as such," said the King menacingly, "I forbid your attendance at court," he rasped at John, "and if you anger me further, you will be expelled from the kingdom. I will throw you on the tender mercies of the German Emperor. He burned Arnold of Brescia for less. Begone you annoyance! Never let me set eyes on you again. If so, I might become violent. Leave this house I say!"

John fell back aghast, suddenly beginning to realize the enormity of his mistake. He would have graveled but the firm old Archbishop and Thomas refused to let him. The Archbishop led him from the dining hall. The King linked his arm in Thomas' who bent down to him and repeated a witticism in his ear. The King roared and they strolled into the great hall as lovers, leaving behind them small groups discussing the tax excitedly or angrily as the composition of the aggregations dictated.

CHAPTER 29

The campaign of Toulouse proved a failure and it heightened discord between my master and the King and between the Queen and the King. We easily crossed the hostile territory claimed both by the Angevins and the Toulousans. The walls of the city were not impregnable and my master was eager to divest the city.

"I will not enter," Henry said sullenly, "I have heard that Louis is in the city and he is my suzerain in Normandy. It would be against all the laws of man and nature."

"Those ideas are going fast, my liege, "Thomas said eagerly, "I am not his suzerain, neither is he mine, I am an Englishman, a citizen of the Angevin Empire. I fight the good fight of the Plantagenet. I owe no one obligations here. I have put into the field seven mounted knights with their retainers and five thousand foot soldiers at my own expense for this campaign. I beg of you my lord, let me take the city. I will bring the insipid French King and the haughty Raymond of Toulouse kneeling to your feet. I will make them swear eternal fealty to you. All this smiling land will be yours. The delicious wines that are fermented in this country will grace your table every day of your life."

"You know as well as I do that a man sworn to fealty to another does not break his oath, whatever the provocation," Henry said patiently, "I desire this land as much as any I have ever seen. It would form a perfect buffer between and France."

"We all know of what you speak," Eleanor said wearily, "what antiquated ideas men can latch onto and use for an excuse not to fight. I am surprised at you, my King, for evading so important an issue on such a flimsy excuse."

"My excuse is not poor," Henry exploded, "I will not be badgered by a commoner and a loose hipped woman into committing an act for which all civilized nations would condemn me. No, dammit, I will not enter. Cease your chatter, Thomas, and madam, belie you to your infamous Court of Love and let your pent up emotions loose in some insipid, bawdy song, sung by some spindly legged, mewling coward. I think I will return to Normandy, visit my mother the Empress and return to England. May the scrawny little Capet and that obstreperous uncle of yours, rot in hell. Should I catch his ass abroad, he will never live to see this obnoxious city that blocks my access to the south!"

"How wearisome," Queen Eleanor yawned, "this then, is goodbye for now. I will travel without delay. I long for the comforts of my palace and for news of the world. At least I will rest for a few weeks in my own Heaven on earth."

"Mind you," warned the King, "start or foment no rebellions. My mood is deadly and I could watch the execution of many and not regret it. The Tower always awaits uncontrollable Queens and I am prone to use it if need be."

The Queen snatched her horse in the opposite direction without a word. Little did the King know that she was pregnant by him for the fifth time.

"I father no bastards by any man," the King yelled vulgarly after his wife's retreating back. She turned and waved gaily and sat very straight as her flowing garments of pale pink and green softly billowed about her.

"A fine woman," Henry told Becket congenially, "but oh so headstrong. She would have her way with any man if he allowed it. She is a born Queen but too strong minded for her own good. She must be watched as one watches a wild animal at all times. I don't believe she would breed with just any man, but she can constantly create the impression that she is in heat. That king of woman is fine to have around if you can take the time to bed her frequently so that she will stay in hand."

"You are so correct as usual about all women," Thomas smiled patiently, "but my mind is for the fight. If not here, somewhere. I have never before had the chance to prove my mettle. I am not particularly liked in the court by the members and I feel that this would be the chance to show them of what I am made."

"I regret that I cannot let you take Toulouse," Henry said sincerely and apologetically, "but you can fight up and down these damn marches as much as you please. In order to make it official, I order you to do so. Whip anything that moves, especially any man who swears allegiance to Louis. I will more than reward you for any accomplishment, large or small, but you don't have to fight to prove yourself to me, dear Thomas. I am happy with you just as you are, and if I hear any criticism leveled at you, they will feel the effect of my flat broadsword, be he bishop of serf. But fight, man, bring peace to my borders. Pacify the bastards. Make them love the Plantagenet. I would have the House of Anjou overlord of all Europe and the East also."

"Thank you, my King," Thomas answered him happily, "I will do all I can."

"Take care," warned the King, "I would have no mishap come to you. I think I will ride north this very day. It is beautiful and dry. If I make good time I can be with the Empress in two days. I need her counsel badly. Nothing official, mind you, and it is nothing that I am keeping from you. Every man needs the comforting voice of his mother from time to time. I am sorry that you have none."

"I too," smiled Thomas sadly, "but I will secure the peace of these frontiers, then join you wherever you are, or if you send for me."

"You are my military governor here, you have the power of life and death over anyone who contests you," the King said.

He gave a long halloo and his chamberlains and barons came galloping to him. He gave the order to ride and his vast army was on the move with little effort. The military captains would dissolve the mercenaries as they rode along. This system was proving successful beyond the wildest dreams of the King and the Chancellor. All Europe was agog with the idea of hiring fighting men and keeping food production up at home. It was revolutionary. Thomas had tried the idea already for the King by using Welshmen for fighting the French and vice versa. This gave him ample opportunity to see if the system could be applied to any nationality. It was wonderful. The loose Flemings, Milanese, Bolognese, Aquitanians, Danes, and Germans answered the call to fight for pay with alacrity and in adequate numbers. They were very controllable, also, with their loyalty only to the King and not to some great baron on whose estates they lived.

My master gave instructions that his army would move up to the north and east along the Garonne River. Here he would establish camp and pacify any insurgent areas that came to his attention. The French drew up an army across the river. The air between the opposing forces grew tense with the approaching certainty that there would be a fight. A huge, towering knight of a somewhat formidable local reputation sallied forth on his side of the river.

"I challenge your puny, effeminate commander," he roared, "I will tie a woman's skirt around his hips and make with the horse."

My master ordered Baron Walter de Holingshead to answer the braggart in turn and arrange the challenge to be accepted at sunrise the following morning.

"Begin the combat," my master roared to the opposing knight Serge de Tralier and they rode at each other full tilt. I trembled as the early morning sunlight glinted from the perfectly burnished armor of my master as he thundered toward his opponent. Generally, these tilting charges are battles more of horses than they are of men. The brute force of the fighting destriers was something to dread by a man on foot and they could maneuver very well for their size. De Tralier's horse was the superior in every sense so my master had to help his lighter and wearer mount. As the lances at rest met, my master shifted his body and the Frenchman's lance glanced from him swinging high into the air, sending both man and horse off balance. The Chancellor quickly dropped his lance which he had hardly attempted to use and wheeled his horse quickly and charged at the off balance man and horse with his wickedly swinging mace. He struck his opponent a blow squarely on the chest and the knight tumbled to the ground in an almost unbelievable easy fashion. He was now at the mercy of my master's wicked broadsword which he unsheathed as if by magic.

Thomas Becket majestically straddled the dazed warrior and put his sword point at his throat. The fallen man plead for mercy. It was granted.

"You must pledge two things," Becket said, "they will be painful but not undignified."

"Anything, anything," the man lying on the ground muttered.

"Are you the leader of this disaffected group of people?"

"I am the King's general, yes."

"Then you must order your people to stack their arms in the open. Arise, and do so now."

The poor Frenchmen were pathetic in their eagerness to dispose of their fighting weapons. Soon there was a huge pile of bows, pikes, shields, and swords before them.

"Order your forces to withdraw a hundred yards," Becket ordered the conquered Frenchman.

As this was done, a line of our armed men quickly crossed the river and interposed themselves between the defeated and their arms.

"Now search their persons, their baggage, and their billets," the Chancellor ordered, "they are not to retire with one offensive weapon. When that is done transport all across the river and pack the weapons to be sent to my King.

Thomas Becket handed the reins of his horse to me. I was the only person besides the Chancellor and the horse's personal ostler who would dare to come near him. He would bite, kick, and trample if a person fell beneath him as he was trained to do so. Today, he almost refused me as I sought to soothe him until the groom came up to lead him away. As it was, he almost engaged in combat with de Tralier's horse who was just as eager to fight as he was to stand. My master went over and forcefully grabbed the reigns of his opponent's horse. The horse attempted to rear and paw, but my master twisted the bit cruelly, and although he was not strong enough to make the horse sit on his haunches, he did make him back up which was impressive, because destriers are not trained nor are they accustomed to retreat. They prefer death to submission. My master mounted the saddle easily after the horse stood quietly.

"This is my prize," he announced proudly, "hand me my lance. This is a man's horse, and I will add him to my stables. He will become famous as the fightingest horse in the Angevin Empire. Go," he ordered the knight who stood in a weary, defeated attitude, "return to your royal master and give him the news that should he choose to resist the Angevins, he will lose all. Your people must return to their homes, to be freed from the obligation of fighting. Take the oath in front of witness."

The entourage of clergy that had stayed with us, and Manassere Biset, the King's personal Dapifer who always stayed with the Chancellor to witness all legal documents, displayed himself prominently in order to show to all the observers that this contract had the blessings of the King. The knight swore to eternal peace and to the release of the fighting forces. He walked dejectedly to his people and ordered their retreat. We heard that Louis put him in the dungeon as punishment for yielding to his social inferior, a commoner. Louis also abrogated the oath immediately and mustered the fighting men back into the ranks.

We had been campaigning in the marches of France for about ten months when all became serene and the hostiles sued for eternal peace. My master came down with the sweating fever. He had never done this before and I feared for his life. Not only did I pray for him, but I sent for an entire troop of Hospitalers and engaged them to nurse him through his illness. I sent a message to the King, imploring him to come, lest it be my master's last days on earth. He came immediately, bringing Louis of France with him. Louis offered his sympathies for a rapid recovery, but Henry came in, brushed the attendants aside, and personally bathed my master's face and hands with scented water and chafed his wrists. He refused to leave his side. The following morning, Thomas seemed to have affected an immediate recovery. The King ordered him moved into the sunny courtyard, protected from the breezes, and they sat there for an hour, smiling at each other and talking in low tones. The King sent word to the French King that they could depart at his wish. The French King came immediately.

"This is my life," Henry said unabashedly to Louis, "better the kingdom lose me than him. I could not wish to live, were not Thomas with me."

My master smiled weakly.

"We must go," the King said to him kindly, "I believe you will recover now. If you receive a setback, I am to know immediately." He looked at me meaningfully as I quaked in my boots. The King had never acknowledged my presence before and I was frankly terror struck to be saddled with so grave a burden.

"I will recover now," Thomas said in a strong voice, "now that I have been near you for a while, your strength will buoy me up."

"That's my man," the King said and kissed him full on the lips. He mounted his horse without another word and the vast train rode away in a cloud of dust.

Within a week, Thomas Becket was his usual self, conducting all the delayed King's business and dispatching orders to all parts of the empire. The King sent word that we were to proceed to Le Mans and join the court for the Christmas celebrations.

"Theobald grows old," Henry told my master as they strolled together among the tents of the royal enclosure," I fear he is failing fast. He has sent me a letter importuning me to send you to him. I cannot spare you now. The order of the kingdom overrides at the moment, any illness short of yours. We have much to do."

"I will do as you command, my lord," Thomas said sincerely, "as ever I have."

They stepped as a messenger stepped to hand Thomas a letter. Without asking the King's permission, he immediately opened it and read it silently.

"It is an urgent letter from John of Salisbury, stating that Theobald pleads with me as his dearly beloved son to come to him before he dies. There is also a veiled hint that I face possible excommunication," he explained to the King who stared at the missive.

"Is not this the same John whom I threatened with expulsion?" the King asked becoming red in the face.

"It is," Thomas told him soothingly, "but do not become angry. John of Salisbury can harm no one, not even with his pen. He is scholarly and we need such men as he. They bring credit on your kingdom."

"I wish the credit," the King said sourly, "but I will not tolerate that snotty scribe to demean me nor will I suffer him to demean, threaten, or order you around. I need you, Thomas, in all seriousness, I need you. The Exchequer must be seen to, there are new laws I wish to promulgate. The Queen and the justiciars can run England. An old, dying man is important, I agree, but the business of the Angevin empire is more so. I need you, do not go. I will not forbid you, because I know the Archbishop has loved you beyond compare and he has always had your interest at heart. I feel sorry about it, but do not go. The interruption would be irreparable."

"I will not leave you," said Thomas gently to the King, "I never have and I never will."

"It is impossible to express my feelings for you," said the King feebly, "I will show proof of my affection and appreciate by ordering the taxes of the provines of Essex, Kent, and Bed be paid into your personal account. I will have ordered for you a bracelet of matching emeralds that will exceed in value the one you are wearing and they will match the piping of your present costume."

"Do not do so, your highness," laughed Thomas, "I have more money than I know what to do with it and you and everyone in the world knows that I spend it freely. My chest of precious stones is so large now that I forget what I own. I intend to clean it out by giving a great number to the princes and princesses to wear."

He stood in the brilliant sunshine in violent contrast to his dun colored king whose beard needed trimming and his clothes were absolutely filthy. Thomas Becket, on the other hand, had on sage green clothes piped in the darkest green. His Spanish leather boots were dyed to match the color of his clothes and they too were edged in dark green. The Angevin leopards rampant, were exquisitely appliquéd on his sleeves and on the back of his extravagantly scalloped cloak. He moved as easily as did the sunlight as he and the King strolled arm in arm beyond earshot.

I was shocked at this callousness on the part of my master. Theobald had been so very good to him and to me. I felt it a sin not to go to see the dying man. We had crossed the channel many times on less pressing matters. I felt that the dying wish of the Archbishop far exceeded in importance a trip across to England just to check on tax payments or how well justice was administered. I went quickly to find a scribe to send John of Salisbury a note warning him to watch his pen and his tongue lest he be banished from England.

CHAPTER 30

We had been on the continent for almost three years, and except for small visits to see that the government of the island was operating properly, we had not returned. This made the terminal illness of the Archbishop the more bitter. Our absences from our native land that was so near became almost a matter of indifference. The turbulence of government lay on the continent because of the pressing concerns of Capetian expansion. We had almost established a permanent residence at Rouen and when on campaigns or itinerary on the continent, we used it as a base. The Chancellor's house was large and commodious. In fact, in size and splendor, it exceeded the houses of the King. The Chancellor's personal staff was much larger than his royal master's, because Thomas Becket required a permanent staff of fifty two secretaries to carry on the correspondence in administering the kingdom. It was seldom now that he referred any matters to the King. His signature with the Great Seal was sufficient to gain the obedience of any baron of the realm, or to have the royal correspondence acceptable to any nation in the world, including the Papal Curia. His word was the word of the King's and any who questioned it, incurred the wrath of Henry Plantagenet.

"The Archbishop is dead," my master told me one day as he came into his private apartments where I was supervising the cleaning and brushing of his magnificent clothing. He owned in excess of twenty changes of raiment and they were so fine that utmost care was needed to keep them in the best of shape. He would become very angry if a spot or careless flaws showed in his dress. A tailor and shoemaker were kept busy supplying him with clothes and necessary footwear. All his apartment floors were carpeted with elegantly processed sheepskins because he abhorred walking on cold, gritty stone. He also hated drafts, so the arrases and drapes were constantly being cleaned, reinforced and sprayed with delicate scents. Nothing was stale or sour in this house as was so common in other great houses, including the King's.

"God bless the great man," I intoned piously crossing myself, "may his soul rest in peace."

"I must needs go to the chapel and light a candle for his soul's repose," he said despondently, "I will make a special novena for him. I wish now I had forced the King to go with me to visit him before he expired. It may be sin that will forever lie on my soul."

"That is not so, my lord," I remonstrated, "you did as you were bid. The Archbishop understood even if he was angered and saddened with your actions. He always held to obedience regardless of the circumstances."

"You are correct, I suppose," he said listlessly, "but we will grow old someday and we will be separated from the able and young. I wonder if Henry will visit me when I take to my death bed. The difference of twelve years in our ages would leave him still agile and young when I am called to my maker. I cannot help but wonder if he will respond to my plea to visit me. If he did not, it would break my heart and I would die the sooner. I hope I have not made a great mistake that will haunt me to the grave."

"Grieve not, master," I soothed him, yet I too wondered if this very same action might not arise in the future. I felt as if I knew the King's mind well enough to see that he had no time for the weak and the ill regardless how much he cared for anyone. He tended to avoid visiting his old and enfeebled mother more and more. We were interrupted by the King strolling into the apartments unannounced. This was most irritating to me, but these men never seemed to mind if one interrupted the other. Regardless of what the other was doing or whom they were consulting, they would halt whatever was the action and give the other complete attention. My master always announced himself to the King but Henry and his entourage always grossly intruded. My master did not stir, but looked lifelessly at his royal sovereign who was followed by the saintly Bishop of Bayeux, the puffing insincere Bishop of Lisieux, Robert of Newburgh, Seneschal of France, and a score of lesser nobility and court hangers-on.

"Are you mulling over the Archbishop's death?" the King asked him bluntly.

"It does affect me somewhat," my master said to him with tears springing to his eyes, "I loved the old man. He was ever good to me as would be a second father. The same as you have been my brother. I have been so fortunate all my life. I have not shown proper gratefulness. It troubles me."

"Oh come, my wonderful and shining Chancellor," Henry said, "I have ordered a special mass for his soul to be conducted personally by the Archbishop of Rouen with six Bishops in attendance, and a special concession just for you and you alone, the Queen and I will attend. I wish all activity in my entire empire to stop for five minutes at high noon ten days from now. The whole of my people will pray for the repose of his soul. Will not that be sufficient? Do you think you can distribute the order fast enough for all to obey?"

"It will be sufficient," Thomas smiled wanly at him, "I can distribute your orders in sufficient time." He knew that Henry was making a magnificent effort just for him and him alone, because one could see that the attendants Churchmen were a little annoyed at this concession to a member of minor orders.

"You are my one and only Chancellor," Henry explained loudly, "had it not been for my express wishes, you would have been on attendance to the great Archbishop. I needed you more and you stayed with me. I am grateful to have one man in my kingdom who puts me first above all considerations. The services will be held day after tomorrow. The Archbishop says he must have time to prepare. Meanwhile, let us go to the chapel and light our candles. At least, we can observe the amenities."

"Well said, my lord and master," said Thomas rising.

I immediately stepped forward, brushed imaginary flecks of mar from his immaculate clothing and put his lavishly scalloped robe about his shoulders and hung a great chain of gold about his neck from which was suspended a magnificent cross set with pearls and rubies. This was one of the finest crafted ornaments that any one had ever seen and I could see the crowd gazing at my master with critical attention. His clothing was of the deepest brown. His surcoat which was a bit longer than was the fashion was of quilted silk embroidered with gold thread. His hose were so finely knitted that the wool was lighter than gossamer yet very warm. His shirt was of the same material although he reveled in wearing silk next to his soft and deeply glowing skin. The ever present Plantagenet leopards rampant were appliquéd on his shirt sleeves and the back of his cloak. They were in brown silk almost black. All the assemblage followed the Chancellor and the King to the cellar chapel where they would crowd in and pray diligently as true worshippers should.

The year following the Archbishop's death was a quiet one. The only disturbance was the ambitions of clergymen who wanted the Archbishopric and the fulminations of the Archbishop of York who constantly contended both vocally and in writing that his See was superior if not the only great

Church capital in England. Things became uneasy as the King impatiently brushed aside every petition. He would not even entertain the pope's personal ambassadors if he knew their mission was to appeal to him to nominate a primate for England. The ancient Empress and the Queen were at him constantly to appoint someone. The Queen now had eight children by Henry and with the two that she had by Louis of France, that household was getting crowded. Betrothals were in the offing and they needed the concurrence of an Archbishop of Canterbury. It was becoming urgent that the young prince, Henry be crowned in order to insure the succession and avoid anarchy in case of the sudden death of the King. Henry at last made his move. It was in the vast audience chamber and combination dining room in the royal palace at Le Mans. All had eaten and been dismissed except the Queen and the royal children who were racing about the hall with abandon. Only the most personal servants were present. The wine was special and cool, the fire reared in the great fireplace to ward off the early April chill. The promise of spring was not far off. One could smell the green in the air.

"I need an Archbishop of Canterbury, Thomas," the King said as the Queen looked on interestingly.

"I know my liege," Thomas answered him directly, "and there are many capable candidates. Gilbert Foliot of London, Robert of Lincoln, Henry of Chichester, and many, many more.

"Yes, but will they be loyal to me, support me in my intentions to bring law and order forever to my kingdom. Will they dispute me or enforce my commands? It will take someone who had depth and breadth in all matters to be sufficient. I have seen no one to date who measures up to such qualifications. They all fall short of the foresight and vigor that I require."

"There are too many good men not to find one," Thomas remonstrated, "England must have a Canterbury.

York grows too strong and vociferous. If he is not checked, there will be confusion in Church matters. He wishes to convoke a great assembly of Churchmen to establish his claims. We will have trouble in that area if we do not act quickly."

I do not fear York," the King mused, "I can control Roger by dangling a plum of promise before him from time to time. He is pliable and manageable. It would be distasteful to me if he gets the pope involved in my kingdom but until he shows signs of doing so, I shall let him have all the rope he wants. He can be put on short tether easily. But you, my Chancellor, why not you as the Archbishop? You are eminently skilled in both canon and civil law. You know my every whim and demand. With you as my Chancellor and archbishop my empire would be in safe hands. You could rule without interference even from me. I could concentrate on the Capet and Spain and be free from the worry of revolt. Do you not feel that you are the one? You are my man you know."

"I am without question your man, sire, to the death that someday will part us. I have neither kith nor kin who are not cared for. My sisters are secure and all my relatives have livings. But I am not your man. You should know that too well. Have I not clung to you whether you were right or wrong? Have I not yielded in every instance when we had differences of opinion? And look," he said as he stood and spread wide the flowing troubadour cape that he had been holding against himself as if he were chilly. He had on black velvet banded in white. The white collar, cuffs, and footwide band around his surcoat were sewn seed pearls. He was truly startling. He had even had triangles of pears sewn onto his stockings immediately below the edge of the coat. It was the interior of his cape that caught everyone's attention.

"Ermine," breathed the Queen heavily, "why I cannot afford that. Only my ceremonial robes are tipped with ermine and here a commoner, a mere minister of the crown has the inside of his cloak lined with it! I did not know that there was that much ermine in Christendom. No, Henry, my lord, my king, she said waspishly, "your Chancellor, for once in his life is absolutely correct. He is not the man for such an influential and holy position as Canterbury. He wears a ransom on his back! No, no," she said, her voice rising, "I will never agree to his appointment. I will petition the Holy Father in Rome to refuse your request."

"Oh quiet woman," Henry said testily, "you are only good for breeding and a show of temper. Would that I had a capable wife who could be objective and control her emotions! I am merely sounding him out. I have not mentioned an appointment, but rest assured, you nor my mother will affect my decisions. This is work for a King not concerning females in the least. I am a good enough judge of character to pick my ministers and Churchmen. The decision will be mine alone."

"In this matter, it will not be you alone, your Highness," Thomas said boldly, "God will enter into it and I'm afraid He is higher than all of us. I am single minded as you well know. I serve only one man well. I cannot serve two."

"Why he is the least inclined Churchman in the kingdom," Eleanor said with conviction, "he cannot even preach well in the required Latin. The only good I know of Thomas Becket is his continence and his failure of dealing venality in his Archdeaconry. He abhors simony as all know, but he is a pluralist. He is slow to fill church vacancies so that he can pocket the money."

"That is untrue," the King said heatedly, "and I command that you cease such scurrilous charges. My Thomas does not need such a common thing as money. I have personally seen to it that his income exceeds my own personal payments. He does not condescend to stoop to such vulgar practices. The appointments have been more promptly made than ever before. The Church's revenue is greater than ever before, even the Archbishop of York cannot deny that. Oh, they yawl and groan about the Toulousan scutage, but they lie and I know it. If Thomas sold his land and jewels that I have given him personally, he could buy all the lands of Spain or France and still have plenty left over. He is constantly returning my rewards by giving expensive gifts to my churchmen and magnates. The most beautiful jewelry and clothing the children of mine wear are paid for by him personally. He feeds and clothes more beggars and cares for more poor than any of my subjects. If you must accuse him, do so with truth, not with exaggerations or lies. That I will not tolerate from anyone. Oh hell," the King profaned wearily, "let us break off this troublesome subject. I am in the mood for lighter stuff. I thought I could settle this matter easily, but you Eleanor, always the female, complicates my mind with unnecessary detail and trivia. I warn you all, when and if I make my decision, it will stand and I will brook no criticism or argument."

"So be it," Thomas said solemnly, "but the all powerful God rules us all and He is a most demanding Master. I would fear for my ability if I were required to serve the man I most respect and love and the God who made us all. It would be impossible not to choose. I am happy as your servant, my liege, I would not voluntarily change it."

"He is absolutely correct," Eleanor said with relief, "but I too am weary with argument. I find too that I do not grow younger. I tire more easily. If am permitted my lord, I would retire to another part of the hall and enjoy the entertainment on a more comfortable couch. Come sit with me and we will speak sweet nothings as we watch the jugglers and listen to sweet songs from the southern climes."

"And I my lord," said Thomas seriously, "if it does not offend you, I would have the necessary papers that must be read and signed brought in while I observe and listen to the amusement. There is much that needs doing. I can look, listen, read, and direct the sealing of your orders while dictating other matters."

"Oh, do as you please," the King smiled resignedly, "I will stroll around, play with the children, and visit with each of you and observe how you both live."

"I am not for playing," Thomas said, "I fear my age does show itself. I find more gray at my temples each day and my energies run lower and lower. Do you realize, my lord, that I have been in your service for more than eight years and we have never been apart more than three months at a time during all these years?"

"You have seen him much more than I," Eleanor said, "but that is no matter. I have borne his children, as is ever the way between man and woman. I do bless you, dear Thomas, because you have been and are the best royal minister and servant that has ever been born. It is only natural that I would be envious and jealous of your apparently unassailable position. I envy beautiful clothing. Please forgive my ungovernable temper, it is a part of my inheritance. I forgive and forget as quickly as I speak. I mean you no harm and I hold for you the greatest respect and admiration as my lord and master, the King, will so readily attest. I am woman, sir, and the hot blood of the Aquitaine troubadours flows richly in my veins. It would be unnatural if I were otherwise. I would die if I were one of those stodgy, northern women who are more cows to be serviced as need be."

"Thank you, my lady," Thomas bent low over her hand, his ermine lined cloak flaring dramatically, "I understand. My loyalty to you is as strong as it is to my King."

"Beautifully put," Eleanor smiled at him engagingly. Her age was really beginning to show. It was obvious that her hair was dyed, that the rouge spots on her cheeks were artificial and the inevitable crow's feet showed around her eyes and the corners of her mouth. Her artful makeup concealed these flaws until she was closely observed or thrown into the unmerciful light. She was ever careful not to expose herself when her deficiencies were clear. I knew that I was far past my youth. My hair was heavily sprinkled with white and mornings had been coming when my arthritis ached my joints unmercifully. I had begun to long for sunnier lands and less onerous duties. I almost demanded full rest and had become adept in avoiding the hellish progresses and campaigns that the still youthful King perpetually conducted.

My master and the Queen busily ordered their servants about their duties. The minstrels and entertainers filed in and began to amuse. The dining tables were cleared, wiped clean, and the Chancery clerks brought in sheafs of documents that they were preparing. My master seated himself at the lower end of the table. Two scribes attended him as he dictated contracts or the King's orders as were required. Three bishops sat down the board on his left and below them, the constables, Dapifers, and Chamberlains. The activity of processing and legalizing documents went on apace. The King was boisterously playing ball with the royal children who were romping and shouting with glee. The Queen had retired to a silk covered couch amid a multiplicity of cushions where she listened to a sensuous love song sung by a long haired man who was indecently attired in his skin tight fitting clothes. This was to be the last merry, happy scene in this royal house for a long time to come.

CHAPTER 31

I was serving my master some light food in his house one early summer afternoon as he was selecting some new clothing. He had his bedroom ranged in a most peculiar fashion. He required some type of fabric on the floors of his personal bedroom instead of the usual stone floors or floors covered with rushes as could be found elsewhere. The large pieces of cloth, usually sewn in a quilted fashion by a multitude of tailors, were very difficult to handle, but they did not get really dirty, because he required that all shoes, except the King's, to be thoroughly cleaned before anyone entered the room where he slept. Further, my master required the use of many braziers to keep his sleeping quarters warm, and many lights to keep it bright when he was awake. The floor covers numbered three. One was yellow, one was blue, and the other was red. Even the Queen was known to remark that his ostentatious Chancellor lived better than royalty. It was required that the floor covers be changed weekly and thoroughly cleaned before they were put down again. Common people, such as servants, outfitters of the Chancellor, and petitioners for problems, delighted to call on him in the bedroom just to get to walk on the covered floors.

My master's bedroom also had several large tables on which documents and writing materials were meticulously placed. Often, he would have a group of his clerks copying or writing in there rather than in his large official chambers in the palace. Here, he could eat in private, converse with anyone he wished, and supervise the activities of the empire. My master hated drafts and the cold stone walls seeped chill and allowed wind to circulate around them. Consequently, he had arrases hung from ceiling to floor, and his bedroom looked like some vast tent that was styled after those of the infidels in the east. They were effective, though, because they trapped air and the room stayed warm from not being disturbed by chill winds. He further required that a giant screen be placed about six feet from the door to the bedroom and all visitors were seated between this barrier and the door until he was ready to see them. It was very easy to dart behind the arrases when one appeared to go out the door and stay concealed for any period of time. When I was on attendance to the Chancellor he often directed that I leave the room understanding perfectly that I would hide behind the cover to hear what was being said.

On this particular day, the windows were open to air out the staleness of the room, but low coals in the braziers kept the place warm. The King came striding in, unannounced as usual, and the clerks and outfitters scurried out the door as fast as I could dismiss them. The King went over and stared out the window. I brought up a chair for him and he seated himself without a word, which I took to be my dismissal. I went behind the screen and quickly concealed myself behind the arras.

"I must have an Archbishop for Canterbury, Thomas," the King said peremptorily, "the master can wait no longer. I wish to have Prince Henry crowned in my lifetime, and I do not wish the See of York to grow too strong. There are many changes in the law that I wish to bring about. One especially pressing problem is that of members of the clergy committing crimes and only having their wrists slapped by the temporal courts. My civil courts punish the lay people severely, while these degenerates parade throughout my kingdom immune from punishment. I will not have this. I wish to return to the ancient customs of my grandfather, and I must have a greater separation of Church and State in the law courts especially."

"I agree with you my liege," Thomas said sincerely, "I have made many nominations to you of many good men. The Queen and the Empress and the Pope have done the same. So far, you have not chosen to have any of the candidates put forward for election."

"I am not pleased with any of those people," the King said petulantly, "I have asked you before to take on this responsibility, because I must have one in that position who is trained in the law and one in whom I have complete confidence. It takes more than one person to administer to my vast lands. The other administrators must be of the caliber of men who are capable and worthy."

"To become the primate of all England would take a godly man devoted to the service of the Most High. He must be saintly in some respects, and he must be dedicated," Thomas explained patiently to the King, "he must be extraordinary. I am not that. I am too worldly. My affections are with the throne, not with the Church. I am of one mind, and I recognize it as a weakness. I can be no other way. I am just as indifferent to the services of the Church as you are my lord, even if I am perfectly aware that yours and my inattention in the chapel are a sacrilege. I still choose to sin and go with you. It is a wonder that we retain a chaplain of any stature. I have noticed that our chaplains have very nervous habits after serving us for a while. I would like to calm you during services, particularly when you wish to converse or move about. It is very distracting to the poor priest who is duty bound to preach as best he can."

"That is one thing that concerns me least. Look at me, Thomas. Do you not see that I incline to fat? I will not be so if I can help it. I do not eat prodigiously or frequently, yet I am somewhat corpulent. If I were muscular, I would not mind. But I will not be fat. If I sat still through those interminable mutterings of these long winded priests I would eventually go insane. It is with great difficulty that I restrain myself. I intend to in time," said the King, "to have you sit down and draw up a schedule of services for these insufferable bores, and make church time attendance standard throughout the empire."

"I could not sire," smiled Thomas affectionately at the wild haired, dusty sovereign, "the Holy Father in Rome would never approve of it and to promulgate such against his and the Church's wishes would be blasphemy of the worst. We would live in dread of a possible interdict."

"That is what I mean," the King said bounding up, "pour me some wine and have meat and bread brought in. I don't remember if I have eaten all day. Suddenly I am hungry. But to return to the other matter. A nation cannot have two masters with overlapping functions. The Church must confine itself to its matters, while the State must function in the civil areas. A ruler cannot protect and lead his people if there is a competing authority. The King should be able to direct his country and the Church should keep to its duties of saving souls. I will not, I will not," the King said heatedly, "be dictated to by some milksop in Rome or here in my own lands. It gravels my very soul to see common criminals walking freely in my lands. It annoys me to the point of apoplexy to think that my hands are tied in the matter of bringing law and order to my kingdom."

My master listened patiently to this tirade then came to the door where I told him that I had already ordered the food which would be forthcoming immediately. I had the servants go into the room, clear a table, and spread fruit, hot meat pies, wine, and cheese for the King to choose from. He hardly noticed anything as he paced the room with gravy dribbling down his chin from attempting to hold a hot pie in one hand and wine in the other. My master smilingly took a great linen napkin, wiped the royal face and clothes clean and tied the napkin laughingly around the royal neck. He began to peel fruit and slice the bread and cheese for the King's selection. Their sameness of mind amazed me after the eight long years of their association. One would perform the humble tasks for the other without bidding or thought. The King was just as likely to serve Thomas as the Chancellor was to serve Henry.

"The service to God is a very serious undertaking, my liege," Thomas said, "one cannot serve a King and God. One must be sacrificed for the other. The Lord is demanding in his work. If one does not fulfill his duty, he is in danger of eternal damnation. I would fear for my sanity if I took this appointment. I love you too much to endanger our relationship. It is not within the realm of my ability to attempt to wear two such onerous robes. I am too worldly. I love luxury. I am vain, egotistical, and proud of my physical appearance. I am not of the material required to perform the services required by God. What He wants would lie too heavily on my conscience. We would conflict, my King, in what we wanted, because I would also be duty bound to the Pope, God's vicar on earth, to obey his commandments."

"Oh Thomas," said the King beseechingly, "quit clouding the issue. You yourself convince me more and more that you are the man for the Archbishopric. You can discern where it would be most effective to yield in the laws both temporal and secular. I must have that kind of person at Canterbury. Should I become incapacitated before one of my sons reaches his majority, I must needs have a man who can rule and who will not encourage an usurper to take the inheritance of my children. I cannot rest until this matter is accomplished. I urge you, my beloved Chancellor," the King said as he grasped my master's beautiful, soft olive complexioned hand, to accept my offer. Do not make me offer it so. A forced Churchman is not reliable. Make it your conscious choice. If nothing more than to please me."

"I hesitate, my lord," Thomas said looking deep into the grey green eyes of this short, stout red faced Anjou, "you have ever been most kind to me. My rewards in your service have been without measure. But the dead Archbishop was also kind to me. I deserted him when he wanted me for you. Can you not see, my master, that God can be just as demanding. Can you not see, that I must needs make up my mind to serve one or the other?"

"You brilliant charlatan," the King smiled at him, "here, drink from my cup," and the Chancellor sipped daintily, "you of all people can perform the stupendous tasks required of me and of the Church. I will help you as I always have. We will work in the same harmony and concert we always have. There is no issue that we cannot resolve. With you as the head of my State and my Church, we will accomplish my desires. We will separate all matters where they belong and all people will stand before the law in equality."

"Please do not say 'my Church', my King," Thomas cautioned him, "it can only be God's church. He is a jealous God and what you say is carelessness, is blasphemy. Your contempt for the clergy and religion will someday get you in serious trouble if you do not guard yourself. I cannot imagine the shrewd, careful King of England, Duke of Normandy, Anjou, and Aquitaine being so free with damaging statements."

"I will not repeat such again," the King promised, "if only to please you. If you will accept this position, I would have you draw up the directions to the monks of Canterbury to elect you. Also draw up the documents for the Bishop of London to consecrate you as priest and send the necessary information to Rome informing the Pope of all the actions."

"Me, my lord?" laughed Thomas heartily, "is it fitting that I author documents to promote myself? It hardly seems fitting because it smacks of political chicanery. Any person who wished to disagree with your decisions could contest these matters on the ground that I was personally involved."

"No one would dare do so," the King said menacingly, his face verging on the choleric, "you are my Chancellor and you are empowered to conduct all my matters of state, foreign policy, nominate all clergymen to vacant Church positions, sign all my official documents, review and reverse if you see fit, decisions of the lower courts, see that my Exchequer functions adequately and that monies are in my treasury as fit my needs. Dast anyone question the King? I would live to see the day that even the Pope meddle in my civil administration. Does that satisfy you? You are ever acting under my direction and approval and no one in all Christendom dare gainsay you."

"That is a wise latitude for anyone," mused Thomas, "I only hope that I have never overstepped my authority."

"You did twice," the King reminded him, "once in that silly marriage of King Stephen's daughter and that time in the matter of the invasion of Toulouse. I am not sorry about our disagreement and I am still convinced that I was correct in my decisions. However, these are bygones so let us let them be."

"I must needs go to England immediately on inter with the Justiciars, my liege," Thomas told him in a businesslike fashion, "it has been overlong that judicial matters must be seen to. I would like to get my inspection tour over before we begin the Michaelmas collections at the Exchequer. We cannot let the kingdom's business lag."

"How did I ever find such a man," Henry said in wonderment, "I know my work will be easier when you are Archbishop. How can it help but not be? We will surely earn the respect of all our people and insure peace and security within the realm for all time."

"I fear, my lord," Thomas said quietly, "I fear."

"Fear not, my beloved," the King squeezed his arm, "all will be fine for the future. You," the King ordered me as I came from behind the screen that blocked the view from the door, ostensibly to rearrange the food, "admit my Chamberlain."

I hurried to do as I was bid. The Chamberlain stood in readiness just beyond the door. He bowed low as he entered.

"Summon the Curia Regis," the King ordered him, "Include the Archbishop of Rouen and the barons of England. Have them to attend me within the week. I have weighty matters to attend to. The Archbishop of York is at Court, we ask him to remain awhile longer. I would consult with him in the next hour."

The Chamberlain bowed himself out.

"Well, Thomas," the King paced nervously, "I must depart for a while, you will not attend me? We'll go for a fast and swift gallop to prove which is the better horse, my French bay that Louis has sent me or the fighting Arab stallion that you purchased from a Crusader. They tell me that that horse is the terror of the stables. He would if he could, have all the mares stabled with him. Would that I could do the same," laughed the King, "but the Queen grows more jealous as time passes and the Lord knows she delivers my children almost without cessation. It is hard for a hot blooded stallion to remain continent. I can understand the beast. What have you named him?"

"He is not named as yet, sire," Thomas smiled, "I have been too busy taming his lusts and curbing his craving for action. He is swift and of great wind. Were he not so lightly constructed, he would be a magnificent destrier. He can change directions with the wind and literally fly. I am very satisfied with him."

"Why do not I acquire such animals?" the King asked as he pouted.

"You can have him if you wish," Thomas said magnanimously as he placed his arms around the King's shoulder, "if you desire it, I will gladly make you a present of him."

"No, no you will not," the King remonstrated, "he pleases you, thus you will keep him. I am not envious, I assure you, it is just that my personal servants annoy me at times by not informing me of such matters!"

"I was not informed," Thomas said, "I happened to see the man riding the beast in the countryside. It did not occur to me that you were interested in horseflesh at the moment. Our nights, lately, have been spent in reviewing the beauties of France. I thought that was what you wanted."

"A man can like horses and women simultaneously," the King said bracing his hand on his back and leaning backward, "that wench last night was overambitious. She squeezed too hard. I might perhaps have her back again this evening. The Queen is very, very pregnant as you know. Better to let me have a little tether than to have me lose control. By the way," he turned to Thomas, "I think that I will let di Luci escort Eleanor back to England. I wish this child to be born at Westminister. From now on, I want all the royal births to be in England."

"How many more do you expect, sire?" Thomas asked, "The Queen is not a young woman."

"You had better not let her hear you say that," the King warned in all seriousness, "she is a vain Aquitanian and she spends a fortune keeping her face and hands looking young. As for children, how would I know? She has turned out to be a fine brood mare, easy to fertilize, would that poor Louis of France could be so lucky as to marry a woman who could give him heirs."

"You sound remarkably casual," Thomas said, "She would think we were discussing dumb animals instead of Queens of the realm."

"One is no different from the other," the King laughed, "besides, in this matter, my dear Chancellor, I am your instructor. Were it not for me, you would not be so well informed on this subject. You disappoint me constantly when you refuse to sleep with one of my chosen wenches. I could think of nothing more delightful than us sharing a common bed with a lustful creature. Say you will and I will surely reorder that mink I had last night. Whew!" he groaned, "she was a true bedful. Couldn't stand much of her too often. Getting to the age where I have to have a little sleep, too."

"You are not yet thirty," Thomas smiled.

"Sometimes I feel sixty," the King admitted. "You're not so old yourself. About forty-two if I remember correctly."

"Near to that, give or take a few months," Thomas agreed with him, "but I can still take you on and thrash your bottom, Henry the Plantagenet, Lord of all He surveys."

With that, the King charged him and they fell on the bed with a tangle of arms and legs. They rolled on the floor, upsetting the food table, then they fell against the wall, ripping an arras from its moorings. Finally, winded and sweaty, they went to stand before the window to cool off. I motioned in two personal servants with two linen napkins to wipe the sweat from the combatant's brows. The King turned to leave.

"I feel sixty two at this moment," Thomas smiled.

"And, I, too," the King remarked as he strode from the chamber where his entourage awaited to join him.

CHAPTER 32

The next convocation was one that will be remembered forever in history. The King immediately breached the consecration of my master as priest. The Archbishop demurred. The Archbishop of Rouen agreed to officiate at the ceremony as did the Bishops of Bayeux and Lisieux. I thought to myself that Arnulf of Lisieux would ingratiate himself in any manner with the King. Before the sun had set that day my master was a member of the Holy Church and could perform Churchly functions. We left the next week for Canterbury where my master, as Chancellor of the Angevin empire, with all the great barons of the realm, swore undying fealty to the young Prince Henry and the crowning date for the youth was set for December 1162. The monks of the chapter of Canterbury house, after due deliberation and with some argument, duly did as their King bid, and elected Thomas Becket to the Archbishopric. He was consecrated in this position by the Archbishop of York with some reluctance, and the palls arrived from Rome in three months.

My master devoted most of his first months as Chancellor. He immediately went with the Earl of Leicester on a tour of the northern counties where he sat in judgment on all the serious law cases. He toured the churches in his Archdeaconry and inspected his castles of Berkhampstead and Eye to see that the lands, livestock, and equipment were being properly utilized and maximum production was achieved.

The thing that disturbed me most though was that he extended visits to my sisters and to his sisters who came from their convents to have a reunion with a man they scarcely knew. He installed many cousins as his assistants around the cathedral. He began to spend more and more time in his devotionals. The King's visits became less frequent and often the visits were not satisfactory.

"You go to church too much Thomas," the King would say. "You spend too much time reading and fasting. You are becoming thin from fasting and you always appear to be tired. The old times have gone. I miss them."

"I am the Archbishop of Canterbury, the servant of God," my master would say, "how else can I save souls and lead them in the right way if I do not do so myself? I find great satisfaction in prayer and contemplation. I enjoy the quietness of the mass and the solitude of my quarters. I am delighted at getting the opportunity to wash the feet of the poor people and feed them and look to their comforts. I know this is the work the Lord commands me do."

"You are also my Chancellor and don't forget it," Henry told him lightly, "but you sound as if you are becoming a fanatic about religion."

"No one is a fanatic about religion," Thomas told him as he began dropping the King's proper titles from his conversation, "there is a lot of satisfaction in getting to know your Maker. I find great consolation in contemplation and prayer. Perhaps I have found my true calling in life. The constant search for the love of God and the guiding of lost souls on the way gives the utmost satisfaction. There is something that is very pleasant to know that I seek the true light. I no longer care for the finery and frippery that I once knew. Plain clothes and plain food are my fare. It is a happy and contended life I now lead."

"Beware that you do not let your administrative duties lag," the King warned him, "and do not let England become unruly. Also, do not become attached to Canterbury, I prefer to work on the continent. I might have need of you any day and I hope that you would come to me as promptly as old."

"I will come when you call," Thomas assured him, "but please remember that I have my obligations to God and the Church. It might take me longer than it has in the past because many functions require my attention now. I am pressed to get out the royal correspondence, attend the sessions of the Exchequer, receive foreign visitors, preach mass, and attend to the suffering."

"You were ever the busy one," the King smiled, "that is why I chose you above all others. You are, in my eyes, perfection. I would have no other near me but you."

"It is gratifying to know that I enjoy your confidence," my master returned, "I am weary of the Church courts. There are so many cases to be heard. Couple them with the civil cases, and one can become rapidly overloaded."

"What about the Church cases?" asked Henry, "surely you keep the civil separate from the Church?"

"Indeed I do," replied Thomas with enthusiasm, "all clerks are referred to the proper ecclesiastical courts while all laymen are tried by civil judges."

"Do you mean that criminous clerks are tried by Church courts against my will?" the King asked with some heat.

"Matters of the Church are kept within the Church," my master spoke to him in great dignity, "the province of the kingdom of God is all about us, and it is the responsibility the Church to see that is properly cared for."

"You know it is against my will to allow criminals go free," Henry said with asperity, "and I make no qualifications. A man who commits a crime in the kingdom of Henry the Second is going to pay society in kind. I will devote my last ounce of strength to see that the law is administered. Take care, Thomas, you know my mind better than I. Do not let me hear of the Church excusing some lowdown, cowardly member of the clergy for murder, thieving, or robbery. I will not tolerate it, even if it were you. I own this kingdom, and my will be done."

"Take care that you don't endanger your soul, my King," Thomas said with vigor, "no man owns the land. Only God has permanent ownership. We my utilize it for the short space of our lives, but we never own it. You endanger your soul to hell fire and eternal damnation if you attempt to usurp God on earth."

"Don't be ridiculous," Henry snapped, "you sound as if you need confinement. Surely you are not mouthing such nonsense to your bishops and priests. If you are, I will act promptly and accordingly. You will have to leave my domain even if you are Thomas Becket, former alter ego of the King. I cannot and will not tolerate sedition and treachery from the Pope himself."

"I do not intend to go contrary to your wishes," Thomas said piously, "but I must serve God as I see fit. It would be hard for a lewd and lascivious King to instruct me."

"I do believe you wish to anger and antagonize me," Henry said, his eyes becoming mere slits in his face.

"Never," Thomas assured him, "I love you too much. I would never knowingly antagonize you. But as I've said before, I cannot serve two masters. The kingdom of God calls me. I must answer that call."

"Well do as you see fit," Henry said with finality, "you have ever known best. I must leave now. I wish to go and hunt and see how the improvements are coming along in the Tower. I have a presence that I will have need of that edifice sooner than I think. I wish it to be commodious and reasonably comfortable."

"The Tower is in the best condition it has been in years," Thomas told him, "I have had it under repair for almost three months. You wished it so. I did it. I would appreciate your viewing my work to see if it is satisfactory."

"My blessed and efficient servant," the King said with affection, "will you not ride with me please? We can wench, eat at a good tavern, and perhaps make a good kill."

"I cannot go this time," Thomas said to him smiling, "too many things must be done. I would not anger you by being inefficient. Perhaps another time."

Their obvious affection for each other made me feel much easier. I felt that at one time the Archbishop might have angered the King. The strange developments in my master's life were disturbing and I know that his will was developing as one of steel. The clash of wills between him and the King could not be forestalled forever. I would find relief when I could.

"He does not know it," my master said to me, "but it is my attention never to kill a living creature as long as I live. As soon as I can, I intend to wean myself from eating meat. For some reason, I am losing my taste for the flesh of a once living creature."

I shuddered at this revelation and did not answer him. I did not wish to subject myself to conversation of this sort, because it would lead me in a direction in which I was not sure that I could compete. I was never sure that I understood my master these days. I wondered at times if he understood himself. A monk came and told us it was time for prayers and we went obediently to the chapel. My master was more and more beginning to stay before the altar of the cathedral or in the chapel. I rubbed his knees with soothing ointments constantly and I had just found out to my horror, that he had donned a hair shirt. I insisted that he buy another one, so I could change them from time to time to keep them free of lice. I knew also that he scourged himself, although he would not admit it, neither would he let me treat his wounds. He would dismiss me gruffly. He now bathed and dressed in solitude and his garments, other than those he wore to High Mass were of the coarsest and simplest sort.

The King had only been gone for three days when he came riding angrily into the courtyard where everyone was listening to a learned visitor and the Archbishop discussing the Marian theory. I as well as the monks and friars scattered as leaves before the wind to escape being pounded by horses' hooves. The King threw John of Salisbury a wicked glance as if to say, 'I'll persecute you later. You have yet to escape my wrath.' John trembled and broke into a sweat under the angry gaze of this agitated King. Without ceremony, the King dismounted and faced the Archbishop who had risen with a distressed look on this face.

"Do you defy me and conceal a scoundrel who wears clerk's clothing, who rapes and murders innocent women?" he literally screamed at my master.

"I am not sure that I understand you," my master said to his sweetly, "we cannot discuss any matter when you are in this state."

"We will discuss what I please when I please," the King shouted, "if you or any of this scum so much as turn your backs on me, it will be the Tower at once and hanging soon after. Answer me, you pompous ass, do you conceal criminals in the so called houses of God in my kingdom? Are the Churches refuges for murderers and scoundrels of any stripe, just because they toady to some scurrilous priest?"

"You have my head reeling, my lord," Thomas answered calmly, "I am not sure of what you speak."

"Oh yes, you do, you lying spider," the King hissed, obviously bringing himself under control, "you tried the case yourself. That foul monk who strangled that poor woman in London just a week ago. You knew of the case when I was here last and deliberately concealed it from me. How could you, of all people turn your back deliberately to me when I have trusted you so completely and put such faith in your sense of fairness?"

"Oh that man," Thomas answered suavely, "he has been adequately punished. He will do the most severe of penances."

"Do you mean to tell me," demanded the King, "that I am to hang a common layman for murder on Tyburn Hill, while one of your robed bastards walks free under the sentence of penance?"

"The courts of the Church are adequate," Thomas said with asperity, "God's work has functioned for many centuries without criticism from the laity. I tell you he has been punished and will not be harassed more. He has repented his crime and is on the road to rehabilitation and the saving of his soul. That is all Our Lord asks. The case is closed and will not be reopened."

"It has not been closed," Henry began to froth at the mouth. You have no authority to supervene my secular courts, and you will not free criminals in my kingdom and live. None of you, if I have to execute every living clerk and begin again. Bring forth the criminal," he ordered.

"I will not obey that command," Thomas spoke to him sternly, "leave this house of God, lest you desecrate it and bring penance onto yourself. Go, I say!"

"You contemptible, stupid priest," the King making a magnificent effort to bring himself under control, "I don't fear you or any man who walks. What has come over you Thomas? You have gone mad and if you have, I will have you confined. This is not right and you know it. Stand aside, all of you," the King ordered and we all horded into a corner of the churchyard, "guard them well," he instructed some rather belligerent knights who dismounted and came at us as if they would relish doing bodily harm, "into the house, the rest of you, and don't leave a stone unturned until you find that sniveling wretch and bring him to me. Nigel de Broc, don't you dare return without that lowborn creature."

"I will find him, my King," de Broc said forcefully and led other soldiers into the quarters of the monks. I knew that their job would be easy, because the scoundrel who claimed to be a friar was scrubbing the kitchen floor, in supposed humility, but anyone could tell that this was an unrepentant criminal. I had remonstrated with my master on the leniency of his punishment, only to have Thomas Becket to fly in a rage and threaten to dismiss me because of my uncharitable and unforgiving attitude. If that scum had not heard the conversation, he would be scrubbing and probably planning his next criminal escapade. He must have been located easily, because the soldiers returned swiftly with him in the midst. The knights were smiling broadly and the monk was ashen faced with fear.

"Those who enter God's house do so in danger of excommunication," warned the Archbishop, and those who interfere with God's servants are doomed to eternal hell fire."

"Shut up, you addled prelate," Henry ordered, "you have fasted too much already. It is affecting not only our good judgment, but your mind. I think I despise you at this moment."

My master looked as if the King had struck him squarely in the face. He actually stepped back to be supported by two sturdy monks. It was obvious that John of Salisbury was seeking a place where the King could not see him at all. The King took the vacant visitor's seat and motioned de Broc and the knight Tracy to sit beside him. He crossed his arms.

"I now convene the Curia Aulia," he said firmly, "it has the power to render decisions on all matters of the kingdom, excluding the ecclesiastical. Bring the criminal forward!"

The scurrilous monk was forcibly brought in his presence where he fell on his knees in abject terror and supplication.

"What have you to say, you manger dog?" demanded the King acting as his own prosecutor, "do you deny raping and strangling a poor hopeless woman, you cur?"

"P-p-p-please spare me, your Highness," blubbered the terrified man, "I have sinned, confessed, and am now doing penance, I wish to dedicate my life anew to the service of God, sp-sp-sp-spare me," he prayed.

"So you have the unmitigated gall to admit to a heinous crime," the King said contemptuously, "the verdict is death at once."

The man began to grovel in the earth and scream.

"Gag him," ordered the King, his eyes blazing like green fire, "hang him on this tree."

"Oh no," Thomas cried coming forward, "do not murder here. This is hallowed ground dedicated to the service of God."

"Sit down you feebleminded one," the King said sternly, "or the Tower will be your fate. You can contemplate how you can save criminals in other ways. I am surprised at you Thomas. Your confidence must be colossal. I can forgive you anything except that not even you will transgress my laws. String him up I say! Be quick about it, the scum is not worth this much trouble. I should have simply had one of the retainers slit his throat, except for this once, this will be my Tyburn Hill."

My master stood as if transfixed. He looked first at the King, then at the monk who had finally submitted to the noose that was placed around his neck. One of the men scrambled up the great oak and caught the rope end that was slung up to him. As he brought the rope over, a knight rode up and fastened it to his pommel. At a signal from de Broc he lashed his horse into a lunge. The criminal's feet immediately shot into the air as he was jerked from the ground. The horse was halted as soon as he swung in the air. The air was rent with the odor of released feces and a brown stain spread rapidly over the front of the cassock of the swinging man.

"He is dead," announced the King, "and a far more merciful death he had than the poor woman he abused and strangled. I wish this to be published throughout the kingdom," he ordered my master, "I will have wanton murder to cease in my lands."

"You have sinned grievously," Thomas intoned still stunned.

The King mounted his horse.

"Inform the Pope of this if you wish. If he condones murder then he and I will have a dialogue on the matter. I will truly scourge and unfrock every religious person in all my empire if necessary. Prepare yourself. After the Council of Tours, which I understand you intend to attend, I will hold a Council at Clarendon. There I will explain to the barons and the Justiciars and the Churchmen that law will prevail everywhere for everyone alike, whether they be high or low. I will clearly delineate the responsibilities of Church and State. My greatest disappointment is that you will not be by my side, as you have so obviously demonstrated. I have one consolelation. You will make a worthy opponent. It should be an interesting contest. Bury that wretch if you will, if not, throw him on the dung heap for the enjoyment of the vultures and the dogs."

The horses clattered from the courtyard and the flies began to settle around the smelly, crumbled heap of flesh that had so immediately been a live, breathing man. My master stood transfixed as if he had been stunned. I mentioned to the monks to remove the body elsewhere.

CHAPTER 33

The Council of Tours came on us apace. It actually arrived before we were ready. When we arrived the crowd of Churchmen assembled was huge and the accommodations were awful. Nothing was really accomplished except that all the prelates swore obedience to the Pope rather than to their secular rulers. The Pope had all his powers reconfirmed as the overall ruler of all men on earth, knowing full well that the Emperors of the Holy Roman Empire would not agree with him. He lived in constant terror of one of the more aggressive and vicious Germans sending an army to put him in seclusion and to question his ability to defend himself. My master was specifically involved in this affirmation and I learned with horror that he resigned his Chancellorship to the Pope.

"But master," I questioned him a quavering voice, "is this not dishonorable? Should you not have notified the King? After all, the Chancellorship is strictly a civil position. It has nothing at all to do with ecclesiastical matters."

"The King and I have lost all communication," he answered me, "the Pope will be our intermediary from now on. I would love to talk to the King as we did in the olden days, but he is hostile to me and all the Church stands for. It is useless to counsel with him. It only opens the rift between us and makes old wounds flow. I miss the only man whom I have truly loved. It makes me ill to think that we are separated on so vital an issue, but the Church and God are supreme in this world and all people must recognize this fact."

"I have never heard the King dispute this," I told him cautiously lest he flare up at me. Since he had become ascetic his temper was constantly on edge and it took little to rouse him. "The King only seems to be concerned with civil law."

"When anyone contests the Church on any issue, he transgresses," the Archbishop told me severely, "and I represent the opponent to see that God's property and laws are not violated whatever or how little it might be. I would be less the man if I stood idly by and allowed laymen to violate His domain."

I kept my silence and was thoroughly mystified when the Archbishop informed me that we would return to England by way of Normandy where the King was quartered at Rouen for the time being. This meeting proved to be sad and tempestuous. The Archbishop, after securing an audience with his ruler opened the debate in a hostile manner.

"I am surprised that you would come to me through an appointment," the King said kindly, "you have ever had ready access to me."

"I felt the more formal approach would be better," Thomas said, "since I come chiefly on matters of the Church. The de Brocs have occupied Saltwood Castle at your command. You know full well that this castle has been under the governorship of Canterbury for the last twenty years. I wish them removed."

"Let us understand one thing, Archbishop" the King spoke firmly, "that which does not belong to the Church will be administered by me if I see fit. Any decision I make stands. Saltwood Castle is and has been demesne property and I shall dispose of it as I see fit."

"I have no choice other than excommunicate them," Thomas said with finality.

"Try it and even the Pope will not be able to save you. I hold the sword hand in my kingdom and I do not hesitate to use on any one who will dispute my authority. Saltwood Castle will be administered by the crown. Prepare yourself. Any other lands that are mine will also be disposed of, regardless of how much your greedy nuns and monks cry. I will not countenance opposition in my government."

"It is hard to keep the old love alive," Thomas told him, "I feel as if I do not know you anymore."

"I the same," the King readily agreed, "You are not my man anymore. You have become strange and hostile to me."

A messenger interrupted the conversation to hand the King an urgent message. He read it then and there.

"Well," he said sadly, "you have finally resigned the Chancellorship. Strangely enough, it comes as no surprise. My mother and the Queen have warned me repeatedly that you would come to this. I too have had a premonition that this was to come. And of course, you had to do it to the Pope. You did not have the guts to face me. You are losing swiftly, Thomas Becket. Once my anger is aroused, I will hurry you from the face of this earth. Take my advice please, and remain the Archbishop only. Meddle not in my government. I tell you now, and I tell you plainly, the Archbishop of Canterbury will not be the first advisor to this crown. I now divorce myself from you now and forever. I will choose a minister of my own. Your advice is neither wanted nor welcomed."

"I am a man of God," Thomas told him, "can you not understand that? I went to great pains to explain that to you before you made me become the Archbishop. When I was Chancellor, I was your man. Now a higher authority commands me and I must do as I see fit to serve my spiritual master."

"You can serve anyone whom you choose," the King told him evenly, "just leave the kingdom of Henry the Second, King of England and the Angevin Empire alone."

"I have no intentions of interfering in your business," my master declared, "I serve only the gracious God above. I am not concerned about earthly matters except to lead all the lost souls to the Master."

"Then the issue you have raised about Saltwood is unnecessary," the King rasped.

"The kingdom of God is here on this earth as well as in Heaven," the Archbishop said patiently, "it is the responsibility of his delegates to safeguard and add to his domain. We must ever do so. Everything to his praise and glorification is necessary. The Church cannot stand idly by and watch itself become stripped of its every possession. Government is just as necessary as is soul saving. The poor vicar of God has to wear two faces."

"The Church is corrupt and contemptible, and you know it," the King said objectively, "simony is rampant. There are as many whoremongers among clerks as there is among laymen. The churches cheat and steal shamelessly from the poor and ignorant under the guise of expulsion from Grace. Why do you not concentrate on reform instead of agitating a secular matter. I have read my missiles as well as you. Jesus preached humility and charity, not greediness and riches. I cannot agree that Churchmen should travel in the same manner as titled royalty. It does not make sense that a Bishop or high ecclesiastical official should make demands of luxury equal to the richest monarchs on earth. They should be simple, unassuming people, instead of the gaudy, spectacular manners which are affected."

"The glory of God is reflected in his creatures," my master said.

"Glory and ostentatiousness are not compatible with denial and holiness," the King rejoined, "look at yourself for example. There are as many people in your entourage as there are in mine. The clothes you wear are the finest Flemish woolens, the softest Spanish leathers, and the costliest of jewels. You look the same as some eastern potentate would. If there is anything of the servile and humble in you Thomas Becket, it has yet to show. The sums you spend on your own glorification to impress people would feed the poor of London town. Preach not to me of humbleness as long as you and your peers and the Holy Father can put to shame Christendom's richest monarchs in dress and elegance. There is nothing humble in this, it is greediness and pride in man beyond belief. If the poor people were not so fearful and stupid, they would rebel and bring all of you proud princes of the Church to your knees. This is not God's work nor His desires, and it is useless for you to tell me so. Your interpretations of your highborn manner of living is that of greedy, intemperate men who must live and batten from the ignorant and fearful."

My master bowed his head and acknowledged that he could not compete in this reasoning. He was clothed in the costliest of woolens and brocades and jewels. He was a truly child of light. A king would be hard pressed to try to match my master in dress or personal tastes in any manner.

"I bid you goodbye, sire," he said weakly.

"So now it is goodbye," Henry remarked, "it used to be until we meet again. You are introducing many new finalities in our relationship, Thomas. You are finally making me see that you have deserted me and your intentions are that I will become hostile despite my wishes. You are fast gaining your intentions. I love to love if I am allowed, but if I must hate, I can hate with the best. I could never hate you, or do you bodily harm, but do not send any of your deputies to speak for you, lest they lose their heads."

"I am not afraid to face my tasks," the Archbishop said proudly, "it is just that I am embarrassed to quarrel with you. It wracks my heart to dissent from my beloved. I must get accustomed to opposition. I have not learned the techniques yet."

"Whatever your excuses are to avoid me and to antagonize me," the King said in a hard tone, "result in the same analysis. It appears that we have set our courses to collide. I hope and pray you do not suffer too much. I reiterate, I shall bring law and order to the land by sword and fire if I must. No person will escape the full responsibility of the law, regardless of the status. I shall also reclaim the demesne lands and dispose of them as I see fit. Warn your churchmen. If they resist my agents, the news you will receive of them will be of their deaths. Punishment will be swift and final."

"It pains me to hear you talk in this manner," my master expostulated, "I or no one under me has any intentions of resisting you. It is a requirement that we guard and husband Church property to the best of our ability. You are wrong in wresting Saltwood from me by force. All donations and care of the Church will resound to your eternal glory. I am doing all I can to correct the abuses in the Church as you desire. I have expelled and excommunicated thousands of reprobates. I hold Court continuously and pray ceaselessly that I can alleviate the corruption in the Church. It is not easy. It takes much time and distractions such as you seem determined to inflict on the Church slow me down, considerably."

"If you can remember that I am King and you are priest, we will have no trouble," the King said, "but you seem to forget it. Your own Bishops do not support you in your contentions. Foliot has not forgiven you for that scutage, and that scurrilous John of Salisbury curries your favor to keep me from hounding him from my dominions."

"There are opportunists and opponents in all walks of life," my master said.

"Don't platitude me, my dear Archbishop," Henry said with some warmth, "remain within the areas of intelligence.

Indulge in all the stupidities with your Churchmen if you like, but don't foister mealy mouthings off on me."

"I beg your pardon," the Archbishop said seriously.

"To change the subject," the King said briskly, "before you leave, have you thought on my Great Council? I intend to hold it within the coming year. I am specifically designing it to clear up any misunderstood matters pertaining to my government. I plan to have my proceedings and decisions published throughout the kingdom, so that all men might know of them, and that there will be no confusion about the law."

"I have not made any plans or thought too much on it, to be truthful," my master told him, "because I cannot envision any problems. We have ever been of one mind, and I do not feel that we will divide on any matter."

"I bring this up now," explained the King, "because we have already differed on the punishment of criminals and the administering of demesne lands. The meeting will be stringent as regards the function of the courts. I do not intend to interpose on ecclesiastical matters, but there will be clearly defined areas for all executors of the law to follow. I wish there to be no conflicts. I have sounded out many Bishops, and they, as you, do not see any troublesome differences. It is my wish that all procedures go smoothly. I am willing to truc criticisms, but I do not intend to brook any arguments where there are clear delineations of the law."

"I understand your desires perfectly," my master assured him, "the Church wishes to see law and order maintained. I can assure you of my approval and support."

"It has come to my attention that Henry, Bishop of Chichester has absconded to Louis' kingdom with all his wealth," the King said severely, "it appears that any trouble I seem to have comes from the Church. Of course, in this case, it is good riddance of the bad blood of the Blois. I shall never let any of that family enter my lands again, on any pretext, and if

Louis does not force that renegade to divulge and gains he extracted from English lands, I shall put the entire family under ban and expropriate everything they own. They are a sly bunch, intent spreading confusion and destruction wherever they go."

"I did not know of this," my master said surprised, "he must have left while we were in conference with the Holy Father. I did not know he had any intentions of fleeing the kingdom. I have myself, prompted him to tighten up his supervision of his See. I did not know that he was as unsettled as this, although I have never fully trusted him since Theobald gained the legatine commission. That family is truly power hungry. I have numerous candidates to suggest to you as a replacement."

"I wish him to be a true and born Englishman," Henry said in a positive manner. Somehow, I love that little island peopled with law abiding and respectable people. I feel that it has gained the right to be governed by its own native born officials. It gives the most loyalty and the least concern of all my possessions. I intend, in the future, to fill all vacancies, both governmental and ecclesiastical, with people of the island. I believe that to be the best policy."

"It is the best, beyond doubt," my master heartily agreed, "since my appointment as the Archbishop of Canterbury, I find myself becoming more and more identified to the ideals and aspirations of the native born islanders. They are a stolid and loyal people, a marvelous base on which to build a future stronghold of government. They are truly loyal to the House of Anjou, and as you know, they love you not only as a King, but as a person beyond all degree. It should please your majesty that an entire nation thinks so highly of you."

"It is most gratifying," the King, "my last progress there was almost disastrous," he smiled, "they mauled me and pulled at me very energetically, in the most pleasant of manners, of course. It was never hostile. Neither did I hear a criticism while I was there."

"You should not allow your person to become injured," Thomas lectured him, "you are too precious and too valuable to be harmed, even by the mobs who adore you. You must take more care in the future and have your guards schooled in your protection without injuring their feelings."

"Do I hear my old Chancellor directing my every thought and move?" the King teased him, "have you not lost all feeling for my welfare in the press of your religious obligations?"

"Nay, say not so, my liege," my master spoke warmly, "your welfare is ever my first concern. I could never relieve myself of the responsibility of caring for you. Whatever may betide, I will always be at your beck and call. Should you suffer injury or illness, no power on earth could keep me from your side."

"I hope it will remain so," the King said with much feeling.

"I must beg to be dismissed, my lord," Thomas said bowing low, "I must needs depart and look to my flock. They call for me after so long an absence."

"You are free to depart any time you choose," the King said kindly, "I know that you personally officiate at all your masses and sermons. God go with you."

"And with you, sire."

We left without further ado and our ships carried us over the channel with ease. We landed at Sandwich, the Archbishop's city and proceeded to Canterbury. Just as night fell, we were attacked by a large force of brigands who did little injury, but were apparently intent on cowering the Archbishop. They couldn't have been more wrong, and he became incensed when it was reported to him that some mules in the baggage train had been deliberately mutilated. Other reports told him that the de Brocs and the Tracys had been recognized as the leaders of the assault. His answer was to send an angry missive of complaint to the King. The Sunday following our arrival, he excommunicated all those whom he knew to be involved. The kinsman of the excommunicated fled to the countryside and over the seas to avoid the angry Archbishop who had such a formidable reputation as a warrior and leader of armies. The King was very angry over the Archbishop's excommunication and expressly forbad him to reinvest Saltwood. The angry prelate answered his sovereign to the effect if more unfair harassment followed, he would petition the Pope for an interdict against the kingdom of the Angevins. The King, after reading this hostile missive, counseled prudence and moderation. The inevitable and fatal split among previously good friends had begun its inevitable course.

CHAPTER 34

The Council of Clarendon proved a disaster. It started off well enough. The King brought up fourteen points that he said were parts of the government of England during the reign of his grandfather, Henry the First, and were ancient customs that all know about. These customs dealt chiefly with a definition of crimes punishable by the State and the areas of tax collection. The King said his desire was to clear up any shady areas of authority and to remove the Church from the burdens of criminal punishment or the collection of taxes thereby freeing the Church to the greater service of mankind. The Archbishop at first demurred, claiming that the rights of the Church were being infringed upon and that he would have to consider all proposals before rendering a decision. He declared to all assembled that he did not come to the council prepared to yield the prerogatives of the Church. He withdrew from the assemblage of barons as soon as he decently could and retired within his tent, barring all visitors, including myself.

"Do you agree with my proposals, good Archbishop?" the King asked him the next morning when the leaders of the realm assembled.

"I do my liege, with reservations," my master answered him.

"What are those reservations?" the King demanded.

"I cannot define them, my lord," the Archbishop answered with knitted brows, "they are complicated and evasive. I need time to study them. They should have been submitted to be before the Council. I am confused and fear to make you angry."

"They are not confused and complicated," the King said loudly and stoutly, "they were in effect during my grandfather's time and the simplest serf understood them. Are you sure that you are not just stalling the assemblage? If you do so, you will pay the bill in the most severe manner of which I can think. I cannot afford to convene these assemblies and let one inconsiderate person waste their time. Think hard, Archbishop. Now listen" the King said in a loud voice, "we will adjourn for the day and reconvene tomorrow. All those that sit with me will be for my proposals. Those that oppose will sit opposite."

It was a miserable night. The Archbishop prayed continuously for guidance, while I lay turning ceaselessly unable to sleep. We were a ragged group when we presented ourselves to the King's audience. All the magnates and Churchmen sat with the King. My master sat apart and alone.

"Well, my Archbishop," the King said turning on him, "how do you sit, today? Never here nor there?"

"I will agree with your proposals, my lord," Thomas said in a weak voice.

"Completely?" queried the suspicious monarch.

"With reservations, sire, I must seek direction from Rome," Thomas looked him squarely in the eye.

"From Rome?" the King reared, "I will not have my lands run by Rome, were it staffed by a thousand popes. What I do is none of Rome's damned business!"

The assemblage gasped at this blasphemy. All began to look around to seek an avenue of escape. Not one Churchman came to stand with my master.

"I will so inform the Holy Father," Thomas said positively, "I don't believe he will mind placing any obstreperous monarch under an interdict to discipline him."

"Discipline be damned," the King sat down and began to froth at the mouth and to clutch at the reeds on the tent floor. My master went to him and I darted off to summon servants to bring towels and cool water and strong wine as we had done many times in the past. When I returned, the King's head lay in my master's lap. I bathed his face while the Archbishop fed him cool draughts of sweet wine. Soon he calmed down and forced himself rudely from us and left the tent without saying a word. He sent word by a chamberlain that the meeting was dissolved and that he would not receive for at least a week. We left to visit some outlying churches. As our van left, the Queen's arrived and the Bishop of Lisieux and the Bishop of London hurried to receive her. The King departed for the continent within the week. I was horrified to find that the Archbishop had secretly mailed both the King and the Pope a long letter refuting his agreement with the Constitutions of Clarendon. His answer from Henry was the banishment of the Archbishop and all his kin from England.

We fled immediately to the safer havens of Louis Capet. He received us cordially and dispersed the several hundreds of dependents of the Archbishop. I did not see the multitudinous cousins of his ever again. In fact, I did not see his sisters nor my sisters anymore. They sought the security of the convents and did not identify themselves to the public. The French King assured us the kingdom was ours to command. My master requested that a conference be arranged with the Pope. This was done speedily.

We had brought uncounted for sums with us abroad and the revenue poured in until an order by the King Henry stopped our income. My master still lived in outward splendor, but what the public did not see was that he wore a hair shirt that chafed him constantly and he prayed ceaselessly for guidance. I feared that his knees would become infected. I designed pads to soften the hard boards he knelt on, but I had to many times go and help him rise after hours of prayer. He would be so stiff he could not manipulate his joints. His hair rapidly turned gray and deep lines etched his ascetic face. His age was coming on him fast. The Pope came to see my master exactly fifteen months following the French monarch's request.

"We cannot have dissension between the secular and the temporal," he informed my master and the Capet.

"I do not wish friction," my master said, "but shall I yield the rights of the Church, master? Shall I stand by and hold my hands and see the world of God abused by a worldly monarch? If so, you must instruct me in writing. Give me guidance. I will do as I am bid.

"The Church does not wish to become involved in this matter," the pontiff informed him, "it is not of such a nature that our intervention is needed. This is a matter between two men, strong minded men, yes, but not a problem that cannot be resolved."

"I have been expelled from my See on pain of injury or of death, Father," Thomas said to him, "my sheep cry for me. They must be sheltered and guided. It will take the threat of an interdict to bring Henry Plantagenet to his senses. I need one, Holy Father, I need an interdict badly. He must be disciplined and harshly. I know him too well. He is an obstinate and fearful man when aroused. He will never yield to ordinary counsel and he sees no reason in any other manner."

"Interdict is not a lightly taken manner," the Pope counseled, "it cannot be used unless matters get much worse. Would you agree to a meeting?"

"I would agree to anything to get to return to my people who are suffering for me," Thomas said with tears in his eyes.

"We will humiliate him in some manner, will we not, Father?" Louis asked impishly.

"I will humiliate no one, knowingly," the pontiff said, "it is not my intention to humble or intervene."

"I know the revenue of England is important," Louis said sharply, "but France does not give you the trouble as does my cohort. If he is disobedient and forces your representative into disgrace, why should he not be forced to yield?"

"Henry of Anjou has yet to go the last mile," Pope Eugenius said, "this is a difference of opinion and I wish to resolve it. Will you use your good offices, my son Louis, and arrange a meeting in my presence between the Archbishop and his sovereign? You will be remembered in our prayers and special blessings will be asked for the salvation of your soul. Will you do this, my son?"

"It will be difficult, Holy Father," the French King said, "you must remember that I had harbored the Archbishop these many months after the Plantagenet specifically asked me not to. He very possibly will not receive my emissaries, but if you feel that he will, I will be glad to attempt it."

"Try," the Pope urged him, "tell him I will be here in person to witness and to attempt to reconcile. That should entice him. Henry the Second of England is one of the wisest of men, he is not one to flout a chance to secure peace for his kingdom."

The King readily agreed to an immediate meeting. It was to be held at Tours, as neutral a ground as could be found for these antagonists. It was a meeting charged from the beginning. An air of unease hung over all the area. The Pope had a vast group to attend him. The French King appeared to have his entire kingdom turned out for the occasion. Henry of England brought unnumbered people. Thomas Becket was attended only by myself and two lowly monks. The

Archbishop had committed a kingly act just the night before this meeting.

"I would have eels for my evening meal," he announced to the prior of the monastery where we were staying.

"Eels are not in season, your eminence," the good man said, "they are hard to procedure even at best in this part of France."

"I would have them," Thomas told him positively a flash of the elegance of the Chancellor returning momentarily.

There was nothing to do except for me and the prior and the monks to hold a hurried conference to see if eels could be found.

"I know a vendor that can furnish them," the purchaser for the monastery said, "but they will cost dear."

"Get them," I ordered him, "money is no object."

This would be the first solid, enjoyable meal my master would have had in over a year and a half and I was anxiously hoping to revive his appetite. I was not prepared for the demands of the greedy fishmonger. I paid one hundred pound of silver for a very small mound of eels! I paid him without argument and had them stewed in milk and wine as I knew my master's tastes. He ate the meal without asking the cost. The monks looked at him enviously as he ate delicately, apparently enjoying each bite.

The morning of the meeting broke fair and cool. The sky was cloudless, yet the world seemed to frown for me. I was not anticipating whatever was to happen. My master had a face of steely resolve. Henry the Second was definitely belligerent. Louis of France smiled in hopes of a disagreement. The Pope wore an anxious frown. The Pope walked to the center of the arena and beckoned all to their knees. He prayed for peace and understanding. My master mounted his horse. Louis and Henry dismounted and came to his side. Each grasped a stirrup as I guided the horse forward. The kings were superb in expressing their humility. The Archbishop dismounted.

"Are all at peace and in agreement?" the Pope asked gently.

"I am," promptly returned Louis.

"I am," my master said proudly.

"I am, Henry said gruffly and without grace.

"Then give the kiss of peace between Henry and Thomas," the Pope ordered, "and let this felicitous greeting bind up all wounds for all time."

My master gingerly approached the King, stooping to kiss him on the mouth as was the custom to end quarrels between men. Henry turned his head slightly and the assemblage gasped at this obvious rebuff. My master stood proudly and smiled. He stood in the radiance of his dress ignoring the meanness of the English monarch. I had dressed the Archbishop with especial care this day. He wore the simplest black velvet robe that fell from neck to ankles. It was fitted to perfection. His heavy gold chain with his mother's emerald gleamed from repeated polishing. The simple white cord sash with the suspended cross emphasized his elegance of dress. Henry looked at it disdainfully.

"Is the return of the Archbishop safe?" the Pope insisted.

"He can return to his See if he agrees to abide by my laws and puts aside his ostentatiousness. He is supposed to be the poor priest, yet the garments he is wearing are worth a king's ransom. I presume they have been purchased with the vast sums of money that he insists on having at all times. Many is the time I have felt he was directing money to his own purse at the expense of the royal coffers. This is not the abject, ragged person who applied to me for the position of Chancellor. I see before me a prince dressed in robes more precious than those of State."

The Pope led the man to the pavilion that had been erected and motioned for all to be seated. My master was speechless at the careless accusations of the King.

"My lord," he cried to Henry, "I earnestly earn all that I spend on myself. You have always smiled on me before. I have never stolen or taken one coin from the realm of which you did not approve. I did not come to you as a poor man. I had the income of my Archdeaconry and many other preferences, plus my inheritance. You knew nothing of my background but I defy you, as you well know you cannot, to have the Exchequer examiners report to you of one thing, money or otherwise that I have filched at your expense. This breaks my heart, my liege, I cannot return to England with such a horrendous charge against me."

"Are your accusations well founded and true?" the Pope asked Henry severely, "I will not send this man back into your custody to be harassed by untruths. You can get your soul consigned to the depths of hell for such matters, you know. This could seriously affect the succession to your throne. No ruler can survive an interdict, my son."

"They are not true," Henry said offhandedly, "the Archbishop is truthful and honest, if nothing more. I spoke in haste and in anger. No harm will come to him in England while I live. All know my feelings for Thomas Becket."

"But you refused him the kiss of peace which is important," the Pope insisted, "without he can only suffer from indecision and fear."

"I am not ready to yield all the way," Henry explained, "I gave enough for him to know that he enjoys my protection if not my love. This is a two way proposition, Father. He must yield also. I will not have my people excommunicated without my knowledge. I will have my laws obeyed and taxes collected in what I have concluded to be the proper manner. No Churchman has the authority to administer my kingdom."

"That is true," the pontiff agreed with him, "you are charged Archbishop of Canterbury to refrain from irritating you liege sovereign. You are wise enough to distinguish between that which is man's and that which is God's. I enjoy you both to keep this peace, however tenuous. I must return to Rome. Go, all of you with my blessings and my instructions."

We left immediately for England after thanking the French King in the proper fashion. As we left, the campsite, the French and English sovereigns were sitting in the sunshine and enjoying what appeared to be an affable conversation.

CHAPTER 35

We passed two peaceful, uneventful years in England. It was a period of unease, because the King nor the Archbishop corresponded with each other. The King appointed his illegitimate son by Rosamond Clifford, Geoffrey, whom he had legitimized as his nominal Chancellor, but he kept the Royal Soul, foreign affairs, affairs of State, and the Judiciary firmly in his grip. He never did release these powers to another individual other than Becket until his death. I became painfully obvious that the civil courts were persistent in prosecuting clergymen who transgressed the law in criminal areas. All the Bishops yielded to the sentences but Thomas Becket fulminated against them in the pulpit. Also, all lands that were not deeded to the Church but had been controlled by it, were being taken over by appointees of the King. Even the Pope complained about the serious loss of revenue to the Church. The King sent some unlanded Norman barons to England and instructed the de Brocs and others who were intensely loyal to him, to seek out undeeded lands and uninherited areas and claim them for their own. My master brooded over this and one Sunday morning in 1158, he blasted the desecrators of the Church in unusually strong terms.

"I excoriate all people who defame the mother Church," he roared, "before this day is over I shall publish the excommunication of all offenders and damn their souls to eternal Hell. Beware my children," he counseled his audience, "do not transgress against God's property. You endanger yourself beyond all belief. It is a living death you face, never being able to absolve your sins. I abhor and abominate willful seizure of God's lands and revenues. The Kingdom of God is above all and no man should attempt to contravene that which is His."

"Did you see the great numbers of the King's henchmen leave the church as you preached?" I asked him.

"Yes, I saw the infidels," he snapped, "I should have named them publicly as transgressors and assessed a penance on them. I am equally angry with the priests and Bishops who tolerated this travesty. They are as guilty as the sinners. The Archbishop of York never has, and never will, assist me in curbing this trend. I am alone in this world fighting the fight of the Lord with no one to turn to. Even the Pope puts revenue ahead of discipline. The King and his magnates no longer heed my advice. It was a sad and mistaken day when I accepted this appointment. I am now committed to God and will die in the attempt to salvage and protect His worldly possessions."

I did not remark on this tirade, because he was now the most austere man in the whole kingdom. His personal eating habits were of the meagerest. He fasted entirely too long and too much. His body was fast melting away under the rigorous punishment and his personal beauty had long gone. He had aged twenty years in the last six years. He was bent and inform from self-inflicted punishment and starvation. Within a week after his sermon, I heard that huge groups of laymen and clergy from England had arrived at the King's court in Normandy, petitioning the King for relief from the Archbishop's threats. Within the month, the King arrived in England asked the Archbishop for a conference.

"We are at the same old game, Archbishop," the King opened the meeting without ceremony, "you still have not learned that I command my lands and that I will rule my empire whatever the cost. I have told you repeatedly that the threat of an interdict does not frighten me overly much, and if I am to be excommunicated for resisting a troublesome priest, so be it, but the Pope understands quite clearly that if he concurs in your denunciations that all revenue to Rome from England will cease. I will not pay one cent to something that will deny me the salvation of my soul."

"I do not resist you, your majesty. I only decry desecration and unlawful seizure. I did no more than this when I served you as a layman. I over protected the Church but was fair in requiring it to pay its rightful share to your Treasury. You can name no instance when I did not support your requests or demands. I was scrupulous to see that the burden was fairly shared by all. Now, it is different. Those rapacious Normans you send over with instructions to defy me and to ravage the countryside, dispossessing the hardworking monks or nuns, are merciless in their depredations. Why cannot it be as old? What has come between us or has changed so drastically that we cannot be of the minds as we were formally? I still love and respect you more than any human on earth and I would never go against your will or desires. But sire, I cannot yield the Church's prerogatives and instruct the clergy to disregard all that the Church has stood for over the years. I sincerely believe that the Church ca punish its own. I recognize the faults more clearly than anyone else and you know I am vigorous in ferreting out misdemeanors and crimes. The Pope has chastised me more than once for vigorous prosecution of offending clerks. What more do you want of me? Of course, I am concerned about the Church's property here on earth. All land is God's. We only hold it temporarily while we live as humans. But the Church is eternal and its possessions should not be violated, ever. I cannot abide willful acquisition that which is the Lord's. Did you not ever realize that all workers of the Lord face the same problem? Is the Emperor of the Holy Roman Empire's problems any different than ours? Does he not wish to usurp the Pope's authority in the area of investiture? I have heard that you support the Barbarossa in his scandalous persecution of the Holy Father. It is not a layman's right to consecrate or invest servants of God. That is a specific duty of the servants of the Church who are appointed to see that the work of Heaven is properly executed. You accepted your rightful succession to the crown of England at the hands of the venerable Theobald. Why am I to be any different? Do you condemn because I wish to do any less? Are those irritants sent to this island to constantly harry and annoy me? I plead with you for protection and relief from their machinations and depredations. You do not even deign to answer my supplications. Yet, when I attempt to protect the Church, you encourage them to make scurrilous throughout the countryside and to malign my name. It is good that I have truly taken up the Cross instead of the Sword. I can assure you, I can call out an army of loyal people and defeat the mightiest of your barons. You know well that I can fight, but you also know now that I am dedicated to peace and the Church. It is against that is good and holy to take a life or unduly punish an offender of the law. It is God's will that all be returned to the fold."

"You speak true, Archbishop," the King said uneasily, "but I cannot allow your persuasions to unseat my logic. I do not contest the legal realm of the Church. I do not envy it its enormous revenue that it milks from my domains at every turn. As you know, as you and I set out to accomplish in our early days, I am still intent to reclaim for my people questionable lands that have been either seized or appropriated by your greedy monks or nuns. There is much land claimed by the Church that should be royal lands or lands that should belong to private individuals. The seizure of those lands was illegal in the eyes of the civil law, regardless

of what any Churchman might preach. The threat of
excommunication by a priest or Bishop is not the way to
acquire property. Neither should a dying man or woman be
persuaded by an unctuous prelate to yield an inheritance to be
a particular church or ecclesiastical establishment. I desire that
the sale or award of land be made through my civil courts or
myself. I will not deny the Church its rightful place in the
competition for purchasing unless the Church has
accumulated unfair amounts of money or unwieldy plots of
land. It is not within my concept to allow a powerful
organization to overrun or intimidate individuals. You know
full well, that I keep those greedy Hansa merchants and the
powerful guilds in close rein. They will never become too
powerful for my armies or servants of the Crown to handle.
All of them know that to resist my desires results in a quick
and early death by sword or by rope. I still get incensed when
I think of the unnatural ways in which the Pope creates
reasons to pay revenue into the Church. They are illegal and I
know it. Those payments keep me and my people in a
perpetual state of penury. They must be stopped or at least
controlled. I am simply not going to tolerate a supposedly
Holy Man to walk the roads of my empire when I know him
to be a murderer or a thief. There is nothing in all your
religious knowledge that frees a man from the penalty of
losing his life or property when he has deliberately taken
some other life or property with malice and intent. Your
punishments by religious methods are not adequate to suite.
A convicted murderer or thief can ease his conscience and
save his living skin by making excessive donations,
confessionals, or devotionals to the Church. As I see it, he is
still not expiated in the eyes of the law. Why, I can have my
Justiciars cite you innumerable cases where the vicious and
intemperate curs who hide behind the skirts of some priests,
repeat their crimes over and over. There are still also, the very
lowest and worst of criminals in the kingdom who wear the

robes of some religious order. My agents have captured and hung many of them and I admit that heinous crimes have decreased, but I shall not rest until all are brought into the light of the full justice of the law. I do not see that my ideas are in conflict with yours. You have become fanatical, Thomas. You have reserved the right for yourself, without the advice or permission of any one to administer my kingdom both ecclesiastically and civilly. I will not permit that. You have no provisions in your Church to administer the daily affairs of men and you should not concern yourself with it. I advise you strongly to desist. The wise men in the Church in England are those clerics who keep their actions within the bailiwick of their authority. I have made no unfair decisions. I have issued no orders that conflict with any Church affairs. You and I spent too many hours on this matter for me to change drastically. My program is no different from what it was when you were Chancellor. I am still King and I shall remain King. The only mystification to me is why you have changed so. I cannot understand why your resistance has grown so. It is not my intention to destroy you, why do you wish to destroy me?"

"I emphatically deny all your allegations, your majesty," my master said sadly, "I would give my life before I would do you harm, but I must be true to God, I must defend Him here on earth and those dastardly knights of yours are wrong in thinking they can expropriate Church property and go free. If they do so, only anarchy can come to the land. Once unwarranted seizure sets in without being checked, we will return to the days of Stephen, whose history you know only too well."

"I feel the same as you do about your criminous clerks and the unlawful acquisition of the Church of demesne property," the King told with some heat, "my people merely repossess lands that once belonged to the crown and they do so at my instructions. Surely you do not send abroad beasts in the guise of Churchmen to rape and pillage defenseless people. Those men who have committed some of the awfullest crimes in the history of this kingdom and still walk the lands free, cannot possibly do those acts in the name of the Church or of the Archbishop of Canterbury. I will not believe that."

"You belabor the point, my King," Thomas said as he rose to pace the floor agitatedly, "no one who does the work of the Lord is instructed to transgress the laws. They are properly punished. It is much better to try to regenerate people than to take their life. The old theory of an eye for an eye was dismissed long ago. It is the responsibility of the Church to instruct and lead the erring into the paths of righteousness."

"I will belabor the point forever, then," the King snorted, because no man or woman, be it whomever, shall walk the lands of my kingdom, who has committed a capital crime and will go unpunished. That will lead to anarchy and the destruction of all legitimate authority. Lives will never more be safe. The aggressive would wantonly slay the weak and then plead forgiveness in the Church. I will not have it so. There is a definite place for the ecclesiastical and the secular, and you must bring yourself to realize it Archbishop. I will still reclaim the lost and my courts will still seek out and punish offenders of the law. I have spoken. The Church will not become a sanctuary or haven for craven criminals."

"We will never find a common meeting ground again," sighed Thomas, "we have our duties to do as we see them. There can be no meeting of the minds that once were in so close a harmony. You are cutting away my heart, my liege, and you are shortening my life. There is no one for me to turn to except God and seek my salvation and that of all the poor unsaved souls of your kingdom."

"You are absolutely correct," the King spoke with asperity, "there is no common ground for us anymore and in those circumstances there is no place in my kingdom for a hostile element who insists on supervening my authority. If you wish to rule, you must seek unconquered lands elsewhere, England is not your proving grounds. If you choose to remain in my lands, I will forcibly unfrock at least half of the leeches that wear holy apparel and divest the Church of its excess property."

"What do you say?" Thomas stood still rearing his head, "are you saying you intend to start a pogrom for persecuting the Church because of me? I will leave, Henry Plantagenet, never to return to my home. I would suffer eternal wandering lest I bring unhappiness to the least man or woman in your kingdom. I beg of you, do not make the land unhappy because of our disagreements. I will go and never return. You know as well as you know anything that an interdict will fall on you if you contest with Rome, and a populace with unshriven souls will not remain servile under any human alive. You will engineer your own destruction. I will leave. At once if you desire."

"Anything will be better than the unsettled conditions that you have brought since your appointment," the King said, "therefore I pronounce the sentence of exile on you, your relatives, and those who are loyal to you. When you have thought the matter over, you may return if you can find yourself capable of promising not to stir up any trouble. I will give you exactly thirty days to set your affairs in order. I would divest you of your Archbishopric if I could, and I know the Pope would never do it because you have done nothing to offend the Papacy. Leave, man, leave. Should I find you in residence a month from now, I will bring an adequate force and stretch all the bodies of your precious monks and yourself around the grounds of the cathedral to warn all that to incur the King's displeasure will be to incur certain death. Go, I beg of you go. Your obstinacy will not avail if you remain."

"I have said I will go," Thomas said humbly, "it will not take a month for me to depart. The French King said it will ever be his pleasure to harbor so honorable person as the Archbishop of Canterbury."

"The Capet does this just to annoy me," Henry snapped, "and you don't fool anybody with those pious claims. You are an expensive liability, Archbishop. Your income far exceeds the poor Frenchman, yet you apparently enjoy leeching on him as long as his benevolence allows you."

"What horrid things you say," Thomas said appalled, "I have never imposed on anyone. The Barbarossa will receive me or I can reside in Rome under the direct eye of the Holy Father. You don't need excommunication, Henry of Anjou, you have already condemned your soul to the eternal fires of Hell. I have never reproached you for the continuous carnal sins you commit so casually. I can only hope that God hears my plea to forgive me for condoning them. You are not without sin and never forget it. I predict a great and sorrowful disaster for you in your time. It is bound to come. You have earned it."

"Now you are the seer," Henry said noncommittally, "please get your bag and baggage and leave England's shores forever."

"I will remain the Archbishop of Canterbury until my death," Thomas said, "you must promise me that York will never supersede me or usurp my rights as a Churchman."

"That will be easy to do," Henry promised easily, "after my experience with you, no Churchman under my surveillance will rise so high or assume so much authority."

"I bid you farewell," Thomas said bowing, "we will never know the kiss of peace. I beg of you to have your permission to pray for your success and welfare."

"You do not need that," Henry said in a steely voice, "you know you have it."

The King turned and wheeled from the reception room of the Archbishop. There were tears in the eyes of both men. This breech would never be healed. Their love was being turned to hate. I dreaded the inevitable clash. For one who has ever sought to avoid conflict, I was one who was ever involved in it. My forebodings on leaving the England that I loved so well bore on me as heavily as a physical weight.

CHAPTER 36

The French King did not receive us directly this time as he had done before. He sent an emissary who was cool and noncommittal. I believe it was painful for my master to realize that we had worn our welcome out in France. We were adequately provided with funds so my master chose an obscure monastery on the outskirts of Paris. He prayed and fasted as much as he was allowed to. Penitents and Englishmen who loved him streamed constantly to the monastery to seek his counsel and ask for his blessings. His sermons were made to standing room only. People would crush into the small chapels he was allowed to use. The French would not dare to let him become too popular due to chiefly the jealousy of local Churchmen and fear of angering the mighty Angevin.

The monastery thrived on the great influx of visitors. The monks worked day and night to present a pleasing appearance and they repaired and enlarged their buildings from the payments of grateful visitors. They acted as appointment secretaries and guardians of the Archbishop's health and I believe Thomas Becket enjoyed this exile. He began to fleshen out on the exotic dishes I had prepared for him and he reveled in the rich gravies of French origin. He had not brought a large staff with him and I missed the absence of a kitchen staff, one who was skilled in the preparation of English dishes. We brought no fighting men with us and absolutely no English prelates. He had learned of the perfidy and ambition of those men. They had deserted him in his hour of need and had taken the side of the King. He had come to dislike them and many stood on the verge of suspension and excommunication and they knew it. The King sent his appointments to the Archbishop just as if nothing had happened and business of the Church was conducted in an efficient and stead manner.

We had been there exactly eighteen months when the deed occurred, in fact it was months old before the news reached us.

King Henry had persuaded the Archbishop of York, the Bishops of Bayeux, Lisieux, London, and Lincoln to officiate in the crowning and consecration of the young Prince Henry as his successor. This was the sole prerogative of the Archbishop of Canterbury as all Christendom knew. The approval of the crowning of a King of England by any other person, including the Pope, was unheard of. This was no ancient custom of the kingdom as Henry the Second full well knew. The news made my master ill. He went into his bedroom and forbad the entrance of anyone for three full days. He even refused bread and water or strengthening soups.

I was amazed at his deterioration when I finally persuaded him to let me enter. His voice was weak and it was apparent that he had not had any sleep in all this time. He left me feed him some warm bits of bread soaked in beef broth fortified by wine. I was also granted permission to bathe him. I took great joy in flinging that awful haircloth out into the sunshine to let fresh air kill those pesky lice. I put a new one on him, but had little hope that he would remain vermin free for very long. One of the monks came to me with a small vial of a sedative which I dropped into the master's glass of wine without his knowledge. He went to sleep almost immediately. I let him sleep until the sunset the day following, then aroused him on the pretext that pressing business matters awaited that could not await resolving.

When he became full awake, he became fully wroth at the King and Churchmen who had dared to usurp his singular and prideful privilege. He paced the floor angrily and called for a scribe. He ate prodigiously which I was glad to see. His color returned and so did his color. He ate as he dictated. It was a long letter to the Pope explaining the details and agreements of his exile. He also informed the Holy Father that he intended to excommunicate all the English Churchmen involved and would possibly call for an interdict to bring Henry to his knees. The scribe paled at the strong language, and I feared for all the innocent people who would be caught in the swirling vertex of the maelstrom that was to come. He next had a letter prepared which he sent to the Angevin King using all the caustic terms he could employ and warning him that the battle was now joined. He also informed the King that he was publishing the denial of his official blessings to the crowning which would definitely put the succession to the throne by the young Henry in jeopardy.

Thus went the first day of strenuous activity of the aroused Thomas. After much silent thinking, because he conferred with no one, nor spoke to no one, he dictated another long and detailed letter to the offending Bishops warning them of his intended action and denying to them some of the many privileges that they had enjoyed. This letter was enough to set the entire country agog. All the Angevin Empire rocked when the letter was read from the friendly pulpits of the priests who supported the Archbishop. Henry was reported to have suffered one of his worst seizures and called for a council of war on France to dislodge my master so he could be burned at the stake as had Arnold of Brescia. The Pope sent a letter of condolence to Thomas Becket, a strong letter of admonition to Henry, denying the legality of the coronation, a letter to be read throughout the empire censuring the Bishops, and a letter to Louis Capet ordering him to protect the Archbishop's person. The lowest and most ignorant peasant in England and France was apprised of the contest between these two antagonists. Louis summarily hung some Norman knights who had penetrated into his lands who were threatening the Archbishop. Henry was apparently paralyzed by the commotion he had caused and in his disappointment on the lack of support by the Pope.

"I shall return to England," my master informed me one day, "it is at times like this that my flock cries for me. Every day I am besieged by requests beseeching me to return and give confidence to the faithful. I shall write a letter to Henry requesting permission to return. He will not dare to refuse me because he fears the Pope and internal revolution. I feel the urgency to return and stand before the unprotected."

"Do not hasten," I advised him, "counsel with your friends and ascertain the King's temper. Remember, not only will you die if he seizes you, but all who remain faithful to you. I am old, master, my age is showing, I could not stand much torture or confinement." He laughed heartily for the first time in many years.

"Ever the man who thinks of his own hide and seeks to avoid conflict," he chided me.

"Not that," I hastily informed him, "but I fear I do not have the strength anymore to swing the battle axe or sword."

"There will be no fighting," he said emphatically, "I laid aside the sword many years ago. If God above cannot prevail, then I am ready to lay down my life. I do not fear death, my beloved servant, it does not scare to anticipate death. Perhaps this is my destiny. I have stood on God's side, and will ever do so. The pain of the piercing blade, the agony of the stake or the wheel do not terrify me. I am strong in spirit if frail in body. My will is of iron. No earthly mortal can make me crawl in terror as Henry the Second will soon find out. The only way he can prevent my return is to physically bar the way which he can do easily enough if he is smart enough to ascertain my method for return. My people will know of my returning but they will keep their counsel."

"I hope you know whereof you speak," I anxiously answered him, "I definitely dread all the things you mentioned, but I will stand by your side. I have gone too far to retreat. If you go, I go."

"Bless you my good and faithful man," he answered me putting his arm around my shoulders, something he has never done since we were children. I supposed he missed the shoulders of the King whom he had loved so devotedly. "You will get your reward in Heaven, I assure you. It is far more pleasant and rewarding than anything you have ever known on earth."

I kept my counsel on this matter. Although the thoughts of being hacked to pieces or spitted on a broadsword of one of the King's henchmen, hade my knees weak, I was determined to stand this time and not to run. I was facing the greatest crisis in my life and I prayed that I would have the courage not to quail.

The Archbishop kept his counsel but remained very busy. Again visitors streamed to and from the monastery. Letters arrived from the guilty and gutless Bishops and even one from the Archbishop of York begging forgiveness for their actions and explaining why they followed the King's orders. They did not deign to answer their writings. He was too busy formulating a quiet, unannounced, triumphal return to England in defiance of the King's band which I knew was not ended because Henry did not send a communication of any kind. Word had reached us that he had overcome the shock of the Pope's threats and would willingly risk interdict to capture the recalcitrant Archbishop if he had the temerity to put a foot on his soil. Thomas laughed and proceeded with his plans. The French King, by this time, belatedly realizing that the Archbishop was more of an irritant to Henry than ever before, sent envoy after envoy to consult with him on any matter and they brought costly gifts and sympathetic attitudes. These visits received much publicity throughout Christendom. At last we received a letter from the Pope promising ecclesiastical protection and the Archbishop was jubilant over celebrating the Christmas Holy Days in Canterbury.

We arrived at Sandwich, the Archbishop's port on the fifth day of December in the year of Our Lord 1170. It was a bitter and raw day. The snow was flying and the wind was whipping up great gusts of snow and slinging it about heedlessly. Huge multitudes greeted Thomas Becket, and wrapped in warm furs, he made what amounted to a royal progress to Canterbury, being greeted at all times by great crowds who sought his blessings. The services that he held from that time on were before as vast an audience as could be crowded into the great hall of the Cathedral. He was sad at times because even if he enlarged the seating capacity, the listeners could not hear the minister. As the worship season for the Savior's birth approached, he sent letters to all his ecclesiastical colleagues and their workers that this season would be strictly religious with a minimum of roistering and drinking. He was strangely cool to all the Bishops who came for a visit and curtly dismissed requests from the Archbishop of York and the Bishop of London when they asked for consultations.

His apparent happiness disturbed me. He kept his own counsel but taught and instructed the monks of the Canterbury chapter day and night in the proper manner of worship. He constantly interpreted the canon law and the Bible to all who were in his audience. His sermons were particularly filled with sweetness and the love for one's fellow man. I could feel him tensing as the days passed as no word came from the King but his henchmen were always present in any audience where the Archbishop preached, as were representatives of all the leading canons in England. I knew that not one word that passed his lips was allowed to rest until they were repeated to the King who was in residence at this time at Le Mans. My intelligence, which I had scattered throughout the chief ports on the channel constantly sent me reports of the King's loyal subjects leaving and arriving in England. The very air was filled with suspense and the antagonism towards the Archbishop was scarcely concealed by the de Brocs and the Tracys who said what they pleased throughout the kingdom.

My master had the announcement published that he would preach his Christmas sermon on the twenty second of December and that all England was invited. The crowd started gathering in the sawn hours as we were getting out of bed. Thomas Becket ate heartily and it took six men to dress him properly for this appearance. His robes were spotless clean and gleamed from repeated brushings where he imagined he saw a mar. His mitre and crozier glowed as would the purest gold and they were studded with precious gems. His pale skin was lustrous and his hair was glinted with light from careful and repeated brushing. He was the beautiful Thomas Becket as of old, proud, witty, and full of life. He exuded the air of the Holy Crusader and this mood was quickly transmitted to the throng that packed the Cathedral. Many reached out to touch his garments and he took a great while reaching his pulpit as he stopped to dispense his blessings to all who asked.

This was one of his most stirring sermons. He placed the Kingdom of God above all else and he explained full that the birth of the Savior was a manifestation of the Kingdom of God here on earth. He denied the superiority of the secular and declared that all mortals were subservient to the vicars of the Lord. He reached his climax when he unfurled a long list of clerics and laymen who were to be excommunicated for their participation in the crowning of the young Prince and for their harassment of the Archbishop. These people would be denied the celebration of the Holy Days and were declared inoperative in their duties until reinstated by the Archbishop. The audience gasped repeatedly and constant rustling revealed many leaving to report immediately to the King.

Strangely enough, no strong words came from Henry. My agents in the Court sent me the message that a group of knights, intensely loyal to the King and who had been rewarded with great and rich fiefs in England, detailed the Archbishop's excommunication to their sovereign. Henry was said to have one of his true epileptic seizures. He was ill for several days. At the height of his illness he was reported to have remarked.

"Will no one rid me of this troublesome priest?"

I was warned to insure the physical protection of the Archbishop because many fighting men swore to accommodate the King's request at the earliest opportunity. I lived in a state of constant unease. What could a common ostler who was thrust into the unenviable position of guarding the life of a cleric against the assaults of his sovereign do? He surely could not act against the greatest lords of the realm for to do so would be certain death. He could not go out and hire fighters to stand guard over the Archbishop, because no layman in his right mind would choose to defy the King of England and the Angevin Empire. My master in concert with Henry had taught all the barons this lesson only too well. Now, this very method of control was to boomerang against the man who had been instrumental in instating it. The Archbishop of Canterbury had only his churchly position and the fear of a man for his life in the next world to protect his very life. I concluded that this was a weak barrier against some of the most savage and barbarous men who trod the lands of England.

Life in the Cathedral went on as usual. The preparations for a really religious celebration of the birth of the Savior permeated the entire area and the Archbishop was very busy instructing the monks in the knowledge of the full impact of the mysteries. He planned to celebrate High Mass at six o'clock on the evening of the twenty fifth of December and we all assembled, making sure that the doors of the Cathedral were secure prior to opening them to allow the multitudes in to worship. All was deathly still and the threatening weather outside added to the ghostly gloom of the flaring candles. The Archbishop approached the altar attended by only three monks. One of those was one Edward Grim, a most devout cleric, who had recently come to Canterbury in his intense desire to learn from my master. A commotion in the outer recesses of the auditorium stopped all religious activity. It was unheard of to disturb the Archbishop in his preparatory devotionals.

Four knights dressed in mail and fully armed came into the center of the auditorium and approached the altar with a great clatter. They were swathed in great, steaming robes that revealed that they had just come out of the pouring rain. I suspicioned that they were armed and that their intentions were hostile, yet I and all the timid monks who stood in respect of the coming services at some distance from the altar, also stood petrified in fear of those threatening fighters. The Archbishop turned to face them, raising his crozier high.

"Halt, you intruders," he ordered, "who dares enter the house of God with disturbance?"

"We dare," one of the knights stepped forward menacingly. His face was obviously covered against revelation by his visor.

"We come from the King," he continued, "who is sorely displeased with you. He has ordered us to bring you to him regardless of the resistance you might offer."

"You are no official emissaries of the King," Thomas said contemptuously, "he comes to me in person. He would never belittle my dignity by sending some rabble from his

Court. Begone, you wretches before you reuse my ire. This is a high Holy Day and you defame it with your threats and intrusions. Return for the services and pray that your miserable souls can be saved."

"Will you come with us peacefully, or must we use force? You will attend the King whatever your wishes because it is our mission to see that you do."

"I will go nowhere," the Archbishop thundered, "no man lives who can force the Archbishop of Canterbury to attend him. If you lay one hand on me, the mob outside will tear you to pieces. Your agony will be far worse than that of Our Savior's who died on the Cross. Leave this hall, I order you, on pain of excommunication. It is not my wish on the birth date of Jesus to remand souls to eternal hell fires, but I will do so if you do not retire from my presence immediately."

The knights drew back monetarily from the terrible threat, but they recovered their aplomb and courage shortly and began again to come forward toward the threatening prelate.

"You will go with us," the speaker reiterated, if it is only your body that we take. You will not rule England. Only Henry can do that. It is our intention further that you will renounce your bans and free all from your denunciations."

"Beware, you dogs of Satan," the Archbishop said softly and entreatingly, "this is my last warning. My patience grows thin. Attendance on God waits for no man. Leave I beg you. Do not force me to assign you to eternal damnation."

No one answered him. The four men, in concert, drew their swords so forcibly from their scabbards that the blades hissed. All of the monks cowered in terror except Grim who stood stoutly beside the Archbishop. The knights rushed at the Holy Man swinging their swords. He attempted to protect himself with his crozier, but was struck on the arm by a sword that severed the flesh to the bone. Thomas Becket reeled from the blow and as he did another struck him on the head completely knocking the top of his skull under his skullcap from his head. A terrible thunderclap shook the Cathedral and I fainted at the deafening noise.

I was later told that Edward Grim was wounded seriously while cradling my master's head from further punishment. When the angry knights realized what they had done, they fled in horror to waiting horses that were apparently tethered outside. The monks quickly recovered their wits and concealed my master's body to prevent further desecration from the howling mob who broke through the locked doors and surged forward, dipping kerchiefs and bits of cloth in the blood and scattered brains that remained on the floor before the alter. When I recovered my wits, my master was safely buried and his tomb had become a shrine that only a saint could occupy. Henry fell into a deep coma when he heard the news and for a month they feared for his life. He banished the murderers from his lands forevermore to lessen the severity of the temporary interdict that the Pope immediately lowered on the Angevin Empire. All was confusion and turmoil due to the countless unshriven bodies that were allowed to lie out because they were not allowed to be buried in consecrated ground. People cried repeatedly for relief from the curse of the Archbishop and the Pope hastily reinstated the excommunicated canons and lifted his curse purely to ease the hearts of men.

CHAPTER 37

"I see the old man sleeps," said the young monk to his companion as they idly tossed a sewn leathern ball in the early spring sun in the courtyard of the Canterbury Cathedral.

"He deserves care and consideration," said the other, "he is the last vestige of the great Thomas Becket known living. He was only the ostler to the saint but it is also said he was the nearest person to the great and holy man. Look how he peers from his muffled face into the bright sun. He seems to wish to speak to us."

"It is only an illusion," the other said, "he is deaf and has not spoken for years."

They were wrong. I was totally deaf from the thunderclap and the memories of that awful night. In my nights of terror, it returned to me as vividly as if it were happening all over again. I know no peace. Someone had to attend me constantly when I was terror stricken. I fear I was a sore burden on this kindly group of ecclesiastics. I prayed ceaselessly for the care of soul of my master and for the damnation of the souls of Henry Plantagenet and those murderers, although the years had proved the King innocent of the intentions of his hot headed henchmen.

Today I felt at east as I watched eagerly the playful antics of the two novitiates as they scrambled about like two young puppies scuffling for their toy. Somehow, Thomas Becket in all his shining beauty was near me. I saw him in the sunlight. His long tapering hands beckoning to me. The sunlight glowed on his perfectly tinted olive skin. It glinted on his perfectly brushed long brown hair. His large expressive brown eyes smiled gently to me as he stood regally in his bright yellow woolens with the Plantagenet leopards rampant on his sleeves and down the back of his extravagantly scalloped cloak. They were appliquéd on in a brilliant contrasting red fabric. The great golden chain with the huge emerald hung in perfection on his chest. The huge jeweled rings on his fingers created small temporary rainbows of light as he turned and postured in his call to me. The Great Seal of the Angevin Empire and the Seal of Henry the Second formed an aureole over his head. A glass of scented lime water was held in his left hand as he sipped and beckoned to me smiling gently. His yellow woolen hose and soft yellow Spanish boots fitted him to perfection as he revolved in the golden sun as would a true prince of Heaven.

"I am coming master," I called to him as I hurriedly brushed my new green clothes to please him with a neat appearance. I gathered his gloves that he eternally used to protect his hands from the roughage of leather reins, placed my hat on my head and picked up his jaunty hat with the eternal pheasant's feather. I shook the hat to give it a more jaunty appearance and to bring the feather to a true erection where it would wave and snap in the breeze. We descended the stairway formed by the sun's rays. I exactly two steps behind him as we were ever seen in public.

"I believe the old man sleeps," said one of the youngsters as they paused from their exertions.

"If he does, it would be perhaps to move him inside against the rising chill of the breeze."

"I believe he is dead," exclaimed the monk who came over to pick the old man up and carry him to warmer quarters.

"Let me see," Gilbert Foliot approached in all his majesty as Bishop of London accompanied by the famous scholar and writer, John of Salisbury who was now the official correspondent.

"He is dead," announced the Bishop, "may God rest his soul. Take him to the charnel house and prepare him for burial." He directed the young monks eager to please so august a person.

"He will be buried in the tomb of his Archbishop," Foliot explained to John, "beside the body of his master. These are the express orders of the King."